Yearnings

C000096671

t

By Isabella TaniKumi

In deference to privacy, some of the names used in this narrative either have been fictionalized or omitted. Any association of such names or characteristics to individuals outside the purview of the text is purely coincidental and unintentional.

ISBN:0615577768
ISBN-13: 978-0615577760

DEDICATION

To my son and daughter, hoping that they will understand my journey.
With all my love

CONTENTS

ACKNOWLEDGMENTS

In honor of the Peruvian people all over the world who are rejoicing in the centennial celebration of the rediscovery of Machu Picchu and its recognition (as of 2007) as one of the New Seven Wonders of the World

ISABELLA TANIKUMI

If you perceive yourself to be lacking in self-worth, stifled by fear and beset by vulnerability in confronting the past, it is because you, and only *you*, have created that image. The chance to enhance yourself always lies before you. Life is a landscape. Paint it with all the colors of your heart. Believe in and be uniquely yourself, and see yourself in a new light – ever growing and becoming.

Isabella TaniKumi

Preface

To reach the point of self-awareness – and, as a result, this writing – I had to travel a seemingly endless path. Transitioning from one place to another – geographically and, particularly, emotionally – was difficult and often painful for me. My story began in a small rural town in South America. Then, my life took shape in Lima, Peru's capital and continued in a large U.S. metropolitan area. My initial inspiration for writing this book was a broken heart, which allowed me to explore the many buried traumas of my past, from which I emerged a more whole, integrated person, with a heightened level of self-appreciation, respect, and ability to move forward, in spite of many hardships. I have learned that how one defines oneself and one's destiny in life is not so much a product of what others believe – no matter how hard we humans strive for external validation. I've come to acknowledge that loss, devastation, disillusionment and betrayal can serve as building blocks for self-development – springboards from which to launch.

Like a phoenix, I rise from the ashes of my past to use my life as an example to others and to declare my wholeness and healing – to myself, as well as to my children, who now witness the triumph within me, glowing forth to the surface. It is this process of growth that I wish to share with them – and with you, who now hold these pages in hand, as a source of inspiration. In

1

this state of enhanced self-understanding, I can now address the root causes of some of my greatest disappointments, while rejoicing in my blessings and accomplishments. My fervent wish is that at least some of my words will resonate with downcast hearts, and let them know that they can beat and sing in sweet cadences again - stronger and more melodiously than ever. The opportunity to evolve lies within and before you.

Isabella TaniKumi

Chapter 1

Marcelino's Song

I recall a time when life was simple – a moment so fleeting that I hardly knew it existed. Once it passed, the idyllic vision of what once was quickly transformed into wispy memories, teasing me with tiny droplets of sweet nostalgia, covered in ash and debris. Huaraz, Peru, my birthplace, my little Shangri-La, still lingers in my mind like an old friend. That is why, in this narrative, I refer to that quaint, beautiful city before the destruction as my old Huaraz. I mark time either before or after the earth shook and subsumed in its grasp our very foundation, our way of life – taking nearly everything and everyone we knew. That is why memories of my past are shadows, blocked out by painful recollections that I have, until now, wished to forget. This writing is my tribute – not only to those I have lost, but also to those I love who have edified and shaped me since.

For centuries, my people have endured the storms of change. Our ancestors, the Incas, were of a culture rich in myth and symbolism. An intensely strong people, whose former empire spanned from Quito, Ecuador and further south to Argentina's Tucumán Province, they were some of the world's most adept engineers. They developed irrigation systems which, to this day, still exist in the region of Cuzco Machu Picchu. This same resourceful culture took a great interest in agriculture, soil fertilization and enrichment, producing the potato, maize, and a

3

variety of other crops. The Incas also created a means of communication with quipus (also known as "talking knots") made of colored spun string, llama hair or cotton. Our people's creativity and industriousness were suppressed by the Spanish Conquest in the sixteenth century. The entire country was subsumed in illness and disease which the conquerors brought into the region. Without the immunization of measles vaccines, and faced with imminent danger from the spoilers' guns and horses, our ancestors fell prey to their captors, watching helplessly as their gold and other precious metals were confiscated. The remains of Peruvian gold and artifacts are enshrined in Lima at the Museo del Oro (the Gold Museum). I often wonder whether the Peruvian Indians' history rendered them submissive throughout time, as they viewed Europeans as superior beings, to be idolized and feared. Perhaps such impressions are indelibly imprinted in their genes – remnants of past subjugation. Who is to say?

Allow me now to take you back to my own uncomplicated past, so brief in time, yet still resonating in my memory like Marcelino's song – the crow of my handsome pet rooster, my faithful companion, who followed me everywhere. A province located in the Andean valley of Callejón de Huaylas, in the state of Ancash, my small town was widely known as the Peruvian Switzerland, demarcated by the Cordillera Blanca and the Cordillera Negra (the white and black mountain ranges). The place teemed with life, refinement and camaraderie. Visitors there were never considered strangers. The consistently balmy, spring-like climate matched the temperament of the population.

Most of the houses in my old Huaraz were made of colorfully painted adobe – local mud and brick – and red tiled roofs, each adorned with balconies, over which the neighbors could lean and converse with one another. Before our world ended, my parents had purchased a huge mansion, painted light green, with my father's wholesale grocery store situated in front. My siblings and I often played there in a back room, where Mom diligently supervised us. We had a menagerie of animals, including adorable kittens and one hen who brought my treasured mascot, Marcelino, into the world. Every morning, he served as my alarm clock, admiring himself in the mirror at the bottom of my bed frame, singing at the top of his lungs. At times, I covered my head with my pillow to drown out the noise, but it was my wake up call to life, and I was grateful. My big sister, Laura and I also loved to play at the side of our patio, near a small spring of shallow crystal water – a place my parents called el pozo (the pit). Long ago, it was used as a water source, but when municipal water flowed into our homes, it became obsolete. There, in that small hideaway, we used to feed one lonely fish, swimming wistfully along. Somehow, that creature is part of my most vivid memories of those early days – perhaps, because, in a strange way, I related to him. In my mind, he was a prototype of myself – a lone wanderer in my little world, sometimes ignored but, overall, content with what I had.

Our house was always alive with activity. Grandma would visit us from her home in the remote mountains of Huacachi, filling the air with the savory redolence of her fresh homemade bread and butter. I always bonded with Grandpa in my youthful days. His formula for longevity was to "eat breakfast like a king, lunch like a prince, and dinner like a pauper." Well, this regimen (which sometimes consisted of steak for his morning repast) truly worked. Like many of his peers from the same region, he lived to be one hundred fifteen years old, on a ranch, surrounded by pristine air, nature, horses, and livestock. Life was enriched and prolonged by these vital fundamentals.

I vividly remember our day trips to visit my grandparents, traveling along narrow paths on horseback, ascending into the highest mountains, which clandestinely horded some pre-Inca ruins. If we dared to look below us, we would see a frightening, cavernous abyss. To say the least, the journey was not for the faint of heart. On breaks, we would stop to refresh ourselves and the horses while we contemplated the natural beauty of the surroundings. While the horses grazed, we satiated our hunger with fiambre (consisting of dried toasted corn, cheese, and beef jerky) and chicha de jora (a special punch for adults, flavored with a bit of alcohol). None of life's surprises and alterations ever will deprive me of those cherished memories.

When I say life was simple, I mean that it wasn't abundant in material goods, and we really didn't have a need for anything. Perhaps, this was because things weren't as important as people

– family and friends. I remember our time with Dad, when he would pick us up from school, buy my sister, Laura, birthday presents, and take us for ice cream and Jell-O. For these and other special occasions, Grandma made her special, natural homemade Jell-O, a savory concoction of spices, created with a strainer made of cheese cloth. Drop by drop, the mix would fall into a pyrex, served with biscuits, exploding with taste. The nectar still remains on my tongue – and oh, her Lúcuma ice cream, made from a tropical orange fruit! After so many years, my mouth still waters at the mere thought of it!

In the light of my sister, Laura (who was like my twin sister, due to our closeness in age), I was always a spectator. My parents lavished her with recognition, while simultaneously ignoring me – as though I were an insignificant bystander, a passing observer of their parental focus and adulation. For example, when I was very young, I received leftovers at dinner, never asked, like the others, which piece of the chicken I preferred. My sister, on the other hand, was the nucleus of Mom's heart. Her birthday was always celebrated, while mine was intentionally forgotten. The cause of such favoritism is speculative, but valid – especially since, throughout our lives, no other reasons have been offered or explored. Apparently, when Laura was very young, she fell and hit her head. Riddled with guilt over the accident, Mom and Dad, along with other family members, doted on her with loving care and attention, neglecting me in the process. Never did I harbor resentment toward my

Laura directly. How could I? She was my best friend in the world, and we entertained a reciprocal love and respect for one another that sustains me still. Two years older than I, she was very pretty, with a tan complexion, slanted eyes and wavy black hair. As she grew, she became the town's beauty queen. Her outward appearance was matched only by her easygoing, friendly personality. I was Laura's foil, with blondish hair and lighter skin. I always suspected that I was adopted because I had a fairer skin tone than the rest of my family.

Lacking in conventional toys, Laura and I used our imaginations to invent various means of diversion. One of our favorite games was our best-dressed paper doll competition. Lined up and sealed in notebook pages, those inert beauties would miraculously come to life through a simple pair of scissors and our fine motor coordination skills. Carefully and meticulously, we would cut them out of paper or pre-cut sheets, and prepare them for their runway debut on our dining room table. Our limited resources called for unbounded creativity, of which we had an abundance. Truly, we wanted for nothing. Those few tangible possessions that we did have were treasured beyond price. I will never forget one Christmas, in particular, when our father placed two huge dolls under our beds – for Laura, one fair-skinned and, for me, one dark, to offset our distinct complexions. We were so excited, and squealed with delight upon holding our babies. These gifts represented but a few of the instances in which we were both equally acknowledged. Though we didn't expressly say so, the dolls were special because they seemed to be replicas of us and, as my story will reveal, each had her own destiny.

In contrast to my sisterly symbiosis with Laura, my brother, Tomás and I seemed to be divided by galaxies. Seven years older than I, in his own world of studying and socializing, he enjoyed his status as our father's favorite. Rarely did he interact with me. I attributed his aloofness as much to our age disparity as to the fact that he deliberately set himself apart. I learned to cope – and still must, to this day.

There was a vague – but very real – tension, as well, between my parents and me. My mother, a light skinned Spanish-looking woman, always was – and remains – very attractive. An orphan, raised by her elder half-sister, she never had a role model and, therefore, did not project herself as such. Eager to marry her off, her guardian encouraged her to wed my father, a frequent traveler from his remote mountain town of Huacachi to the larger city of Huari. There, he set his sights on my mother, and asked for her hand. Of South American Indian and Spanish origin, with eyes resembling those of Japanese heritage and a Native American complexion, I don't wonder that his eclectic, exotic appearance must have more than slightly intrigued my mother. His authoritative nature commanded respect and attention. In his presence, negotiation never was an option. So, my mother dutifully threw herself into the marriage with calm, philosophical resignation. "Your father is a good man.

I learned to love him with time," she told me when I expressed surprise that she married her first suitor, eleven years her senior. In my mind, it was difficult for me to apprehend that notion. I believe that love is an emotion which germinates deeply within your heart and never leaves you. It is a longing to be with someone unconditionally, and without compulsion. Love should flow naturally and easily – not as something to work toward but, rather, a gift that simply is. My mother didn't have that luxury – and didn't seek it, I suspect. She always spoke of her marriage as a matter of course, a kind of surrender to an unchangeable fate.

For some inexplicable reason, my mother and I never connected. She perceived me as the strongest of her children, able to fend for myself and less in need of maternal nurturing. Therefore, she often ignored me, and dispensed with the customary caring and attention which are every child's rightful expectation. "Don't worry about Isabella," I used to hear her say. "She is very strong." So, I developed a tough veneer and made her statements self-fulfilling prophecies while silently cowering within, avoiding rejection, at all cost.

My pervasive fear of alienation and rejection also stemmed from a pivotal event in my infancy, which took all of a few seconds, but changed my life forever. Due to the fact that I was only three or fours years old, I do not have an independent recollection of the incident. Virtually all of my knowledge about the matter comes from my mother's accounts. Apparently, while I was sitting in Laura's lap, I toppled face down into a pot of scalding hot custard which someone had placed nearby. I was rushed to the hospital, where Mom learned that I had sustained second-degree burns. I was treated with a medication called Bepanthen, designed to sooth and cure my skin damage. I'm uncertain as to whether or not the ointment later caused the emergence of unsightly blotches on my lower lip and mandible – dark brown, irregularly shaped blotches spotted my lips and trailed down my chin and onto my neck. Sunlight exposure accentuated them even more. For an adolescent dealing with all kind of social issues, these blemishes were a source of enormous anxiety and distress. During that period, therefore, I was in a constant state of uncertainty and trauma, second-guessing myself, and wondering whether the visible, external flaws triggered every instance of rejection in my life. In those adolescent years, I spent countless hours attempting to cover up the spots, and, with them, submerging my self-perceived inferiority.

To compensate for my feelings of inadequacy, I placed emphasis on my education. In truth, I had a natural proclivity for academics, and I excelled in every subject. As I write and tap into my self-laudatory inner voice, I cringe. You see, I still have issues with my successes, given that my parents always subordinated me to my siblings – particularly Laura. I unconsciously – or, perhaps, purposefully – placed myself on a self-imposed pedestal, in order to insulate myself from extrinsic judgment and reproach.

11

Santa Elena, my Catholic grammar school, was located in the center of my old Huaraz. A typical Spanish monastery, it resembled that of Fraulein Maria in "The Sound of Music," only smaller, with a main patio and metal doors. The surrounding buildings had secondary doors in each corner, with entrance stairs leading to the second floor. The main patio was the center of activity, including our daily lineups, where the nuns would scrutinize our hair and clothing. If they thought our skirts were too short, the wrath of heaven would descend, as they ripped open the hems in front of everyone to teach us the virtues of propriety and modesty. The slightest transgression was met with disproportionate punishment, such as slapping with a ruler, the demand that we kneel on a hard cobblestone patio for lateness, or banishment in a corner for any type of misbehavior. Such is how I was socialized: to fear wrongdoing like the plague. For the most part, I monitored my every move – though I did, at times, make an attempt at defiance, such as when, in the second grade, I tipped my friend's chair onto the floor, with her in it. Oh, did the Mother Superior make an issue of this! She even called my parents in to meet with the principal. I was mortified, and vowed never to commit such a felonious act again. Given the level of stringency in my environment, it's a miracle I didn't turn into a rebel. My grades spoke for my commitment and dedication, and I was always poised and ready to assist fellow students with their work. I even skipped a level in kindergarten – the prelude to my early high school graduation.

Those school days were tinged with a powerful mix of joy and sorrow for me. When I was not being teased for my facial spots, I enjoyed playing with friends and going on field trips. On a typical day, Antonio, one of my detractors and my desk mate in the early years, would do anything to annoy or frighten me. His father was a wealthy rancher, whose prominence mischievous Antonio imputed to himself in the form of scare tactics. Somehow, he always caused a commotion in class, either by bringing in a jarred cow's fetus or a mouse in his pocket. As rogues do, Antonio feigned innocence. The latter incident nearly caused me to lose my wits and jump on top of a desk. The nuns didn't know what happened but, thankfully, one of the girls spotted the mouse scurrying across the floor and put to rest any thoughts of my hallucination.

Was I really there? Thoughts, imagination, memory now fade to black. My mind reels, as I try to recollect other events, but I cannot. My legs tremble as they did on that fateful day, May 31, 1970. I am nine years old again, in that moment, when the earth falls off its axis, wiping away all recollection. My brilliantly colorful, precious Marcelino sings, and I awaken once more – only this time to darkness.

Chapter 2

When the World Went Away

Marina, Inés, and I were inseparable. Each moment of our fourth-grade experience was spent together. We attended a middle school called Santa Rosa de Viterbo, nearly identical to Santa Elena (the grammar school which I described earlier, only larger). There, we took part in school plays and other social events, always joined at the hip. If we didn't get concurrent parts in the plays, none of us would participate. In one instance, we played nurses. These fictitious roles conceptually shaped our future careers; but only I fulfilled the dream. At another time, we were three angels, dressed in bright colors.

For my trusted best friend, Marina, being an angel was a natural state of being. She was lighthearted, easy to be with, always smiling, and well liked by everyone. She was my constant companion.   We enjoyed lots of outdoor activities together, including volleyball, hopscotch, hide and seek, jump rope, and playing with her cocker spaniel puppy. I can still envision her lovely face, her beautiful milky white skin tinged with a rose-colored hue, and her thick, shiny black hair, sculpted in a short bob that swayed in the wind. Although she was about three years older than I, she was very protective of me. Whenever kids commented on "the dirt" on my face (referring to my spots), Marina was the first to shield me from emotional pain and encourage me to ignore their negativity. On the day before our world ended, she was preparing to participate in el festejo, an African-Peruvian dance. Wearing a polka dot red and black costume, a turban on her head, and her face painted with black shoe polish, the angel stood about five feet away from me – and I said nothing. You see, a day earlier, we had a childish quarrel – a falling out over nothing. Marina later attempted to send me a note of reconciliation, but my foolish pride restrained me from answering. Little did I know that I had a chance – a fleeting moment – to talk to her, to say goodbye. That was the last time I saw her. The sands of time just slipped through my hands and, with them, the most cherished friendship I had known. That which we can't fathom emboldens and hardens us to the cruel realities of life. We feel invincible; yet, all we are, at any given moment, is a composition of molecules, occupying the infinite vastness of time and space. We stop for a while to listen, to learn, and to love – and, then, we take the route of eternity. For my dearest friend, Marina, it was all far too soon.

When the clock struck 3:10 p.m. on that May 31, 1970, Laura, Tomás, and I piled into my father's truck to visit our Mom in the hospital. Mom's sudden minor feminine issues required medical intervention and treatment but, thankfully, she was improving quickly from one day to the next. This development (which I later acknowledged as a supreme blessing) interrupted the normal flow of my routine. So many preoccupations beckoned my attention: homework, uniform preparation, and an invitation to a party in honor of the Mother Superior at Santa Elena, my alma mater. She had just returned from a trip to Lima, and we were all invited to regale her. I looked forward to the event, and had resigned myself to the fact that I was too young to visit Mom's ward. The day before, a nurse there had told me as much, and her sternness commanded my compliance. I tried to persuade my father that I simply couldn't go, but I knew that the effort was fruitless. No one contradicted Dad, especially not his nine-year-old.

When we arrived at the hospital, I sat on Mom's bed, talking and laughing with my siblings. All of a sudden, my Aunt Julia walked in, irate and flustered. "Why was I not informed of my sister's admission to the hospital?" she demanded to know. "I had to find out through secondary sources, and…" Her speech trailed off, as the clock struck 3:23 p.m. Surely, Aunt Julia's anger can't be so strong as to shake the bed and the entire room so fiercely, I thought to myself. In the next minute, I heard the rumbling noise of a huge storm approaching. Then, the windows shattered, and the water tank in Mom's bathroom began to leak. "Stay calm! This is an earthquake! Let's all move to the main door!" my father commanded. In an instant, I followed instinctively heeding Dad's imperatives.

As we huddled at the room's main entrance, we began to pray. "Thank God, I took communion this morning! I'm ready to die, if I have to!" My angel big sister looked at me with a glare

16

of resolve. I hugged her close, praying and cowering in fear. I couldn't bear to lose her or my own life – to surrender all that I so loved. Fog, dust and dirt filled the room, engulfing us in a dream – the nightmarish truth of nature's wrathful dominion. Chaos ensued, as blood poured on the floor – remnants of life so sacred – mothers giving birth in the adjacent maternity ward. In Spanish, to give birth, dar a luz, literally means "to give to the light." What greater life source can there ever be than light itself? But, in those moments, surrounding us, obscurity reigned, and voices cried out in confusion and agony.

Dad, our valiant commanding officer in battle, was the pillar of strength and poise. "Remain calm!" he continued to call out, as he attempted to find a sanctuary. At first, we decided that we would proceed down the stairs from which we had entered, but Mom suggested that we go through the back patio behind her room, to a garden that had been filled with beautiful flowers. After the cataclysmic event, life was literally uprooted, the place cruelly transformed into a mass grave, subsumed in fog and dust. My stomach rose to my chest and a current of electricity seemed to pass through my entire body. The smells of decomposing corpses overwhelmed my olfactory senses, as my ears filled with the victims' cries of anguish, fear, and defenselessness. As I struggled to catch my breath, my entire body trembled, but I managed to move forward, like an automaton programmed to survive. Young children, asphyxiated by the dust and bloodied from head to toe, lay helpless, their lives tragically cut short in the flower of youth. All around us, emergency workers and volunteers piled the corpses of victims into a mass grave. No one – let alone children – should have to endure or witness such despair and pain, but we had no choice. We were like puppets at the mercy of Destiny – that sometimes heartless mastermind and orchestrator of lives. At one point, a defense mechanism was triggered within me, and I dissociated myself from the disaster, focusing only on my own life and that of my family. My father's attempts to keep us safe were constantly intercepted by aftershocks, which sent us into heightened states of alert and panic.

Suddenly, I spotted a man whom my brother later recognized as his teacher, carrying his mortally wounded wife on his shoulders. "Please, somebody, help me!" he pleaded. "My wife is dying and my kids are still at home! I have to go back and help them!" My mother offered some water which she took from her room; but there was no hope of resuscitating the woman. Moments later, she expired, and her bereaved husband hurried home to rescue his remaining family. Later, we discovered that he died in the attempt – a martyr, whose heroism I will never forget.

That night, we camped outside the hospital in Dad's truck, which he covered with a canvas tarp, used for the protection and insulation of foodstuffs. Sleep was impossible, as the earth relentlessly continued to shake. Everywhere, the air reverberated with the cries and moans of desperate survivors, and we seized every opportunity to sit up and say the rosary. Mom was – and is – deeply religious, and that was her only means of solace.

The next day, determined to spare us from witnessing further tragedy, Dad took us to a place outside the city of Huaraz. Although Ernesto, a distant uncle, lived nearby with some remains of his home still intact, the structure was in peril of collapse in the wake of aftershocks. Not wanting to take the risk of remaining indoors, therefore, we made our temporary home on some hospital blankets in the open air, amidst the corn husks which typically sprinkled the ground at harvest time. Thank goodness the rainy season wasn't upon us. Like drops of a magic potion, small miracles were welcomed and valued in those moments. To say the least, food was scarce, but Dad managed to get a box of apples, crackers, and chamomile tea. Someone gave us a mud pot, and Mom cooked on the ground with stones to support it. Dad found wood for the fire, and we muddled through our improvised living, grateful to be alive.

About five days after the world came down upon us, in the midst of the mayhem, my paternal grandfather appeared, clad in his alpaca coat and poncho, riding his trusted horse – his faithful friend and companion, Mauro Mina, named for a famous Peruvian boxer. What powerhouses both of them were – our shining angels of mercy, approaching us fatigued but forthright through the dust. We looked at what we thought was an apparition and choked back our tears. The solid, unshakable oak of our family had come. But how? How could this be? we thought, barely able to breathe. It was impossible to believe that my grandfather had traveled such a long way from his remote home in the mountains of Huacachi, along extremely rough, difficult terrain. But, yes, it was he! In vain, we searched for a place for Grandpa to rest his exhausted head, to take off his shoes and raise his feet – blistered, no doubt, from walking through the narrow, arduous paths where Mauro Mina couldn't carry him. What sacrifice! What greatness! When we had all settled down from the shock, we discovered the reasons for Grandpa's perilous journey. He thought that we had all perished, and had come to recover our bodies. This resolute, incredible man who would live to be one hundred ten years old – almost to the very last in possession of his full faculties – broke down then, amongst his loved ones, and sobbed. I will never forget the vision of Dad's eyes glazing over with tears at the sight of his adored father. "Papá!" he cried. For the first time in my young life, I saw my two pillars of strength fall into each other's arms and crumble before my eyes. Little did they realize that their instinctive surrender to emotion was just another aspect of their mutual strength and courage. All of us embraced and cried in surprise and awe. Such glorious moments those were – even in the midst of such disaster – for we were breathing, ready to carry on somehow.

During his two-month stay with us, Grandpa endured conditions of which he had never dreamed. In the great outdoors, he lived a life graced by clean air, water, exercise, and wholesome food. These basic elements defined not only his life course, but his very identity. One may imagine his shock and consternation, therefore, when the typhoid vaccine was forced upon him. He believed that this was some sort of conspiratorial plot by civilization to destroy the fundamental happiness of those who resisted conventional medical intervention, like vaccines and medicine. I understood Grandpa's reservations but, in truth, he had no choice under the circumstances. The consequences of defying his convictions could have been fatal. With this realization, he overcame his grumpiness, and returned home, safe, sound, and relieved to have escaped the clutches of death.

Since the roads were blocked, and our power lines had been entirely destroyed, we had no recourse for gathering food and supplies. The only source of such luxuries were planes stocked with canned goods, meat and milk, which were periodically dropped down to us. Later, when the government finally assessed the magnitude of horror and destruction, the military arrived and set up tents as temporary homes. We remained there for a few months, until prefabricated dwellings were built. As time went on, humanitarian aid arrived from various countries. I especially remember the intervention of people from Russia, who didn't speak a word of Spanish. Our non-verbal communication, through gestures, worked miracles, helping us to access food, clothing, and other necessities.

We made do with what we had – devising creative means of diversion, as well. Our paper glamour queens suddenly were replaced by corn husk dolls and, sometimes, were even replaced outshone by mud games. Laura's precious baby doll that Dad had bought her that one joyful Christmas had been irretrievably lost, but her counterpart had been spared, thanks to Dad's ingenuity in returning to the spot of our dilapidated home and retrieving her. Mom made an effort to repair my wounded companion, and Laura and I played with her together. We also played in the creek and climbed trees, where I, specifically, was sent to procure delicious wild cherries, called capuli. After eating too many of these delicacies one afternoon, I descended from the tree feeling slightly lightheaded and out of sorts. Though I didn't enjoy the sensation, my appetite for the delectable fruit had been well satiated. After the world went away, everything we did was a manifestation of hope – the essential building block for our shattered lives.

Life breath was, truly, all we had. We yearned for a tiny space of land to call home, but such was a mere concept, at first. Our adobe paradise had been completely demolished, its splattered remnants paving the narrow streets of our neighborhood. In hindsight, I realized that even if we had escaped from the house, we would have been buried right there, on the street, entombed in a mass grave. Only Dad and Tomás went to witness the disaster and carnage of our destroyed neighborhood. In so doing, they most likely had to summon the courage of decorated soldiers; but they displayed such unparalleled stoicism that we never knew what was going on inside – the extent of their anguish and intense emotion.

In all likelihood, Dad found the remains of our beloved animals – including my handsome Marcelino, who had sung for the last time on that horrific day. Not a word was spoken of their demise, however. Ever with our interests in view, Dad absorbed the tragedy unto himself – many times in silence. Sometimes, in our limited human experience, words are inadequate tools with which to access the inexplicable, indescribable truth. Suffice it to say that all who perished live still in my heart.

During this time, a lot of imposters entered the town – those who feigned their status as victims but who were, in reality, unlawfully trying to procure land and personal property. When Tomás tried to recover some of our possessions from the rubble, he witnessed the intrusion of these strangers first-hand. A fraudulent victim approached him, claiming that his family was buried in that area and that he needed help in finding them and their personal belongings. Tomás confronted the man, asking, "Who are you? What are you talking about?" Catching the man in a lie, he declared, "Neither my father nor we, his family, are dead." Upon hearing these words, the nefarious intruder fled the scene. Tragedy brings out either the best or the worst in people, and particularly in the earliest hours and days following the disaster, humanity displayed its full spectrum of flaws and attributes.

So much confusion and destruction attended the earthquake, that the government, unable to verify or corroborate incoming information, allocated land to anyone who claimed a right to it – even if they had never lived a day in old Huaraz. As a result, my father lost the big mansion that he had purchased through hard work and sacrifice. Not only had we lost our home, our personal effects, and my father's business, but also this prized acquisition – a symbol of and testament to his tireless efforts and sterling reputation. Prior to the quake, we had looked forward to moving onto the property, which had been located right next to our family home. Once owned by Lima's elite, it was rented to the Ministry of Agriculture. Sadly, the place was not destined to be ours. I was so sorry for my father but, at that tender age, I learned how to put life into perspective. Resilience was an essential component of survival, and no one exemplified that trait more than my father. We took from his example. Before the huge cleanup of the old city and the government's disbursement of lands to the displaced, we settled for a couple of years on the outskirts, in a place called Nicrupampa. We managed to subsist there in a tent, grateful for a simple roof over our heads – and the enormous privilege of life breath.

Though our surroundings and way of living had changed drastically, in the sphere of my subconscious, the world was renewed, and Marina was well. In my dreams, I sought her out and asked where she was. Her mother always came back with the reply, "She is in Europe, and will return any day now." I earnestly believed in my reverie, until one day when a school friend told me the horrible truth: Marina had perished alone at home with her dog, while her two sisters succumbed to the devastation in different locations. Miraculously, her parents and two brothers had been close to the main plaza, and had managed to survive. I was beside myself at the news, and hardly could believe it. Many times, I saw Marina's father, always dressed in black – a sign of perpetual mourning. He had worked at the superior court, and had a makeshift office built nearby. I could have had many opportunities to speak with him, but I wouldn't dare approach him or broach the subject for fear of hearing those cruel words again: Marina was gone. Her mother seemed like shadow in my midst, consumed by the loss of her three daughters, living in an abyss of grief. At one point, I even spotted her brothers walking in the town. Their quiet reserve spoke volumes. Words failed, leaving a vacuous chasm of feelings unexpressed – especially to Marina, herself. Never would I have the chance to tell her how I felt – how sorry I was for not reconciling with her over our foolish dispute. Guilt pervaded my entire being, but it was, simply, too late. I was too young to cope or have the ability to analyze the meaning of death. The concept of finiteness was anathema to me, but I was learning – far too quickly.

Later, I discovered from my friend Inés's cousin what had happened to her family. Apparently, the quake did not hit as severely in Yungay but, ten minutes later, a piece of the largest glacier, Nevado Huascarán, fell into Lake Yanahuin, causing an avalanche. In a panic, people ran in various directions until, finally, someone guided them toward the cemetery, Yungay's highest point. There, a statue of Christ with open arms (which stands in the exact spot today), welcomed the refugees. Everyone ran to this area, except Inés's father, whose weight would not allow him to continue. As he was following his family, he suffered a heart attack and, seeing the end of his life's path, told them to go on without him and save themselves. Before they did, they witnessed his death. The insurmountable pain of that tragedy remained with the family forever, including Inés, whom I met nine years later when I was a military nurse. She had come all the way from Trujillo, where she and her family had moved right after the quake, to visit her mother, who was convalescing in a hospital. At that time, I was dressed in my military garb, manifesting an old childhood aspiration. Our eyes met, but Inés didn't seem to remember me. The mind has a way of shielding itself from those insufferable memories, too powerful to relive. I suspect such was the case with her. Her father had been our family physician, and her mother was Mom's close friend. Because our lives had been so intertwined, I knew too much. Our paths never crossed again and, somehow, I understood why. I had been part of a world gone away in the mist – a distant memory of what no longer existed.

And what of Santa Elena, my old grammar school, celebrating the return of its Mother Superior? The whole building collapsed, with a couple of thousand people inside, a stony tomb for many of our country's innocent and some of their brave parents, who had attended the day's festivities. The enormous death toll was largely due to a well-intentioned, but foolhardy nun, who told everyone to remain calm and insisted that the large metal door leading to the outside be shut. The main plaza was just within reach, but because of the nun's tragically poor judgment, almost everyone died. Some fortunate few kicked out the door's glass bottom frame and escaped – orphaned and alone. My middle school, Santa Rosa de Viterbo, also collapsed, but a prefabricated structure was erected on the outskirts of the city. Later, a permanent building was constructed on the original spot. That school still stands to this day – a living monument to the power of the human will and spirit, just like the families who, like mine, defied the earth's ire and lived – against all odds.

Every single second became precious in those days, and for a seemingly endless time thereafter. The tragedy had taught me the notion of impermanence – something to which most children are barely accustomed. Even more than before, I came to understand the inherent value of people – those loved ones who meant so much – who, in the blink of an eye, could just vanish from the earth. Arriving at this realization, I sensed the importance of self-cultivation – those human attributes which would guide me through life: self-sufficiency, empathy, compassion, and love. I hardly knew where or how to channel such feelings then. Every day became a process of growth and understanding – an evolution into an entirely new way of life.

Chapter 3

Life-Force Energy Amidst the Ruins

In the days following our apocalypse, it was difficult to delineate where death ended and life began, and vice versa. All I knew was that, we – everyone in our immediate family circle – had survived, when so many others (an estimated seventy thousand people or more) had not. The devastation of our world as we knew it was of such a magnitude that it defied all comprehension. The spoken word, too, never could adequately depict the calamities that surrounded us – illness, mass graves, closed roadways, scarce resources, and general upheaval, the likes of which no human being should ever have to face; but there we were, alive, in the midst of it all. Our gratitude was as infinite as the universe itself – that vast expanse unaffected by disaster (was there really such a place in existence then?). Given our state of supreme thankfulness for every breath, we refrained from commenting on our plight – to each other or to anyone else – and simply remained in a state of quiet patience and acceptance. Of course, for me, the loss of my dear friend, Inés, and my cherished friend, Marina, caused unspeakable anguish, but I endured – in silence. Amidst the chaos, there wasn't any counseling, and we had to deal with our trials on our own terms. To say the least, this was not an easy task for those of tender years – but what choice did we have? For about a year, my dream of Marina's return home from Europe continued. Tragically, its sweet culmination would ever be confined to the realm of my imagination alone.

One important source of sustenance during those times was my friendship with Adriana, a girl whom I had known since kindergarten and one of the few students from Santa Elena who had survived the quake. This miracle was due the fact that her home was located in El Centenario, away from where most of the devastation took place. Her father, a veterinarian, used to own a store located across from Dad's in old Huaraz, where he sold all kinds of agricultural products. After the earthquake, Adriana and I reconnected. Dad had a provisional supermarket, where he also sold groceries wholesale to retailers. Adriana's father owned the adjacent store, a simulation of his former workplace. Both were located in Avenida Fitzcarral, on the periphery of Huaraz – far enough from the city to have escaped destruction. Adriana, her sister and I used to help in the respective businesses. Often, we would get together at lunchtime to talk and conjure up images and memories of the past. How strange to be so young and so pensive! Youth shouldn't have a past, but ours was permanently etched in Peru's collective consciousness – regardless of who was doing the thinking – and we treasured those moments gone by, when perpetual contentment seemed nothing short of a certainty. When Adriana left for school in Lima, we parted, meeting up again on her intermittent visits to Huaraz, always maintaining our fast friendship. During that period, her sister,

Barbara, and I spent even more time together in our city. It was a great comfort to have her around. Later, Laura and I also attended college in the capital, but Adriana lived too far from us in Lima to continue our get-togethers. So, we waited for holidays to come home to our small town of Huaraz, where socializing with family and friends was a matter of course. Somehow, my connection to Adriana and Barbara was – and has been – indelible. I suppose all that we had mutually endured inextricably bound our hearts together. To this day, Adriana and I remember those early days. She now lives in Switzerland and we catch up through the incredible medium of Facebook. What a trajectory of lasting memories! Time has wings and carries us on its back, but the constancy of love anchors us to the familiar, the shared experience.

Aside from Adriana and my beloved sister, Laura who, no matter what the circumstance, shone with love and joy in simply being, I drew most of my inspiration from Dad, whose stoic resolve in adapting to our situation was truly heroic. Like his father, he was a rock in those times of emotional draught and stifled chaos – a trait that still resides within him. His strength of character and physical fortitude were and are matched only by his courageous, unshakable principles. A case in point: several years ago, one of his employees (whom co-workers playfully nicknamed Mala Noche, or Bad Night, for his unrelenting complaints about unpleasant evenings) had an accident outside of the workplace. Moved by his misfortune, Dad took it upon himself to provide for Mala Noche and his family during his recovery period. When people questioned Dad's actions – particularly in light of the fact that the injury occurred in off hours – our father clearly and decisively replied, "That man is a good man. He doesn't have anyone, and someone needs to help him and his loved ones." That's all there was to it. Who could argue with pristine reason?

Demonstrating such conviction right after the quake, Dad never complained about our losses. More than ever before, he became like a soldier in battle – a man of deeds rather than words. As the weather became more and more inclement and survival in the tents grew increasingly uncomfortable, our consummate protector took us to a small piece of land in Nicrupampa, away from the major catastrophe. As I mentioned earlier, living in my uncle's home, still valiantly standing, was not an option for us then. The mere thought of being indoors for any length of time – let alone for dwelling purposes – was unthinkable to us. Therefore, our little patch of civilization became our home, where we had the luxury (by no means do I use the term loosely here) to plant corn, potatoes, carrots, and all sorts of herbs for our nourishment. It was here where we used to come during the harvest to consume delicious pachamanchas – baked meats of various kinds, cooked with heated stones (the word literally means earthen pot).

Our temporary home was made of straw, mud, and an aluminum roof, called techo de calamina, made of corrugated tin, anchored by nails to secure it from huge gusts of wind. Our charcoal stove, which Mom called a vicharra, was extremely rudimentary, made out of adobe. Mom used to cook all of our meals on this apparatus, using ollas de arcilla (clay pots), her eyes tearing profusely from the smoke as she stirred with a wooden spoon. One would, reasonably, tend to believe that food prepared under such conditions would be unsavory but, in fact, the opposite was true. The aroma and substance of Mom's flavorful cooking defied all atmospheric obstacles. To compensate for our lack of electricity, Dad bought us a gasoline-operated lamp with a cloth-like light bulb. That little light in the darkness became our sanctuary, where we gathered to talk, play cards, or read at night. Its cozy glimmer was our metaphor for life energy, inhering in our collective resilience and ability to adapt, through love and solidarity. Self-initiative and ingenuity were key components of survival in those times. I recall standing in long lines with my family to get clean water from relief tankers, then carrying buckets of water back to our shack. The weight of those buckets equaled my own. I suppose that this explains, in part, my present upper body strength. We executed these tasks diligently, so as to avoid water contamination which had infiltrated the creeks and generated diseases, such as typhoid fever.

By the grace of fortune, life-threatening afflictions managed to bypass our door. At night, however, a horrible feeling in my throat, accompanied by an unusual choking sensation, persistently descended upon me, as if the overwhelming shock of the earthquake were still lodged in my throat – a literal manifestation of my state of shock in the aftermath of my world's collapse. All of a sudden, I would wake up frightened, gasping for air, trying to determine the cause. I also awakened my parents who, alarmed at the unanticipated interruption of sleep – their only respite from the struggle to survive, rushed to my side, just as afraid – and equally oblivious as to what was wrong. Now aware of the techniques and philosophies of traditional ancient Chinese medicine, I realize that my Qi (also Chi) had been disrupted by the influx of stress and other strong emotions. Qi is the life-force energy which circulates throughout our bodies. Disease and other toxins can interfere with the flow of this energy and cause the body to react negatively. When Qi becomes stuck or stagnant, illness ensues. When disease is present, the flow of Qi must be restored. To do this, the interference must be removed. In Peru, women called curanderas (loosely translated as curative ones) were well versed in the art of restoring energy flow. In hindsight, I view them as versions of their ancient oriental counterparts – only armed with other kinds of methods. For example, they rubbed fresh eggs all over the body while in prayerful contemplation, or they introduced live guinea pigs to do the work. Even contemplating the latter methodology still makes my skin crawl, and a graphic depiction would not serve here. Thankfully, in my case, Mom called upon a curandera to use the egg/praying technique, while administering calming herbs. Voilà! After a couple of months, I was cured. Not too long ago, someone in my office with the identical symptoms experienced complete wellness after I gave him acupuncture. The success of the treatment bore out my theory that the interference of life-force energy can cause illnesses. Mud treatments, yet another healing method, helped with digestive problems. I can still remember Mom putting mud on my stomach, waiting for it to dry, and then peeling it off. The treatment worked, and I always felt restored. In later years, I saw, first-hand, the ameliorative effects of alternative medicine, and I truly believe that its use should be respected as much as traditional Western techniques.

Despite the post-traumatic effects of the earthquake, we did have some measure of levity, which arrived most conspicuously in the person of Uncle Ruben. His Baptist church was housed in a nearby tent, where preachers would come and give sermons to an admiring crowd, seated in chairs, meticulously lined up. Ruben, who lived with neighboring relatives at the time, frequently visited us, with his bible in hand, cheerfully coaxing Laura and me to sing devotional hymns. Mom allowed us to participate in Ruben's songs and sermons on condition that we would remain Catholic. Of course, we agreed, and formed a little congregation out of respect for our fascinating uncle. Ruben's story is extraordinary in that his basic precept was, originally, atheism – that is, until he fell madly in love with Rubi, a staunch Baptist. Ruben converted in order to continue his life with her and, in so doing, became more entrenched in the faith than some who were born into it. Dad's sister, Aunt Enma, told us the story of her attendance at Ruben's baptism ceremony into the faith. The ritual entailed multiple submersions into a pool of water, which rendered the erstwhile non-believer into the most ardent practitioner. Such is the transformative power of love!

Such is the river of life, inching along, changing everything as it flows on its course.. Slowly and incrementally, circumstances altered for us, too, and our days at the mercy of the elements came to an end. At last, existing became less of a conscious effort. With the aftershocks dissipating, we grew more comfortable with the thought of staying inside. Uncle Ernesto put us up in his dilapidated home, with a large bedroom, closet and a basic kitchen. Surrounding the main dirt patio, rose bushes and other flowers fragrantly bloomed, bursting with life, in defiance of nature's recent eruption. In that illustrious spot, amidst the rose blossoms, a deeply unfortunate event took place – one which, quite literally, scarred me forever. It was a beautiful day, with bright, blue skies – one of those afternoons where all seems to be right with the world. I had come home from school in El Centenario, where Santa Rosa de Viterbo had been temporarily reconstructed. I was dressed in my uniform – a starched white top and a dark grey skirt, tightly fastened at the waist. Mom greeted me and asked if I could reach into an old cabinet and get some rice. I did so dutifully but, after several minutes, I simply couldn't find what I was looking for; so, I decided to try each container. As I bent over, a mouse scurried onto my starched collar and down my back, becoming imprisoned by my tightly cinched skirt. In my mind, I heard the creature yell, "I'm stuck! Help! There's no way out!" – or was that my own terrified voice? In a panic, I began running in frenetic circles, until I became so dizzy, that I ended up in the rose bushes with a thorn in my left earlobe – right behind the pierce for my earring. Blood rushed from what seemed like every pore. My shirt was bloodied entirely on my injured side, as if I had been torn apart by shrapnel. I stood up, in complete shock and disbelief, to find that my attacker had vanished, never to be seen again. Needless to say, from this day forward, I developed a strong aversion to mice – and, quite frankly, roses, too – and if ever I dare, for a second, to forget that this incident ever happened, I only need to look at the evidentiary proof – a scar behind my earlobe – the insignia of truth.

Like all things in life, a source of pain in one instance can also be a wellspring of pleasure, in another. In one corner of that very patio stood a device which Ernesto called el batán, a large oval, egg-shaped stone, which he used as a kind of blender to concoct the most delicious chili sauces, made with herbs from the garden. After the stone's cleansing, Mom mashed hot peppers into it and placed them into a separate container, adding lemons, salt, spices, fresh cheese, and scallions, creating her famous aji con huacatay, delicious Peruvian hot sauce with potatoes. Huacatay, my favorite herb, is related to marigold and tarragon. I don't have to strain my memory to smell the aroma again, traveling across eons of time, linking me to a moment gone by...but has it? As I allow my cognitive/olfactory journey to continue, I detect the savory scent of Mom's biscocho, sweet bread made of eggs and raisins on an adobe brick oven. Every Saturday, when Mom made this delicacy, we would wait for the dough to rise and then clamor around a wooden table, our fingers shaping the malleable substance into various designs. For fresh fruit, we went right to the source: peach and pear trees on Ernesto's property, which seemed to populate the area and produce their fresh nectar especially for our enjoyment. How could any degree of abundance flow in the wake of upheaval? As a child of nine, I was happily oblivious to this inquiry. Now, having distanced myself geographically, I can peer into the window of my past and have an objective view. Actually, for the sake of truthfulness, I freely acknowledge that I'm much closer to that time than I consciously believe at any given moment. As my hand pens the memory, I live it again, like a bird migrating with the seasons, infinitely regressing to its original home.

If loneliness ever crept upon our doorstep, we could always count on Aunt Julia, the younger of Mom's two older half-sisters, who was in the hospital with us when the quake struck. Incredibly, she and her family of ten children had all survived, due to their geographic distance from the epicenter. On our weekly visits to her house, Mom carried a bundle of sun-dried laundry in her arms, intent on using Aunt Julia's intensely

38

strange iron. To accomplish the simple task of ironing, Mom had to pour charcoal into an opening at the top. Then, in order to protect the clothes from soot, she cleaned the apparatus with wax. After the iron sufficiently heated, she would proceed meticulously to press and smooth our sheets, linens, and clothing. Meanwhile, Laura and I eavesdropped on the ladies' lively gossip. At times, our cousins would come to our home for a day of hide and seek, tree-climbing and fruit-picking. I distinctly recall playing in the fields, with our mouths smothered with raspberry, yellow, green, purple or orange pear juice, the latter of which was derived from the prickly pear, a peculiar-tasting, exotic fruit which grew in the upper regions bordering the creek. Covered with tiny thorns, it was high in vitamin C. Laura and I peeled each one with great care, so as not to injure ourselves before ingesting them – which we did either out of sheer necessity or hunger. We laughed at the myriad of colors adorning our faces, making us look like little circus clown nymphs of the field. We were children of the earth – that formidable Mother who had so recently betrayed us. It was difficult to comprehend that She who nurtured us could have caused such upheaval.

Resuming our lives' routine was almost surreal – particularly with regard to school activities. Though the school's name was identical, its inhabitants had changed. Everyone was new – nuns, teachers, classmates – as though they were produced by the reconstruction itself, planted there as fixtures, as if to declare, "welcome to your entirely new, completely strange, reconstituted world!" Nothing felt the same. People may have feigned a kind of artificial normalcy, but we all were keenly aware of what no one wanted to admit: our lives had died and could never be reclaimed. Still, we had to move on. We had been given a second wind, and there was no time to waste.

For obvious reasons, it was difficult for me to make new friends at that time. When the impact of loss is as great as we had experienced, it's extremely painful – and seemingly impossible – to overcome the fear that nestles in your heart, whispering, "Beware! It could happen again!" Even now, this faint reverberation of doubt creeps in at various points in my life, appearing in the midst of different relationships, determining how I react to given situations. I will return to this personal epiphany later on, but, for now, suffice it to say that in those early days after the disaster, I mostly kept to myself. I did, however, strike up an acquaintance with Singa, a tall, bright girl, who continuously defeated me at chess. For all of her intelligence, I perceived Singa to be slightly self-conscious, owing to her stooped position. She had every reason to stand at her full height, but, since nature had endowed her with feminine anatomical gifts (which, I believe, she considered to be too prominent), she deliberately bent over, as if to cover herself up. Why her mother never admonished her about her posture – both emotional and physical – was beyond me.

On second thought, I was no stranger to more than a small degree of self-consciousness, myself. As I grew, the spots on my face began to be more obvious, rendering me awkward and uncomfortable, especially in the presence of the opposite gender. But, for the time being, I just focused on academics, which always had been my strength. For some reason, though, I fell short in geography, and my Dad was called in to speak with the teacher. Well, let me rephrase that. I absolutely knew why I was distracted and couldn't focus: Mom was pregnant. After eleven years of being the youngest, the presence of new life energy was about to assume dominion over the entire family. As Mom became bigger by the day and couldn't walk anymore, she decided to take Laura with her to Lima for some rest and to see my brother. Tomás had already gone to the capital city to attend a prestigious Jesuit school. So, I was left alone in the house with Dad and Victoria, a young, uneducated housekeeper. The timing could not have been worse. One morning, I awoke to find myself in a pool of blood. I'm dying, I said to myself, not knowing what to do next. In my terror, I couldn't understand why Victoria jubilantly celebrated the arrival of my womanhood. I felt miserable. Why hadn't Mom spoken to me about this? Why did she have to leave at a time when my pubescence raged and took over me like a fire-eating dragon, threatening to devour my youth? All of these questions overwhelmed and confounded me, and I felt totally alone with yet another sign of Mom's neglect, perhaps the biggest: her absence at a life-changing time. I was relieved to see Victoria wiping away all indicia of what had happened, vowing to keep the secret from Dad. I cringed at the potential embarrassment of such a revelation – especially to my austere father, who could have offered me absolutely no comfort. How could he? If such subjects were taboo for Mom, how could I possibly broach the subject with Dad? After being alone and pensive for a while, I managed to pull myself together and understand (although I don't know how) that, like everyone else, I was a pilgrim traveling through the world. With that perspective in view, my geography class dilemma finally diminished and, thanks to the help of a tutor, my final grade was more than respectable.

Then, the day arrived. Dad came to me and said, "Mom had twins!" I was floored. A surge of excitement welled within me. The mere thought that I had two brothers – one light complexioned, the other, dark – was truly amazing to me. It was as though Santa Claus had arrived early and managed to defy all obstacles – even broken pathways. Well, at least, the sky was clear – at least, as far as anyone knew. Mom and Laura had to stay in Lima for a while because one of the babies had minor complications, which he fortunately overcame quickly.

When Dad and I went to meet Mom, Laura, and the precious new arrivals at the airport, I was filled with joy and enthusiasm. I had missed Laura's presence so much and as she emerged from the terminal, carrying one baby in her arms, my heart raced. Mom followed close behind with the other. Our reunion was sweet. Suddenly, my eyes wandered and I noticed the attractiveness of the people around me – the good-looking pilots and the stewardesses, in their pretty dresses. Wow, was I jealous! The thought of my blemishes and spots surfaced again, and I cowered inside, feeling self-conscious and alone. Then, my mind traveled to that forbidden place – that dark, vacuous space of self-doubt, telling me that the twins, in all of their innocence, would rob me of what I craved most: Mom's attention. In fact, neither my family nor I realized how much responsibility would be involved in caring for twins, but, ultimately, the extra work didn't matter. Love often overcomes challenges and, again, as ever before, I found my way.

When I was eleven, while awaiting our return to a permanent dwelling in Huaraz, my family and I moved to another piece of land in Nicrupampa, and resided there for three years, in an adobe house built by my father. The place was somewhat more comfortable, with such conveniences as indoor bathroom facilities, running water, and vastly improved kitchen appliances for Mom. In the realm of relative comfort, our family continued to grow. Two years after the twins were born, along came Beatriz, my parents' last child and the adored baby of our group, who looked remarkably like Laura.

The presence of new life was restorative for all of us. Laura and I doted on our little siblings as if we had birthed them ourselves. Our lives resumed a sort of settled character, as if our tragedy had occurred in a landscape on an impressionist painter's canvas – misty, but infused with color, painted with a brush of hope.

Chapter 4

In the Shadows of the Harvest Moon

I don't know the precise moment when the first sign of womanhood took hold. It simply crept up on me, like the little mouse that had found a home in my starched white shirt in Uncle Ernesto's garden. Looking in vain for someone to turn to for answers, I found Mom – but she wasn't there. Although her physical presence stood before me, her lack of emotional support made me feel needy. As she attended to Roberto, Juan, and later, Beatriz, I felt increasingly isolated. Though I adored my twin brothers and little sister, I must admit that I was jealous of their position at the center of Mom's world. Thank goodness, with the intervention of Victoria, the young housekeeper, and the occasional enlightenment of the family health education instructor, I had my first exposure to the subject of human sexuality. In truth, the whole conundrum was foreign to me. Feeling hindered by my facial spots and severe acne – the blights of my life, I yearned, like most pre-adolescents, to be liked and admired.

Instead of being nurtured, I was ridiculed by a person who should have known better – one of my instructors, no less, whose deliberately blatant, insulting remarks about certain students in front of the whole class, made me cringe. When my blemishes popped one day, leaving embarrassing red marks on my face, the instructor just couldn't keep silent. "What happened to you?" she exclaimed, as though I had fallen into a bucket of paint. Intuitively more versed in the art of tact than my elder, I refrained from a reply. The next morning, retribution swooped in, like a bird on the wind, as the instructor marched into class with a black and blue eye. I truly didn't wish her harm, but I couldn't help but perceive irony in the situation. More than anything, I wanted to return the question, "What happened to you?" but, again, discretion dictated otherwise.

By that time, at the age of eleven, I was attending my first year of high school. It is important to clarify here that, in South America, fifth grade is the final year of middle school, after which students enter el primer año de secundaria (literally, the first year of secondary [education]). While awaiting the rebuilding of Santa Rosa de Viterbo at its original site in Huaraz, I went to class in a prefabricated structure, located on the outskirts of Nicrupampa. As mentioned, life was not easy for me then, but I immersed myself in extracurricular activities as a way of diffusing and escaping from the sea of emotions and concerns plaguing me at every turn. I learned to play the drums – a feat which was not often encouraged and cultivated in girls. The feminine species had its place, and was not supposed to strive, but I excelled at and thoroughly enjoyed this skill. It was important for me to defy odds, to actualize my talents and proclivities, in spite of socially imposed limitations, and I never stopped. In my second and third years, I cultivated my affinity for volleyball, becoming captain of the team, awakening at 6:00 for training. This structured schedule gave my life context – and a sense of purpose, besides serving as an enjoyable hobby. I also joined the church choir and learned how to ride a bicycle, which involved straining my short stature to reach the pedals of my brother's bike. Was that tough! No matter; I welcomed the challenge.

Around this period, I met two sisters, Anna and Mariela, with whom I practiced riding. Anna attended school with Laura, and Mariela was in my grade. Tragically, Mariela died of appendicitis at age 13, a loss which devastated all of us. Although she was a casual friend, no life passes through this world without leaving a unique spark of light. I remember Mariela to this day. The sorrow of her loss is difficult to forget. Anna was magnetic – at least, to the male persuasion. She was the life of every party, and the guys just pivoted to her, wanting to chat or dance. As for me, the self-consciousness which my spots produced never could be overstated – but, since I couldn't really confide in anyone (except my beloved sister, Laura) I outwardly stated nothing, and spent most of my time wondering whether I had adequately concealed my insignia of shame. Thankfully, Laura always came to my rescue, introducing me to all of the guys, helping me to overcome the inner turmoil which only she could sense – and cared to address. At every turn, she tried her best to rectify my plight. If I would say, "I like that guy. He's cute," "that guy" would (not so coincidentally) show up at one of her parties. "Come here!" Laura would excitedly beckon the subject of my attention. "I want to introduce you to my little sister!"

Shy and self-conscious, I responded tepidly, but proudly, for I was standing next to my big sister,. She was ever my icon of beauty, good sense, and intelligence. Any awkwardness I felt was mitigated by her open, gregarious nature. In Laura's absence, though, I had to fend for myself in the romance department. When I was fourteen, I met Carlos, one of the most enigmatic figures I had ever encountered. He was a sweet boy, a year older than I, with whom I had been friends for a year. Our connection began in the choir, when a nun paired us to procure contributions for the church. Many people thought that we looked alike, with our dirty blonde hair and light complexions. Tall and handsome, Carlos always had the appearance of a young nobleman – very neat and spiffy, with not a seam out of place, his clothes ostensibly imported from a foreign land (this notion was purely conjecture on my part). If someone could have been chosen to walk out of a fashion magazine, Carlos would have been the perfect model of dignity, respectability and good looks – though, I must admit, without an intellect to match. For what he lacked in gray matter, he more than made up for in personality. His background remained a mystery and he never spoke of his parents or lineage. Supposedly, he resided with his aunt, but I never saw her. Somehow, Carlos' clandestine nature enshrouded him in intrigue. Everyone – including all of the girls, of course – liked him immensely. Perhaps, for the same reasons, my parents were endeared to him. Dad enjoyed his help at the store, and appreciated his ability to ingratiate himself in the most amiable way. In short, there wasn't anything not to like about Carlos.

What my parents didn't know about my friend – aside from his mysterious ancestral heritage – was that he had become my boyfriend. We had a kind of puppy love liaison, which began with my first kiss. As we walked home from school one day, with my books in Carlos' arms (as per his custom), we detoured into a small wooded area, where he kissed me. I was terrified, as I conjured all sorts of things – particularly that I could become pregnant with that kiss. I was so overcome, that my legs shook in the same manner as when the earthquake took place. Only Laura was privy to my secret, and she repeatedly reassured me that my fears were baseless. I felt awkward and silly, not knowing what to do. Nevertheless, unbeknownst to my parents, we continued to see each other.

One afternoon, we were scheduled to go to a movie matinee, and Laura walked with me to the movie theater. Already a college student, my sister was home in Huaraz on vacation from her legal studies in Lima. She never took our time together for granted, and provided support at every opportunity. Suspense began to build, as we waited…and waited. After ten minutes, Carlos was a no-show, and we left. You see, in my culture, it was unacceptable for women to wait for men. So, steeped in disappointment, I just had to accept that I had been stood up, let down, and all manner of other idioms used to connote the seesaw of emotions which inevitably culminated in overwhelming feelings of rejection. In truth, I never loved Carlos – how could I? At that point, I barely knew what the term meant – let alone the feelings that went along with it. Still, what had happened was a blow, and I knew that I would recover – I had to. So much life lay ahead of me. My physical body was changing, and although I didn't fully understand my natural physical evolution, I intuitively felt that I simply had to surrender to the forces of life – those in my external and internal worlds.

Ever coming to my rescue, Laura, my guardian angel, invited me to a party that evening, attended by college friends of hers, all of whom were older than I. In fact, I was the only high school student there. Within a short time after my arrival, I spotted a tall, dark, slender, exquisitely handsome man of about twenty. Laura read my thoughts, and introduced me to him. "This is Lorenzo," she said. "He's a law student in Trujillo." Lorenzo asked me to dance and, in those moments, unspoken feelings were communicated. A lot of dancing took place in my homeland of Peru. It was our way of having fun and meeting people. For me, that interlude was one of the most pivotal events of my life.

Lorenzo and I instantaneously bonded, and he asked to walk me home. Laura and her boyfriend, Xavier, walked in front of us, as silent chaperones. When we stopped at my door, Lorenzo asked to see me the following day. In that instant, I fell completely under his spell, enraptured by the request – and honored that such an accomplished man would want to date me. I eagerly accepted Lorenzo's invitation, and spent the rest of the evening in wakeful anticipation of our next meeting. Over the course of one month, we dated many times, sharing priceless moments – the remnants of which still linger in my memory like wispy sprites, teasing and taunting me at intervals, reminding me of a past so distant in time, yet always resonant in my heart.

To illustrate how deeply ingrained my formative experiences still are, a digression is in order here. For that purpose, allow me to journey to the present – the only real reference point for past or future timeframes – and the ultimate revealer of truth. The other day, as I was sitting on a park bench, making notes for this book, two elderly ladies, whom I knew, approached me and asked what I was doing.

"I'm writing a book," I answered, making room for the ladies to sit next to me.

"What about?" they each asked, almost in unison.

"I can't tell you now. It's a secret," I replied, smiling.

"Well," said one of the ladies, looking at me intently. "We'll read it only if it's racy."

Though I'm fluent in English, there are still some words which require dictionary clarification. When I found out the meaning of the word racy, I laughed uncontrollably, and decided to consider their request. Now, as you know, I was raised by nuns, in a society grounded in rigid – and, I dare say, oftentimes dictatorial – codes of conduct, particularly with regard to minors. Therefore, you can imagine my degree of hesitation in recounting anything remotely salacious. Besides, what good does it serve, I ask rhetorically? Well, now, I know. It serves, presently, to satisfy the mildly prurient curiosity of two venerable elder women – and, possibly, other readers whose interest in subjects of a romantic nature needs to be addressed. Therefore, in deference to these individuals – and, at the same time, dispensing with all need for propriety, generally, I hereby relate the story of my love affair with Lorenzo, the man to whom I first entrusted my heart.

For about a month, we experienced dating bliss. He held and touched me in places I never knew existed, kindling within me the feeling of what it truly meant to become – and to be – a woman. When he kissed me, the entire world seemed to vanish, when he whispered loving words in my ear, the very earth shook – this time with excitement, rapture, and longing. I experienced, in effect, an inner earthquake of a magnitude far beyond anything the written word can depict.

One evening, after a sporting event at my high school, Lorenzo picked me up and took me for a walk in the shadows of the harvest moon. Sensing our need for privacy, Laura left us alone, agreeing to meet us back at the house. Such romance as I experienced on that night had never even entered my wildest dreams. Our physical chemistry was, literally, palpable – an enchanting formula of tender embraces and passionate kisses, that melded us into one. Wrapped in Lorenzo's warm, loving arms, I saw the moonlight reflected in his eyes, assuring me of his heart's constancy. His voice spoke words of a forever love. "I will take you with me everywhere I go," he promised. Permanently imprinted in my soul, Lorenzo's speech and conduct gave meaning and context to the pubescent changes taking place within me.

Time and again, Lorenzo was there for me, loving me, making me feel special. On walks in the woods, he serenaded me with love songs, playing each guitar note in my name. He claimed my being with soft kisses behind my ears and on my neck, blanketing me in ecstatic caresses, making me dance on Cloud 9. I was living a dream, the fantasy of every young girl – to be wanted – completely. For a brief period, I cast off all feelings of self-consciousness about the spots on my lower lip and mandible. Lorenzo's love rendered them almost imperceptible to my vision. That's what love can do: peel off the layers, the façade of so-called imperfection, to reveal the essence of an individual – in my case, that of a fifteen-year-old girl, madly in love and bursting with more emotion than she had ever felt before. But, when Dad saw a love bite on my neck one day (broken capillaries, caused by one of Lorenzo's ardent kisses), that was the prelude to my joy's end. Dad effectively put a stop to Lorenzo's phone calls, insisting that he was "too old" for me – and far too persistent. He banned all of our conversations, admonishing Mom not to allow Lorenzo to speak to me. So, I began to see my love a escondidas – hidden from my parents. Friends came from school to take me to him. I didn't know what else to do. One night, a serenade brigade congregated outside of my window to sing for Laura and me. Dad was snoring, but I knew that he was, secretly, awake and in full possession of his senses. He had to have heard the music – we all did, for, the next day, we had black circles under our eyes from lack of rest. Customarily, the father of the girl being serenaded would invite the suitor and his followers in for coffee or tea – but not in Dad's case. In matters of the heart – especially when guarding the heart of his daughter – Dad was unyielding.

After that glorified month of passion and promise, Lorenzo had to return to his law classes in Trujillo, about eight hours from Huaraz. He said that he would write, pledging his unwavering love. I believed him. For a time, the letters came, four in all – rife with poetic refrains and words of commitment. Then, all of a sudden, his correspondence ceased. When I went to the post office in expectation of a letter, I came back empty-handed. Even the postal worker felt for me, her eyes lowered in dejection, as though she were mirroring my sorrowful spirit in empathy. Without reason, cause, or explanation, Lorenzo had disappeared from my life. As anyone may imagine, I was heartbroken.

Then, one afternoon, out of the blue, I spotted Lorenzo, walking on the street in El Centenario, on the opposite side from where my mother and I stood. I thought that I had seen a ghost, but upon closer inspection, I knew that it was, indeed, he – in plain view. "What's wrong?" Mom asked. I was speechless at the sight of him – that cruel purveyor of broken hearts – my heart! How could he? How could he be with…that beautiful woman on his arm whom he embraced seductively, passionately? That could be me! my heart cried in anguish. I felt so small, so unworthy of Lorenzo. He saw us, but pretended to be oblivious. What had I done? Was I unattractive? Did I make him embarrassed, uncomfortable? Beside myself, I felt a torrent of misery well up inside of me, obscuring all of the unbridled euphoria of libidinal energy that he had once evoked – and still did. I couldn't help myself.

Graduation was drawing near – a time of celebration and partying. I didn't want any part of it, but my friend, Charo, persuaded me to forget my troubles by going to one of the gatherings. After a lot of arm pulling, I finally conceded. As people started to dance, I looked up to behold…none other than Lorenzo, walking in with the same vision of loveliness whom I had seen with him in town. Cowering from the mere thought of being in the same room, I wanted to be swallowed by Planet Earth. So, Charo whisked me away to other quarters, where I drank more than my share of Sangria. A short time later, Laura came to pick me up, and she and Charo brought me to a cafeteria, where I was restored – but only topically – by a cup of coffee and mounds of mint chewing gum to mask the scent of alcohol. To face my parents in that condition would have been a disaster – my emotional death knell. When we arrived home, Mom asked about the party, and I replied that I did not feel well. After taking some warm tea from Laura, I went straight to bed – to sob for the entire night. Only my sister and Charo knew the truth of my harrowing ordeal.

Soon, prom time rolled around, and I didn't have a date. I was stunned when Laura suggested that I ask Lorenzo. Everything in me dictated against such a move, but in the absence of options, I reluctantly followed through. One last hurrah, my sister thought, would do my heart good before departing for school in Lima, where my studies, new friends and new school would vanquish all thoughts of Lorenzo forever.

I picked up the phone with shaky resolve (a contradiction in terms, but my soul was filled with oppositions then). "Lorenzo," I said, upon hearing his voice. "My brother, Tomás, was supposed to take me to the prom, but he couldn't make it back from school in Lima. Can you take me?" What are you doing? my quivering heart asked. I barely had time to formulate a thought, when Lorenzo replied, "I'll call you back." As I waited, I repeatedly mulled over his possible reasons for rejecting me – again. Then, when the phone rang, I ran like lightening to answer – only to hear the voice of Alfonso, a family friend. "Hi, Isabella. Lorenzo is unable to take you to the prom, but I will."

What just happened? I asked myself, in shock and amazement. Then, I determined that I had no other recourse than to pull myself together and simply show up at the prom – and I did. My parents had no objection to my attendance with Alfonso, who was a respected friend. Adorned in my beautiful red velvet dress and long, wavy hairstyle, I felt almost ethereal, ready to enjoy – or at least, muster some strength to endure – what should have been one of the most memorable nights of my life.

The definition of the word memorable is crucial here, given that the evening was, indeed, unforgettable – but not in a pleasant sense. As I was dancing with Alfonso, and casually assimilating in the crowd, there he was again – yes, Lorenzo! I couldn't believe it – and, this time, with another girl, perhaps more beautiful than the first. Alfonso and I continued to dance, the cadences of the music reverberating up and down my spine – or was that anger? I had been rejected – yet again. After about three or four dances, Lorenzo approached and asked me to dance. I don't know why, but I instinctively agreed. I suppose that I had left my heart in the shadows of the harvest moon. The season had changed, but my love remained constant. Youth is foolish, blind, impetuous, and unstoppable – even in the presence of flagrant dismissal. About halfway through the dance, Lorenzo blurted out the spontaneous, declarative utterance, "Tu eres solo una chiquilla" ("You are just a little girl"). I believed that his words were cruel deception, masking his true feelings: that I was ugly and undesirable. Instantly, my spots came to mind. He's pitying me, making my age an excuse for what he really thinks, I told myself. This was too much for me to handle; so, after a brief pause, I retorted, "You are a very complicated man. I don't understand you, and it would be best if I never saw you again." With that, I picked up my coat, and asked Alfonso to take me home. Inside, I was dying, experiencing a kind of second earth-upheaval, the shattering of a planet – the microcosm of my own little world. I yearned for the Lorenzo I knew – the man who, beneath the moonlight, vowed to love me eternally. My feelings vacillated between longing and retreat. It was not in my nature to beg and, besides, had I done so, I would only have caused myself further grief and degradation. No! I had to hold my own – to claim my right to my own identity, free of Lorenzo. He didn't really know me, and to be honest, I had yet to discover myself. I had my whole life ahead of me, but I didn't know that then. All I knew for certain was that I felt utterly, desperately miserable, a shadow of myself. My sole distraction was the fact that I had a future awaiting me in Lima, the capital city, where I was about to explore a whole new world – a place which would spread out a tapestry of different experiences at my feet – a hodgepodge of joys and sorrows, the magnitude of which, in those moments of isolation and heartsickness, I never could begin to comprehend.

Chapter 5

Springboards For Evolution

As time evolved, so did I. At the age of fifteen, my dreams shone before me like the sun's morning rays, each passing day beckoning me to soak them up and create my future. In truth, however, I was still a child in many respects, always in Laura's shadow, thrilled to be included in her world and accepted by her peers. Unlike most older sisters, she unashamedly involved me in everything, cultivated my happiness, and tended to my comfort with such love and regard as I received from no other human heart. Laura's delicate sweetness and affable personality endeared her to virtually everyone.

It was no surprise that my sister was my parents' darling, often to the negation of Mom's attendance to issues concerning me. I never questioned why my beloved Laura held her distinguished position. I only pondered the reasons for my own dismissal. It would take years for me to come to terms with this complexity and, as I will narrate, in due course, I did. Closure eventually comes to those who probe and, then, quietly wait for answers naturally to flow. In my adolescence, however, this realization had not yet formed. It was extremely difficult for me to comprehend my status, in everyone's eyes (except Laura's) as the strong, independent sort, who could fend for myself, without maternal intervention. Mom's conspicuous lack of involvement in my world occurred even on such momentous occasions as my fifteenth birthday or quinceañera (analogous to "sweet sixteen" parties in the United States). Though I never could quite ascertain the cause, I was left alone on that auspicious day, to drown in my solitude – literally, in a bottle of whiskey, with which I chose to experiment for the purpose of making myself more content. I took my example from various adults whom I had observed, and I didn't see why that method wouldn't work for me. The odious concoction almost made me gag and in an effort literally to sweeten the agony, I added sugar. The difference was, of course, negligible, and after I swallowed my share of the horrible potion, I fell asleep. When everyone came home to find me in my stupor, they explained that Dad's store had been burglarized, and that this unfortunate event had precluded my celebration. A likely story? Perhaps – and I don't question it now; but it was painful to believe that I had been robbed of recognition on such a pivotal day in my life. Laura had been absent from home on this occasion. To be sure, she never would have allowed anything to mar my joy – not even a burglary.

My sister and I were like twins. Every chance we had, we were together. On one very memorable afternoon, while walking out of a store in El Centenario, we ran into Enrique, the boyfriend of Laura's friend, Elena. I recalled meeting Enrique the year before at one of Laura's parties. At that time, the tall, wavy-haired, light-complexioned boy who fawned over the enormously popular, beautiful Elena, hardly recognized that I was alive. Naturally, I was envious of Elena's feminine magnetism, and the fact that she had such a handsome boyfriend. On the occasion of our chance meeting outside the convenience store, Laura introduced me as her little sister. After a passing exchange of pleasantries, Enrique went his way – only to appear again when I attended nursing school in Lima, to serve as my ubiquitous friend and tour guide – well, at least at first.

As the days went by, I hearkened back to those childhood plays with Marina and Inés in which the three of us were nurses. I pledged to fulfill those early dreams, and at the same time, actualize my potential and inclination for the practice of nursing. Without reason or cause to defer what I perceived to be the inevitable, I applied, at age sixteen, to a military nursing school in Lima. So ventured the mountain girl into city life.

What an atmospheric and cultural transformation! The very air that I breathed was thick with vehicular fumes – particularly in the downtown area – expelled from wall-to-wall cars and buses. These vehicles were jam-packed with passengers, like sardines, swarming every which way to various destinations, at a pace that would make one-hundred-meter-dash runners gasp. The city's pulse was so charged that suffixes were often omitted from words. Why bother to enunciate what everyone easily could guess? There was simply no time. To witness and experience all of this was more than my small town heart and lungs could bear.

In truth, I was miserable – nauseous, dizzy, and generally ill to a degree that I never had experienced before. Fortunately, my home which I shared with my brother, Tomás, and Laura was located in a suburb about thirty to forty minutes away from the city center. Tomás was studying medicine and Laura was completing her pre-law classes.

Living with Tomás wasn't easy. At every turn his modus operandi was to keep his younger sisters on the periphery of his influential circle – as though our presence somehow would diminish the standards that he and his friends always strove to establish. Often, my siblings' verbal altercations made me feel displaced and extremely uncomfortable. As for me, my spots instantly came to mind as the cause of my brother's maltreatment. I dare say that Tomás' scornful scrutiny of me formed a deeper internal scar than my more obvious ones. I was mortified at the mere thought that Tomás relegated me to the sidelines. I believed that he was ashamed of me, that I wasn't good enough. These feelings of inadequacy only served to compound my already existing fears of being in a new environment and having to confront new people who would, no doubt, judge me as well.

For a moment in time, I believed that I had a connection, via across-the-room eye contact, with Paulo, one of Tomás' friends – a cute, blonde-haired, blue-eyed youth, whose engaging looks would appear before my eyes again in later years – not in the person of Paulo himself, but, rather, someone who very closely resembled him. It's funny how life comes full circle. Again, my thoughts are running away with me. Anyway, the issue here is that Paulo was, therefore, like a phantom – harboring, perhaps, what may or could have been if I had found the courage to speak with him. Contingencies very often don't take shape into reality, even when we want them to or entertain hope that they will.

Not only did the changes in my immediate world envelope me, the differences in the entirely strange and new ambience overwhelmed me even more. Everything was distinct from all that I was accustomed to hearing and seeing – the music, the food, and even the style of dress. In an effort to stave off the heat, most people wore light clothing. My red-complexioned face created by high mountain oxygen seemed incongruous with the tanned visages of city dwellers. Still, despite all of the anomalies and disharmonies around me, I knew that I was where I had to be – in a place in which to cultivate my future.

The prestigious nursing school issued a couple of thousand applications for only fifty or so vacancies. I'm uncertain of the precise data, but the number of vacancies was small when compared with the magnitude of candidates. My fervent hope of attending was almost dashed when I failed the physical exam because of my height. Being told that I was too short was devastating. Someone advised me, however, that exceptions had been made in the past for this technicality. So, Dad appealed to a high-ranking officer with whom he was acquainted, and persuaded him to allow me to take the academic and psychological portions of the test. If I failed academically, that would have been it for me. I was so grateful for the opportunity, and worked my heart out to fulfill my ultimate goal. I had to wait three agonizing weeks for the results – probably the longest time span of my entire life. As usual, Laura, my guardian angel, waited with me and, at the appropriate time, accompanied me to school to view the postings. I nearly fainted when I learned the news: I had been one of few students accepted to the program. Brimming with joy, my sister and I called Dad to share the news. It was truly a time of celebration.

By this point, to meet the requirements of the stringent program, my long, flowing blonde locks had been truncated into a short bob, like that of a boy. It was during this time of transition that I became reacquainted with Enrique, my guide to fun in the sun. Our connection quickly blossomed into a steadfast friendship. He showed me around the city, taking me to places that I never even imagined existed – the zoo, fancy restaurants, and shows. We frequented the movies, chatted, engaged in childish banter, and just enjoyed each other's company. For some inexplicable reason, I felt comfortable with the intensely engaging boy who seemed to know everything – at least, in my estimation. By that time, Enrique and his girlfriend, Elena, had broken up. She had gone to study abroad in Russia – a decision which caused my friend no small measure of distress. In his sorrow, he confided in me and was grateful for a listening ear. For my part, I was only too glad to divert my thoughts from my recent heartbreak over Lorenzo. I guess you might say that Enrique and I were in the right place at the right time for each other. For reasons that I still cannot define, he never seemed to mind my spots, which were visible then, without a hint of coverage. Enrique just accepted me unconditionally. When I cut my hair, he was shocked, but ultimately declared that "it's just hair, and I'm sure you can let it grow in no time again when you are done with school. I know how much school means to you. So, congratulations!" I was pleased with this endorsement, grateful that, with Enrique, I never had to strive to be someone other than myself.

Having an ally, though of enormous comfort, still couldn't shield me from the harsh realities of my new surroundings. The idea of sunscreen was inconceivable to me – a mountain girl who thrived on fresh air and radiant sunshine, without any fear of burns. Was I in for a rude awakening! One day, two of my classmates, Carolina and Linda, invited me to the beach – in those days, a novel concept to me. When I returned, I noticed that my skin had turned very red. A few days thereafter, it turned dark and began to peel. I didn't think anything of this; but, about a week later, after I ventured to the beach to sunbathe again, I had to go to the emergency room and was diagnosed with a second-degree burn on my back. Sleeping on my back was incredibly painful and, for two weeks, I had to wear bandages and gauze pads. Just imagine! In the middle of the intense summer heat, I had to walk around Lima like an American football player! That experience taught me to be far more careful and study the landscape a little more before going to a new place. More than I ever could contemplate at the time, this lesson would serve me immeasurably in my future. The cliché is true: sometimes, pain is a necessary precursor to gain – especially when the discomfort engenders awareness.

Once I cleared the hurdle of being admitted to nursing school, I confronted the even greater challenge of remaining in the program. During basic training, many failed out, and a couple of students in operating room instruction dropped out, as well. I vividly recall that after observing heart surgery in our first year one of the girls suddenly turned pale and fainted on top of me. She and a couple of other students never returned after that incident. I, on the contrary, was intrigued by the entire experience of witnessing for the first time a human heart as it pumped autonomously the life force throughout the body. How perfect is nature's intricate and mysterious design. For me there was no question of whether I was in the right place – this was certainly my calling. I thoroughly found the whole experience deeply moving. Such an experience gave me increased motivation for studying even more intensively. What little time was left I spent socializing, making lifetime friends – all while maintaining twelve-hour days, five days a week, and half days on Saturdays. Our training was almost as rigorous as that undertaken by medical doctors in the United States. Under the military government, we received monetary assistance with purchasing our books and uniforms, along with room and board.

Living one block away from school was a luxury. I could literally roll out of bed into class. Notwithstanding this convenience, I had a tendency toward lateness – a habit for which I nearly received serious reprimand. Perhaps, on a subconscious level, I used my freedom of independence to compensate for all of my years spent under the nuns' iron rule. My one source of sustenance and security was my ability to excel academically. The youngest and shortest in my group, I sat in the back of the room with a contingent of taller friends. When my father came to school one day to inquire about my progress, he learned that I was among the top in my class. Later, he stopped by my apartment and left a package with a note at my door. "I am very proud of you. You are among the best students in the program, but you must get to class on time." The package contained a large alarm clock – my warning device for keeping to my schedule and my implicit promise to Dad. His approval and pride inspired my compliance, and I was never late again.

When it came to studying human sexuality, I turned crimson with embarrassment. With the nuns, the subject always had been taboo. Desperate to avoid the wrath of ages, some girls in my high school who had become pregnant dropped out and got married, never to return. The openness with which the subject was addressed in medical school, therefore, was an entirely new dimension for me – one to which I had to adjust, slowly and incrementally.

As I think back, my reticence was due, without question, to a particular incident that occurred in the fourth grade, a year before the earthquake, while I was attending Santa Rosa de Viterbo. Like all young children, the human form was intriguing to me. Perhaps, the fact that we couldn't speak openly on the subject with adults made the pursuit of knowledge even more enticing. Rummaging around one day in the attic of our family business, I found what I believed to be a cartoon comic book, depicting dorsal nudity. No one in my immediate family ever read such material, and I attributed ownership to one of the workers. As a child of about eight, my understanding of the actual photographs was limited to vague amusement. In fact, what I witnessed was pornography. I giggled at the sight of the bare anatomy. The next day, I made the fatal mistake of bringing my "comic book" to school. What did I know? I thought the photos would get a laugh out of my classmates. At first, their reaction was precisely what I had anticipated, but when Carla, the teacher's pet, set her eyes on the book, the atmosphere changed entirely. When she presented the incriminating evidence to Ms. Cecilia, a stone-faced spinster and the strictest of teachers, I felt my heart quicken. Then, Ms. Cecilia gazed knowingly into my eyes. At that moment, my life had come to an end. I was called out and hit with the dreaded ruler, which mercilessly struck my hand many times. I withdrew that beleaguered hand, only to be struck twice as hard. The humiliation was unspeakable. In front of everyone, I was demeaned, belittled and debased, as though I were a common felon. Is this the way to treat innocence – a misdeed perpetrated by sheer unawareness? The question is more than rhetorical; it begs for a resounding answer in the negative. The next day, while I was in class, I spotted my mother walking into the principal's office. By her solemn expression, I could tell that I was in serious trouble. Apparently, Ms. Cecilia, who was one of Mom's acquaintances, had summoned her immediately. More demoralization followed as I was made, once again, to feel diminished and unworthy.

Across the conduit of time, history repeated itself – only this time, neither as severely nor as bitingly – though there was a parallel. Just like in the fourth grade class, conduct in nursing school was monitored for the slightest transgression. A case in point: one day, I was joking with some friends about a nephrology professor's pronunciation of the word, haya (the first- and third-person subjunctive conjugation of the verb haber, to have). The professor, whose Spanish grammar was less than pristine, consistently said "haiga" for haya. At the precise moment that I pointed out this unintentional slip to four of my classmates, he blurted out the word again, sending us into gales of laughter. Noticing the disruption, the professor demanded that "the young lady with the light brown-blonde hair, please stand up and share the joke with the class." There I stood, mute, not being able to say what was the subject of our ridicule. At the professor's command, my three friends also stood, one by one, equally incapable of uttering a sound. There was no turning back. We had been insubordinate – an intolerable offense, warranting a report to our superiors and banishment to four consecutive days of manual labor – the cleaning of hospital instruments. Although my friends were upset, their loyalty to me – and vice versa – prevented any of us from revealing our secret. We simply had to bear up under our lesson in conforming to the establishment. What didn't hurt us made us stronger, I suppose. Besides, a bit of levity had to factor in to offset the seriousness of our studies. Dealing closely with life and death situations called for reprieves now and then – even if this meant engaging in passing improprieties. I was stronger than that crestfallen fourth grader, prepared to meet any challenges, and if that signified doing some community service, I relented – willingly and resolutely.

Anyway, steeped in my books, I barely had time to take such things seriously. The "haiga" episode just served as a reminder of how not to let minutia get to me – and as a clear indication of my increasing personal fortitude in standing up to life. No longer was I the little girl victim. I was a full, validated participant in the human experience. As such, my chief preoccupation was living up to the honor of being in the nursing program and being the best at my profession. Enrique, who was studying industrial engineering at the time, was always attentive to and respectful of my commitment to learning. I was still in my first year when he came to my home and kindly took along some books to assist with my psychology research project. At the time, we had an honored guest: Grandpa who, quite against his will, had come to stay with us to see a local orthopedic doctor for his hip, which he injured while riding his faithful horse, Mauro Mina. His injury was an aberration – something so out of the ordinary. Grandpa seemed untouchable, but we were glad to accommodate him as he convalesced. Anyway, as Enrique and I sat on the living room couch in close proximity in order to see by the dimmed lights, Grandpa walked in and began his verbal onslaught of Enrique. Addressing my friend sternly, he bellowed, "I know what your intentions are with my granddaughter, and I must warn you that this is my son's house. As his father, I assert the right to tell you that you are to leave the premises immediately." Without a sound, Enrique complied. Grandpa's unfounded overprotectiveness caused such unjustified embarrassment that I began to sob. Instantly, my sweet Grandma (who, of course, had traveled along with Grandpa as moral support) came to hug and comfort me, while scolding Grandpa for his behavior. Right before my eyes, that grumpy, seemingly intractable old man transformed into a demure lamb. It was amazing to witness my delicate flower of a grandmother subsume the behemoth in her grasp. While she made Grandpa believe that he was in charge, she gently, unassumingly assumed dominion. For me, such was an unforgettable example of the inexorable triumph of grace and beauty over the illusory dominance of masculinity. I say this not as a feminist, but as a humanist – firmly established in the opinion that kindness and strength are not mutually exclusive – irrespective of gender.

Naturally, I apologized profusely to Enrique, who never wavered in his friendship toward me. About a year or so later, he asked me to go for a walk with him on the beach to look at the sunset. Pulling me in front of the ocean's boulders, he held my hand for the first time. As we contemplated the beauty of the setting sun, Enrique kissed me. I was mesmerized – and intensely surprised – for I had always considered him just a friend. I responded, feeling that the evolution of our relationship was as natural as the impending dawn. We began seeing each other more often. Enrique picked me up and took me home after dinners and dates, which made us feel like a couple.

Later, however, I began to notice Enrique's affinity for alcohol – a tendency which I found unacceptable. I had to face the undeniable fact of his blatant alcoholism when he took me to a formal party with his parents. Leaving me alone the whole evening with them and, basically, ignoring me while he drank with friends, he spoke incomprehensibly and acted like a buffoon. Such behavior was an abomination. You see, in Peru, when a young man takes you to a stately gathering with his parents, you are his official girlfriend and prospective fiancée. It soon became clear, however, that Enrique was taking me for granted, dating me on the rebound from his relationship with Elena. In hindsight, I can say that I was not in love. In coming to this realization, however, I must admit, in all fairness, that when he was sober, Enrique was the consummate gentleman, every woman's dream. He was very romantic (though not quite as ardently passionate as Lorenzo). He told me that he loved me several times and treated me with special care. The extent to which he came under the influence, though, proved to me that he loved alcohol more than anything or anyone. I just couldn't compete. His parents were, clearly, embarrassed by his behavior at the party that evening. His father apologized and drove me home, but I remained indifferent and just went with the flow. I continued to go out with him and enjoy our time as a pair, but I was not tied to him in any way. My heart wasn't invested. Now I know, unequivocally, that my apathy was a sign of detachment. When all was said and done, we were good friends, and for a considerable period of time, we occupied a special place in one another's hearts. I always will be grateful for the time we shared together.

When I was not in Enrique's society, my self-consciousness about my spots seemed to be a never-ending concern. Despite my best efforts, I was always reminded of that which I perceived to be an inescapable imperfection. As a result, relating to the good-looking doctors and officers around me (the latter of whom either were visitors or patients at the hospital) was an immense strain. Some very insensitive residents and doctors sometimes seized the opportunity to make a spectacle of me – in conversation with one another, no less – for the purpose of evaluating my condition. I felt like a case study, an object being held up for scrutiny quite against my will, but no one seemed to care. Especially when I was in clinical training, self-aggrandizing doctors would blatantly point out my spots, as though I were not even there. One painful incident particularly stands out in my mind: a doctor held my chin in his hands, and without consulting me, spoke to his residents and asked, "Is this melanosis or melanoma? Retracting slightly, I was able to remove my face from his grasp. I was humiliated and demoralized beyond measure, internally questioning myself: Why me? This scenario served to exacerbate my feelings about Lorenzo's rejection. Surely, my appearance was the cause, I thought. Fear of being ostracized and romantic rebuffs engulfed me like a dark cloud, and I shielded myself yet more with my own self-imposed shroud of aloofness (or so my behavior seemed to others) by ignoring anyone who might have been remotely interested in me. I related to and empathized with those who had indelible scars, for it seemed that my humiliation could not be erased.

My feelings of inadequacy were compounded one afternoon when a young boy came into the pediatric unit and remarked, "You're pretty, but you have to erase all of those marks on your face." When I told him that couldn't be done, he just looked at me quizzically. Up went the shield again – crafted of iron. By the time I reached my second year and a handsome resident approached me on clinical rounds to ask me out to dinner, I dismissed him outright, stating deceptively that I was seeing someone. Without another word, I left. In my quiet moments, I cringed at what I had done – no, I hated myself. My self-esteem had been so comprised that I couldn't even allow myself the pleasure of male companionship. Around my co-workers, I was equally uneasy – unless, of course, I knew the people whom I was with. At all times, I carried lipsticks and concealing makeup. Without these instruments of defense, I was bare – discovered, as if my spots were indicia of criminality. This sense of diminished self-worth was the hallmark of my conduct in subsequent relationships, upon which I will elaborate later. Suffice it to say, though, that what I thought of myself in those early days – essentially, my formative years – clearly manifested and profoundly shaped my later life.

I'm proud to say that, today, I have evolved, and I wear my self-confidence like the finest gemstone. If anyone ever dared to treat me now as that supercilious doctor did those many years ago, I would speak my mind and assert my personhood. "Take your hands off!" The woman of the Now would declare. "I am not your display object! Pay heed to people's feelings before you decide to use them as guinea pigs. The worth of every individual cannot be measured. How dare you treat anyone as a freak of nature!" By the way, the woman who would, hypothetically, utter those words no longer has her facial spots. Now, as I peer into my past, I clearly discern that the source of my enormous pain was, in truth, a catalyst for my growth.

Some experiences, however, serve no ostensible purpose at all – except to demonstrate the arrogant self-possession and lack of tact within certain individuals. One decisive example comes to mind. I continued to acclimate to the city by going out with my friend, Carolina, who was about seven or eight years older than I. I perceived her and her friends to be very sophisticated, and it was a pleasure being around them. One evening, we went to a discotheque where one of the naval officers, dressed in full uniform, asked me to dance. I conceded. The dance floor was dark but, by the contours of the officer's face, I could tell that he was extremely handsome. He pulled me close and deliberately collided with me several times. Then, he gently took my hand and slowly guided me to the nether region of his manliness – which, I can only say, as I search for delicate phraseology here, was at its height. "This is the effect that you have on me," he said. I didn't know this man from Adam, yet, I doubt that even if I had been in the Garden of Eden at the Genesis, I could not have discovered a more salient expression of masculinity. Far from being flattered, I was repulsed and offended by the officer's forwardness. How could he? No doubt, he saw me as an object instead of a human being. Confused, shocked, and afraid, I told Carolina that I wanted to go home. Not until this day have I recounted the story. I supposed that I had to await my rebirth – a kind of resurgent, personal genesis, with introspection and insight about the world from which I came and the future to which I was heading.

Yet more springboards for evolution awaited me when, in my third year of nursing school, Carolina (who, by then, worked in the Neurology and Neurosurgery Departments), introduced me to the rotating doctors and nurses there, who invited me to be part of their team. In my first assignment as a young nurse, Carolina introduced me to Dr. S., a fascinating neurosurgeon, whose looks were surpassed only by his intellect. I believe that I was, indeed, attracted to him, but he was more of a mentor figure to me than a prospective romantic interest. Though he was single at the time, he later married one of my co-workers in the Neurology Department.

Once, when I was on the night shift, Dr. S. assisted me in tending to the body of a deceased patient. My supervisor was incensed, and chastised me severely for "not doing my job." Instantly, Dr. S. came to my defense. "Isabella did not ask me to help," he insisted. "I offered. She is new here, and I wanted to assist." I was deeply moved, and never forgot Dr. S. for his kindness.

Tragically, Dr. S. was, ultimately, a victim of self-imposed destruction. As brilliant as he was, his addiction to Valium and alcohol did him in. I learned this quite by happenstance, when a male nurse's aide, walking at a very fast pace into the unit one day, collided into me and a tray of Valium spilled all over the floor. When I asked whom the drug was for, he quickly answered, "They're not for me. They're for Dr. S. He takes them quite often." I was shocked. I told Carolina, who knew the facts – as did everyone else. However, no one bothered to make an issue of Dr. S.'s addiction, for he was highly functional – even, apparently, when he performed neurosurgery under the influence of prescription drugs and alcohol. Notwithstanding this stunning truth, he was always the best doctor in the hospital. His genuineness, too, was a constant, and everyone had nothing but good things to say about him and his methods of treatment.

When I mention that his addictions did him in, I mean this quite factually. Many years subsequent to my departure from Peru, his wife tried to awaken him one morning, but found him nonresponsive. Evidently, the evening before, he had come home in an inebriated state, and choked in his sleep. Like everyone who knew Dr. S., I was overcome by disbelief and sadness. I asked myself how alcohol could rob such a bright, handsome, accomplished individual of life. I never could wrap my mind around such devastation.

In hindsight, remembering the horror of Dr. S.'s untimely demise, I juxtaposed my erstwhile affinity for Enrique. I realized then that, had I remained with him, I would have ended up just like Dr. S.'s wife – a bereaved widow, bemoaning the senseless death of her husband in the very prime of his life – and for what purpose? Surely, not for love! Certainly, I was not in love with Enrique, and being with him would have meant undeniable sacrifice. Besides, if he really had loved me as he professed, he would have done everything in his power to conquer his addiction – for the sake of love, if for nothing else. That is what love signifies – transcending weaknesses and foibles for a greater, mutual good. Perhaps this sounds idealistic, but especially if, in the name of commitment, one cannot seek to achieve the highest standard of conduct, how can we humans hope to attain lasting relationships? Love should be give-and-take, an unconditional exchange – in all respects – but with eyes wide open and readiness to rectify blatant imperfections which stand in the way of real happiness.

I now understand that all of my nursing school experiences served as a sidebar to truth. By this I mean that, as I witnessed and experienced, I silently internalized, in a dialogue with myself. Without defining my actions or intentions, I was taking stock of my past which, while I lived it, was a rote, mechanistic expression of who I truly was. The mirror images that resurfaced for me in the prelude to my professional career – insecurity, fear, self-doubt, a broken heart – placed in perspective everything I had gone through as a child. I was ready to move forward. What I didn't realize was that life's cruelties could strike in ways that my heart could barely sustain – circumstances that would challenge me even to breathe – even when the darkest days beset me and I couldn't find the rhyme or the reason....

Chapter 6

Of Cowards and Heroes

Had I not decided to become a nurse, I most certainly would have studied veterinary medicine. I always was – and still consider myself to be – adept at working with and interacting with our four-legged friends, our fellow inhabitants on this planet. Part of being a caretaker and healer is the ability to empathize with all living things. Cross-species respect and love are integral to the whole human experience. In writing my own story, therefore, I would be remiss were I to omit mention of some special beings in my life who left permanent imprints on my heart – each in distinct, but very significant ways.

One such valiant creature in my world was Clipper, my cherished blue-eyed mutt, whom I taught to dance and pretend to smoke a cigarette, while standing on his hind legs. He was adorable. I had this dog when we were in Nicrupampa. At that time, he was a veritable cottonball of fluff, my steadfast companion, who rode with me in the back of Dad's blue pickup truck, enjoying the wind currents through our hair and fur, my long locks flowing behind me and Clipper's soft mane fluttering in like fashion. After the earthquake, we walked together through the slushy, soaked and muddied streets of Nicrupampa, like two waifs in a lost world. Sadly, I had to leave him in my mother's charge while in pursuit of my nursing career in Lima. I should have known better, for Clipper disappeared from the house and no one knew what had happened to him. I was heartbroken.

When I came home for vacation in my second year, I visited the open market with my mother and Victoria, the young housekeeper who had helped me through my pubescent episodes. Suddenly, a scruffy-looking dog came up beside me and began to jump up and down. At first, I was afraid, but soon recognized the precious canine to be none other than my long-lost Clipper! Awestruck, I began to pet and speak to him, until a rather corpulent lady came over and asked, "Who are you? Does my dog know you?" "Your dog?" I queried. "I am the owner of this dog." The lady proceeded to tell me that she found Clipper a year before. He had been roaming as a stray, so she brought him home, and mated him with her dog, who had puppies. Clipper is a father, with a family of his own! I silently gasped. With a heavy heart, I bid farewell to my Clipper and his new guardian. What other choice did I have?

Clipper gave me that choice. Unbelievably, while I was home for about a month's stay, Clipper showed up at my door, bloodied, with a cut and lacerations under one eye – the apparent insignias of a dog fight. Even in his distress (or, perhaps, because of it, in an attempt to seek help), Clipper remembered where he lived and who his original master was! No coward was he. He knew where the heart was and where to find proper treatment. As I write, I swallow my tears at the very thought of his immeasurable devotion. I took him in and went to the pharmacy to buy necessary items for his care. Donning clean gloves, I tended to his wounds, washed, and placed him in a comfortable, padded box. I kept him there, under close watch, on a regimen of soft foods. A couple of weeks passed, and as he increasingly felt well nourished and loved, my Clipper began to heal and run around the house, as good as new. During the recovery process, his beautiful blue eyes seemed to cross, and formed a winking expression. I had to laugh, for he was more endearing than ever.

To my sorrow, Clipper's homecoming endured only as long as my hiatus from school. When I departed for Lima, he decided to return to his family. Though I never saw him again, his memory ever flashes in my mind's eye, always resurrecting a joyful time – one that never can be recaptured.

I was in my third year of nursing school when I was graced, yet again, by another treasure of our terrestrial ecosystem. Laura and I decided to go up to our terrace to observe the day of commemoration for Capitán Miguel Grau, hero of the Naval Battle of Angamos, which took place during the War In the Pacific (1879-1884). During this celebration, people could be seen saluting, with their palms to their chests, in solemn remembrance. As we looked around us, Laura spotted a little green parakeet. He seemed rather demure and in need of a home. That was what our hearts told us, anyway. So, Laura threw her sweater over the bird, and we took him downstairs. So began beautiful little Miguel's stay with us. Yes, he was named for a hero, and he certainly lived up to that nomenclature. At first, of course, he was timid; but after we clipped his wings and fed him breadcrumbs and fruits, he seemed to adapt well to domesticity, and became a wonderful pet. When I came home from the hospital, there was Miguel, greeting me. I used to put a paper towel on my shoulder, which he used as a resting, launching, and landing pad, flying to and fro, like a tiny jet. He was a real charmer. I tried to teach him to speak, but he was, somehow, not genetically predisposed to elocution. Finding that lack within himself, he heroically attempted to make all sorts of sounds to please me – gurgles, whistles, rumbles, and tweets of all kinds. His devotion to us was unflagging. Even when his wings grew, he never attempted to leave.

Miguel did disappear for one entire day, leaving me beside myself with anguish. When I came home from school, he was nowhere in sight. Even our housekeeper had no clue as to where he had gone. Toward evening, I began to worry, and offered a reward to those neighborhood kids who would find him for me. He must have flown away, I thought to myself, vainly trying to fend off my grief. Late that evening, I went on our terrace, where Laura and I had first encountered our winged companion. Softly, I called to him and heard…"peep!" Then, again, "peep!" I followed the sound, which I detected to be coming from the attic. As I followed the whistle, it grew closer and closer. Then, from under a blanket, the noise seemed to emanate even louder… and there he was, my hero, almost asphyxiated beneath that covering. He flew out, happy as a lark – or, I should say, a parakeet – so grateful to have been found. I later discovered that, when the housekeeper had gone into the attic, Miguel must have followed her and become ensnared in the blanket. I can still feel my heart quicken when I think of our happy reunion.

For about a year, my delicate friend continued to be source of entertainment to all who knew him. A neighbor next door had several children who took an enormous liking to Miguel, and asked their absentee father (who was known to visit only once a month) to get them a parakeet just like our little one. The father, who apparently gave in to all of their wishes, came home one day with a full-grown, talking parrot. This bird was loquacious. He could have run for political office, so imposing was his status and ability to speak. (I mean no disrespect to office-holders, of course. Any who might be so affiliated would be rather flattered by a comparison to this splendid feathered creature.) The kids insisted that I bring over his diminutive counterpart for a visit one afternoon – I suppose with the intent to show off their ostensible differences. Miguel wasn't a fancy bird – he was, well, himself, never trying to impress, just hoping to please. Having nothing much better to do on that particular day, I conceded to the request. I will never forget how my cute little hero took one look at that formidable bird and began to run away. The latter waddled close behind, yelling, "Cobarde, cobarde!" ("Coward, coward!") The episode was so hysterical, that it brought tears to my eyes – but Miguel wasn't amused. I had to take him home immediately.

Several months later, my brother Tomás' dog, Ramón, a dachshund, or perro salchicha, was playing roughly with Miguel, as he was accustomed to doing. When I arrived home, I found the housekeeper crying, with our beloved bird in her hands. Miguel was expiring. Apparently, Ramón had bit him too aggressively in the wrong place. Laura and I sobbed. It was amazing how this little creature had touched our hearts and our lives with his incredibly dynamic personality and tenderness. What surprises nature can grace you with, if you just open your heart – even to the tiniest life forms! We all have something to teach each other, and my hero taught me this great lesson.

We wanted to bury Miguel in our garden, but observing how sad we were to have lost him, a friend insisted upon taking his body away from us. We had no idea what his intent was, but we entrusted the precious earthly remains to him. Two weeks elapsed, and he returned with the likeness of Miguel, sitting on a branch – a creation of taxidermy. Then, we had to give him up again, when Dad took and kept him in a glass cabinet in his office. Beneath the tiny bird was a plaque inscribed with his name, the date on which we found him, and when he died. Thus had our friend been immortalized. I really didn't know whether to be repulsed or grateful, but I suspect that, after all these years, the latter feeling holds sway – along with our endless memories of love, fun and laughter.

It may seem odd to juxtapose a human story to those narrated here and, in fact, there isn't any ostensible correlation

between them and the event which I am about to recount –
except the very telling truth that, as you will see, all of these
relationships were infused with three elements: immense love,
loss, and letting go.

I was born to be a care provider and throughout my life – to
this very day – I remain committed to that goal. Being such a
practitioner requires the vital characteristics of compassion,
resolve, and sense of purpose, which I employ in all circles and
at all levels of interaction – a selfless, unconditional exchange
with humans and animals, alike. As between humans, mutual
love and regard are forces which, when sincerely communicated,
give us an opportunity to transcend all other forms of exchange,
and achieve the highest level of expression.

With Lorenzo, my first love, I had that chance – twice. The
first occurred as a young teenager, newly in love, exploring the
reaches of my burgeoning adolescence and yearning for affection
and validation. The second episode happened in my last year of
school, at age eighteen. For me, during the second interlude,
things had changed. Quite out of the blue, I received a call from
my aunt, who had been dating Lorenzo's uncle. She frenetically
told me that Lorenzo and his new girlfriend, Zoila, had been in a
horrific accident. They had been crossing a street, when a car
with one light (which they erroneously thought to be a
motorcycle) hit them, head on. Without any chance to move to
the roadside, both were impacted. Miraculously, Zoila only
suffered lacerations and a concussion, but Lorenzo was in dire

straits. He had multiple facial wounds and corporeal fractures, the most severe of which was to his femur. To make matters even worse, he was rendered unconscious and remained in a coma for fifteen days. Realizing that Lorenzo needed immediate expert medical intervention, my aunt prevailed upon me to have him admitted to my hospital, one of the most prestigious in the country. The problem was that Lorenzo wasn't in the military, so, with emotional tour de force – and more than a little good fortune, – I had to pull a few strings.

As luck would have it, Ana, one of my classmates, was in a relationship with the hospital's CEO, whom I will call Dr. B. Boldly summoning my courage, I requested that Ana arrange my introduction to the eminent physician, for the purpose of discussing Lorenzo's urgency. She did so, and I went to Dr. B.'s office – dressed to the nines and fortified by deep conviction. I explained Lorenzo's situation, and asked whether "my cousin," notwithstanding his lack of military status, could be admitted. Winking at me impishly out of the corner of one eye, Dr. B. replied, "For your cousin, of course." Breathing a sigh of relief, I went home to inform my aunt who, in turn, broke the good news to Lorenzo's father. The gratitude of that man was, truly, overwhelming. I was all too happy to oblige. The heart never forgets, and always maintains an open door – if not romantically, then in other, even more meaningful guises.

So, my erstwhile love was transferred from a hospital in Trujillo into the specialized care of my facility. By then, he had emerged from the coma, and I was excited by the prospect of seeing him after a long while. Of course, he was still very weak and out of sorts, but he recognized me. The details of his past, however, still remained sketchy. His faithful girlfriend, Zoila, came religiously every day to keep vigil and attend to him at his bedside. She even applied for and got a job as a nutritionist at a nearby institute. Star-crossed in love though I had been, I was profoundly moved by her attention to her boyfriend. One may imagine, therefore, how stunned I was to witness Lorenzo's cruel rejection of her when he gained full strength and cognizance.

"Do you still love me?" he cried one day, grabbing my hand when I went to visit and check on him in the recovery room.

What? I said to myself. Was I hearing properly? How could this happen? I had been in love with a womanizer, and, had I remained with him, my heart would have been torn to pieces – and, possibly, my life would have been bereft of quality and the chance at other meaningful relationships. Lorenzo was a phantom, a mere figment of my youth – though, undeniably, someone to whom I had given my heart without regret. At that moment, there in the hospital, I stood mute. My silence spoke infinite truth. It just wasn't meant to be. I was somewhat older then, definitely wiser, and more capable of making sensible choices – and I did. That was a turning point, and I was undeniably proud of myself. In that moment, I rescued my own heart.

As with Clipper and Miguel, I had cared for Lorenzo, loved him with all of my heart, made sacrifices and exceptions for him – and then, I had to let him go. Again, I must explain – but I make no apology for – the apparent incongruity of Lorenzo's story with those of my beloved pets; but the three elements of love, loss, and letting go were irrefutably present in each instance. Isn't that what the whole conundrum is often about? Maybe, but I had so far to go and so much to discover. My heart wasn't finished experiencing yet – not nearly. What I could not possibly have known was how much I had yet to invest and, tragically, to relinquish.

Chapter 7

The Dove

La Paloma

Si a tu ventana llega
Una paloma,
Trátala con cariño,
Que es mi persona.

The Dove
If a dove comes to your window,
Treat it with affection,
For it is I.

Sebastián Yradier, composer (1809-1865)

Life is a series of diametrical opposites – emotions, feelings, and events which often descend upon us all at once – admixtures of joy and sorrow, pain and pleasure, loss and gain. It is therefore natural, dear reader, that my own story contains an amalgam of these contradictions. I arrive now to a place in my narrative filled with sadness; a chapter in my history where sorrow alighted at my window like a dark apparition, taking me to the lowest depths of my soul. Before I moved forward, I had to visit that place –

quite against my will, and despite enormous desperation and pain – until, once again, I could emerge into the light. You needn't refrain or cower from what I am about to recount, for I'm certain that you, too, have experienced life's fluctuations in many forms. Who among us is immune to them? Take my hand and travel with me through a tunnel of grief, so that we can emerge again into the sunshine, together.

Sights, sounds, smells – all teem before me now as wispy memories of my past – all parts of the conundrum of opposites. Just yesterday, as I was on my way to a painting class, a waft of succulent Chinese food filled my olfactory senses. Yum! Kan Lum fried wonton, that crispy, crunchy victual – Laura's and my favorite! Where can I find it? I asked myself. Until yesterday, no Chinese restaurant that I've tried in America could accommodate my request. Just yesterday, a familiar craving entered my brain, triggering a memorable moment gone by, never to be recaptured – until yesterday, when I experienced the taste again. In my first year of nursing school, I had tried that delectable dish, in secret. You see, at the time, I had my tonsils removed and was on a strict diet of Jell-O and liquids. Hunger overtook me like a ferocious monster, subsuming me in its clutches. Enter, my sweet sister to the rescue, as she was always wont to do. She visited me in the hospital one afternoon – at a moment when my hunger must have appeared in my facial expression.

"How are you, Isabella?" my sister asked tenderly.

"I'm so hungry, but I'm not allowed to eat, and I can't take it anymore."

"What can I do for you?" asked my benevolent resolver of all ills.

"I'm craving Kan Lum fried wonton." I salivated, almost tasting the delicacy.

"I'll be right back."

My sister hurried away and soon returned to manifest my wish. She always met – and surpassed – my expectations. I hid the Kan Lum fried wonton under my covers – just in case the nurse walked in and found me perpetrating the crime. Agent Angel Sister stood at the doorway, on the lookout, smiling and admonishing me not to crunch too much. "Quiet!" she gently commanded, holding one finger to her lips. Sure enough, just when I finished devouring the forbidden meal, a nurse came into the room. "Something smells good in here," she declared, eyeing me suspiciously. Laura and I just looked at each other without saying a word. What a savory misdeed – and I was worse for the wear! A couple of anti-inflammatory throat medication doses later, I felt as good as new.

It was just yesterday...or was it?...when I bit into that familiar Kan Lum fried wonton, and relished the flavor. Wait! How did I get there – here? Oh, yes, it was she, again, my sister. It was she who brought me to America and my present consciousness. It was – and always will be – my sister.

One morning, clad in her hand-knitted green sweater, black pants and shoes, with a large purse on her right shoulder, Laura ambled sideways, out the back door. "Chao, Isabella!" she said, wistfully looking at me askance, as though sadness enveloped her entire being. I wondered why…and I still do, though it's not such a mystery to me now. That state of being was not characteristic of my usually blithe Laura. Other than that brief farewell, everything about the day was unremarkable. At the time, I was a registered nurse, working at the officer's clinic. It so happened that I was off that day, just relaxing or watching television. To tell you the truth, I can't remember now. I basked in idleness, pondering nothing, enjoying my sheer lack of contemplation.

I didn't bother to recall that, just two days before I observed my sister's unusually sorrowful expression, she had a nightmare of such a magnitude as to cause her to sleep next to me, in my bed. "I had a terrible dream!" she cried, in deep anguish. "I dreamt that something very heavy pressed on my body, and I couldn't move. I'm so frightened! Please let me stay with you!" I didn't stop to remember that fifteen minutes thereafter, both of us let out bloodcurdling screams when our brother, Tomás, pounced on the bed with such force, that we imagined another earthquake. Seeing Laura's bed covers half unfolded that morning, and believing that she had left to attend a party with Xavier, Tomás had come in search of our sister. "How dare you frighten us so!" I exclaimed. After many seconds of terror, I realized that he was just being as he always was.

I didn't pause to reflect upon how, several weeks before, Laura had run into a clairvoyant in the main plaza outside the Supreme Court, where she was doing her legal practicum. The woman stopped my sister serendipitously – quite against her will, as she was about to board the bus – and offered this word of advice: "Be careful, child!" she said, taking her hand and looking at her palm. "You won't have a very long life. Take care!" This encounter was terribly odd, especially given that so-called fortunetellers didn't simply offer their skills or advice without compensation. Laura certainly didn't seek, or even want the lady's counsel, and didn't pay a penny for her unsolicited comments.

Beside herself with fear, Laura came home in tears and told me the story. "If something happens to you, I couldn't live!" she cried, hugging me. "I hope that I die first, because I couldn't bear to lose you! I love you so much!" Then, she added, "Should something ever befall me, think of me, Isabella, and know that I am with you. I will give you a sign."

I recall that my sister used to sing a song about a dove, called "La Paloma," well-known in several countries throughout the world. I always associated the song with Laura, somehow. It seemed to befit her so well.

Si a tu ventana llega

Una paloma,

Trátala con cariño,

Que es mi persona.

At the time, I knew that the symbol of the dove had special significance, but I never knew what a profound impact it would have on my life.

As Laura's little sister, the mere thought of her absence sent me into a panic. I became extremely upset, and told her that she mustn't speak or think in that way. We had endured so much together, including the catastrophic earthquake that destroyed our youthful dreams of perpetual happiness, we lost acquaintances and friends, withstood heartbreak, resurrected laughter from the ashes – and, ultimately, survived! At any given moment, therefore, the thought of not having Laura at my side was inconceivable. Through all of the smiles and tears, she was there for me, as my public relations manager, my confidante and companion – the best friend with whom I chatted until the wee hours of the morning about everything – books, movies, life itself. Being naturally predisposed to seeking pleasure – as we humans all do – I chose to evoke the nectar, the sweet contemplation of that day in Miraflores, an upscale district in Lima, with boutique dress shops and other luxury stores. As we walked along together, I looked up and spotted a beautiful, elegant, blue couture dress with a sash at the waist. My eyes must have lit up, because my sister looked at me knowingly. She sensed my every emotion. "Don't even look at it!" I said. "It's much too expensive!"

A short time later, Laura received her first paycheck for selling appliances at the World's Fair. Instead of spending the money on herself, she thought of me – just as she always had. When I came home from school, I found a huge box on the table near my bed. I opened it to find…the dress! I was so excited, and nearly cried for joy. Inside was a beautiful card, which read, "To my little sister from your big sister, who loves you."

I can't remember anything now, except that love…and except that on the evening of that seemingly ordinary day, at 9:00 p.m., I was washing my hair, leaning into the tub, when there came a loud banging at my door. It was Tomás, screaming frenetically, holding my sister's black shoes and large purse.

"Laura has been in a very serious car accident! The police just came with her belongings, and she was taken to your hospital's emergency room! I'm going there right now!"

Apparently, a doctor at my hospital was driving the automobile – a dangerous instrumentality, made so by his probable drunkenness. Later, I learned that after hitting my sister (who had been walking near the road), the doctor panicked, exited his car, picked her up off the ground (an uncommon act, under the circumstances), and brought her to the ER.

I was stunned. With my hair drenched and disheveled, I grabbed a towel and ran, for one block, to the hospital. When I entered the ER, dazed and soaked, I heard my brother, screaming, "No, no, dear God, no! My sister is dead!" Upon hearing these words, I collapsed to the floor. There, in my anguish, I opened my eyes to catch a vague glimpse of a familiar face – that of Carlos, a physician and family friend. He barely recognized me, but when he finally did, he exclaimed, "Oh, my God! This is Laura's little sister, Isabella!"

Under intense sedation, I remained overnight at the hospital. It seemed that no amount of medication could assuage or take away my mental and emotional distress. Feelings of shock washed over me like a tidal wave, robbing me of my aliveness, my center. My anchor, my sister, who had been so much a part of me was irretrievably lost. All night, I stayed awake, screaming and crying for my sister. The next day, as a friend walked me home, I encountered my father entering the hospital. "Oh, Dios mio! Mi hija está muerta! No puede ser!" ("Oh, my God! My daughter is dead! It can't be!") I heard him say as we briefly embraced.

There wasn't any way to deal with such a horrible tragedy but cry, and cry I did – for days on end. I'm certain that the tears never stopped; they just dried up in my heart's reservoir, where they sometimes well up again, when the sights, sounds, smells, and remembrances of my youth come gushing toward me, like torrents of rain – and rays of sunshine – more examples of the juxtaposition of opposites.

When my dove flew away, she did so with military honors. The hospital staff were so shocked by my sister's death that they gave her an illustrious funeral and burial. As I mentioned, I was already a nurse at the military clinic, and the doctor whose car hit her also worked at the hospital. So, the administration believed such an elite tribute to be appropriate. Although I was deeply grateful for such displays of respect and affection, I barely could entertain a thought or a feeling as I struggled against slipping in and out of consciousness, collapsing at every turn. At Laura's funeral, I saw the sleeping beauty dressed in white, with a blue belt around her waist, holding roses in her hands. I suspect that my aversion to this type of flower has origins in sorrow.

All the while, I felt dissociated from my body, as though my brain were protecting me from the deep emotional pain occasioned by the moment – the sights, the sounds, the smells, the entire experience. It was as though my body and mind had, somehow, detached from one another in an effort to keep me earthbound – and yet, somehow, not completely present – there, in the space of unspeakable mourning.

Laura was buried on the fifth level of an elaborate mausoleum, located about half an hour from home. On the night before we interred her earthly form, I sat on our terrace, imploring her to give me some indication of her eternal presence. "Please, please send me a sign! You said that you would let me know! I can't live without you!" Just at that moment, a piece of a metal rod that had been leaning against the outside sink crashed to the ground. Startled, I ran back into the house, without breathing a word to our multitudes of guests. Surely, they would have believed that I lost my mind – but I knew what I felt. My sister was with me. I did, however, confide in Carolina, my good friend and colleague. Throughout our tragic ordeal, she was with me, even assisting to prepare Laura cosmetically for burial. Carolina told me that, on the third day of a loved one's death, the departed walks through phases of his/her life before entering Eternity.

On that third day, our house was, once again, filled with people – relatives and other mourners from Huaraz and various towns. With scarce room to sleep, Carolina and I were relegated to the trailer outside of my house. This vehicular dwelling, equipped with beds and other comforts, was owned by Dad's brother, Luis, who lived in America. He had hoped that, perhaps, my father could sell the trailer for him. For the time being, though, we were grateful to use it as sleeping quarters in the absence of alternatives. All of a sudden, as I dozed under the influence of a sleeping pill, I was awakened by a distinctive voice, whispering my name, "Isabella! Isabella! Isabella!" My body shook and, thinking that it was Carolina in the bed across from mine, I quickly glanced in that direction. My good friend was sound asleep, oblivious to the voice. I began to cry, shouting, "Laura is here, Laura is here!" Carolina awoke and rushed to my side to comfort me. Just at that moment, we heard the plaintive wail of a dog outside, "Auuuuuuuu!" In my country, there is a pervasive belief among elders (sort of an old wives' tale) that, when a dog howls in that way, it has seen a ghost.

Whether there is any truth in this is anyone's guess. All I knew that night was that my sister was very close to me – close enough to say her last goodbye.

A few weeks later, still at the mercy of indescribable grief, not being able to sleep or eat very well, I saw Laura, my dove, right before my eyes. Whether she was a figment of my tortured mind or an actual presence, I know not. I was in my room, lying next to my sister's empty bed, when she appeared, as real as anyone I had ever seen, sitting at her desk, studying her law books. I tried to speak, but couldn't form words. All I could do was scream.

"Laura, Laura, she's…here!"

Dad came running in, took me in his arms, and hugged me close as I sobbed uncontrollably.

"I already lost one daughter, and I don't want to lose another," he said, looking at me tenderly. "This may be a good time for you to visit Uncle Luis in America, as you often spoke of doing in the past."

Without the presence of mind either to agree or decline, I went along with Dad's suggestion. I knew that, as always, he meant well, and I couldn't take issue with anything he said – especially when he had my interests at heart, which he always did. So, without having a full opportunity to mourn my great loss, I had to prepare to leave. My father made arrangements with Uncle Luis and the Lions Club for me to obtain my student visa, and Dad paid considerable money for my ticket, plus all expenses. My future – at least my immediate one – had been decided for me.

Like my dove, I was flying away, to a far away land, high above the clouds, where grief and pain couldn't touch me….But, no! I was intensely earthbound, still prey to my irrepressible sorrow. Laura was free – and, in that respect, perhaps, more fortunate than I. I had to go on – but how? I knew that she missed me, that she was thinking of me, loving me ever as much as I loved her. Oh, but for that one last chance to tell her! How did I know that it would be the very last time? How do we ever know? Yet, my sister lived – as she ever does still – in this heart of mine; and, as I will reveal, she returns over and over again in mysterious, intriguing, and profoundly poignant ways.

Chapter 8

Transformations

When my beloved Laura transcended to another sphere, so did I – to America, a wonderful, mysterious place, of which I had absolutely no cognizance in those early days, where modes of communicating, interacting and living were utterly foreign to me. I was twenty-one when I took that interplanetary journey, via Ecuatoriana airlines (a now defunct carrier), to Kennedy Airport. The trip was my very first time on an airplane. The feeling of being completely weightless and not in control of my destiny was daunting, to say the least. In my heart, I carried a weight that would most likely have overwhelmingly enveloped any place – let alone an aircraft cabin – but I wouldn't dare admit its presence – not even to myself – that pervasive, all-encompassing grief of mine. I felt very small, but not insignificant. I knew that something – perhaps, something surprisingly pleasant – awaited me, but this was just a fleeting speculation. In truth, the experience was one huge question mark.

Coming from an entirely different climate, clad only in my alpaca sweater with Peruvian designs, I looked as though I had just dropped out of a time-culture capsule from another world. Bewildered and frightened (who wouldn't be?), I waited in anticipation and suspense, for my Uncle Luis to pick me up. It was 10:00 p.m., and I was cold – a feeling so rare and uncomfortable. Suddenly, a respectable, distinguished-looking, middle-aged gentleman approached and began speaking to me in broken Spanish.

"How can I help you?" he asked. "Is everything all right?"

There was something in the man's face and mannerisms which inspired my trust.

"It's getting very late, and I'm worried because my relatives who were supposed to come for me have not arrived." I must have looked at him like a lone deer in headlights.

Immediately, the man sprang into action and spoke with a Puerto Rican family – a couple with two daughters, whom I will call the Ortegas.

"These nice people will stay with you while you wait for your uncle. You are in good hands," my ally reassured me.

Then, the solemn, resolute Good Samaritan shook my hand, wished me good luck, and took his leave. Never will I forget him. Thank you, Sir, for being my prelude to an amazing journey – one that ever continues!

We waited for about an hour, without any sign of Uncle Luis. So, the Ortegas helped me to use the phone. Given my inability to speak English, that device was a terrifying instrument.

Mrs. Ortega left a message for my aunt Carmela, my uncle's wife, and provided our location at the airport and the family's contact information (including their address). At about 1:00 a.m., when there was no sign of my benefactor, the Ortegas decided to drive me to their home, about half an hour away. I had no idea where they lived. In fact, I was clueless as to the distance between New York and New Jersey, where Uncle Luis lived. Apparently, everything was very spread out, and my spatial and distance perceptions on my new planet were, as yet, nil.

An hour after my arrival at the Ortegas', in walked Uncle Luis, at last, looking like an Eskimo in his huge winter jacket. Seeing him was like spotting a familiar face in a desolate tundra. Pleasantries were exchanged, and Luis expressed his extreme gratitude for my friends' hospitality. I also thanked the family for all that they had done to make me feel comfortable. It is rare, indeed, when you find people who genuinely care and cast off all façades and feelings of restraint to reach out to someone in need. Across the bridge of time, thanks again are in order for those extraordinary hearts who so extended themselves to me.

And, so, there I found myself, in Uncle Luis's posh SUV, with electronic windows, doors, and all manner of sophisticated technology, the likes of which I didn't even try to comprehend. That which I witnessed outside of my window pane was even more engaging: tall skyscrapers, vast roads, and signs everywhere in English – that intensely difficult and frightening mode of communication which seemed to be beyond my grasp. What amazed me most was our drive through the Lincoln Tunnel. Uncle Luis turned to me and said very matter-of-factly, "We're driving under the Hudson River." "We're under water? No!" I replied, with a gaping expression. I can't be sure, but I imagine that for quite a while during my initial stay in the United States, my gaze was transfixed for much of the time.

My stay at my sponsors' home was brief – only a few weeks. Although they were kind to me, they had financial constraints and couldn't afford to sustain me for an extended period. Their home was small, and I had to stuff my belongings into tiny closets. Still, with the passage of days, I began to settle in. Seeing all of that beautiful snow on the second day of my arrival was a particularly awe-inspiring vision. Never before had I witnessed such a phenomenon. It was January, the cold, blustery month. In Peru, we had glaciers, of course, but the snow was always high above us – never beside us, on the ground. In its glistening coat of wintry splendor, the new planet looked quite inviting. If only I could have shared it with Laura!

With the help of destiny and Aunt Carmela, I enrolled in a language program and put my student visa to use. We were sent some forms to fill out, after which I attended a language school about forty-five minutes from home. I felt awkward calling anywhere other than either Huaraz or Lima "home," but I simply had to abide by the whims of destiny. At the language school, I encountered a very pleasant woman, whom I will call Mrs. N., who didn't speak a word of Spanish. Somehow, though, her heart spoke louder than any words could. Inherently, she understood my plight – the fact that I was alone and needed a friend – so, she decided to introduce me to her daughter, Julie, who, at the time, had taken a semester off from college.

Elaboration upon this friendship deserves particular attention, since it was – and remains – a true blessing in my life – the best thing that could have happened to me, at a time when I was most in need of emotional sustenance, understanding and support. At 5'7", with blue eyes and blonde hair, Julie's external beauty was matched only by her unstoppable energy, vivacious personality and contagious good humor. Although we initially spoke not a word of each other's languages, we communicated through gestures, photographs, and pictures – a continuous game of charades, which we thoroughly enjoyed. Gradually, as I began to learn English and taught Julie some Spanish, our communications became more fluid and our interactions more extensive.

During this period, I began to work as a live-in au pair, tending to two delightful children, Cameron and Melissa, ages six and eight, respectively. I doted on and became very close to them and vice versa – to such an extent that Cameron asked whether I would become his mother.

"Dad," Cameron said reflectively in the middle of dinner one evening, "if Mom dies, can you please marry Isabella? I want her to be my Mom."

Everyone fell silent.

"Cameron, I said, looking at him firmly, but benevolently, "I love you very much, but I am not your Mom. Your Mom is sitting right next to you, and no one can take her place."

Though my English was halting, I believe that my message was clearly understood. I realized that Cameron's mother must have been daunted. I did my best, therefore, to be deferent toward her. All the while, I felt intensely flattered, sensing that Cameron's remark had sparked my maternal instincts – however minutely at the time – like flowers germinating beneath the last snow of winter.

Speaking of the changing seasons, that phenomenon was a complete mystery to me. When winter turned to spring, Julie and I jogged together in the park. Enthusiastically, like a child witnessing an awe-inspiring event, she pointed out the cherry blossoms – the enlivening of trees, dormant all winter long, transforming into magnificent arrays of cherry blossoms, which populated the branches like little sprites impishly displaying their magic! Never had I seen such a miraculous sight in my entire life. As nature transformed, so did I, gradually assimilating and melding into my new world.

As the days evolved into months, I continued to learn English via home instruction which, owing to my lack of transportation, the language school provided. I couldn't wait for the arrival of Mrs. D., my home tutor, a wonderful lady who not only instructed me in the language, but also exposed me to American culture. It was an exciting time, and my pangs of grief, if not dissipated, slowly began to become part of my emotional fabric – something I lived with, as opposed to an enemy combatant. This transformation was due in large measure to

Julie's shining presence and her ability to make me feel comfortable – no matter where we were together.

Soon, I began to take night classes in English as a Second Language at a local school. There, I met people from various countries – Colombia, Italy, Greece, India, and a host of others. One special man, whom I will identify as János, was a handsome student pilot from Hungary, with whom I became steadfast friends. He took me out to dinner and plays in New York City and, within a few months, we were officially dating. Although I diligently obscured my facial spots, the issue was moot with him. I felt at ease and intrinsically knew that János liked me for myself. He even told me that, if ever I had bouts with insomnia, I could call him at any time of night. At one point, I took him up on his generous offer. You can imagine my astonishment when a woman answered, declaring herself to be his girlfriend, whereupon I ceased to see János again.

After about a year of working as an au pair, my full-time services were no longer required, as the mother of the family began to spend more time at home. I gratefully took my leave, bidding the children farewell with every ounce of love and goodwill.

In the next phase of my evolution, I worked for Mrs. C., an eighty-five-year-old dynamo. Mrs. C. was a thin woman, with blue eyes and wrinkles that were most prominent when she smiled. With her gray hair piled in a bun, she was the depiction of graceful old age. In her mannerisms, however, she was quite idiosyncratic, but I loved her for that. Her favorite pleasures were chocolate and Bible readings, both of which she freely shared with me. Her odd juxtaposition of temporal and spiritual matters always made me laugh. At night, she came to my room on the second floor, opened my bed hotel-style, and left milk chocolate on my night stand, along with an occasional glass of Harveys Bristol Cream Sherry. The chocolates and the liquor were sometimes excessive, and I had to hide them from myself, so as to prevent overindulgence. Mrs. C. spoke to me for hours, recounting the adventures of her youth and family life. She called me "deary," and doted on me like a daughter. As if I were her child, she even imposed a curfew upon me. If, God forbid, I didn't come home at 8:00 p.m., she had the entire neighborhood police department looking for me. It was a wonder that she didn't call out the National Guard. We enjoyed many pleasant times together, attending the nearby church, watching our dog run around in the yard and, on rare occasions, shopping in department stores. Mrs. C. was the definition of selflessness, always buying sweaters or dresses for me, while refusing to purchase anything for herself.

. Mrs. C. encouraged my education, for which she paid, along with my room and board. She even took an interest in my love life. She wasn't shy about noticing János's good looks. It was amusing to see how she gaped at him, almost like an awe-struck youth. Yes, János actually came to visit, asking me to come back to him; but that wasn't going to happen. The relationship was never too profound, and therefore, it wasn't difficult to relinquish my ties to him.

On one memorable occasion, Mrs. C. took me to visit her daughter in a neighboring town. There, I met Henry, Mrs. C.'s grandson. His cordial, welcoming manner made me feel at ease. About a week later, Henry's mother stopped by, telling me that her son found me attractive, and wanted to take me out. Anxiety seized me, and given my scanty vocabulary at the time, I could only reply, "Aw! He is so cute!" Apparently, my reaction was received as a rejection, for neither Henry nor his mother broached the subject again. Owing to my low self-esteem, I brooded upon the miscommunication – and the possibility that I, in fact, was the rebuked party. You see, the mere idea (let alone the existence) of my spots still created subliminal, as well as overt, feelings of inferiority, which I either subconsciously or deliberately used to justify rejection. Alternatively, I sometimes employed my feeling of low self-worth as a shield against a potentially broken heart. Such was the case with Henry – and, as you, dear reader, shall see, others, as well. I also entertained the notion that Henry's mother may have discouraged a prospective romantic liaison between us due to my status as a health aide and my disparate socioeconomic circumstances. The family was very wealthy and I was not; so, I reasoned I was not good enough for Henry. Such was the devastating mantra of my diminished self-confidence. Thank goodness, the tune has changed now.

One of the highlights of my stay with Mrs. C. was our adopted shaggy black mutt, Maggie. She was very attached to me and used to sleep on a long sofa next to my bed. We were inseparable, and I always played with and tended to her. Unfortunately, this ordinarily sweet mascot abhorred Father Othello, the head of Mrs. C.'s congregation who, along with other priests, used to come to the house to give Mrs. C. her daily Holy Communion. My fairy godmother was very religious, avidly read the Bible, discussed the Book with me, and practiced her diurnal ritual of receiving the Eucharist. On one particular day, I looked out of the window and saw our escaped mutt chasing Father Othello around the lawn, with his clerical garb flailing in the breeze. A bit overweight, the poor clergyman stumbled over himself, as he tried to avert Maggie's wrath. Though the incident was no laughing matter, I couldn't refrain from seeing hilarity in it. Later, Maggie reentered the house with a prize dangling from her mouth – a piece of Father Othello's black attire. Oh, no! We're in trouble now! I thought. The phone rang, and it was none other than the beleaguered Father himself, vowing never to return or to send another priest to the house, unless we "got rid of that beast!" Deeply upset, I feared for Maggie's fate, not knowing what Mrs. C.'s intentions with my faithful companion would ultimately be. When I returned from school one day and ran to play with my friend, my greatest apprehensions were realized. Mrs. C. broke the news. "Maggie has gone to live with my relatives in another state," she said, with compassion in her voice. I never saw Maggie again. Yet once more, I had to part with another of my four-legged friends.

Tears fell prodigiously that day. I just couldn't help it, but I knew that I had to let go. I was learning that, like everything else, impermanence is part of the endless cycle of that continuously edifying and deconstructing entity called life, a voyage on which we each travel divergent paths. If we're lucky enough, various roads converge and footprints form, side by side, signifying friendship and love. Through the tears, the laughter, and many transformations within and outside of me, my personal journey had only just begun.

Chapter 9

Breaking Away

There is no doubt that my father's desire for me to depart my home in Lima had a very pragmatic, reasoned purpose: to dissolve the all-encompassing grief in my heart. However, I discovered that there is really no means of escape from those feelings which perpetually form an integral part of one's emotional makeup. Somehow, I had to get on with my life, in spite of pervasive, insurmountable heartache. My sister was never coming back, and I had to face that horrible truth.

Aside from my best friend and chief source of solace, Julie, my career was a particular focus. I applied and took prerequisites for a physical therapy program – the only one of its kind in the entire state of New Jersey at the time. I had heard that the prerequisites for admission were extremely rigorous – often grueling. However, I was determined to study until I was blue in the face to prove myself to myself, and to everyone around me. On vacation from school, I decided to return for a brief visit to Peru – that source of so many memories. I had come so far from home and, after some deliberation and soul-searching, I ventured back to the piece of earth that had given and taken from me so very much. Julie accompanied me. She knew about my emotional pain ensuing from the loss of my beloved sister, Laura. Empathizing deeply, she cried with me and, with all of the love in her selfless, beautiful heart, offered to fill the void that was left inside of me. How? By being my sister. Truly, she was as true as any sister could be to me; and, to this day, I cannot ever forget her extraordinary acts of kindness and devotion. Never could I imagine the extent to which this one shining presence in my life could so positively impact the course of my destiny. We never know when angels alight in our midst. Julie was – and is – mine.

When we arrived in Lima, we visited the house where I used to live with Laura and Tomás, and took buses downtown. As I looked around, I was overcome by a sense of loss, as though parts of my internal anatomy had been wrenched from inside of me. Everywhere I peered, in every corner and crowd, my sister was missing. I took massive doses of prescription Valium to cope with my emotional pain, while gasping for a breath of oxygen. The very air that I had inhaled with Laura not very long before literally choked me in her absence. Panic attacks and palpitations seized me to the point of near suffocation, triggering my need for an electrocardiogram. I was rushed to the hospital – the very facility where I used to work and was well acquainted with the staff, and where I had received the life-altering news that Laura was gone. I had returned full circle to that place. It was as though fate were mocking me. A cardiologist examined me and prescribed large quantities of Valium. From then on, I was hooked. Popping Valium constantly to mask my inner turmoil, I was on a downward spiral, until one day, Julie helped me to break free. She took the Valium from my hands, seized every bottle that I had and, right before my eyes, flushed the pills down the toilet. "From now on, you won't need these," my angel affirmed. "I will be your Valium."

Dispensing with the medication saved my life. The symbolic act of flushing away the pills also signified a purging of my sorrow. From that moment on, the crutch of taking medication to camouflage my grief became a thing of the past. I was, in effect, cleansed of the toxicity of the bottomless sadness which had consumed me from within – that silent anguish, suppressed by my precipitous departure from Peru, only a couple of weeks after my sister's death. Not until that moment, when Julie spoke those words of love and salvation, could I free myself from tacit self-destruction. If only the world – anyone suffering pain of any kind – could have a support system such as I had then – someone to say, "I care! Please don't hurt yourself anymore! I love you!" Thank you, Julie for helping me to face my inner torrent and lead me into the light. Were it not for your wisdom, empathy, concern and love, I could not be who I am today, composing these pages, and living my truth.

Once I was extricated from my emotional abyss, our journey continued to Cuzco and Machu Picchu. We were accompanied by Carolina, my trusted friend from my nursing school days. First, we flew from Lima to Cuzco, in order to adjust to the high altitude. Everyone who visits the region affirms that this is the best course of action before traveling on to Machu Picchu, where the considerably higher altitude can be jolting if you're not prepared. Carrying our sweaters at all times, we were able to withstand the cool temperatures, ranging from about 10 to 20 degrees Celsius. It was my first time there, and my eyes consumed the beauty around me as nourishment for my soul, filling me with memories to last a lifetime. Bright blue skies danced overhead, as if welcoming us to the region, filled with ancient structures built in the days of the Incas, my ancestors. In ancient times, Cuzco was the capital city, the hub of activity. The word Cuzco (or Cusco), itself means navel in Quechua, the Incan language, connoting the heart or core of the nation. Today, the mountainous peaks, majestic temples, and structures of sculpted and carved stones harbor secrets of the Incan Empire – a past that I never knew, but to which I was honored to be privy by witnessing the splendor of the place. The earth has a language of its own there, and if you listen, you can hear echoes of truth, wisdom, suffering, and triumph.

We stayed in Cuzco for a couple of days, where we took day trips to Urubamba Valley, with its breathtaking river and Sacsayhuamán, a huge fortress with stonework nearly thirty-three feet high, that looked as though it were built by giants. In the shape of a lightening bolt, the walled complex had nearly half-mile-long symmetrical entrances and exits. Altitude adjustments and my inner emotional turmoil rendered me incapable of climbing a small pyramid, which Julie and Carolina encountered without incident. Upon our return to Cuzco, I gradually began to feel restored, as I drank mate de coca and periodically carried a small portable oxygen tank to assist with my residual anxieties and altitude sickness.

The following day, we went to the sacred city of Machu Picchu, built at the tip of a mountain ridge. No one can explain the reason for the awe-inspiring stone city's location. Upon our approach, we saw a military fortress built into a single rock, the famed Temple of the Moon, with its intricate, exquisitely constructed caves. During the highlight of the trip, my intrepid friends and I climbed the Intihuatana pyramid and saw the solar clock. I was so proud and happy – all the while wishing that Laura could have shared that awe-inspiring experience with me. The next day, we returned to Cuzco for the last day and night of our journey. There, we socialized with some very cute fellows, one of whom accompanied me back to my hotel. Julie and Carolina continued to party the night away, while I felt the need to go back to my hotel and sleep. Such was the case, notwithstanding the fact that a handsome young man expressed an interest in me. Politely taking my leave of him, I returned to my room, while my friends enjoyed a night of revelry. On the following day, we boarded a return flight to Lima, and my friends slept on the plane. Since, on the previous night, I had opted for more sedate activities than they, I was wide awake and eager to visit my family. Carolina returned home, while Julie stayed with my family and me for a couple of days before flying back to the States. A week later, after my visit with family and a brief trip to Huaraz, I left for my new home. After my days in communion with nature and the sights of my historic homeland, I felt renewed, leaving, as ever, a piece of my heart there.

Back on the new planet which I had come to call home, I discovered, to my surprise and delight, that I was admitted to the elite physical therapy program. My diligence and hard work had paid off.

Soon after, learned that my brother Tomas had decided to come to the United States to further pursue his career as a medical doctor. He informed me that he needed a place to stay. I was able to secure his residence with the unparalleled Mrs. C. who out of deep affection for and courtesy to me, gave my brother free room and board.

Solving many problems kept me busy, yet the trip to Peru brought back sharp memories about the loss of my beloved sister Laura. No matter how hard I tried to deflect my emotions, I some times thumbled into a cavernous abyss of grief. Even though the trip to Peru had been a catharsis – thanks, most of all, to Julie – I couldn't entirely avoid feelings of desolation. No doubt, Tomás felt this, too, but his feelings went unexpressed. Perhaps, if we had been able to communicate more openly, we could have bridged the gap between us.

You see, after Laura left this earthly plane, I perceived her belongings to be empty shells, meaningless nothings, in disuse without her. I came to understand that things are, after all is said and done, utterly superfluous and that the saying, "You can't take it with you," is truer than any of us care to face. My sorrow was that Laura herself was not there to experience life with me –

to celebrate triumphs, to despair over trials, and to be my confidante, as she always had been. The mere mention of her name sent me into the depths of sorrow.

At about this time, I had been in a car accident, which completely totaled my vehicle, but from which I emerged, thank goodness, in one piece. With the insurance money, I purchased a brand new Toyota Supra, a stick shift car, equipped with every possible state-of-the-art amenity. The possession of this car was brief, however, because Tomas quickly found a way to have my new acquisition. This forced me to buy a beat-up old mustard-colored station wagon for $200 from Mrs. C.'s daughter-in-law. The only reason that I made such a purchase was that I required transportation to and from school. As Tomas took ownership of my new car, I spent agonizing summer months with my head popping in and out of the window of my dilapidated station wagon trying, in the absence of an air conditioner, to breathe in some fresh air. By that time, I was driving my second-hand red Honda Accord (a replacement for my extinct mustard station wagon, which I triumphantly drove with a stick shift – sweet revenge. My self-taught efforts had panned out well). I had been studying for a Gross Anatomy exam, dissecting cadavers, and feeling particularly susceptible, as though my own heart had been lain bear on a table, for all the world to see.

Such residues of my past – the subjugation I felt in my brother's presence, and so on – all were transposed like dissonant musical notes into my new world. It was at about this time that I met Eduardo Davidio. As I mentioned, I had been attending an extremely competitive physical therapy program. Coursework entailed taking some of the same classes as first-year medical students (e.g., Gross Anatomy and Embryology). As I walked to class on one unforgettable Thursday afternoon, I saw a tall, strikingly handsome, blue-eyed young man walking in the opposite direction. Our eyes met, and I instantaneously felt that he had surreptitiously peered into the portal of my soul. My mind was transfixed, though my body remained in motion, as I continued toward my destination. That state of oblivion lasted for the entire duration of the lecture, as I sat daydreaming about the Adonis whom I had encountered. In my reverie, he asked me out, showed me tender attention, admired me, and made me feel special. "But wait!" my insecure, shy, heartbroken self cried out. "How can you have such dreams when you have ink-like spots on your face, when you have been rejected, when you have been injured in love consistently, when you barely speak English?" The negative voice in my head and heart drowned out all possibility of hope. That voice of fear and self-abnegation was a liar, but I never knew it.

The next day, my classmate and friend, Sarah, asked me to go with her and a group of other girls to a Mexican restaurant near our school. I hesitated, acknowledging Mrs. C.'s penchant for keeping tabs on me, and also out of self-consciousness about being in social situations which, at least in my mind, literally and metaphorically meant having to cover up my insecurities.

Nonetheless, with a little coaxing, I decided to go along. A short time after arriving at the restaurant, I saw him again – the Adonis himself, walking toward me, like a hologram emerging from my dream. Scarcely believing that his eyes were focused on yours truly, the mountain maiden, I turned to look behind me, wondering about the identity of the lucky girl who awaited him. When I saw no one there, I quickly deduced, to my surprise and amazement that, indeed, I was the object of his attention. After initially introducing ourselves, we spoke for a long time, with the ease and naturalness of old friends – those who were, undeniably, attracted. I dared not admit this to myself, lest the manifested dream would disintegrate right before my eyes. We spoke about Peru and its culture, which seemed to captivate Eduardo's interest, while serving as a comfortable topic of discussion for me. My broken English suddenly assumed a fluid character when speaking of my homeland, since I had written school essays about my experiences and had developed a comfortable vocabulary on the subject.

Suddenly, I noticed the time and said that I had to leave. Eduardo had been so attentive and the night's discourse so wonderful, that it was difficult to pull myself away; but I had no choice. I explained that the elderly woman with whom I lived expected me home by 8:00 p.m., after which she would call the police and practically report me as a missing person. Reluctantly, though graciously, my friend acknowledged my pressing situation. He walked me to my car and gave me a kiss on the cheek as his sweet farewell, asking whether he could call me the next day. I was so flustered and excited, that I could hardly breathe. The air around me seemed to change, as if something spectacular were about to happen. There he was, the protagonist of my youthful dream, actually articulating the words that my mind had conjured only hours before. He was real, and he wanted to be with me – with me!

I'm a little embarrassed, even now, to confess that the phone could not ring soon enough. I conjured that ring, as though it were a meteorite about to fall from the sky and impact my life forever. When the call came in, my heart raced like a champion thoroughbred about to claim a blue ribbon. For some reason, from the outset, the quality and depth of this connection had meaning beyond any feeling that I had ever experienced. We agreed to meet for a casual dinner – just a burger and fries. Somehow, that decision seemed appropriate for the brief length of our acquaintance.

So, at 7:00 p.m. that evening, Eduardo showed up at Mrs. C.'s door. When he entered the main hall, he and Tomás briefly shook hands. As I came downstairs, I spotted my date standing next to the door, in a royal blue winter jacket. Even in casual dress, he looked dashing. My brother comported himself very stiffly. To make matters worse, the hour beckoned Mrs. C. to her usual ritual (one among her many humorous, though intensely idiosyncratic habits) of placing her nightgown over the window curtains, so as to shield potentially nefarious spectators from peering in at night. This odd state of things would be much too much for any ordinary guy – let alone for someone who made my heart skip several beats. Therefore, when Eduardo came to the doorway, I hurried out, shutting the door behind me, saying nothing more than, "Let's go!" We entered the car and, of course, desperately seeking a way to compensate for my lack of hospitality, I attempted an incomprehensible excuse.

"I'm sorry that I didn't let you come in. I would have…but we have a lot of antiques in there."

I looked rather sheepish and wondered how in the world I could have concocted such ineffectual reasoning.

"But I like antiques," Eduardo replied, looking at me quizzically.

Keenly aware of my deliberate omission and sensing that I had no means of escape, I didn't force the issue. It would take a gargantuan marine mammal to wrangle out of that net! So, we continued on our way to the restaurant and, though Eduardo's puzzlement didn't abate, he couldn't have been more courteous. Once at our destination, Eduardo's body language spoke volumes. In an attempt to put his arm around me, he sat close, fed me French fries, and behaved in such an engaging, charming manner as to render me completely smitten. My heart fluttered, as butterflies made their way through my stomach walls, teasing me with tingles and nervous sensations that I couldn't control, even if I tried – and, believe me, I couldn't even make the attempt. The little winged creatures enveloped my entire being, leaving me helpless – almost defenseless. Love's force can be overpowering – more intense and dynamic than the most powerful chemical reaction. I suppose that's why the attraction between two people is called chemistry. The surrounding lights weren't bright, so I had no cause for second-guessing or embarrassment about my facial marks; yet, there was so much that I wanted to say, but couldn't – so many inhibitions that couldn't come to the surface, owing to my lack of language fluency. Most especially, I was haunted by the pervasive fear that the magic would vanish in an instant – just as it had with Lorenzo, my adolescent paramour, who broke my heart. I could hardly trust, therefore, that intense aura of attraction, evident in Eduardo's every glance – the profundity with which he looked at me, as though he looked through me, to the core of my being. "But no!" my insecure self admonished me, subsuming me in its ominous control. "Don't allow yourself to be emotionally injured again! Guard your heart under lock and key! Never, in your past, were you deemed worthy – not by Lorenzo or by Tomás and his friends; particularly Paulo, that cute, blue-eyed aristocratic youth, of whom your present company eerily reminds you! Love hurts! Beware! Keep your distance!"

Later, we went to a nearby nightclub. The lights were dimmed, rendering me less inhibited – well, slightly. Heeding the lies of my fearful heart, wearing my invisible armor of self-preservation, I took the dance floor with Eduardo after our casual repast. Intense, intertwining emotions of attraction and fear engulfed me, with trepidation emerging victorious in the battle. All attempts to conquer this foe eluded me. Wallowing in an emotional pit of negativity, I hurried back to our table as soon as I felt that forbidden sensation: closeness and…love. Dare I say love? Why is the word so taboo to me? Yes, I loved Eduardo! However doubtful one may be of love at first sight, it can and does exist. My date had an intensely puzzled look on his face. The confusion seemed to be indelibly etched in his astonished expression. "What's wrong? Why did you run back to the table so quickly?" In a moment charged with feeling and reciprocal perplexity at my own behavior, I was speechless. I simply didn't know what to say. I felt as though I were surveying the emotions of someone I hardly knew – myself.

Fast-forward about three decades, and sit with me, dear literary spectator, in my rehabilitation center office. Witness an octogenarian couple, two people who love one another with as much ardor and sincerity as the day they met. "I loved him from the first moment I saw him," the woman declares to me on more than one occasion. The gentleman echoes his wife's precise sentiments, with equal tenderness. The pair travel home together in a taxi cab, fawning and doting on one another like two teenagers. What a sight to behold!

Contrast my reaction on that memorable day – on that first date with Eduardo. Remember the child whom I encountered in the pediatric clinic, who suggested that I erase my spots – a veritable impossibility (or so I thought, at the time), a stigma to be concealed at all cost - even at the risk of appearing eccentric at twenty-three years old. "Love hurts! Beware!" my beleaguered heart repeatedly chanted.

Understandably, Eduardo was perplexed. As urgently and fervently as I wanted to, I couldn't break through, so I broke away – without adequate explanation. In hindsight, how could I have permeated that iron wall of fear, edified by a heart filled with pain? I had neither the emotional power nor the resources to decipher such complexities – at least consciously – long enough to lift my head and declare my truth to the man I loved. So, he was left in the dark, while I concentrated on a clean break, free of anguish. In truth, though, I was dying inside. He took me home and, with a kiss on the cheek, we parted, our silence charged with feeling.

Two days later, I saw Eduardo yet again, while he was sitting, in plain sight, in the school cafeteria with a group of his friends – all medical students. I had ample opportunity to approach and speak with him, but I avoided what should have been a welcomed icebreaker. Materializing through the corridors of my past, thoughts came rushing back, resurrecting the cruel doctor who held my chin in his hands, requesting a diagnosis from his residents – as though I were an inanimate object, to be dissected by cruel scrutiny and callous judgment. The object of my secret affections looked at me incredulously, with a huge question mark on his face, wondering why I had changed so drastically since two days before.

Still, Eduardo was relentless – but in true gentlemanly fashion. Stealthily, he headed toward the cafeteria's exit door to wait for me. When I was about to leave and spotted him looking at me with his characteristic poignant gaze, I felt like I had stepped into a bed of quicksand. All of my makeup had disappeared and, without sufficient concealer, I felt like a sketched figure, awaiting the artist's brush and palette. Though I was in a room filled with people, I felt alone, bare, yearning to hide. Standing there was Eduardo, looking more perplexed than ever. I had no choice but to fly away – as much from myself as from him - to break free of the shame and sadness whose origins where permanently etched in my history. Several more times after that incident, whenever I saw Eduardo with friends, I made every effort to avoid him – and he knew it. In one instance, as I was about to enter Anatomy class, I felt a gentle tap on my back from none other than Eduardo, offering to help with my Myology studies. Not knowing how to respond, I turned crimson and was unable to speak to anyone, as I impatiently waited for the door to swing open so that I could break away. Any other young man, with far less sensibility and compassion, would have run for the hills in the wake of such unusual behavior. Instead, he persisted, casually appearing in front of me, pursuing me gracefully – in vain. That is not to say, by any stretch of the imagination, that I was indifferent. On the contrary, I was stymied by self-imposed feelings of inadequacy and trepidation –

those two malevolent specters of my own creation, ever hovering over me.

Time and again, I lost my chance, until one day, with my spots well camouflaged, I encountered the Adonis once again, in a lab customarily occupied by medical students. There, standing behind my instructor, eight feet away from me, I spotted my ubiquitous, benevolent suitor. His expression beckoned me to him, as though he wanted to speak with me. I wanted to run again, but his penetrating blue eyes captivated me. Later, when I met him in the hallway and walked with him to his locker, I mustered up the courage to ask whether he wanted to come with me to my best friend Julie's Christmas party in New York City. At first, he hesitated, but then agreed, stating that he had to be home early to prepare for a final exam the next day. Later, when we ran into each other in the hallway again, he requested that I meet him at his apartment, which was more in proximity to New York than mine. Going against my inherent beliefs and practices, I agreed, feeling that complying was the least I could do, in light of the pain that I had undoubtedly caused him. Truly, this was the farthest thing from my intentions – the call of that insidious mantra, "Love hurts! Beware!" My modus operandi always had been and ever shall remain to treat all people with due respect and regard – especially those whom I love. Indeed, I must have entertained the latter feeling for Eduardo, given that I had never initiated a date or ventured to a man's house alone. This was truly a first for me, in all respects.

Dressed in a Peruvian outfit of a friend's creation (a black skirt and a wooden vest, with a light blue cashmere sweater beneath), my hair curled and falling below my shoulders, and sporting my decent-looking second-hand car, I presented myself at Eduardo's residence. I spotted my date through a window panel as he approached the door. Clad in his dress pants, without a shirt, he looked like a vision of masculine estheticism. In more colloquial parlance, he had a very handsome physique, which I couldn't help but notice. Eduardo requested that I remain in the living room while he changed. When he emerged from his bedroom, I noticed that he carried a guitar, which he played, while singing the Bee Gees' song, "How Can You Mend a Broken Heart?" This melody was apropos of my unintentional aloofness. Eduardo began to caress my shoulders in intimate fashion; then, all at once, we noticed that it was time to leave for the party.

We mutually decided to take my little red Honda, which Eduardo drove adroitly. Along the way, at his request, I read questions pertaining to his final Anatomy exam, tentatively pronouncing English words, but more efficiently managing those with a Latin stem. I was slightly nervous, but my companion's gentleness and supreme gentlemanliness in holding doors for me and, generally, making me feel like a lady, placed me in a zone of comfort and security. At the party, we were separated in the crowd, while dear Julie introduced me to some of her friends and my date mingled. Since we didn't have a chance to communicate alone, and given the pressures of the following day's exam, we decided to leave early. Much to my amazement, I accepted Eduardo's invitation to his apartment. I cannot tell a lie: I was anxious, but my sense of connection to my new friend transcended any misgivings – yet another first.

Once in his apartment, we entered Eduardo's home office. There, on his computer, he displayed a one-page letter which I assumed had been composed for me. My heightened excitement, coupled with my scanty English vocabulary, prevented me from reading the entire missive; however, my eye wandered to the signature line, "Your secret admirer." I must have shown some measure of discomfort, for we wound up in a small living room area, where I sat down. Just as Eduardo began to massage my shoulders, I said that I had to go. I rose and my companion walked with me to the door. Tenderly, unassumingly, he tried to kiss me. I offered my cheek. Eduardo's expression turned solemn, and I could tell that he was sorely disappointed. With a heavy heart, I left. Again, another missed opportunity slipped through my fingers like elusive butterflies.. I simply couldn't – or, rather, wouldn't – allow myself the closeness that I so coveted – not just with anyone, but with the most giving, enchanting man I had ever met.

The cycle of rejection continued, as I persisted in my attempts to ignore Eduardo. Each time I ran into him, I ran circles out of my way to avoid him. Never did I, even for a moment, dismiss him from my mind. In fact, he flooded my

130

thoughts like a deluge of emotions, drowning me in an ocean of feelings. My grades began to plummet, and I feared expulsion from the program. Trepidation, self-degradation, past loss – all submerged in my heart's cavernous abyss. Perhaps, in hindsight, my stance could be viewed as a defense mechanism. Before being rejected, I wanted the upper hand – the empowerment of being the person who walked away. I didn't want to be left alone again – wondering, brooding, questioning and doubting myself to the nth degree – all for naught. In so doing, I misled my suitor, falsely deceiving him into believing that I was detached. In reality, however, my insecurity was the culprit, the source of my feigned aloofness. I couldn't fathom how a shy, unworldly mountain girl could appeal to an attractive, preppy guy. By projecting my own self-doubt onto Eduardo, I sabotaged myself and my chance at true love (that is, what I *thought* the definition of "true love" should be: unconditional acceptance and enduring commitment). Whenever I saw Eduardo, a flood of emotions pervaded my being, leaving me at his mercy – as though I were adrift on a vast ocean without a life raft. Yet, I felt anchored by a wonderful sense of connection to him, such as I never had experienced before. Because I felt unworthy, however, I wasn't about to reveal my true feelings.

As Eduardo sat on a couch in the hallway one afternoon, I approached him with a letter in hand – a fabricated epistle, filled with lies and more lies – something about a tragedy that befell someone in my past, of whom he reminded me. I made up the story as a means of rehabilitating my reputation with him – not to mention my own sanity. If someone were to ask me to elaborate upon what that letter contained, I couldn't, for when you make up a story, different versions of that narrative surface and boomerang back to haunt you. Telling lies means never recounting the same story twice. If, on the other hand, the truth is on your side, several versions of the same account can be given, but the essence of veracity – the unchanging, empirical truth – always emerges, words that never can be distorted.

And so, with the most downcast of spirits, I broke away, yet again, in a colossal effort to shield myself from what could have been the greatest, most fulfilling relationship of my life. Through a series of fabrications and inner personal wrangling, I ensnared myself in a trap – set by myself – and only through the passage of time did I come to understand that only I could free myself through the continuous, painstaking, joyous, mysterious, and ultimately triumphant process of self-discovery.

Chapter 10

You Were There

A Letter To Julie

Julie,

At this point in my narrative, I decided to pause and pay tribute to my best friend on earth – yes, you! You are an essential source of my courage to write this book – to compose the passages of my history and to revisit some very painful – and joyful – memories. With your selfless heart and unconditional love, you epitomized – and ever shall – the definition of "friend." When I first came to America, self-conscious and shy, you took me under your wing and mentored me, included me in social gatherings and compelled me to mingle with people when I hardly spoke a word of English. My facial scars didn't matter to you. You saw me for myself and brought out the best in me. Through gestures, facial expressions and graphic depictions, you introduced me to my new world. You gave everything a context – labels and meanings – and thereby provided a framework in which I could evolve. You laughed and cried with me, embraced and showered me with support as no one else could. You even alerted me to the changing seasons, as nature blanketed herself in cyclical attire.

133

At my lowest ebb, when the lights of my world dimmed and hope seemed a mere concept, you were there. When sorrow consumed me and I clung to artificial sustenance as my source of strength, you lifted me up and showed me the true meaning of courage – the importance of summoning my inner resolve to confront life head-on, with all of its ups and downs. The day you dispensed with my prescription Valium – the tiny pills that masked the feelings I couldn't face – you freed me from self-imposed harm and showed me the path to life, the road on which I had to walk without my sister, never forgetting her, but treading with conviction and purpose for myself. Had you not been there to enfold and guide me, who knows where I might be today? Who knows how pain manifests when constantly suppressed? I shudder to think – and I need not, for you were there.

Because of your ability to reach out, you rescued me from the ravages of an anguished heart, and evoked the smile that I wear today. You were there – and, so, I am for you – now and always.

Thank you, Julie!

I love you!

Isabella

Chapter 11

Mountains and Valleys

In matters of the heart, I wasn't prospering during this period in my life – largely due to my insecurities about my facial spots. I failed to understand, then, what I now know: that the blemishes themselves were not blots on my life. Rather, the impediment to my romantic bliss was how I perceived myself.

As for Eduardo, I didn't really see him very much after that fateful fabricated letter that I had written – except for a couple of passing encounters. The first time we met subsequent to my written rebuke was on an escalator. As we descended (sadly, in the direction of our relationship), Eduardo stood right behind me.

"Are you still living with that elderly lady?" he inquired.

"Yes," I said, without more.

Eduardo seemed upset and disappointed. "You're going to live there all of your life!" he answered sternly, connoting that I was destined to be an old maid.

Silence reigned for a few seconds until we stepped off the escalator. Eduardo continued toward the exit, while I made a sharp left into the cafeteria. What a tragedy we experience when words fail, when miscommunication or lack of expression obscures the truth of what we want to articulate. Feelings alone don't operate as mechanisms of thought or speech. I realize now that I should have again seized the opportunity to say that which was in my heart, but I just couldn't. The reasons for my reticence still elude me – but then again, maybe not. Perhaps – no, certainly! I had to evolve and grow in order to view the situation – and myself – objectively, and to acknowledge my own self-worth with or without external validation. Still, the pain of losing the man whom I perceived as my ideal was more than I could bear. I was consumed with the fact that I had brought on Eduardo's aloofness myself, and had thereby driven him away – very much against my subliminal intentions. The fact that I couldn't face him emotionally and that my lack of language proficiency hampered any meaningful exchange was, I thought, my fault, and that I had no one to blame but myself. Now, I question myself as to why blame had to factor in at all. What I had with Eduardo was a momentous encounter in my life – one to which I latched on with every ounce of hope and breath – and these feelings lingered and persisted…until I decided to move on. No other choice seemed possible or tenable.

Part of the process of moving forward was solidifying my career in America and taking the nursing boards. Due to my scanty knowledge of U.S. geography, I thought to myself, Why not take the exam in California, a neighboring state of New Jersey? Think again, Isabella! On what seemed like an interminable flight (about seven hours), I flew to California and sat for the exam – the most difficult in the nation. I then embarked on a nine-day whirlwind bus tour. In my travels, I met three eccentric ladies (to whom I will refer collectively as the

Clausens– Jane, Emily, and Margret, the latter being Emily's middle-aged daughter). Discovering that I was a nurse, they clung to me like koala bears, following me everywhere. Their amusing antics made me laugh and took my mind off the stresses of my daily life. At the hotel, they made sure that they took an ample supply of towels and various paraphernalia – habits which kept the housekeeping staff on their toes. Meeting them also made me realize that still waters truly do run deep. Margret, the middle-aged lady, had a penchant for manipulation, which I hardly could fathom.

"We are going to have dinner at one of the most exclusive restaurants in town," she declared to me one evening.

"But how?" I protested. "We don't have reservations."

"Just wait and see!" Margret's stealthy look unnerved me slightly.

When we entered the illustrious establishment, Margret walked up to the maître d' and, with the air of a socialite, declared, "Clausens, party of four."

"I'm sorry, but we don't have anyone on the list by that name," the maître d' replied.

What ensued was the most astonishing Academy Award-winning display of indignation and rage that I ever witnessed, before or since. Margret ranted at the top of her lungs, expressing the greatest displeasure and threatening to expose the gross negligence of the restaurant's staff for failing to book us. People could have heard the ruckus all the way to Wisconsin – and, I have no doubt, they did. In order to avert prolonged agony – for everyone involved – the maître d' showed us to a table. After the episode had ended and we were safely out of the zone, our dramatic companion broke into gales of laughter. I wondered how anyone could live in such a fashion, with such an underhanded agenda – on any occasion. It was truly a sight to behold, and although the meal was sumptuous, I somehow couldn't justify Margret's tirade. That was certainly an experience. I wonder where those ladies are now! I never did see them again.

One elderly woman from the bus tour also gave me a memory for my scrapbooks. During our trip, she hardly spoke a word to me, but when the Clausens and I went to one of the Lake Tahoe casinos, I saw the lady (I use the term cautiously here) playing poker, seated in a crude, manly posture, nonchalantly smoking a cigar. I could not believe that she was one and the same taciturn bus passenger whom I had seen just days before!

Along with these humorous interludes, I paused to enjoy the scenery. California is a beautiful state. The sequoias were especially awe-inspiring. Their majesty, reach, and breath made me realize that we humans are only fractions of the entire spectrum of miracles on this planet.

Once on the home front, I found out that I had passed the difficult California nursing boards and that there was reciprocity with New Jersey. That meant that I could practice my skills in both states. I was on top of the world, feeling defined by my success. At last, I was someone – validated, whole, free to explore the reaches of my potential, and to demonstrate to my skeptical brother that women (even his sister) could, indeed, be career savvy and prosperous.

Of course, I yearned to share my news with my "secret admirer" (at least, I believed that such was the nomenclature he assigned himself in his digitalized letter to me, revealed on the date of Julie's Christmas party). One afternoon, when I saw Eduardo sitting with two of his friends at the entrance to the school cafeteria, I briefly got the chance to tell him that I had passed the California nursing boards. I couldn't avoid him at that moment – and, I dare say, I didn't want to. Something inside of me sought validation from the one man of whom I thought the world. I felt exalted, but my glowing achievement assumed a special character when I thought of sharing it with Eduardo. My inherently diminished self-esteem must have inspired such a wish. Crimson-complexioned and nervous (but with my facial blemishes well concealed), I approached Eduardo, not knowing what to say; so I uttered something foolish, such as, "Sometimes bad things happen to people" (possibly referring to the concoction of fabrications that I had written). I don't know what those particular words emanated from me at that moment. It was as though I were trying to fill space to obscure my hesitancy and awkwardness. Eduardo, himself, looked uncomfortable and confused, as though he were thinking to himself how eccentric and strange I was! Filled with embarrassment, I took my leave –

again at the mercy of my internal feelings of inadequacy, unable to allow my truth to shine forth.

About a month later, as I exited the ladies' room at school, I saw Eduardo hurriedly walking to class. As we briefly exchanged greetings, our paths crossed that one last time, never to be entwined again – at least, so I thought. Serendipity has a way of asserting itself in curious ways. I will not explain myself just yet. For those of my readers not so inclined for suspense, I can only say, alas! You have to wait for my history to unfold.

A few months after this fleeting chance encounter (casual as it was, it was charged with meaning for me), a friend, Ben, approached and informed me that Eduardo had gone to another campus. Ben conveyed the message that Eduardo wished me all the best, and made a point to tell me that he (Eduardo) was engaged to a nurse.

"How do you know this to be true?" I queried, trying to stifle my emotions.

"Well, I saw the girl myself. She had a very nice ring on her hand. You had better get that man out of your head," the friend almost commanded, as if attempting to shield me from pain, while presenting the harshest reality imaginable.

To say that I was crestfallen is a gross understatement. I cried all day – at least, in my heart, unable to focus my attention in class. Such pain encased my heart that I could barely contain myself. Loving and losing had been the leitmotif of my life, and I didn't want that hurt. I wanted to cast it off into a vast ocean to be consumed by the undulations of the deep – instead of the depth of my own soul. I just was not up for the challenge of resisting that which I didn't want to face: Eduardo had vanished from my life – forever. Somehow, I managed to lift myself from the chasm of sorrow that engulfed me – but not too successfully. I had just about finished my classes. I couldn't let everything for which I had strived and struggled go by the wayside.

In the meantime, I was entertaining the hope that Tomás would be luckier than I in the romance department. I don't know why I felt this way. Perhaps it was simply because of our kinship and my desire to be protective of him in some way. In hindsight, I realize that, in all likelihood, he was trying to guard me from life's harsh byroads; however, what he didn't understand was that he was imposing more stress upon me than I could barely handle. His temperament often made life quite difficult, and I wanted to live geographically apart. Yes, that was it! The real reason was I wanted my brother to be married off. I couldn't wait for him to leave. I cannot tell a lie.

For the above reasons, I was relieved when Tomás announced that he had a girlfriend. I sensed that the cause of this decision was my father's urgency for having grandchildren, expressed in a phone conversation, which I overheard one afternoon. "Son," Dad said to Tomás, in his characteristic imperative tone, "when are you going to get married and give me grandchildren?" Subsequent to this conversation, I perceived an increase in my brother's interest for getting married. Meanwhile, my self-interest compelled me to seek my own course in life, as I endeavored to climb the mountain of success. I didn't exactly know where the journey would lead, but I had to find my own path. Certainly, my brother himself was not championing my cause, and if I didn't take the reigns and direct the path of my own destiny, no one would.

Sadly, some are not so graced by fortune as to craft their destiny – particularly the elderly. With enormous pain in my heart, I witnessed my fairy godmother at the mercy of a cruel, uncompromising fate. Throughout time, it became apparent that Mrs. C.'s eccentricities were contributing to her decline. Born during the Depression years, she had learned to skimp and conserve to the point of self-deprivation – especially when it came to nutrition. This lack of self-nurturing was a source of great concern to me, and I did everything in my power to contribute to my benefactor's wellbeing. Sometimes, however, when people are set in their ways, no amount of intervention can make an impact. One day, I heard a loud thump, and ran to see what had happened. There, on the floor in her room, I found my esteemed Mrs. C. on the floor, writhing in pain. Apparently, she had fallen, perhaps while attempting to plug something into a wall. I checked her quickening pulse, and noticed that she absolutely couldn't move. Her shoulder looked like it had been displaced from its socket. The poor lady looked disoriented and in intense agony. I suspected a fracture, coupled with a stroke. Immediately, I called 911. As it turned out, my diagnoses were correct. In the aftermath of those moments, my beloved Mrs. C. went into a downward spiral. She was transferred from the hospital to a nursing home, at which point our communications and interactions steadily decreased. Such circumstances were due to the fact that Mrs. C.'s family descended like vultures to devour whatever personal effects and assets she possessed. Whereas they had been aloof and detached during her years of vitality and health, Mrs. C.'s family members viewed her weakened condition as an opportunity to confiscate, dispose of, and claim her belongings as their own. I believe that my attachment to her and her affection for me were seen as impediments to that goal; so, the family did everything possible to distance us from each other and prohibited my visits.

Striving to muddle through, I continued with my studies, while working at a local hospital as a Registered Nurse. Tomás had already moved into an apartment nearby. As for me, I made just enough salary to pay room and board at my new home with Mrs. Alan. One of the major drawbacks of living there was that I had to surrender my cherished dog, Shaggy, who had been my companion at Mrs. C.'s residence. The Benji-look-alike tragically ran away from the family to whom I had surrendered him, and I had no hope of ever seeing him again. One afternoon, as I stopped by Mrs. C.'s residence to pick up something that I had left there, I walked in to find painters preparing the house for sale. They asked whether I owned a dog.

"I *had* a dog," I replied.

"Well, this crazy dog came into the house, went to that room, began to bark at us non-stop, and then ran outside, still yelping like there was no tomorrow," one of the painters said, pointing in the direction of my old room.

I began to describe Shaggy, and indeed the painters confirmed that he had been there. My eyes filled with tears. I decided to sit and wait to see whether Shaggy would return. All of a sudden, one of the painters shouted, "There's that crazy dog again!"

"Shaggy!" I cried, unable to contain my emotions. My little mascot was so happy to see me, he jumped up and greeted me as though his wish to find me had been granted. His loyalty and gratitude overwhelmed and overtook my very being. Had circumstances been different, I would have kept him. To my deep regret, however, Mrs. Alan couldn't have dogs. My heart tore into several thousand pieces as I realized the inevitable: I had to give Shaggy up – again. The house was about to be sold, my studies were on the line, and there was simply no other option. So, I took my faithful companion to the nearest shelter, beseeching the lady there to call me immediately when she found a home for my treasured pet. The next day, the call came through. A lady and her son had adopted him. Yet another goodbye. I was confronted with another mountain to climb, and I faced it with the courage of one who had been on that journey before.

Yet another drawback of living with Mrs. Alan was her loquaciousness – which nearly drove me to distraction. In her presence, my studies were always intercepted by incessant conversation, and I could never get anything done. Still, I persevered, always hearkening back to my days with Mrs. C., whose generosity had galvanized the pursuit of my education and career path. Once when, in spite of the family's dictates to the contrary, I did call on my dear friend, she clung to me, asking, "Where have you been? Are you my Isabella? When can you take me home? Call a taxi! Please take me back to our home! Please don't leave me here!" she cried. My heart sank. I just didn't know what to say, except that her request was not possible. How could I tell my fairy godmother that her house already had been sold and there was nowhere to go? I couldn't bear to see her in that state, and I was helpless to change her situation. With a very heavy heart, I gave her a hug and a kiss goodbye, never to see her again. A feeling of desperation pervaded me, but there was nothing that I could do. I could only love that beautiful heart – and say goodbye – as I had done in so many ways and in various instances before. It was as though endings and beginnings, highs and lows, mountains and valleys were the leitmotifs of my life.

One afternoon, in my last year of studies, just before graduation, I was passing a pharmacy near Mrs. C.'s former home. Quite by happenstance, the owner addressed me with a compassionate look.

"Hi! I haven't seen you in a long time! I'm so sorry to hear about what happened!" she said, as I paid for my item.

"What happened?" My startled expression surprised the pharmacist.

"Don't you know?" she asked.

"Know what?"

"Mrs. C. passed away." The pharmacist handed me the day's paper.

"When?" I inquired, consumed with sorrow, barely glancing at the obituary.

"Recently. In fact, she is being buried today."

I felt as though a momentous portion of my own life had just come to a close. Ascertaining the time of Mrs. C.'s interment and, realizing that I had enough time to pay my respects, I got into my car and headed for the cemetery. On my way, I stopped to buy a red rose. When I arrived at my destination, I noticed that the casket had already descended six feet into the earth. The ceremony had just ended, and no other friends or relatives were around. The coffin's clean, shiny veneer still remained uncovered. At that moment, my belief in purposeful times and seasons for everything was solidified. It was as though Ms. C. had said, "Wait! There's someone special to whom I have to say goodbye." The men asked me if I wanted to be alone. I said yes. In those moments, I poured out my heart, thanking my fairy godmother for all that she had done to edify my life – particularly by conferring the gift of my education, which was so important to me and served as the foundation for my future career. I expressed gratitude for all of the good times that we had shared together – the laughs, her Bible readings, the English language instruction – everything. Then, as I left and allowed the men to cover up the casket, a sense of peace enveloped me. I was so moved that Mrs. C. had given me that gift of goodbye – that last expression of homage, which was so much her due. Although I was sad to have lost her, the opportunity to have engaged in private reflection healed and filled me with fond remembrances and gratitude. Mrs. C., I shall forever hold you in my heart!

So, as one chapter closed, another began. Tomás tied the knot – much to the delight of my parents, who traveled in from Peru with my twin brothers and younger sister for the great event, and stayed for about two weeks.

While waiting for Tomás big event, I had to watch over my siblings. In order to avert their boredom, I managed to enroll them in a parochial school, taking charge of their activities and diversions in the interim. I was so busy with school and tying up loose ends, that this added responsibility was quite an impediment at such a crucial time – although having the younger ones around me was otherwise a source of joy. My family accused me of being selfish and distanced from them when, in truth, all I wanted was for my parents to embrace my plans and prospects as being equally as momentous as my brother's. Therefore, after the wedding, my family left for Peru, leaving me with just a few of my friends to celebrate my life's passage. To make matters even more unsettling, the photos that Tomás was supposed to take of my special day were either entirely destroyed or blurred when he opened the camera. Thus, nothing – not even the pictorial memories of that momentous occasion – remained. To say the least, I was devastated, but at the same time proud to have arrived at that moment. After all that I had endured, descending into the valleys of suffering, fear, and aloneness – especially without Laura – and climbing emotional mountains into the sunlight rendered me stronger than I had ever been. Along the journey, I was grateful for the support of my staunch allies – Julie, her mom, and my beloved Mrs. C. – fortresses even more powerful than that which I beheld on my trip to Sacsayhuamán. I had a long way to go, many valleys to traverse, and many mountains to climb; but armed with the essential building blocks of love, hope, and self-belief, everything and anything seemed possible.

Chapter 12

Freedom and Entanglement

Thus far, my life had been a series of full-circle moments and epiphanies, some of which came at my own instigation, and others which were simply purposeful designs of the universe. Over time, I have discovered that the more one strives for something to happen or forces the issue, so to speak, the less likely the desired end will manifest itself – no matter how concerted the effort. A case in point was my self-image, marred by that fateful day in my childhood when I fell into a pot of hot custard, which subsequently resulted in the appearance of facial blemishes, areas of dark hyper-pigmentation resembling ink blots. In countless symbolic, as well as literal, ways, that single event directed my life's course. As a result of low self-esteem and a tarnished image (which, as per the little boy's assessment in the pediatric clinic those many years ago, had to be corrected through spot erasure), I could not fully be myself, free to interact, socialize and project myself on the world as my natural inclinations dictated. The visual blight of the facial marks transformed me into someone I didn't recognize and didn't want to be, constantly running for cover – quite literally, always having to carry concealer, lipstick and other forms of masking tools to camouflage the topical stigmas which impacted nearly every decision and every move I made.

One day, when I least expected something momentous to occur, as I was standing in a grocery checkout line, I spotted a photo of a girl with a mark on her cheek very similar to mine. The headline referred to the skillful removal of such marks by a renowned New York City dermatologist who, by means of an electro-cauterization procedure, was able to burn off the unwanted scar. Practically trembling with excitement, I bought the magazine, and rushed home to delve into the article. Not wasting any time in deliberation, I was soon off to the Big Apple for my procedure, instinctively feeling that my entire life was about to change. I undertook this life-altering step without any accompaniment. For reasons that I could not articulate – perhaps because explanations and emotions shared would, somehow, diminish the intensity of what I was about to experience – I decided to encounter this deeply personal journey alone.

As I sat in the chair with my eyes closed and shielded, the doctor burned my blemishes off, one by one. Each ounce of pain I felt (and, yes, there was pain – even though I was anesthetized) was an exercise in waging mortal combat against the enemy: the stigma of my scars, which had blotted my countenance like spiteful dirt marks refusing to be wiped away. In countless theaters of war, those paper-thin nothings rose like insurgents to conquer me and thwart all present and impending joys. They robbed me of my self-esteem when the doctor at the hospital in Peru held my chin in his hands to display to his residents, as though I were a sideshow participant; they made me cower in front of suitors, and were, in my mind, the cause of Lorenzo's rejection. Most significantly, they made me cower and run from Eduardo, someone whom I held dear and with whom – but for my pervasive feelings of inadequacy – I may have been able to build and sustain a lasting relationship. I'll never know, and speculation on this point only allows those specters of my past to rise again; but in those moments when the treatment was underway, I felt a lightness and sense of purpose. The psychological and emotional implications of what was taking place can only be described as rebirth, renewal, and ultimate triumph of the will over adversity. Of course, the doctor had little or no idea that every motion of his hand was crafting my new sense of personhood. The exorbitant cost was incidental to all that I was experiencing inside – the joy and exaltation of an entirely new destiny.

After the treatment ended, my lip and lower mandible were protruded and swollen – not a pleasant sight. I went home and ensconced myself in my four walls for about two weeks, so as to escape sunlight and resultant irritation. Such were the doctor's express instructions, and I paid heed with every ounce of fortitude and resolve. As the blemishes healed, they became dark scabs which, after two weeks, began to peel and magically fall away, like the skin of a molting snake. By the third week, my facial swelling gradually began to decrease. Free at last! Every fiber of my being proclaimed when the last piece of unwanted skin descended. The enemy had effectively been defeated, leaving the host country in a state of peaceful bliss and renewal. The spoils of emotional turmoil and the rivers of doubt and self-consciousness deconstructed and dried out like the ruins of an antiquated, forgotten realm of existence. In its place, a new zone of confidence emerged, no longer in the shadows, fully embracing the light, and resonating with life-force energy.

With my renewed sense of self came my desire to purchase a townhouse of my own and declare myself to be fully autonomous. Oh, America the Beautiful, Land of Opportunity for those who strive, I thank you! My generous Dad assisted me with the purchase, though I was making a good salary working as a physical therapist at a local hospital. A friend of mine told me about a property which she discovered through her realtor husband. The house was being sold through a lottery, and just as I was all set to make the purchase and sign the contract, someone with a lower number than I showed up and virtually snatched the contract from my hands. To say the least, I was disappointed, but as fate would have it, when that door closed, another literally opened. My friend then pointed me to a property which was twice as large, in an ideal location for my daily activities and lifestyle. I am a firm believer in the yin-yang pull of life, and that we shouldn't fight those polar opposites. The reason is that, just when you believe that your dreams are dashed, something – or someone – usually comes along to change circumstances for the better. I have always expressed this philosophy to people – and I have seen its confirmation, time and again. Just when you think hope has vanished and rain clouds fill, suddenly they part and, like a beautiful, unwrapped gift, the sunshine peers through and smiles down on you.

As the clouds parted for me, I got on my feet, and took in my younger sister as a charge. This circumstance was due to my parents' insistence that Beatriz was in danger of being captured by Peruvian terrorists pervading the country at the time, preying upon the affluent to surrender large sums of money. They threatened that noncompliance would result in the kidnapping of the families' children, whose whereabouts and school locations were constantly under their scrutiny. Evidently, Mom and Dad were victims of this scheme, and not knowing where to turn, they asked that I give Beatriz a safe haven. Such a responsibility was quite unexpected – and, I dare say, challenging – just when life had begun to assume an even keel for me; but feeling my parents' urgency, I gladly conceded. Until her first year of college, Beatriz remained in my care and looked to me as a maternal figure. We took in roommates, and made quite a cozy home. It was rumored that our dwelling conduced to good marriages, for upon leaving the nest, most of the girls who boarded with us were so fortunate as to enjoy wedded bliss.

During this time, I was in a minor rear-ended accident, and my ensuing back injury and pain put me out of commission as a physical therapist for a while. Still hoping to be resourceful during my period of convalescence, I applied for and was hired as a Registered Nurse and office manager for a local doctor. One day, while opening the mail, I noticed a familiar name in one of the surgical reports. I asked the doctor to describe the resident listed there. The doctor described him as tall, good-looking, blonde, and blue-eyed. At that moment, my heart dropped to my knees, as my stomach ascended into my throat. Eduardo! my heart cried. My lost love, the man for whose presence I longed , the man who barely knew me, but who morphed into the idealized vision that my mind and heart conjured and nurtured – clearly had some connection to the doctor.. That was a full-circle moment, far more than a coincidence. The minute Eduardo's name surfaced, scattered memories flooded my mind, along with more questions than I could, possibly, answer for myself. Would Eduardo come to the office? Would I have a chance to see him again and, perhaps, repair some of the damage that our awkward separation had caused? Of course, I didn't breathe a word to the doctor – or to anyone – about my knowledge of Eduardo or my inner reflections.. Just as these thoughts were beginning to sink in, the doctor approached me and asked whether I would interview someone to work in the office – a woman who…was…none…other…than…Eduardo's…wife. I still cower at the mere thought. I abhorred the idea of potentially having to conduct the interview and explain complex procedures to the woman whose husband I had so admired and for whom I still harbored deep, latent feelings. Worse, I couldn't bear the thought of Eduardo visiting the office and discovering that I was still unattached.

A week after the request to interview Eduardo's wife was made, my injured back miraculously healed, as if by an invisible magic wand, and I was out of there, on my way back to my job as a physical therapist. I needed an escape, and I believe that even if I had been ensnared in a hornet's nest, I would have wrangled my way out at all cost. What had just happened? He was there, but slipped away again; he appeared and, then, vanished once more. The pattern was unmistakable. Was I pursuing a phantom, a mere figment of my imagination, a wish-fulfillment? Then, again, he was married, and I came so close to confronting his wife – for the purpose of hiring her, no less! What were the odds? Was this a cruel twist of fate, offering me a tempting bite of forbidden fruit, and, then, depriving me of the sweetness of fulfillment? As these thoughts pervaded my mind, escape was my only recourse – as it often had been. I was always hiding, running away – as much from myself as from the one I loved. The truth was, however, that I didn't have to escape any more. Waking up each morning and looking in the mirror was no longer a chore or evocative of fear and anguish. I completed myself, for myself. Even though I didn't know it then (what young person, struggling for a place in the world, possesses that awareness?), I didn't require extrinsic adulation. Perhaps, however, I did entertain that idea – at least subconsciously.

Casting off the residue of uncertainty and reflections of my painful past, I decided to celebrate my newfound freedom from the blight of my facial blemishes by taking a three-week trip to

Europe – Switzerland, Italy, France, Holland, Austria, and Germany. Five friends and I embarked on the journey – two medical students, a nurse, a psychologist, and a physical therapist. I was glad to take time off from my daily routine and imbibe the air, in the light. Because of the huge 1989 airline tragedy of Pan Am Flight 103 over Lockerbie, Scotland, I opted for Lufthansa Airlines. My friends, who took a chartered flight for considerably less money, wondered why I had decided to travel alone, at such expense. The answer was that conformism never was part of my nature. I always let my head and heart lead, despite others' protestations and alternative suggestions.

I began to question myself, however, when, upon going through security checks, I was detained and questioned about my expired Peruvian passport. To this day, I haven't the slightest clue as to why that fact escaped me. I was – and am – fastidious about protocol, especially when it comes to adherence to the law. Although I had a current U.S. green card (signifying permanent residency status), my expired passport could have caused my deportation. Curiously, though, something told me to remain calm – perhaps because I had the truth on my side. I attested to my status as a healthcare practitioner and very matter-of-factly stated that I was awaiting my friends' arrival on a Pam Am chartered flight that had taken off from Kennedy Airport about half an hour before mine. Sensing the customs officers' congeniality, I explained my reasons for traveling alone on Lufthansa, and answered all of their questions candidly and without restraint. Upon request, I also provided all of my friends' names. Clearly, I had nothing to hide. As the officers and I engaged in cordial dialogue, they acknowledged my credibility, and provided me with a six-month temporary passport with which I could travel freely in and out of the country. With a hardy, "Welcome to Germany!" the affable officer who granted my freedom shook my hand and took his leave. During the entire ordeal, I had begun to worry that my friends had waited for me, and when I didn't show up, left me there, stranded in strange, unknown territory. Although I was not unaccustomed to such circumstances, I quivered at the thought. The waiting room was small and cramped – not at all equipped with today's amenities. As I waited for half an hour, my heartbeat and pulse raced intermittently. Then, when I had all but given up hope, my friends arrived – albeit disheveled and flustered after their flight from Belgium (which had been detoured due to turbulence). Needless to say, I was relieved on two counts: first and foremost, that my companions had landed safely, and secondly, that I had flown pleasantly and uneventfully on another aircraft. Somehow, I always became entangled in unusual events, but in flight, smooth cruising was the only option I would accept.

Once on solid ground, we dusted ourselves off, and traveled to Manheim. My cousin, Sofia, was studying Economics at the university there, and as my friends went off sightseeing, she and I welcomed the chance to catch up. It was easy and fun to be with her – particularly in a foreign land, where I didn't speak a word of the language and knew no one. Then, again, that was really nothing new for me. One evening, as we were about to go out, I received a return phone call from Johann, a young man whom I had met years before on a visit to my hometown of Huaraz. One of my childhood friends had introduced me to him and another young man, both intensely good looking and personable. My acquaintanceship with Johann, though brief, had been memorable, and as such, merits the following retrospective digression.

At the time of our first meeting in Huaraz, Johann and I, along with others, had been discussing widespread rumors about an indigenous Peruvian Indian, who purportedly had been abducted by aliens and rehabilitated of a serious illness. Now, before you accuse me of literally being out of this world, please know that this story was the gentleman's own account – a man to whom I will refer only as Diego. My Dad and twin brothers vouched for this miraculous event, which they witnessed with their own eyes. One thing was for certain: Dad and my brothers were never given to falsehoods. As the story went, Diego was in close communication with these so-called extraterrestrials who, he claimed, cured his gangrenous arm. Dad told me that when Diego displayed the diseased limb, he (Dad) immediately admonished him about seeing a doctor; but Diego insisted that his alien friends would cure him, whereupon he disappeared without a trace, for over a week. When he returned, he was completely free of disease, thanks to life on another planet (exactly which one still eludes me to this day). I'm a big skeptic about such topics; however, having lived in a place where mysticism was a way of life and occurrences of unknown origin (such as alien sightings) were often accepted as a matter of course, I tried to maintain an open mind – all the while inwardly chuckling at the seriousness with which these anecdotes were recounted – if, indeed, that's what they were. By no means do I intend to trivialize what I heard and saw, but Diego's tale did seem bizarre, particularly to those who heard it second-hand. To compound matters, Diego apparently had the ability to have his voice resonate through a radio receptor by putting his mouth to the wrist of his healed arm. The kids used to joke about this and dubbed that radio station Radio Shankayán, the name of Diego's hometown. Hearing these tales just wasn't enough. Steeped in curiosity, my friend, the two young men and I decided to pay Diego a visit. There we were, engrossed in conversation, when Johann, overwhelmed by the subject matter, stood up and left, saying, "This is all too much for me." We all filed out, leaving Diego to his own devices – or, I should say, electromagnetic connections. To say the least, that was quite an experience. The world is filled with mysteries, to be sure; and which one of us has a monopoly on truth? I certainly don't lay claim to righteousness and veracity. I only live my own truth and enjoy sharing it. Come to think of it, I'm certain that Diego was doing precisely that.

Anyway, to return to my account of Johann: On our way home from our discussion with Diego, he began to show an interest in me and asked whether he could accompany me alone. Perceiving his innate decency, I couldn't refuse. Upon our arrival, I introduced him to my mother, who met us at the door, conspicuously failing to invite my new friend in. Later, she expressed that, much to her dismay, she observed Johann wearing an earring, the insignia of same-gender orientation. You see, in those days, earrings were reserved for women. Mother's assessment was vehement, so as to discourage any further communications between us; however, I managed to maintain the friendship during my two-week stay in Huaraz. Johann was a true gentleman, and asked whether he could write to me in America. I agreed, and subsequently, was the recipient of the most lyrical prose that I had ever read – in perfect Spanish – far more elegant and grammatically correct than any native speaker I had ever encountered. After receiving his first letter, I became so immersed in physical therapy school that I could not answer back. The second missive asked me to be Johann's companion in his travels around the world. I was flattered, but a bit scared, since I hardly knew the man and couldn't possibly consider the proposition. Such is how we lost touch, but I always kept his phone number. You never can tell when fate might conjoin diverged paths.

And, so, it happened. Years later, when I traveled to Germany and stayed with my cousin, Sofia, I took Johann's number with me. I wanted him to see the new me, in full daylight – not as before when, under the cover of night, my dark secrets – my facial blemishes – were well hidden and my feelings of inadequacy enshrouded me in timidity. Therefore, you can imagine my excitement when, all those years later, the phone rang and I heard Johann's voice at the other end! He explained that his attempts to reach me over time had failed, since my phone number had been disconnected and I was no longer residing at the address that I had given him. Surely, he thought, our paths never would cross again. When they did, it was far too late for a romantic interlude – or any sustained relationship. By that time, Johann had married a beautiful Italian girl, with whom he was expecting his first child – a boy. Mixed feelings of joy and sadness washed over me like the waves of life's unpredictable ocean. Love doesn't wait forever, other chances come along, opportunities die, and new hopes are ignited. So it was with Johann, and upon reflection, I could only rejoice at his good fortune.

Little did I realize, in the moments after hanging up the receiver, what awaited me. Unbeknownst to me, during my conversation with Johann, the huge retractable brush attached to the hair dryer that I was using became embedded and entangled in my long hair. All attempts to extricate the brush were in vain. In a supreme act of compassion and resoluteness, Sofia placed a scarf on my head and accompanied me, on foot, through the streets of Manheim. With the brush protruding from the side of my head, I must have appeared like one of Diego's alien friends. In hindsight, the scene was hysterical, but caused a great measure of concern. How will I ever dislodge this apparatus? I asked myself, vaguely listening for echoes of extraterrestrial counsel. Fortunately, I found ample help at the salon, where beauticians worked on me for several hours and, finally, removed the brush. Best of all – well, a close second – I wasn't charged a penny. Everyone was so kind and wished me well in my travels.

What a time to travel! It was a momentous period in history as "Die Berliner Mauer" (the Berlin Wall), eighty-seven miles long and having divided East and West Germany for nearly three decades in the post-World War II era, was toppling right before my eyes! The highlight of my entire European trip was to see the wall and the two sides – the Eastern former Soviet communist Bloc and the West – finally freed from that barrier's oppression. What a profoundly emotional experience! With my own hands, I was honored to chisel a piece off the wall, a relic that I still cherish today. For me, the entire event was symbolic of my own life – the vanquishing of old, misplaced conceptions about myself, and the embracing of new, healthier ideologies that would help me to integrate with the world more freely. As I looked over at what once was East Berlin, I perceived desolation and grayness, a kind of frozen city, with symmetrical building facades – great architectural handiwork, standing like transfixed sentinels – sullen echoes of a time passed, marking the death of division. By contrast, West Berlin teemed with exaltation, abundance and life, as did Koblenz, Cologne, and the Rhine, Germany's longest river. There, people sang and regaled each other in camaraderie, reveling in the tastes, the sounds, and the sights of freedom. So did I, as my own inner walls of self-doubt and oppression collapsed even more. Freedom – that wonderful word, concept, and ultimate reality – inheres in all of us. No matter how entangled we feel by circumstance or imposed burdens of the heart and mind, absolutely no one and nothing can rob us of our individualism.

Speaking of freedom and individual expression, I took some memorable side trips on my own, where people's lack of inhibition completely startled me. I experienced these culture shocks (which were more like lightening bolts) while visiting with old friends. One such experience occurred in the company of Charo, a high school peer, living near Salzburg, Austria with her husband. You may recall that Charo was the heroine who comforted me during my humiliating episode with Lorenzo. Then, many years later – eons after that incident took place – Charo invited me to view her lake property in a town near Salzburg. We traveled there via a very small boat, almost as miniscule as the property itself – a tiny piece of land on which three people could fit, at most. Right next to the property were two men lying on towels, as natural as the day they were born, sunbathing in the nude. I could hardly believe my eyes.

"Is it my imagination, or are those men naked?" I asked, practically choking on my incredulity.

Charo laughed and said, "No, it's true! Seeing naked people is extremely common here near the lakes."

"Really?" I queried, still fairly gasping. "People in America are so much more conservative and would not dream of disrobing in public. No one will believe what I have just seen."

Intent on preserving evidence of the scene, Charo grabbed her camera and began taking photos of the men. Aware of our intense curiosity, the good-natured sunbathers stood up, posed, and waved to us – no doubt, with the understanding that what I had seen was foreign, if not alien to me. For a moment, I sensed the very remote analogue of the experience to Diego's sightings. If only he had a camera! If not for film and digital imaging, proof is a mere idea. All joking aside, that was an unforgettable scene!

When I visited my Peruvian friend, Emilio, a Ph.D. Economics candidate at the University of Heidelberg, a similar scenario awaited me. As we toured the campus, I was amazed to see some students smoking and drinking during class breaks – conduct to which I was entirely unaccustomed. Then, when Emilio and I picnicked on delicious fresh bread and other refreshments near the lake, two women sat close to us and casually proceeded to undress and sunbathe. Emilio thought nothing of this, but to be honest, I felt uncomfortable and took extra large bites of my lunch. Then, I hurried off, as if to shield myself from that which my eyes were loath to observe. Imagine journeying from my conservative upbringing into a culture where liberty meant throwing personal inhibitions to the wind! Little did the mountain girl know or have the capacity to conjure what surprises life would eventually reveal!

In my adult years, as I came into my own, the definition of liberty didn't so strongly signify abandonment of physical restraint as much as personality uniqueness, nonconformity and personal conviction. Part of that definition included clinging to my single status. Although I was free of my facial blemishes, I was still emotionally scarred by past rejections. I wanted to be cautious – perhaps, too much so. Guarding my heart and finding the right life partner was my principal aim. As the clock began to tick more loudly, my parents' concern escalated. Consequently, as I approached the danger zone of my thirties, in peril of being labeled an old maid, Mom and Dad did everything in their power to be matchmakers. I know they meant well – as do all parents who want the best for their children – but who can make better choices in matters of the heart than the individual whose heart matters? Unfortunately, my parents' loving instigation was always at play, and whenever I went home, they always stealthily planned to set me up with countless eligible bachelors.

In the early nineties, I went home to Lima where, by then, my parents were well situated and comfortable. I was greeted at the airport by Enrique, the man whose alcoholic tendencies had detracted from our lasting relationship years before. Upon my arrival at the airport, I saw him smiling, amiable and pleased to see me. He told me that he was divorced, with two children, successfully working as an executive with an international manufacturing company. I was impressed, but cautious, remembering his inappropriate behavior in our youth, when he made a ruckus at the party attended by his parents. The embarrassment still made me cringe, but as an adult, I resolved to forgive and forget. Enrique took me home and visited me every day. One evening at dinner, his attentiveness culminated in a marriage proposal. He was so sincere and serious about the request, that I didn't have the heart to refuse outright, so I said that I would think about it. Given Enrique's social and financial status, I'm certain that anything but a yes came as an extreme shock. Virtually no other girl would have turned him down. I held to my conviction, however, and bided my time – knowing, intrinsically, that he was not for me. When I went home to tell my parents, they were delirious – especially Dad.

"He loves you, Isabella. You should marry him!"

"But Papá!" I protested, "he loves alcohol more than he loves me."

"You are strong. You can change him. He is a good catch, financially secure, and in love with you."

"Please forgive me but, with all due respect, you are not correct, Dad. I would rather be an old maid than risk marrying the wrong companion. I trust that you understand." How amazing it was to me that Dad lifted his marriage ban against divorced men! No doubt, the exception was taken for the sake of his aging daughter. Although he was deeply disappointed in my decision, he rightly sensed that he couldn't sway me.

Dubious about what my answer to Enrique would be and wanting to give my suitor the benefit of at least some consideration, I decided to put him to a test. My younger sister Beatriz's boyfriend, Flavio, graciously offered to prepare a meal for us. The four of us – our chef, Beatriz, Enrique, and I – enjoyed a sumptuous dinner. Then, under the pretext of having to make a phone call, I excused myself, leaving my untouched glass of wine conspicuously in its place at the table. If Enrique drinks that wine before he leaves, I won't marry him, I told myself, alluding, in my mind, to his insatiable thirst for alcoholic beverages. Stealthily spying behind a glass pane, I soon spotted him drinking the wine before he stood up to leave. That was my answer: a resounding no! Still, I was discreet. When we parted, Enrique and I embraced amiably, but I knew, at that moment, that it would be our last exchange of affection. "See you tomorrow!" Enrique affirmed, as if our meeting the next day were a foregone conclusion. I nodded politely, and went on my way to call the airline. Successfully able to book my flight one day earlier, I took off on the wings of freedom, unburdened but sorry that I had to hurt Enrique by leaving so abruptly and with such finality. In fact, he never knew what hit him. I didn't even say goodbye. While I understand my wrongful omission, I really did not see any other alternative at the time. I simply couldn't confront him. What was I going to say? "Your love of alcohol exceeds your devotion to me, and I have to engage in self-preservation?" Any attempts to explain myself in that way would have resulted in Enrique's possible defensiveness, denials, and all manner of cajoling and promising to the contrary. Enrique was – and is – a very good man, but I decided, then and there that unless he understood the meaning and urgency of alcohol abstinence, he couldn't be my husband. Predictably, Dad was terribly distraught – as was Enrique himself. When I returned home, Beatriz found numerous messages from him, none of which I ever returned. My contrition for my silence could not be denied. I never forgot the good times we shared, how kind Enrique was to me, how much I admired his intellect and genuine good heart – especially in those days, when I was a newbie in Lima, and he showed me around the city, making me feel comfortable and secure. Everything has a season, and I was grateful to blossom in his presence and bear witness to his generous spirit.

Ultimately, life has a way of tying all loose ends and filling heart voids, leaving pleasant memories trailing along. Not too long ago, I phoned Enrique's house to find out how he and his relatives fared during the terrible 2007 earthquake in Ica, Peru. Fortunately, everyone was uninjured. His children were attending law school at the time, living with their mother and thriving beautifully. I was so relieved and happy to hear this report from Enrique's mother, who assured me that she would convey my news and contact information to her son.

As it turned out, my erstwhile admirer never returned my call. Like any rational person in my position, I didn't even bother to contemplate the blatant reason. There was too much water under the bridge, and I had navigated oceans away from my days with Enrique. I have yet to narrate the events of those subsequent days, and I cordially invite you along.

Chapter 13

Reversal of Old Maid Syndrome

In hindsight, the fact that my parents wanted to marry me off was truly endearing. What more did that wish signify, after all, than a genuine desire to see their daughter happy? As I think back, as disconcerting as it was to be the subject of their matchmaking, I realize now, more than ever, that they were just endeavoring to secure my future. For my part, however, marriage was not my foremost preoccupation. I had come into my own and was fully prepared to face the world, free of the inhibitions that had plagued my past, and to explore new vistas of possibility. Only then, I thought, could my heart truly be open to love.

As I've mentioned, one of my principal forms of diversion was travel. Experiencing different countries and cultures enabled me to appreciate other mindsets – to apprehend the larger macrocosm beyond myself. Aside from my trip to Germany, my later travels to England with my friend, Donna, were noteworthy. We were able to see many interesting historic sights, such as Buckingham Palace, St. Paul's Cathedral, where Prince Charles and Princess Diana were married, and the awe-inspiring Westminster Abbey, where Prince William and Kate Middleton were wed on April 29, 2011. There, as I stood near the grave of famed novelist, Charles Dickens (1812-1870), I felt the rush of ages. We then traveled to Stonehenge in Wiltshire, the magnificent four-thousand-year-old circular structure reminiscent of the pyramids in Machu Picchu. Like those magnificent creations, Stonehenge was an incredible sight to behold, its construction a great mystery. From there, we drove north through Salisbury, where we viewed a small mountain with a horse in the center. Our guide mentioned that people in that region had reported extraterrestrial sightings. Hmmm…that sounded familiar. How could I ever forget Diego and his alien comrades?

Next, we detoured into Bath, where Prince Charles was scheduled to play in a polo match. We decided to go to the game and, to our surprise, saw His Royal Highness drive up in a dark green Rolls-Royce and, then, stand about eighty feet or so away from us. To catch such a glimpse was a real highlight.

Then we went to France, where we sailed on the Seine River around Paris, and visited such tourist attractions as the Louvre and Orsay Museums. Of course, we saw the breathtaking Eiffel Tower, the tallest building in Paris. That behemoth of a structure opened my eyes to the fact that we are all just nestled in little corners of a vast universe, teeming with excitement. If we dare to look outside of ourselves and allow the world in, our hearts and minds expand to unimagined heights.

Our tour of these fascinating places helped me to gain perspective and prepare for the tasks that awaited me at home. By that time, I was Director of Rehabilitation Services at a local hospital. Our services included physical and occupational therapy, speech and language pathology, and audiology. I also worked privately for a very dear lady, for whom I had cared since I graduated from school. I didn't want to leave the job because the lady was so much fun, and I wanted to maintain my skills as a Registered Nurse. In addition, I had a private practice which I acquired from one of the physiatrists (an M.D. who specialized in physical medicine) at the hospital. His practice wasn't doing well, so he persuaded me to take it on. After our hospital passed the Joint Commission accreditation process with commendations, I felt motivated to try my hand at private practice management. My specialization: physical therapy. The endeavor was daunting at first, but with the help of God and some highly capable individuals working at my side, I was able to overcome the difficulties confronting me – all while simultaneously juggling my responsibilities at the hospital. It is amazing what a person can do in the presence of tenacity and will.

Predictably, my social life suffered during this time. I had little time for anything, and dating didn't factor into my schedule at all. I briefly encountered the dilemma of whether to date or not to date, when a doctor whom I had met some time before opening my private practice returned my phone call (which I had made for the purpose of requesting patient referrals). He suggested "a romantic walk on the beach, and after that, maybe we can talk about business." I was mildly intrigued, for I liked the doctor, too; but I just didn't feel right about conceding. The call was intended for professional purposes, after all, and I didn't want to inject any confusion into the matter. After writing his number on the back of a business card, I replied that I would call him back – but I never did.

Shortly thereafter, I was assigned to attend a meeting/dinner for the hospital staff. There, I spotted a striking, tall man with dark hair, standing next to a blonde woman who, I thought, was his wife. Later, as I was sitting with a group, the gentleman approached and politely requested a seat next to me. I agreed, and we struck up a lively conversation. I soon learned that Richard was a television producer for a Spanish station which, coincidently, aired many of the programs that I had watched in the 1980s. He was erudite, kind, and displayed an impressive body of knowledge about South America – and, particularly, about Peru. Most surprisingly, he spoke Spanish with uncommon fluency for a non-native. His bookishness and ability to hold forth on a vast variety of subjects were very engaging. Although he captured my attention, I cannot say, in all honesty, that sparks flew. Still, when Richard asked for my number, I readily gave it to him, which I unwittingly wrote on the same card on which I had the placed the doctor's number – my would-be suitor, with whom a walk on the beach just was not meant to be. It took Richard a full two months to get a date with me – and, of his many attributes, persistence was a salient characteristic.

As I said, tenacity pays off – as it did in romance. A year subsequent to that first meeting, on Valentine's Day, Richard and I were married. The proposal was typical of the gentleman – elegant and romantic. As we dined at a restaurant, he knelt and presented me with a beautiful ruby heart ring – the precursor to an engagement ring which, he said, I should choose. Being of sedate, uncomplicated taste, I replied that I wanted something small, befitting of my hand size. Richard looked perplexed, believing that most girls liked big, ostentatious rings. As I said before, nothing in my nature adheres to conformism.

Speaking of dancing to my own drumbeat: Before we were married, I did my due diligence in checking out my fiancée's credibility – and his health. The shy mountain girl had turned into a conscientious urbanite. I recognized the risks involved in new undertakings, particularly marriage to someone about whose past I knew little. Therefore, I wasn't about to take any chances. Mustering all of my strength and courage, I called his ex-girlfriend, a talk show host on one of the Spanish television networks that I used to watch. Surprisingly, the woman was pleasant, and had absolutely nothing derogatory to say about Richard. "He is a good man," she assured me. Satisfied, I thanked her for her time, hung up the phone, and told my fiancée exactly what I had done. He couldn't believe my gumption, but I had to do what I had to do. Then, I took Richard by the hand to my primary care physician, insisting upon a battery of blood tests for both of us. "You know that I'm in the medical field, and I need to make sure that we're healthy before we get married," I told him. Richard clearly understood that he didn't have a choice in the matter. When I approached my doctor with my health-before-marriage imperative, he replied good-naturedly, "I've never seen this before! If any woman would put me through these tests, I would leave immediately! This is too much! You are something else!" Then, he proceeded to write the prescriptions, anyway. Fortunately, we passed wellness muster, and were ready to get on with our lives together.

So, with my acceptance secured – and all of the highly important incidentals squared away – Richard called my father and asked for my hand in marriage. "On one condition," my ceremonious Dad replied. "The wedding must take place in Peru." And so it happened, with over three hundred guests, a forty-eight-piece bilingual band in tow, a wedding cake of ten layers or more, and the most elaborately decorated wedding hall imaginable. Suddenly, my biological clock seemed to be ticking counterclockwise, effectively reversing Old Maid Syndrome, and my parents celebrated the event in grand style. My invitations were simple, but elegant – a fact with which my brother took particular issue, thinking that I should have been more grandiose; but that just wasn't my way of doing things. My beloved friend, Julie, was in Washington at the time, and couldn't attend the festivities – but she was there in my heart. My bridesmaids – my younger sister, Beatriz, and our roommate, Clara – looked beautiful. My dress was opulent – a fact which, I realize, contradicts what I said before about understatement. The sole reason for this departure from subtlety was nothing more than impulse – and a bit of "I'll show you" attitude. Beforehand, I had visited a dress shop where an elderly lady criticized my taste in dresses – to such an extent that I rebelled. Her entire stock was outdated and tacky, so, in a moment of frustration, I went to an exclusive store and purchased a gorgeous dress in which to take my vows. The only mishap occurred with my hairpiece, which was switched with another in preparation for my flight to Peru. I had no choice but to wear what I had, and was no worse for it. Sometimes, you have to just go with the flow, and in the scheme of life, minutiae really don't matter. Despite my mother's protestations, I handled my own hairstyling and makeup. Everyone was astonished at how well everything turned out.

Soon after that memorable occasion, I was blessed to welcome my son into the world, and a year and a half later, my daughter. Around the time of my daughter's birth, I experienced headaches, depression, and allergies. A doctor who boarded in our home at that time offered to administer acupuncture treatments. At first, I was skeptical, but the treatment worked magic, while inspiring me to pursue my studies of traditional and ancient Chinese medicine. Mastering these studies has led me to a unique understanding of alternative ways of treating many kinds of ailments, complementing my knowledge of Western treatments. This practice still serves my family and me as a preventative measure, maintaining our good health. I feel deep respect for Eastern medicine. While I went to school, my husband pursued and eventually earned his law degree. Our family flourished, and I rejoiced in being a mother.

My children were – and are – the core of my being, the center of my universe, and the greatest blessings bestowed upon my life – the culmination of everything that I had done right and subsequently strived to achieve. In deference to their privacy, I omit their names. I ask their indulgence, as I share just a few anecdotes about their childhood and how they have evolved. It's one thing to express maternal feeling, but it is quite another to be a fortunate mother who, in addition to guardianship, also enjoys the society of great human beings in whom her legacy lives. I am one of those lucky individuals. I often think about how their Aunt Laura would dote on them, how she would love and shower them with gifts of the heart as much as of the material variety. This brings me to a memory of when my son was born, and the dove visited me again – quite unexpectedly. I recount the story because I know, with every fiber of my being, that Laura was there. I was lying in my hospital bed when, all of a sudden, a dove alighted on my window. I didn't think anything of the incident, until the nurse said that she had never seen anything like that before. Then, I knew: Laura had come to share my joy.

Keenly aware of life's graces, my children are growing up in an environment which nurtures and engages their curious minds. Even when they were little, my son and daughter, each in their own way, demonstrated extraordinary abilities to comprehend and interpret their world with sensitivity and intelligence beyond their years. A case in point: when my son was about three, we were walking in the vicinity of the New York Museum of Natural History. All of a sudden, from his vantage point in the knapsack baby carrier, my son called out, "Mr. Suzuki, Mr. Suzuki!" When I asked, "Who is that?" my son exclaimed, "I know him!" Suddenly, a gray-haired man approached and asked whether we had called him.

"Are you Mr. Suzuki?" I asked, hardly believing what was happening.

"Yes," came the reply.

When questioned as to how my son knew him, my little prodigy declared, "I saw all the tapes of the brain, and you were in them."

We all laughed, and Mr. Suzuki said, "Oh, that was a long time ago. Aren't you too young to be interested in those tapes?"

Apparently, my son insisted that the nanny play those videos, narrated by...you guessed it: Mr. Suzuki! My son had absorbed his image like a sponge, and recognized him even as an aged man.

About a year later, when my son was four, we passed a children's exhibition at the same museum. Walking hand-in-hand, we walked by a stand where the presenter displayed a dinosaur bone. He asked the older children to identify it, whereupon my son popped his head into the group and said, "I know it! It's a patella. I saw it in a book!" How astonishing it was to witness my son's intense interest – and even more to realize that one so young could remember such an intricate fact!

On another occasion, we attended a live animal presentation in an outdoor arena in northeastern Pennsylvania, where my son captured the attention of the entire audience by identifying a ringtail lemur.

"How do you know that?" the presenter queried, in disbelief.

I was amazed. Then, upon further questioning, my little boy's imagination took flight. "My grandfather and I traveled to different countries, and one of those was Madagascar. We saw lots of ringtail lemurs there."

"Oh, really? That is so impressive! And to what other countries has he traveled?" the presenter asked, looking at me.

Not wishing to contradict my son, I covertly smiled and gestured to the contrary. To this day, I still don't know how my son knew about that animal. Certainly, he probably only traveled to Madagascar in his mind – or through pictures.

One of my son's most tender characteristics is his abiding love for his younger sister. Since their inception, he has protected and alerted her to the realities of life – that is not to say that she, in her own right, hasn't always been a powerhouse of intellect and heart. In her own person, she is the very embodiment of these traits; but as the two were growing up (and still today), my son never shielded her from the truth. He shared everything, even when I told him to conceal things from his little sister for the sake of protecting her. For example, one evening, after having lost a tooth, he rebelled against the tooth fairy's impending visit. After tucking him in that night and checking on him a few times, I found him to be fully awake.

"What's the matter, Honey?" I asked.

"I don't want the tooth fairy to come, Mommy. I don't want her to leave me money."

My son was so adamant that, finally, I had no choice but to tell him that I was that spritely entity, begging him not to tell his sister. Brightening, he replied, "Oh, thank you, Mommy! Now, I know that you are not only the tooth fairy, but also the Easter Bunny and Santa Claus." Soon thereafter, I received a call from my daughter's distressed teacher. "Ms. TaniKumi, your daughter has been telling the kids that there isn't a Santa Claus. Can you kindly tell her not to say this? She is spoiling the holiday festivities for the others." I couldn't believe it. My children were in collusion on the Santa secret, and there was nothing I could do about it.

Curiosity always infiltrates a mind hungry for knowledge. As we drove past a cemetery one afternoon, my daughter (about three years old at the time) asked, "Mommy, what is a cemetery?"

"That's easy to explain, I'll tell you what that is!" my discerning five-year-old son piped up. "A cemetery is a large field of grass where people have statues. They go there to visit their statues and pray."

"Oh, thank you so much!" my daughter replied, exuberant at the answer. Little did my son know how grateful I was for not having to explain the somber significance of that place. Somehow, he always had a ready answer for anything – on the spot and on target, with astonishing insight.

Perhaps the most poignant example of my children's closeness to each other occurred when our dog, Magnolia, became ill after a canned food poisoning outbreak. Tragically, Magnolia's kidneys were failing. I didn't want to traumatize my children, realizing that she did not have long to live, so I asked my husband to take Magnolia away to a hospital in Pennsylvania to spend her last days in peace. Showering their beloved pet with hugs and kisses, my son and daughter said goodbye, believing, I thought, that our dog was going to convalesce. About a month later, my son came to me and stated declaratively and with the mature resignation of one far beyond his years, "She's dead isn't she?"

"What makes you say that?" I asked, trying to conceal my amazement.

"Mom, I know you. If Magnolia were alive, you would visit her every day. Since you're not doing that, I know that she's dead."

"It's true," I replied, astounded at my young son's powers of deduction. "I didn't want say anything because I didn't want to upset you and your sister. But please don't tell her. The news would be too much for her to handle. "

About a year later, a woman came into my rehabilitation office with her small poodle. My daughter, who happened to be with me that day, knelt down and began to pet the dog. Then, she looked up at the lady and said, "I had a dog. Her name was Magnolia, but she died a year ago." I could not believe my ears. Such unusual sense, calm resolve, and acceptance were sights to witness. Her brother had revealed the truth, and she accepted it with resignation.

Along with her keen intellect, my daughter's prominent characteristics are her appreciation of life's smallest pleasures, her strong will and tenacity, her alacrity in mastering tasks and conquering challenges with poise and grace, and her rare sense (i.e., common sense, so uncommon in this life). Such traits have evolved throughout the years and have been displayed in every phase of her life. When she was a baby, she observed me removing tags from newly purchased clothing. I took one, picturing a tiny bear, and handed it to my little girl. With the most genuine delight and pathos, she looked up at me and said, "Oh, that's for me? Thank you!" Her big eyes almost welled with tears of joy.

The efficacy of cell phone usage didn't escape my daughter's unstoppable, tack-sharp brain. At about age four, when cell phones weren't as ubiquitous as they are today, my practical girl enlightened my husband and me to the fact that shopping didn't have to be an exercise in logistic gymnastics. We simply had to coordinate our schedules by phone, and meet up at a mutually convenient time. "You're so silly!" she chastised us, when she saw our ill-timed planning.

At about the same age, my girl insisted on learning how to swim on her own. We were at a hotel, and her brother was already comfortable in the water. I asked whether she wanted me to hold her as she made an attempt to swim in the shallow pool. "No, Mommy! I want to do this on my own!" Keeping my eyes on her, I witnessed her strong will and determination to succeed. Then, becoming distracted for a moment, I diverted my glance. When I turned to look back at her again, there she was, swimming by herself.

Within the space of a brief hour, at age eight, my daughter undertook to ride the bicycle that I had purchased for her birthday and hid in the garage. When her special day arrived, two of her friends and I presented her with the gift, which she received with gratitude and delight. Within no time, she mounted the bike, with her friends running at equidistant paces on either side, instructing and encouraging her. A few minutes later, I peered through the window and saw her whisking past, all by herself. Her independent spirit was unstoppable. Memories pervaded my mind about how difficult it had been for me to learn to ride my brother's bike as a child in Peru. My heart swelled with pride.

These stories serve as but a few examples of the vast reach and breath of my children's proclivities and talents. While I admit that they are narrated with a hint of braggadocio, I hardly think my readers will take issue – especially parents who have an inalienable right to tout the aptitudes of those whom they love most in this world. I take special pride in knowing that my blessed gifts, my children, will someday read these passages and realize just how deeply I love and appreciate them, and how much happiness they bring to my world. Such feelings often become subsumed in the din of daily living, but are never lost. I am so grateful for the opportunity to express these sentiments, and to bear witness to my children's growth and evolution. In so doing, I see the future. My son's professorial vocabulary and ever-present brilliance, and my daughter's sensibility and dedication never cease to amaze me. Most of all, the two make me reach for and strive to achieve the best within myself. They always were – and remain – my ultimate antidote to Old Maid Syndrome and filled a void within me that I never before even deigned to recognize.

Chapter 14

The Travesties of Miscommunication

Timelessness also blossoms in the kindness of good friends. Without my confidante, George (whom I've known for about seven years now), I may not be writing this book today. His friendship is that significant to me. He worked in an office next to my former workplace, and our association was originally grounded in his computer expertise. However, as time passed, we got to know each other and became friends. Eventually, he began to visit my office for the treatment of knee pain. An African-American man with a tall, imposing frame, he is as amiable as he is wise, and as kind as he is pragmatic. I respect his opinions, and he freely confers a masculine perspective – a welcomed contrast to and springboard for my own interpretations and perceptions. One evening, as I was winding down my caseload, George, my last patient that day, made a pivotal observation. "You seem so preoccupied. What's on your mind?" Feeling that I could trust him, I answered, as the floodgates to my heart opened wide, ushering forth a wellspring of past and present memories, which took me through the countless, varied byroads of my life.

Admittedly, confiding in George was my only outlet at that moment, and I saw that opportunity as the sole recourse for soothing my troubled mind and heart. I was in a bewildered state,

185

unable to concentrate on work – or anything else for that matter. There, before me, at the end of my workday, was just the friend I needed – a kind voice of reason, and an ear willing to listen to the moral dilemma that had plagued me for a full twenty-six years: I was still carrying a torch for Eduardo. For once in my life, I could express myself fully and completely, and place my heart on the table in front of someone who was, actually, an ally, someone who would listen to me free of judgment and reproach, as a true friend. For two hours, I sat with George and told him about some of the events of my past, and the fact that the flame of love, passion, and longing still ignited in my heart for a man with whom my miscommunication had destroyed the endurance of that relationship.

The odd reality of the situation was that my husband, Richard, knew all about that flame. In an effort to be entirely authentic with him while we were dating, I revealed my ever-present affections for Eduardo, to which he replied, "That was long ago, and you probably will never see him again. Besides, I will make you forget about him." But how could I forget, when there were so many words unspoken, so many feelings unexpressed, so much of a heart-connection which, at the time, I could hardly explore, due to my self-doubt occasioned by my facial blemishes, my language barrier, and concomitant insecurities? I had evolved so far away from those years – and yet they still plagued me like a chronic sensation of something unpleasantly familiar welling in my stomach. My youth had passed. Yet, the sensations still felt so raw. And there was George, dear. friend who patiently listened and provided good, solid advice. I don't know what I would have done without him in those moments!

My response to George's questions, "What's wrong? Why are you so preoccupied?" was prolific. The fact was that I had just come into communication with Eduardo again via our medical school web site, directly linked to Facebook. I hadn't even heard of social networking until my childhood friend, Adriana (who now lives in Switzerland) introduced me to that miraculous utility. Now, I have a whole new vocabulary, with interchangeable nouns and verbs, like "to friend" and "to unfriend." It's an alternate reality.

In all events, we transmitted a series of written messages, which began with a couple of pleasantries. These initial salutations were a prelude to our Facebook exchange. I believe that our communications merit narration here, particularly because my good friend, George, was riveted by them, and because I feel that they are revelatory of my interaction with Eduardo. Come into that mysterious, detached, and strangely intimate world of social networking, and deconstruct the words and images which ignited the ultimate could-have been-romance of the millennium (yes, I'm a sentimentalist, but this is my reality).

Once connected to Facebook, we wrote:

Isabella: "Hi, Eduardo! I came across your picture on the medical school network. How are you? Just wanted to say hello."

Eduardo: "Fine! How have YOU been? I just sent an 'add' request."

Isabella: "*I just finished my work. I was happy to hear from you. Of course, a lot has happened since I last saw you after I graduated from physical therapy school. I worked in several hospitals, opened my own practice, and returned to school to study acupuncture and traditional Chinese medicine. Let me know what's happening with you.*

Without replying, Eduardo waited until that evening to upload a prodigious number of photos to an album, depicting himself at his workplace, his beloved children, hockey games, and all manner of other personal snapshots. Such information endeared him to me yet more – as if that were possible. In the older gentleman, I perceived the kindness and gentility of the romantic youth in whose luminous blue eyes I constantly lost myself – though silently, in contemplation alone. I had been too shy and tenuous to let him know at the time when expression would have mattered most – a tragic truth.

Still, chances must be seized, for the moment is what matters – in philosophical parlance, anyway – and I resolved to integrate that viewpoint into my life, to seize the day. So, when

Valentine's Day arrived, I wasted no time in writing a covert message on my Facebook wall. "I'm going to my secret hideaway – no phones, no computers, incommunicado; but, before I do that, I would like to wish everyone a Happy Valentine's Day. P.S. I am Sarah Palin." In the comments field, I wrote, "Look at my hand." I uploaded a photo of myself in scrubs, taken by my friend for that very purpose. On my hand, I had written in marker ink, "I <3 u" (for the few uninitiated, the designation <3 signifies a heart). With that, I left on a Friday, and returned home on Sunday (Valentine's Day), excitedly checking my page to discover how my message had been received and interpreted. To my disappointment, on that very day, Eduardo had posted a photo of himself and his fiancée, accompanied by the salutation, "Happy VD, everyone!" I read this to be an express message to me – nonverbal communication, signifying, "I am engaged to be married, and am spending the day with my fiancée."

Upset and hurt, my bruised ego dictated that I erase my entire message and photo and replace them with a picture of my husband and me embracing against the backdrop of a cascading waterfall. Once again, Eduardo's photo changed shortly thereafter, depicting him with his son on vacation. Query: Was Eduardo communicating with me through photographs? The following week, when he changed his relationship status to single, I noticed that one of his friends wrote, "I heard that you are no longer engaged." Eduardo confirmed, "It's true."

That Sunday, another posting of Eduardo with his children playing a game was conspicuously displayed in my silent communicator's profile, along with an empty hand gesture identical to the one which I had posted on Valentine's Day – with one conspicuous exception: no accompanying writing. Was this a mere coincidence or the mirror image of my gesture – a reciprocal message of some kind? I ask rhetorically, of course, for I may never know. Does it matter now? I ask myself, again, rhetorically, listening in vain for my own response. My heart, however, remains mute.

A couple of weeks elapsed before the following passage from a book on Buddhism appeared on Eduardo's Facebook wall: "What we are today comes from our thoughts of yesterday, and our present thoughts build our life for tomorrow. Our life is a creation of our mind. We choose to act or speak with a pure or impure mind and that makes all the difference." Captivated by this message, I knew that this was the spirit that had reached mine all those many years ago – the heart that, despite our communication difficulties, saw through the window of my soul, and spoke to me in ways that I never had been addressed before or since. I replied: "Hi Eduardo, I was thinking about what you wrote based on the book you read. It was very profound. I guess we set our own paths in life, and it is up to us to decide our actions and thoughts. Hopefully, with goodness within us, we can be truthful to others and ourselves. I would like to be truthful today, because I do not know what tomorrow will bring. I have thought about you over the years, and regret not being truthful then, due to fear of rejection, fear of failure and embarrassment, fear of not knowing the language well enough to communicate with you. So, I acted very foolishly. I have grown so much now, and I wonder if someday we will get a chance to get to know each other better."

The next day, Eduardo wrote: "What weren't you truthful about?"

"Fair question," I answered. "I feel uncomfortable replying in this setting."

"Email me?" Eduardo suggested, offering his address.

"I think I'm walking a tight rope, without a net below me!" I ventured, tentatively.

"Why?" came the answer.

"Just a harmless expression," I explained. "For me, it means a bit scared and cautious. I guess e-mail would be all right. Just give me some time."

"Send me an email," repeated Eduardo, apparently eager to receive some sort of revealing confidence or insight from me as to what troubled my mind.

In an effort to explain myself, to bridge the gap of silence and miscommunication which characterized our association twenty-six years before, I wrote the following answer, infusing every ounce of heart and effort into each syllable. Considering my former language barrier, the letter was a tour de force, a victory over all of the inhibitions of days gone by. I had found my voice.

"We are the product of our past. Unfortunately for me, that meant a bad relationship when I was fifteen, as a senior high school student. I fell in love with a law student from a prestigious school who later dumped me, without explanation. Having a broken heart at that young age was not easy to overcome. The letter I gave you was not the truth, but it was the only excuse I could come up with at that time. Now that I look back, it was so childish. I am sure you must have forgotten it by now, but I could not forget. I do regret behaving the way I did. I was very fond of you and I found you very charming, attractive, and most of all, brilliant. At that time, I was doing so poorly in school, failing all my classes. I felt that I had to concentrate on school at that time. Now, to complicate things more, my English was so poor. Every day was a struggle. I did not want to look like an idiot next to you. I could not hold a long conversation with anybody, and the last thing I wanted to do was to cause you embarrassment in front of your friends. It was so hard to ignore you sometimes. I was so fearful of embarrassment. I bluffed in my classes and around you. I think I did a good job of pretending. What a difficult experience that was! I look back now, and I see how bad my situation was. I don't know how on earth I succeeded back then. The only regret is that I never had the chance to explain this to you until now. I think it was unfair to both of us. I thought about it over the years. I am very thankful for the writings of Buddhism for opening the door for me to say this to you now. I don't think I could have done it any other way; and if indeed the teachings of Buddhism are correct, I do not want to leave this to my next life to make amends. The most important message I want to give you is that the foolish girl has grown up and needs to apologize for her past actions. It is the right thing to do."

Now, when re-reading this personal epiphany, I can honestly state that, perhaps, it might have been misinterpreted as an apology, underhandedly sprinkled with sarcasm in the phrase, "I don't know how on earth I succeeded back then" (which Eduardo may have construed as a declaration of self-aggrandizement. That is, "I am doing very well, thank you, and I succeeded in all of my undertakings"). Such was far from my intention, and could have been yet another travesty of miscommunication.

Eduardo replied, "There is no apology required! I bear no ill will against you! Continue with your happy life and think no more about the past in this regard, please! I wish you all the best and happiness!"

Then, Eduardo changed his Facebook status to read, "My life is complete….Not perfect, but complete!" On his wall, he wrote something like, "Some people walk up and down the bank, but never have the courage to get to the other side."

With a heavy heart, I clearly discern, now, that my words were interpreted as aloofness – a brief, off-handed apology to someone whom I met casually and with whom I had only a passing association. My heart is not elusive – especially when it comes to people I love. Eduardo factored into that number, and I desperately wanted him to know that, but as much as I tried, I fell short – yet again, I thought. I was hurt that Eduardo misunderstood and wrote back, in frustrated tones.

"I feel as though someone just slammed the door in my face! I am going away for a couple of days. This has been a very rough week for me."

After composing myself and returning home, I noticed a reply to my message. "I remember you, Isabella, but I don't recall the letter you are referring to. Can you refresh my memory?"

How could I remember a lie? As I mentioned, lies are internally deceptive. You can never tell the same story twice. Therefore, faced with yet another moral quagmire, I consulted George, who told me to forget about that correspondence. "You need to close that chapter containing the letter. That isn't important now. You can open another chapter and start anew, if it's meant to be."

As usual, my rational conscience, embodied in the person of my dear friend, had spoken once more. I mustered the courage to answer: "I don't think the letter is important now. I wanted to get something off of my chest from the past. The letter was a way of rationalizing my inconsistent behavior at the time. That chapter of our lives is closed now. Do you agree with me?"

Silence reigned. For several days, Eduardo was nowhere to be found on Facebook. I began to worry, and deferred to George again for advice.

"Give him a couple of days, and if he's still not online, write casually and say, 'Hi, I haven't seen you online lately. Just want to make sure you're OK.'"

Perceiving inherent sense in this phraseology, I did just as George advised, and received an almost immediate reply: "Thanks, I'm fine! Busy, but fine!" From that time forth, Eduardo began to communicate with his Facebook network again, revealing his intention to purchase a motorcycle, which he referred to as "a bike." Therefore, I mistakenly conjured a bicycle.

"Good to know that you are OK," I wrote, delighted to hear from Eduardo again. "Don't overwork. A Chinese master warned me, '[Work] wears down your Yin-Essence and it makes you age very quickly. You still look good, so conserve your Yin-Essence. I noticed you're planning to get a bike. A year ago, I was looking into the Lee Iacocca bike. I think it stores energy when you pedal and I believe there's an electric one that assists you when you're going uphill." Without knowing that the bikes were in second-hand production only, I proceeded to send Eduardo a link. I meant well, at least.

Clearly, time had not hampered Eduardo's athletic prowess. He mentioned that he did, indeed, have a bicycle and that his thighs began to burn while pedaling uphill – an express indication that youth and vigor still graced his stature. I commented a couple of times on the effects of bike-riding, and asked whether Eduardo had read any good books of late (noticing that he had "liked" Barnes and Noble through Facebook). I ventured to ask for book recommendations. I mention this fact because of what occurred next. "It gets curioser and curioser" (to quote Lewis Carroll's "Alice"). One night, I awoke from a dream of Eduardo searching diligently for books on my behalf. That very morning, I rose to find his recommendation of Dan Brown's "The Da Vinci Code" and "Angels and Demons." Speak of mental telepathy! I always felt the power of intuition between us.

More small talk ensued, in which Eduardo asked about my kids and my job, among other things. After praising my children, I observed that I had already discussed my job, and the conversation was becoming circular. I felt that I had been cornered. Around the same time, Eduardo had been communicating with a female friend on Facebook, holding forth on the virtues of directness. "As a goalie, I like when people throw things at me," he said.

I sensed the urgency of action on my part, and consulted my mentor. "It's obvious, Isabella," George said. "He will never ask you out because he's free and you're not. Any decent man would have a problem with this. So, this is your chance to ask Eduardo out!"

I was stunned. The voice of pragmatism was spurring me on toward audacity, to take the reigns. Everything in me – the inhibitions of my past, the ubiquitous strictness and wrath of my teachers (the nuns), the punishment inflicted at the slightest transgression or display of girlish folly – pervaded my every pore and sinew.

"No, no! Me? I can't!" I said aloud; but something propelled me forward – the desire to speak candidly, openly, without reservation. I had come a long way from my mountain-girl reticence. It was a new dawn. Either say what's on your mind, or forever hold your peace, I told myself. I decided to play it safe, however, and I wrote the following:

"It would be very nice to see you again…and catch up."

Twenty minutes later, Cupid's arrow landed right in front of me.

"WOW! That could be very dangerous! You are still pretty sexy!"

Barely knowing how to respond and charged with an ego and energy boost the size of Mount Everest, I waited until the next afternoon to respond.

"I'll take the chance. By the way, the feeling is mutual."

Was that really I,– the timid girl from Huaraz? Surely, that girl had an emotional and/or psychical makeover! It's a good thing that Eduardo didn't see my face turn beet red behind that screen, as I was zapped by a lightening bolt that had for so long remained inactive within my heart. If such feelings seemed adolescent, I freely concede that they were – and I felt them unashamedly, as I allowed my deferred girlish exuberance, bolstered and endowed by my well-established maturity and knowledge, to flow forth like an ocean.

"Double wow!" exclaimed the man who was verbally seducing me. "What do you have in mind?" Then, he quickly added, "Let's use regular email."

I cannot adequately relate my joy during these times – moments when I truly felt liberated, unfettered by my past, and by time itself. Eduardo's acceptance of and desire to see and communicate with me, his flattering overtures and expressions of admiration made me feel whole. I had to pinch myself to realize that the man for whom I had pined for over a quarter of a century had entered my world again. The only void left to fill was my wish to speak with and meet him again.

I went to a local Verizon Wireless store to activate my "secret red phone," so named not for any association to the CIA, but for my clandestine attempt to keep my resumed communications with Eduardo private. A lovely Russian girl (to whom I will refer as Oxana) assisted and took a photo of me, and asked for whom it was intended.

"It's for someone very special from the past, and we have found each other again."

"Oh, that is so romantic!" Oxana exclaimed, beaming.

Because I had to leave for work, I was advised to return that evening for further instructions on how to use the phone. I had given Eduardo my phone number beforehand. That night, as I was driving to the store, Eduardo texted me and asked (alluding to my message the evening before, stating that "I will be dreaming about you"):

"So, tell me about your dream last night."

In disbelief, I pulled over and, at a loss of what to say, I wrote, "I probably have to whisper it in your ear." This was a mere figure of speech. Never, in my wildest dreams, did I think that he would decide to call me; but, when I arrived at the store, just as Oxana was demonstrating the phone's features, a call came through. "He's calling you," she said, spotting Eduardo's name on the screen. Emanating from the other end was his voice. As we spoke, I walked to my car and began to drive, forgetting the stringency of the police about cell phone usage while driving. I didn't even know how to activate the speakerphone at that time. I was simply immersed in the moment. All of the feelings from my past rushed in like a tidal wave. I could hardly believe that I was speaking to him. In our brief conversation, Eduardo asked how my marriage progressed, to which I replied, "It's OK." "If it's OK," he reasoned, "why are you talking to me?" I avoided the question by telling him that I was anxious and asked whether we could speak that evening. He agreed, and I continued on my way to pick up my daughter from softball practice.

Can this really be happening? I asked myself, hardly knowing how to formulate a cogent thought. That evening, I pulled myself together and told my family that I would be working late in my office. This was not an unusual occurrence, but my covert evasion of the truth made me feel uneasy. Still, the overriding, pervasive energy that flowed through me commanded that I proceed with my secret operation – and with my red phone, I was appropriately equipped. So, there I sat, in my office, with the phone in front of me, waiting for it to ring. I stared at it, as though it were some magical creature, holding the secret to my destiny.

At precisely 11:00 p.m. (the exact time when Eduardo promised to call), the phone rang and I answered. There it was – that familiar, though remote voice from my past. I felt strangely complete, yet displaced – caught between the world of yesterday and the rather complicated one that I faced. Though I had so much for which to be grateful, I was filled with regret for what might have been – not really knowing whether my mind had invented an untenable story or whether Eduardo's attention still remained an imminent reality, yet to be. All I knew was that love doesn't tell falsehoods, and what I felt was as real as anything that I had ever experienced.

The two of us had a lengthy, meaningful conversation, in which Eduardo told me of the loss of his father, with whom he had been extremely close, some years before. At the very point of that tragic event, as a newlywed, I remember feeling an inexplicable grief envelop my entire being. I recall that I had been immersed in a TV program, not thinking of Eduardo at that given moment when suddenly, his image came to mind, occasioning tears for him – a kind of mourning that I didn't understand. Was this sentiment prophetic or a mere coincidence? Now, in hindsight, I understand that the feelings must have signaled some intuitive, telepathic, empathetic connection between us – similar to that aforementioned concerning Eduardo's recommendation of books. I never mentioned the incident to him for, sometimes, in the narration of such events, their visceral nature evaporates. Now, however, I am free of restraint – free to live my truth.

In response to Eduardo's revelation regarding his strained relationship with his mother, I offered some personal advice. I explained that I also had overcome a similar hurdle with my mother, which I accomplished by writing her a long, heartfelt letter, pouring out my feelings of neglect and rejection in my youth. Her misplaced interpretation of my resilience and ability to stand on my own left me bereft of maternal nurturing, and her lack of intervention made me feel alone and rejected. "Forgive your foolish mother," Mom wrote back in a moment of personal disclosure. After that exchange, our bond was solidified, and love built a bridge over the pain of our past. We're now good friends. I shared that story with Eduardo because I realized, first-hand, that forgiveness was the greatest panacea for all ills. The following day, Eduardo drove almost two hours to see his Mom. Afterwards, I noticed a posting from his mother on his Facebook wall, stating, "Thank you for the lovely visit." I interpreted the statement to indicate that amends had been made, and I was flattered and happy that Eduardo had taken my advice.

After revealing that my marriage had become devoid of emotional and physical closeness, I heard in my ears that tone of undeniable sweetness and understanding that had engulfed my heart for so many years. Accompanying Eduardo's mellifluous tones of empathy and goodwill came his explicit, passionate declarations of what would occur at our meeting – a union of bodies and souls, described in minute detail. I could hardly believe that such words emanated from the man for whom my feelings had been frozen in time, indelibly imprinted on my heart. Being free of my facial blemishes enabled me to open myself to the possibility of actually being loved and desired by this man. I must admit, however, that I felt a strong level of discomfort in keeping this interlude (which amounted only to a verbal exchange of affection) a secret from my family. Still, I felt an insurmountable compulsion to explore whether my feelings were genuine or whether they were, simply, a byproduct of my past insecurities – that all-encompassing wish of bygone times to fit into the world without the encumbrance of my facial marks. In hindsight, I can say unequivocally that the feelings had only to do with a sincere yearning to connect with someone whom I deemed to be my soul mate.

Eduardo asked to see me, and we agreed upon a Saturday, May 1, 2010. Initially, he asked for a romantic meeting, for drinks and then going to his place; but I just couldn't bring myself to accept the proposition. That is not to say that I was averse to it. My naturally reserved posture just dictated against such an intimate rendezvous. Therefore, we agreed to meet at a mall in his home state, and that I would come out his way for the purpose. All the while, we continued to exchange emails and texts. One of the latter forms of communication came the very next day, after a night of excited, wakeful sleep, in which I hardly could believe the advances he had made towards me. The texts to which I referred were designed, I believe, to awaken my dormant need for physical intimacy – the desire to be wanted and needed. Eduardo produced a rather astonishing resume – the full display of his anatomical accoutrements, at their zenith. Need I say more? In deference to those who may cower at matters appealing to the prurient interest, I ask those bold of heart to use their vivid imaginations here. I refer back to the elderly ladies, who suggested that my book had to contain some racy elements. Well, what I saw amply fits – and far exceeds – that description and, as such, cannot be described extensively by the culturally austere girl inside, whom the nuns would chastise severely for such graphic depictions. Yes, that girl was still there, albeit in a more subdued form, even after my bold recitations on Facebook and via email. You can take the girl out of the mountains, but there are some elements of the mountains and the life that I knew that still cannot be extricated so readily from my psyche.

At last, the day of our meeting arrived. The night before, I writhed in insomnia, tossing, turning, and thrashing every which way, getting only about four hours' sleep. I was literally being torn apart by thoughts pulling me in opposite directions – my tremendous love for my family on the one hand, and my insatiable yearning to be with my long-lost love on the other.

I pause here to reflect upon and give due respect to the praiseworthy qualities of my husband, Richard, as a father – his devotion, care, and love for our children, his commitment and promise to make me forget about Eduardo. He just couldn't – no one could. In deference to my family's privacy, I omit here specific reference to our lives together and what we have been through, stating only that the turmoil I experienced – the longing for true love – was not mitigated by my marriage. As for my children, my world, I don't perceive my love for Eduardo to be a transgression or abnegation of my responsibility and love for my son and daughter. The two loves are separate and distinct, and one variety neither negates nor threatens the other. You can only be the best of yourself when you are true to yourself and what you feel. By expressing myself openly, I confer myself to my children as the integrated whole individual that I am – the entire package, with all of my cards on the table. In no respect or guise does that diminish my depth of feeling for them. On the contrary, I am not hiding anything. I am simply saying, "Here I am! This is who I am and, with every ounce of my heart, I love you."

Such musings raged as I wrangled with myself, mind, body, and spirit. I was supposed to call Eduardo early on the morning of our meeting but, given that I didn't go to sleep until 4:00 a.m.

and arose at 8:00 a.m., that wasn't possible. In the interim, I received a text, saying "Good morning!" from Eduardo at 6:00 a.m., to which I didn't reply. This omission was due to my nerves, extraordinary rush to prepare myself casually for the day, and hurry to my office for an appointment that I couldn't cancel. All of my other appointments had been rescheduled for the momentous occasion. Indeed, I placed my entire life on hold.

My intent to hide my plans from my family obscured all other thoughts. Everyone was at home. I told them that I was going to the mall to meet a friend – a half truth which almost absolved my conscience of guilt, and I took care to ensconce my secret red phone away from their vision. I answered Eduardo's text at around 9:45 a.m., with a return, "Good morning!" Silence spoke volumes. I surmised that Eduardo was upset – as any busy practitioner would be. In our circles (that of healthcare providers), my failure to respond promptly probably was construed as a deliberate, rude omission; but, again, such was not my intent! I was, simply, very excited and nervous. Something told me to change my mind and turn back, but after all those years, I had to give myself this one gift – for my own sake. I dressed inconspicuously, in jeans and a denim top, wearing my hair in a ponytail. Beset by my usual seasonal allergies (which flared precisely on May 1, for some reason), my eyes were swollen. My lack of sleep manifested in bags under my eyes – those insidious robbers of a youthful complexion. Not anticipating romantic bliss that day, I figured that I was appropriately attired, desiring only to get to know Eduardo better. Besides (and this is significant) our meeting was to take place in proximity to my farm; so, if by happenstance, I ran into anyone familiar, I would just say that I had come for a visit there. I had my scheme all mapped out.

After receiving my message, Eduardo replied, "Where are you?"

"I'm on the road."

And what a road it was – filled with enormous trucks and other vehicles careening all around, sending me into a panic, but I mustered the courage to continue.

"Are you heading my way?"

"Yes. I'm not sure about my arrival time. Should we say 1:30, and I'll call you when I get there?"

"Okay, call me then."

My suggestion to phone Eduardo upon my arrival was for his convenience – a courtesy which he seemed to dismiss. I had never initiated such efforts in traveling and waiting for any man. (Except, that is, as a teen, when I awaited Carlos, a no-show at the movie matinee. That was eons ago, and the incident's significance infinitely paled in comparison to what I felt in those moments just prior to reuniting with Eduardo.) If a man really cares deeply for a woman, I mused, he would not concede to her waiting for him as I did. Instead, he would have offered to wait. The entire effort was on my shoulders. I figured, however, that since I had treated Eduardo so poorly during our school days when he tried to approach me, and my persistent avoidance due to my lack of self-esteem at the time, it was only fitting that I exert myself. Still, something just didn't feel right. It was particularly uncomfortable, humiliating, and embarrassing to find myself alone at my destination, awaiting someone who only days before had been so overtly suggestive and eager to see me.

Every fifteen minutes, Eduardo continued to text me, asking, "Will I get you alone?" I answered "yes," thinking that he was referring to my friend who initially had planned to drive me to my destination, but cancelled at the last minute. Obviously, Eduardo intended to have a physical connection

"I'll be there in fifteen minutes." The texts came in waves, as I finally became frustrated by the wait.

"I'm going shopping. Call me when you get here," I wrote.

I took myself to a little shop, where I spotted a metal heart surrounded by the words, "Dream, dream, dream!" How apropos of my situation! In fact, before we met, Eduardo posted on his Facebook wall, "Don't dream it, live it." I was living a dream – perhaps chasing the phantom of my youth. When Eduardo called to say that he had arrived, a battle between head and heart had been waging within me. In my mind, I tried to make excuses (a mind game in which most women engage when they're in love). He's a doctor, after all. Maybe he had an emergency, maybe I interrupted his workday, maybe he was tired, overworked…maybe! My thoughts raced on contingencies.

Then, playing in my head, I began to hear the Bryan Adams song, "Have You Ever Really Loved a Woman," featured in the 1994 film "Don Juan DeMarco," starring Johnny Depp. I saw Eduardo and approached him, advancing in his direction, eagerly awaiting a kiss. Since I had already seen Eduardo's picture on Facebook, his distinguished, defined features, chiseled by some of his boyhood youthfulness did not surprise me. I was, however, slightly daunted when my teeth clashed with his veneers when I attempted to kiss him. His carriage was icy and reserved – like a cold, steel plate. No apologies emanated from him, and nothing was said about his delay: no "I'm happy to see you," no embrace. I felt as though I were about to collapse under the weight of an awful, sinking feeling.

"Are you hungry? Did you eat?" Eduardo asked.

"No, did you?" As I returned the question, pressure rose to my head.

"I already ate." Eduardo said, looking at me as if he had just seen me the day before.

"So, what do you want to do?" I asked, for lack of more substantive dialogue.

We decided upon a casual restaurant, where we would go for cool drinks to offset the sweltering temperatures of that May day. How appropriate! I felt as though I were on a collision course in the middle of nowhere, inwardly shouting, "Mayday, mayday!" We arrived at the restaurant and sat across from one another. Eduardo's glance darted across the room, toward every nook and corner – except at me. I was becoming increasingly ruffled and upset. Yet again seeking a bridge to our silence, I ventured, "So, where are you taking me?"

"Nowhere. I have only one helmet," Eduardo replied, referring to the fact that he had taken his motorcycle. Then, he added, "My son is at home. He lives with me."

At that point, our dialogue had descended into the depths of...nothingness. Was this a bluff? I asked myself, wallowing in embarrassment and discomfort. Fortunately, the conversation picked up as we spoke, for nearly two hours, about our families. Eduardo confided that he had been in an abusive marriage. I wondered how anyone could have treated him so poorly and whether his cold exterior had something to do with his construction of the wall around him.

"How are things at home?" Eduardo inquired, without a hint of his former gentility and charm.

"My parents are doing fine, thank you."

"I wasn't speaking of your parents. I was asking about you and your family."

As we decided to walk around the mall, Eduardo's stern body language and facial expressions became apparent.

"How are things between you and your husband? What does he think of you?" Eduardo was finally hitting upon his point of curiosity. More than anything else, he wanted to know whether he would be taking a chance with a happily married woman.

"My husband thinks I'm irreplaceable," I said candidly. "But I was never sure that I ever loved him."

"Then why did you marry him?"

"My biological clock was ticking.... Who knows?"

"What does he do for a living?"

"He's an attorney."

At that point, Eduardo became uncomfortable, and our conversation diminished and declined again. "Mayday, mayday!" My heart cried, on the collision course to nowhere.

"So what did you buy?" Eduardo queried, without genuine interest.

I showed him the little metal heart, surrounded by the imperative, "dream, dream, dream." Eduardo continued to walk with an arrogant, contemptuous swagger, so distinct from when we were young, so self-possessed and smug. Still, I continued to walk with him. I don't know why. It seemed that I was a glutton for punishment. Perhaps, subconsciously, I felt that this was the result of my past avoidance – but was it? Did the man next to me truly remember me and entertain the same feelings for me as I had for him? Clearly not. Nonetheless, I couldn't bring myself to simply walk away in pain, an act that which would only have served to exacerbate my feelings of loss for twenty-six years.

"Did you ever go kayaking?" This strange question from Eduardo threw me off course.

"No," I replied, by then becoming used to my monosyllables.

"Do you like motorcycles?" Eduardo asked, desperately seeking common ground.

"I'm petrified of motorcycles."

"Why? You ride horses, and they are the same."

"I ride in a controlled environment. I had two friends who died in motorcycle accidents," I offered, hoping that Eduardo understood that I cared for his safety and well-being.

"You can die just crossing the road." Eduardo was decisive, if nothing else.

His words hit a chord with me. I don't believe that he knew of the tragic loss of Laura, my beloved sister.

"Don't you care about your kids?" I ventured, signifying that, if anything happened to him, he would deprive his children of his society, the comfort of his presence, a cherished father – and someone for whom I deeply cared.

Of course, under the circumstances, I couldn't vent my true feelings. Obviously, physical attraction was his sole motivation for our meeting and, for him, I didn't seem to be enough. I, on the other hand, would have accepted him in a bald, antiquated, decrepit state. Evidently, Eduardo was extremely discomforted by my remarks. We walked to the other side of the outdoor mall, silently seething inside. I speak for both of us because I'm sure that we shared a mutual resentment in those moments. Disappointment was my constant guide, and I felt helpless.

"You know," I said, trying to break the ice – a formidable task even for black belt karate masters, "you should be very honored that I came all this way for you."

Eduardo's response was bitingly expressive. He began skipping and swinging his arms, as he said, "Look at how happy I am!"

I had never been in such an awkward situation before – almost feeling victimized by Eduardo's apparent disdain and ridicule. Good sense and reason would have dictated that I leave, then and there, but I viewed this as a cowardly act. I had come so far, and there was no turning back. Something went very wrong, and my irate companion had occasioned a silence between us as dense as London fog. Again attempting to wade through the obscurity, I said something mindless.

"Aren't you going to give me a hug?"

"A hug?" Eduardo thrust his body against mine. He was as stiff as an oak. "Here's a hug!"

This was very bad, very bad, indeed! As the cry of "mayday" resounded louder than ever in my ears, I said, "I feel awkward!"

"Me, too! Where is your car?"

"On the other side of the mall."

"I'll take you there!"

Humiliated and defeated, there was nowhere for me to turn. I should have said, "Don't bother. I'll walk there, myself." However, the desire to conquer adversity compelled me to grind my teeth and stand my ground. So, I said nothing. As we walked to Eduardo's motorcycle, he handed me his helmet.

"Here, put this on! I'll take you to your car with my bike."

I don't know why I complied with this less-than-gracious offer. Climbing on the back, I sat at a remote distance from Eduardo, clasping his sides with my fingertips – hardly touching the man whom I had so admired – the man who had morphed into my detractor. I pointed to my car, we stopped there, and I descended – all while Eduardo remained seated. My ponytail became entangled in the helmet - a cruel metaphor for my web of emotions. Finally, when I managed to extricate myself, we hugged, said goodbye, and Eduardo drove away.

In the sanctuary of my car, I sobbed uncontrollably. I decided to proceed on my way to attend the second night of "Peter Rabbit," my daughter's play, which my husband and I had seen the night before. My heart was in turmoil and I could feel the blood coursing through my veins. Then, with my guard down, I pulled over and texted Eduardo.

"What really happened back there?"

"A few things," Eduardo replied. "I felt wrong about your being married, I didn't feel the sparks between us, as I had expected, and the distance, as well."

"That is exactly what I was afraid of when I was young. This scenario would have devastated me then, but I am older now and I can take it. I need closure to move on with my life. Maybe we can consider just being friends?"

What I thought was Eduardo's silence detonated like a bomb in my heart. In truth, he had answered me, but I had been driving and missed his response. When I arrived at my daughter's school and the lights dimmed in preparation for the play, I sat there, next to one of my daughter's lovely friends, restraining my tears. Never had I felt such gratitude for the darkness. Then, I stood up, excused myself, and went into the bathroom. There, amidst my confusion and sorrow, I saw another text message from Eduardo in response to mine.

"It's best to forget tonight."

Interpreting these words to mean, "Forget that we ever existed," I again broke down in tears. I felt ancient, unsightly, and seemed to have regressed into my former cocoon of self-doubt. I began to ask everyone about my physical appearance – as if the external validation of others determined by self-worth. By sheer force of compulsion, I wrote back.

"Fake boobs, fake nose, fake belly are not who I am! I'm one hundred percent real – swollen, allergic eyes, some wrinkles, some temporary tooth problems – but I am natural and real, and people should just accept me the way I am." I felt beyond miserable. In my mind, my appearance surfaced again as a possible deterrent to Eduardo's affections. I feared the ravages of age and time, and asked everyone around me whether I had fallen prey to unattractiveness and old age. Even when I was reassured that such was not the case, I still felt empty – as though some form of closure and healing had to be reached between Eduardo and me.

A reply to this writing never arrived, but a series of text messages ensued, in which Eduardo told me that my appearance was not the trigger for his aloofness. In turn, I told him that he had to face life as it occurs, to be an open communicator – otherwise feelings fester. I reassured him of my awareness of his abusive marriage and the urgency of his self-expression, which I believed to be repressed. I later wrote again, stating that I had something interesting and of further import to say, but at the time I was preparing for my daughter's birthday party. I felt torn between my need – and privilege – of attending to my daughter, and the pressing longing to speak with Eduardo, to at last smooth over the rough patches caused by miscommunication. Eduardo insisted that our conversations be restricted to Facebook, and that he couldn't be my therapist. I countered that I required no such intervention, as I always dealt with matters at hand by confronting them head-on. I had survived one of the most devastating earthquakes imaginable, faced the loss of a sister whom I adored, shouldered each trial that life had thrown at me with resigned acceptance and poise – and Eduardo boldly intimated that I needed a therapist! At the height of such audacity, I still forgave him. Why? I know not. Perhaps, I was motivated by the image so indelibly etched in my heart – the depiction of that gentle, gracious soul, whom I never had abandoned in thought, despite time and distance.

Regarding that "interesting matter": Because I needed to shop for the party, I couldn't text at the moment that I should have – that pivotal instance, when propriety and opportunity should have merged. I missed the chance. So, as I sat in a store awaiting my daughter, alone in a dark place, surrounded by perfumed scents and loud music, I allowed myself to give vent to my sorrow. I cried and prayed to God to alleviate my intense pain. Later, my daughter came to me and noticed my red eyes. "Poor you, Mom!" she said empathetically. "You must be allergic to something around here." My angel was right. Not only was I allergic to pollen, but also to the sadness pervading me. Again, yet another misstep, yet another omission to write at a key moment had possibly taken away every hope of positive closure. You cannot retrieve moments, but it is never too late to speak your mind.

Some three weeks after our unfortunate meeting, I posted the following message to Eduardo on Facebook: "I am so confused about the 'sparks.' I thought we felt them when we were young. I guess it does not matter anymore, but life is short. So, I thought that you should know this: I know that you do not want to talk to me, and I will not expect anything from you."

Eduardo then had an exchange with a friend, in which he quoted Confucius: "Either you do or you don't. There is no trying." Again, I wondered whether he was trying to communicate with me in some way. Did I have to decode the message, "Either you commit or you won't. I won't go half way?" If his language had been rendered in code, why was it so? Why this game-playing?

About a week later, Eduardo took the bold step of "unfriending" me, a move that rendered me baffled. Still, through the powers of the network, I could view his photos. Something can be said for direct communication, and where there lies a true connection, there is no need for subterfuge or evasion of the truth. Come to think of it, that is what I am doing now, conferring my Eduardo-inspired testimony, telling the whole truth and nothing but the truth, so help me God! In this day and age, the computer often acts as a third party in conferring ideas and sentiments between people. Some things are, therefore, lost in electronic transmission (specifically, the opportunity to hear a voice, interpret an inflection, see a reaction, and develop a genuine relationship with someone).

Later, seeking to reach out by acknowledging Eduardo's birthday, I wrote my message early in the day – as a kind of compensation for my failure to respond in timely fashion to his text on the morning of our meeting: "Good morning! May your heart be filled with loving kindness, empathy, happiness! May you be well! I want all the best for you! Happy birthday! Isabella." My goodwill gesture was met with stone silence. Was this indifference, anger, pain, frustration, or outright rejection? Again, nonverbal evasion or silent communication only caused me further to wonder from where Eduardo's emotions were flowing – or whether, indeed, any feeling other than that of corporeal desire alone were directed at me.

I am guided by the teachings of sages such as the Buddha. I don't playact at love. I don't feign affection – and for me, affection has its foundation in the heart and on humanistic common ground. I thought that Eduardo and I were connected in so many ways – intellectually, emotionally, psychically, and physically. Was that connection mere conjecture, a product of my mind, or an actual byproduct of real, palpable feeling? I can only answer these questions with more questions, and I travel in an infinite circle of whys and maybes.

Perhaps, in retrospect, the journey into the latent recesses of my heart was a cathartic way of regressing into my past and revisiting my youth, when love was a magical concept. When one is young, the notion of love is untainted by facades. As such, it exists in its purest form, and descends like a lightening bolt into one's heart, giving vent to hidden yearnings – feelings waiting to be explored. Perhaps, the woman in mid-life needed to feel the girl inside again, the young woman who still believed in love in its most ideal state, manifested as raw, irresistible impulse.

Life comes full circle, and everything happens with a purpose. When I went to Barnes and Noble bookstore to purchase Eduardo's recommended novels, I realized that I could, actually, write my own. The uniqueness of my reality – the pain, the joy, the yin-yang of life – that is what I wished to share, in tribute to and with love for the catalyst of my broken heart, whether or not he is listening; for surely, each story has a message. Mine has countless ones, namely the literal transcendence from ashes, the tragedy of loss, being held up to ridicule, scorn, and degradation – and still, through it all, the triumph of being myself. Literal and metaphoric chapters are still being written. So, come with me yet a little farther through the corridors of my life, as I offer some final reflections.

Chapter 15

Awakening to Promise

There's a biting chill in the air at this time of year – Christmas time – when the sky portends snow, the gift of the season. In these moments, when mistletoe and magic fill our surroundings, a kind of wistful melancholy descends upon me, reminding me of time's passage and the constant changes occurring all around and within us. It's a time of gratitude, and my heart fills with an ever-present sense of appreciation for so many blessings, chief among which are my children, other family members, friends. I greet my husband as he comes home from a trip. Our exchange is warm, tacitly solidifying the mutual commitment that we share as parents to our most precious gifts, our children. Still, perhaps only in moments of quietude, I think of Eduardo. Only now, I see him through a pane of glass, reflecting shadows of a time gone by. In my present world, as a spectator to all that I felt and experienced, I'm grateful for the opportunity to have seen him again and to have given expression to intense, genuine feelings, nurtured deep within my heart. Few people experience such feelings in a lifetime. The cycle of life continues, and there are seasons of the heart. Longings diminish through time and circumstance, but to negate their existence is to do injustice to the past, present, and indeterminate future.

Although the threads of my life's tapestry interweave between past and present, each strand inextricably wound with another, I am grounded now, content with my life in all respects. I have begun to paint, a pastime which takes me on an inner odyssey and allows me to explore my creative side. I take great pride and joy in the companionship of my horses – those sentient beings whom I came to appreciate through my grandfather. I take joy in my patients and being a practitioner of the healing arts as well, deriving fulfillment each and every day from all of the wisdom and insight of those for whom I care. I also extrapolate from my past the meaning of growing, changing, and learning. The ashes, dust, and debris of the devastating Huaraz earthquake of my youth have cleared to find me in an entirely new country, thousands of miles from my original home, fully grounded and with a thirst for life. I pause to pay homage to the lives lost, and pledge my dedication to them through present and future good works. I still see my beloved Grandpa riding his trusted Mauro Mina, forging ahead against the odds, with pragmatism and resolve. I envision my beautiful Grandmother, gently asserting her feminine power. I conjure my mother, leaving me to my own devices yet, ultimately, cradling me in the warmth of her self-introspection and admission of flaws (no human on Planet Earth is free from them). I hearken to my father's sensibility, his sense of justice, and his ability to think quickly on his feet. Now almost ninety, he still possesses all of the faculties of his youth (except for his sight), with insight that clear physical vision never can provide. I think of my brother who, though estranged from me now in a very palpable sense, has found his place in the world. I hope that, through these words, I can reach out and find him again – to extend an olive branch of acceptance and forgiveness.

I think of my youthful broken heart – the could-have-beens - from Carlos' rejection that day when I waited for him at the cinema to Lorenzo's romantic walk with me beneath the harvest moon as a teen. I still feel the sting of Enrique's kindness, coupled with his vices and transgressions, and Eduardo's icy reception of me at our last reunion…and I am grateful for all of it – the entire conundrum of opposites, the pull-tug of life, for I have learned and evolved from these experiences, becoming stronger and empowered to narrate my story.

And, then, there is Laura, my angel, ever around me, assuring me of her presence. Not long ago, I received a mass mailing from actor Richard Gere, requesting prayers for the people of Tibet. I don't usually read such mail, but for some reason, something drew me to that message. I read every word of the letter and then took the enclosed cloth prayer chain into my hands. Placing it in the center of my fireplace beneath a beautiful mirror, I said a silent prayer of love and goodwill for the Tibetan people, whom I perceive to be peaceful and forgiving. I have always had an affinity for them and their good works. A couple of months later, a new patient came into my office. I was conducting an intake of her history, and when I asked about her occupation, she revealed that she was unemployed. Just then, I had to leave the room briefly. When I returned, I found the woman writing something on a piece of paper. "Actually," she said, "I am a clairvoyant, and sometimes I receive messages that I have to write down. When you left the room, I got a message that I believe is for you from someone very close to you. She said that she was there, by the mirror near the fireplace that day." Immediately, I recognized that, in reaching out to someone well-intentioned (even strangers), there comes an immeasurable feeling of peace, contentment, and connectedness to those whom we have lost. In my heart, I knew that Laura had, indeed, made a silent, powerful appearance. In an effort to maintain professional decorum, however, I refrained from reacting overtly. I maintained my composure, acknowledged what my patient had just told me, and let the matter drop.

In the tangled web of life, the answers reside in subjective truths – the silent whispers within each of us – and the calling to do good in the world by entertaining feelings of empathy and solidarity. It's all here, around and within us, emerging into light when we seek our individual truths. Buddhist writings inspired the expression of my own.

The answers also lie behind closed doors, which have the potential to reopen, with new insight and understanding. Such has been the purpose of this writing, my personal odyssey, with which I called upon history as a springboard for what lies ahead

– ultimately, my awakening to the promise surging in the birth of new days.

My ruminations and conversations with my good friend, George, continue to this day. Recently, I told him of a dream that I had three years ago. I was in a winding maze, through which I traveled to the top of a pyramid. I was told, "You will see him (Eduardo) there." I continued my journey. There, in what looked like a Chinese fortress, I encountered a large door. I knocked, and an elder answered, saying, "Sorry, he's not here!" and slammed the door.

"So, George," I said, looking to my friend for his opinion, "was this reverie a prognostication of reality or did it exist only in my subconscious?"

George lifted his gaze and looked straight at me, knowingly. "Only the future will tell," he said.

Some things must be left floating in the unknown, until the time is ripe for awareness. The door to my mind and heart stands open, welcoming the gifts of life and all they have yet to offer.

Anhelos del corazón

de Isabella TaniKumi

Por respeto a la privacidad, algunos de los nombres empleados en la presente narración son ficticios o se han omitido. Cualquier asociación con dichos nombres o características con particulares más allá de las páginas del presente libro es pura coincidencia casual.

ISBN:0615577760
ISBN-13: 978-0615577760

CONTENIDO

DEDICACION

Para mi hijo y mi hija, con la esperanza de que así lograrán comprender
mi viaje.
Con todo mi cariño.

.

RECONOCIMIENTO

En honor de los peruanos de todo el mundo que están celebrando el centenario del redescubrimiento del Machu Picchu y su nombramiento (en 2007) como una de las Nuevas Siete Maravillas del Mundo Moderno

Si te ves a ti mismo carente de autoestima, dominado por el miedo y acosado por la vulnerabilidad que produce el enfrentarse al pasado, se debe a que tú, y nadie más que tú, has creado esa imagen de ti mismo. La posibilidad de mejora está ante ti. La vida es un paisaje pintado en un cuadro. Píntalo con todos los colores que albergas en tu corazón. Cree en ti mismo y sé tú, mírate bajo una nueva perspectiva, siempre favorecedora y en desarrollo.

Isabella TaniKumi

Prefacio

Para llegar a conocerme a mí misma —y, por consiguiente, conseguir escribir el presente libro—, he tenido que viajar por un sendero aparentemente interminable. Pasar de un lugar a otro —y no geográfica, sino sobre todo, emocionalmente— me ha resultado difícil y, con frecuencia, doloroso. Mi historia comenzó en una pequeña población rural en Sudamérica. A continuación, mi vida tomó forma en Lima, la capital de Perú, y prosiguió en una extensa área metropolitana de Estados Unidos. Mi inspiración inicial a la hora de escribir el presente libro fue un corazón roto, cosa que me permitió explorar numerosos traumas ocultos de mi pasado y, de aquello, emergí siendo una persona más completa e integrada, con un mayor nivel de autoestima, respeto y capacidad para seguir adelante, a pesar de una multitud de dificultades. He aprendido que la manera en la que uno se define a sí mismo y su propio destino en la vida no es tanto el producto de lo que otros piensan, independientemente de lo mucho que los seres humanos nos esforcemos por obtener aprobación externa. He llegado a comprender que la pérdida, la desolación, la desilusión y las traiciones pueden hacer las veces de ladrillos que componen nuestro propio desarrollo personal, trampolines desde los cuales podemos impulsarnos.

Como el fénix, renazco de las cenizas de mi pasado para utilizar mi vida como ejemplo para otros y con la intención de manifestar mi completitud y mi curación, tanto para mí misma como para mis hijos, que son ahora los que presencian mi triunfo junto a mí, surgiendo resplandeciente a la superficie. Es precisamente ese proceso de crecimiento como fuente de inspiración el que deseo compartir con ellos, y vosotros, que ahora tenéis estas páginas entre vuestras manos. En este estado de autocomprensión aumentada, ahora sí puedo afrontar las causas subyacentes de algunas de mis mayores decepciones, al mismo tiempo que me regocijo de mis bendiciones y mis logros. Deseo fervientemente que, al menos, algunas de mis palabras lleguen a resonar en el interior de los corazones abatidos, para que sepan que conseguirán volver a latir y a cantar dulces melodías, mucho más fuerte y melodiosamente que nunca. Tenéis justo delante de vosotros la oportunidad de evolucionar.

Isabella TaniKumi

Capítulo 1

El canto de Marcelino

Recuerdo una época en la que la vida era simple, un momento tan fugaz que apenas me acuerdo de su existencia. Una vez que hubo pasado, la visión idílica de lo entonces fue rápidamente se transformó en un tenue recuerdo, provocándome minúsculas gotitas de dulce nostalgia, cubierta de ceniza y escombros. Huaraz, Perú, el lugar en el que nací, mi pequeño Shangri-La, todavía pervive en mi memoria como un viejo amigo. Esa es la razón de que, a lo largo de la presente narración, me referiré a esta pintoresca y hermosa ciudad antes de la destrucción como «mi vieja Huaraz». El tiempo quedó marcado antes o después de que la tierra temblara y absorbiera en sus entrañas nuestros cimientos mismos y nuestro modo de vida, llevándose por delante prácticamente todo y a todos los que conocíamos. Por eso, las memorias de mi pasado no son más que sombras, bloqueadas a causa de dolorosos recuerdos que, hasta ahora, he deseado olvidar. El presente texto es mi tributo no solo para aquellas personas a las que he perdido, sino también para las que quiero y que, desde entonces, han modelado y dado forma a mi carácter.

Durante siglos, mi gente ha soportado las tormentas del cambio. Nuestros antepasados, los incas, gozaban de una cultura rica en mito y simbolismo. Unas gentes apasionadamente resistentes, cuyo antiguo imperio se expandía desde Quito,

Ecuador, hasta más al sur en la provincia de Tucumán en Argentina, y que fueron unos de los ingenieros más expertos del mundo. Fueron ellos quienes desarrollaron los sistemas de irrigación que todavía hoy siguen en pie en la región del Machu Picchu en Cuzco. Esta misma cultura emprendedora se tomó un gran interés en la agricultura, la fertilización y enriquecimiento del suelo, y en la producción de patata, maíz, y un amplio abanico de otros cultivos. Los incas también crearon un sistema de comunicación mediante quipus (también conocidos como «nudos parlantes») hechos de cuerdas hiladas de colores, pelo de llama o algodón. La creatividad de nuestro pueblo y su diligencia fueron subyugadas por la conquista española en el siglo XVI. Todo el país se vio sumido en la enfermedad y la muerte que los conquistadores trajeron consigo a la región. Sin la inmunización de las vacunas contra el sarampión y enfrentándose al inminente peligro que suponían las armas de fuego y los caballos de sus asaltantes, nuestros antepasados cayeron en manos de sus captores, contemplando sin poder hacer nada como estos confiscaban su oro y otros metales preciosos. Los restos del oro y otros objetos peruanos han sido confiados al Museo del Oro en Lima. A menudo, me pregunto si fue la historia la que hizo que los indios peruanos se volvieran sumisos, pues veían a los europeos como seres superiores a los que había que idolatrar y temer. Es posible que dichas impresiones hayan quedado impresas de forma indeleble en mis genes, como remanentes de aquella subyugación del pasado. ¿Quién podría asegurarlo?

Permitidme que os transporte a mi propio pasado, esa época sin complicaciones, tan breve en el tiempo, pero que, aun así, sigue resonando en mi memoria como el canto de *Marcelino*, el cacareo del hermoso gallo que tenía por mascota, mi fiel compañero, que me seguía a todas partes. Ubicado en una provincia en el valle andino del Callejón de Huaylas, en el estado de Ancash, mi pequeño pueblo era tradicionalmente conocido como la Suiza peruana, delimitado por la Cordillera Blanca y la Cordillera Negra. Era un lugar que irradiaba vida, delicadeza y camaradería. Los visitantes nunca se consideraban forasteros. El clima primaveral permanentemente suave casaba a la perfección con el temperamento de la población.

La mayor parte de las casas en mi vieja Huaraz estaban pintadas de colorido adobe hecho con barro y ladrillos de la zona y tejados de tejas rojas, y cada una de ellas se hallaba adornada por balcones, a los que se asomaban los vecinos y donde conversaban entre sí. Antes de que nuestro mundo llegara a su fin, mis padres compraron una enorme mansión pintada de verde claro, que estaba situada frente a la tienda de ultramarinos de mi padre. Mis hermanos y yo solíamos jugar allí, en una habitación de la parte trasera, donde mamá nos vigilaba con diligencia. Teníamos una colección de animales, entre los que se contaban unos gatitos adorables y una gallina que trajo al mundo a mi adorada mascota, *Marcelino*. Cada mañana hacía las veces de mi reloj despertador, admirándose en el espejo a los pies de mi cama y cantando con todas sus fuerzas. A veces, yo me tapaba la cabeza con la almohada para amortiguar el ruido, pero aquella era mi alarma para despertar a la vida, y me sentía agradecida por tenerlo. A mi hermana mayor, Laura, y a mí también nos gustaba jugar a un lado de nuestro patio, cerca de una fuentecita de aguas cristalinas y poco profundas: un lugar que mis padres habían bautizado como «el pozo». Mucho tiempo atrás se empleó como manantial, pero cuando el agua corriente municipal llegó a nuestros hogares, el pozo se quedó obsoleto. Allí, en aquel pequeño escondite, solíamos darle de comer a un único pececillo solitario, que nadaba melancólico de acá para allá. De algún modo, esa criatura forma parte de mis recuerdos más vívidos de aquella primera época, quizá, porque, de alguna extraña manera, yo misma estoy ligada a él. En mi mente, él era un ejemplo de mí misma: un solitario trotamundos en su pequeño universo, a veces ignorado, pero, en general, satisfecho con lo que tenía.

Nuestra casa siempre estaba viva y rebosante de actividad. La abuela acudía desde su hogar en las remotas montañas de Huacachi para visitarnos, llenando el aire con la sabrosa fragancia de su pan y su mantequilla caseros y recién hechos. Yo siempre me pegaba al abuelo en mis primeros años. Su fórmula para la longevidad consistía en «desayunar como un rey, comer como un príncipe y cenar como un pobre». Bueno, ese régimen (que a veces estaba compuesto por un filete de desayuno) realmente funcionaba. Como muchos de sus coetáneos de la misma región, vivió hasta los ciento quince años, en un rancho, rodeado del aire prístino, la naturaleza, los caballos y el ganado.

La vida se enriquecía y se prolongaba gracias a aquellos elementos vitales básicos.

Recuerdo vívidamente nuestras excursiones de un día para ir a visitar a mis abuelos, recorriendo estrechos senderos a caballo, ascendiendo a las montañas más altas, que atesoraban clandestinamente algunas ruinas preincas. Si nos atrevíamos a mirar a nuestros pies, veíamos el aterrador y tenebroso abismo. Por decirlo suavemente, aquel viaje no era apto para cardíacos. En los descansos, nos deteníamos para refrescarnos nosotros y los caballos, y contemplábamos la belleza natural que nos rodeaba. Mientras los caballos pastaban, nosotros saciábamos nuestra hambre comiendo fiambre (maíz tostado, queso y otros embutidos) y chicha de jora (un ponche especial para adultos, aderezado con un poco de alcohol). Ninguna de las sorpresas o altercados en la vida me impedirá seguir recordando estas preciadas memorias.

Cuando digo que la vida era simple, me refiero a que no había abundancia en bienes materiales, pues en realidad no teníamos necesidad de nada. Puede que esto se debiera a que las cosas no eran tan importantes como la gente: la familia y los amigos. Recuerdo nuestros momentos con papá, cuando nos recogía del colegio, nos compraba a mí y a mi hermana Laura regalos de cumpleaños y nos llevaba a comer helado y gelatina. En estas y otras ocasiones especiales, la abuela preparaba su gelatina casera natural, una mezcla de especias creada con un colador hecho con estameña. Gota a gota, la mezcla caía sobre una fuente, servida con galletas, en una explosión de sabor. El regusto de aquel néctar aún persiste en mi lengua... Y, ¡oh!, ¡qué delicioso era su helado de lúcuma, hecho de esa fruta tropical de color anaranjado! Después de tantos años, ¡todavía se me hace la boca agua solo de pensar en él!

En comparación con mi hermana, Laura (que era casi mi hermana gemela dada la poca diferencia entre nuestras respectivas edades), yo era una mera espectadora. Mis padres no escatimaban a la hora de conferirle reconocimiento, al tiempo que a mí me ignoraban, como si yo no fuera más que un testigo insignificante, una observadora circunstancial de su cariño y adulación paternales. Por ejemplo, cuando yo era muy pequeña, solían servirme la última en la cena, nunca me preguntaban, como a los demás, qué trozo de pollo prefería. Mi hermana, por el contrario, ocupaba un lugar central en el corazón de mamá. El cumpleaños de Laura siempre se celebraba, mientras que el mío caía deliberadamente en el olvido. Solo puedo especular sobre la causa de este favoritismo, pero creo que la conclusión a la que he llegado es válida (especialmente dado que, a lo largo de nuestras vidas, nunca nos proporcionaron ni exploramos otras razones). Al parecer, cuando Laura era muy pequeña, se cayó y se golpeó la cabeza. Atenazados por la culpa provocada por el accidente, mamá y papá, junto con otros miembros de nuestra familia, la consentían agasajándola con tiernos cuidados y atenciones, desatendiéndome a mí mientras tanto. Yo nunca albergué ni el más mínimo resentimiento directamente por mi querida Laura.

¿Cómo podría haber hecho tal cosa? Ella era la mejor amiga que tenía en el mundo, y ambas cultivábamos un cariño y un respeto recíprocos que aún siguen sustentándome. Dos años mayor que yo, era muy hermosa, con una complexión bronceada, ojos almendrados y una ondulada mata de cabello negro. Al crecer, llegó a convertirse en la muchacha más bella de la ciudad. Su apariencia exterior únicamente estaba a la altura de su personalidad dulce y serena. Yo era como la otra cara de la moneda de Laura, con mi cabello trigueño y mi tono de piel más claro. Siempre sospeché que yo era adoptada, porque mi piel era más clara que la del resto de mi familia.

Puesto que carecíamos de juguetes convencionales, Laura y yo empleábamos nuestra imaginación para inventar diferentes tipos de diversión. Uno de nuestros juegos favoritos era el concurso de la muñeca recortable mejor vestida. Alineadas y confinadas a las páginas de un cuaderno, aquellas bellezas inertes volvían milagrosamente a la vida gracias a un simple par de tijeras y a nuestras delicadas habilidades de coordinación motriz. Con cuidado y esmero, las recortábamos del papel o de hojas troqueladas, y las preparábamos para su debut en la pasarela sobre la mesa de nuestro comedor. Nuestros recursos limitados exigían una creatividad sin límites, cosa de la que teníamos en abundancia. De verdad, no echábamos absolutamente nada en falta. Las pocas posesiones materiales que atesorábamos no tenían precio a nuestros ojos. Nunca olvidaré unas Navidades en particular, cuando nuestro padre colocó dos enormes muñecas sobre nuestras camas: para Laura, una de piel clara y, para mí, una morena, para compensar nuestras respectivas complexiones. Nos emocionamos tanto, que chillamos alegremente mientras cogíamos en brazos a nuestros respectivos bebés. Aquellos regalos representaban unos de los pocos casos en los que a ambas nos agasajaban a partes iguales. Aunque nunca lo expresamos abiertamente, aquellas muñecas eran especiales porque parecían réplicas de nosotras mismas y, tal y como mi historia revelará más adelante, cada una seguiría su propio destino.

En contraste con mi simbiosis fraternal con Laura, mi hermano, Tomás, y yo parecíamos estar a años luz. Siete años mayor que yo, en su mundo de estudios y relaciones sociales, disfrutaba de la categoría de ser el favorito de nuestro padre. Apenas interactuaba conmigo. Yo atribuía su actitud distante tanto a nuestra diferencia de edad como al hecho de que él deliberadamente se mantuviera aparte. Aprendí a sobrellevarlo, cosa que sigo haciendo en la actualidad.

También existía una vaga, pero muy real, tensión entre mis padres y yo. Mi madre, de piel clara con aspecto español, siempre fue una mujer muy atractiva y sigue siéndolo. Era huérfana y había sido criada por su hermanastra mayor, por lo que nunca contó con un modelo a seguir, y ella misma no se proyectaba como tal. Ansiosa por casarla, su tutora la animó a que se desposara con mi padre, un viajero frecuente entre su pueblo remoto de montaña, Huacachi, y la ciudad de mayor tamaño, Huari. Allí, se fijó en mi madre y pidió su mano. De origen sudamericano, indio y español, con ojos rasgados similares a los de los japoneses y complexión como la de los nativos americanos, no es de extrañar que su apariencia exótica y ecléctica hiciera algo más que intrigar a mi madre. Su naturaleza autoritaria infundía respecto y atención. En su presencia, la negociación nunca era una opción. Así, mi madre, con diligencia, se metió de lleno en el matrimonio con una resignación tranquila y filosófica.

—Tu padre es un buen hombre. Con el tiempo, aprendí a quererle —me dijo cuando yo expresé sorpresa por que se hubiera casado con su primer admirador, que tenía once años más que ella.

Para mí, resultaba difícil comprender aquel concepto. Creo firmemente que el amor es una emoción que germina profundamente en el interior de nuestro corazón y nunca nos abandona. Se trata del anhelo de estar con alguien de forma incondicional, sin obligaciones. El amor tendría que fluir de manera natural y fácil, no como algo en pro de lo que hay que esforzarse, sino como el don que sencillamente es. Mi madre no pudo permitirse tal lujo, y sospecho que fue algo que tampoco buscó. Siempre hablaba de su matrimonio como algo que daba por hecho, una suerte de rendición ante un destino inalterable.

Por alguna razón inexplicable, mi madre y yo nunca conectamos. Ella me consideraba la más fuerte de sus hijos, capaz de arreglárselas sola y con menos necesidad de cuidados maternos. Por esta razón, solía ignorarme y me despojaba de la protección y las atenciones que habitualmente se supone que los niños deben recibir legítimamente.

—No os preocupéis por Isabella. —Solía oírla decir—. Ella es muy fuerte.

Así pues, desarrollé una capa dura e hice que sus afirmaciones se cumplieran proféticamente, al mismo tiempo que, en mi interior me retraía en silencio, evitando el rechazo a cualquier precio.

El origen de mi omnipresente miedo por sentir alienación y rechazo también residía en un acontecimiento fundamental que tuvo lugar durante mi infancia, no fueron más que unos pocos segundos, pero cambió mi vida para siempre. Dado que solo contaba con tres o cuatro años de edad, no poseo un recuerdo propio de aquel incidente. Prácticamente, sé lo que sucedió por boca de mi madre. Al parecer, mientras estaba sentada en el regazo de Laura, me caí de cabeza sobre una fuente de natillas hirviendo que alguien había dejado en las cercanías. Me llevaron corriendo al hospital, donde a mamá le dijeron que se me habían formado quemaduras de segundo grado. Me trataron con una pomada llamada Bepanthen, diseñada para calmar y curar las lesiones cutáneas. No estoy segura de si fue aquel remedio el que posteriormente me provocó la aparición de unas antiestéticas máculas en el labio inferior y la mandíbula, unas manchas de forma irregular y color marrón oscuro que me cubrían los labios y se me prolongaban por la barbilla y a lo largo del cuello. La exposición a la luz solar las acentuó aún más. Para una adolescente que tiene que enfrentarse a toda clase de problemas sociales, aquellos estigmas eran fuente de una enorme ansiedad y angustia. Por lo tanto, durante aquella época, me encontraba en un estado constante de incertidumbre y trauma, autocensurándome y preguntándome si aquellos defectos tan visibles y externos desencadenarían todas las situaciones de rechazo en mi vida. Durante aquellos años de adolescencia, pasé innumerables horas tratando de disimular aquellas manchas y, con ellas, de sofocar la inferioridad que percibía en mí misma.

Para subsanar mi sentimiento de encontrarme fuera de lugar, centré mis esfuerzos en mi formación académica. En realidad, sentía una propensión natural por lo académico, por lo que destacaba en todas las asignaturas. Mientras escribo esto, sacando a la luz mi autoelogiosa voz interna, hace que me avergüence de mí misma. Ya veis, mis logros aún representan un problema para mí, dado que mis padres siempre me subordinaban a mis hermanos, especialmente a Laura. Y yo, inconscientemente —o quizás a caso hecho— me emplazaba a mí misma en un pedestal autoimpuesto para aislarme de las críticas y los reproches extrínsecos.

Santa Elena, la escuela católica de primaria a la que asistía, estaba ubicada en el centro de mi vieja Huaraz. Se trataba del típico monasterio español y se parecía al de Fräulein María en *Sonrisas y lágrimas*, aunque más pequeño, con un patio principal y portones metálicos. Los edificios circundantes contaban con puertas secundarias en cada esquina, con escaleras de entrada que conducían al segundo piso. El patio principal era el centro neurálgico de las actividades, entre las que se incluían nuestra presentación diaria en filas, durante la que las monjas nos inspeccionaban el pelo y la ropa. Si pensaban que llevábamos la falda demasiado corta, la ira de los cielos recaía sobre nosotras, y arrancaban el dobladillo de cuajo delante de todo el mundo para inculcarnos las virtudes del decoro y la modestia. La más mínima trasgresión recibía como respuesta un castigo desproporcionado, como pegarnos con una regla, exigirnos que nos arrodilláramos sobre los duros baldosines del patio durante varias horas o el destierro a una esquina por cualquier tipo de mala conducta. Así era como yo aprendí a relacionarme con los demás: con el miedo al mal comportamiento como a la peste. Durante la mayor parte del tiempo, procuraba controlar meticulosamente todos y cada uno de mis propios movimientos, aunque a veces, en ocasiones, hacía algún que otro intento de rebeldía, como cuando, en segundo grado, incliné la silla de mi compañera de clase tirándola al suelo, con ella encima. ¡Oh, vaya revuelo montó la madre superiora por aquello! Incluso convocó a mis padres para que se reunieran con la directora. Me sentí mortificada y juré que nunca jamás volvería a perpetrar un acto tan atroz. Dado el nivel de rigor de mi entorno, es un milagro que no me convirtiera en una rebelde. Mis notas demostraban mi responsabilidad y dedicación, y siempre me comportaba con aplomo y estaba dispuesta a ayudar a mis compañeras con sus deberes. Incluso me adelantaron un curso en la guardería, cosa que fue el preludio de mi graduación temprana en el instituto.

Aquella época escolar está teñida de una poderosa mezcla de alegrías y penas para mí. Cuando no se burlaban de mí por mis manchas faciales, disfrutaba jugando con mis amigos y yendo de excursión. Durante un día típico, Antonio, uno de mis enemigos y mi compañero de pupitre durante mis primeros años, hacía todo lo posible por importunarme o asustarme. Su padre era un acaudalado ranchero, cuya importancia el malicioso Antonio se atribuía a sí mismo poniendo en práctica sus tácticas para amedrentar a los demás. De algún modo, siempre causaba conmoción en clase, por ejemplo, trayendo el feto de alguna vaca en un tarro o un ratón metido en el bolsillo. Como todos los matones, Antonio simulaba ser inocente. El incidente del ratón casi hizo que yo perdiera los estribos y me subiera de un salto sobre un pupitre. Las monjas no sabían lo que había sucedido pero, por suerte, una de las niñas localizó al ratón correteando por el suelo, cosa que me tranquilizó, pues me confirmó que yo no había sufrido ninguna alucinación.

¿Estuve realmente allí? Los pensamientos, la imaginación, los recuerdos... todos se tiñen de negro. Me da vueltas la cabeza mientras intento recordar alguna otra cosa, pero no lo consigo. Me tiemblan las piernas igual que aquel fatídico día, el 31 de mayo de 1970. En aquel momento, tengo nueve años cuando la tierra tiembla sobre sus cimientos, borrando de un plumazo cualquier recuerdo. Mi precioso *Marcelino* de colores brillantes canta, y yo me despierto una vez más. Pero esta vez, la oscuridad es lo único que me rodea.

Capítulo 2

De cuando el mundo se derrumbó sobre sí mismo

Marina, Inés y yo éramos inseparables. Pasamos juntas cada momento de nuestra experiencia en cuarto curso. Asistimos a la escuela secundaria llamada Santa Rosa de Viterbo, prácticamente idéntica a Santa Elena (la secuela de primaria que he descrito anteriormente, solo que más grande). Allí, participamos en las obras de teatro del colegio y en otros acontecimientos sociales, siempre cosidas con pespunte. Si no nos daban un papel a cada una en las representaciones, ninguna de nosotras tomaba parte en ellas. En una ocasión, hicimos de enfermeras. Aquellos papeles ficticios determinaron conceptualmente nuestras futuras carreras, pero yo fui la única que cumplí ese sueño. En otra ocasión, fuimos tres ángeles vestidos de colores brillantes.

Para mi fiel mejor amiga, Marina, ser un ángel era su estado natural. Era alegre, resultaba fácil estar con ella, siempre sonreía y gustaba a todo el mundo. Ella era mi más leal compañera. Disfrutábamos juntas de multitud de actividades al aire libre, entre otras, jugar al voleibol, a rayuela, al escondite, saltar a la cuerda y jugar con su cachorro cocker spaniel. Todavía me acuerdo de su hermoso rostro, su preciosa piel nívea coloreada por un rubor rosáceo, y su espeso y brillante cabello negro, recortado en una melenita corta que se mecía al viento. Aunque era casi tres años mayor que yo, me protegía mucho. Siempre que los niños hacían comentarios sobre «la guarrería» de mi cara (refiriéndose a mis manchas), Marina era la primera en protegerme del dolor emocional y en animarme a ignorar los comentarios negativos de los demás. El día antes de que nuestro mundo llegara a su fin, Marina se estaba preparando para participar en el festejo, un baile africano-peruano. Con un vestido rojo y negro de lunares, un turbante en la cabeza y la cara ennegrecida con betún, el ángel se encontraba a metro y medio de mí... Y yo no le dije nada. Ya veis, un día antes, tuvimos una pueril pelea, una discusión por nada en particular. Más tarde, Marina intentó enviarme una nota de disculpa, pero mi estúpido orgullo no me dejó contestarle. Poco podía imaginarme que aquella sería la última oportunidad —un momento fugaz— de hablar con ella y despedirme. Aquella fue la última vez que la vi. Las arenas del tiempo se me escaparon de las manos y, con ellas, la amistad más preciada que había conocido. Aquello que no comprendemos nos envalentona y nos endurece ante las crueles realidades de la vida. Nos sentimos invencibles y, aun así, lo único que somos, en un momento dado, es una composición de moléculas ocupando la infinita vastedad del tiempo y el espacio. Nos detenemos durante un momento a escuchar, a aprender, a amar... Y entonces, tomamos el camino de la eternidad. Para mi queridísima amiga Marina, todo aquello sucedió demasiado pronto.

Cuando el reloj dio las 3:10 de la tarde de aquel 31 de mayo de 1970, Laura, Tomás y yo nos metimos apretujándonos en el camión de nuestro padre para ir a visitar a mamá al hospital. A mamá le había hecho falta intervención y tratamiento médicos a causa de una serie de repentinos problemas menores femeninos, pero, por suerte, estaba mejorando rápidamente de un día para otro. Aquella circunstancia (que más tarde comprendí que había sido la máxima bendición) interrumpió nuestra rutina habitual. Yo tenía muchas preocupaciones que ocupaban mi atención: los deberes, la preparación del uniforme del colegio y la invitación a una fiesta en honor de la madre superiora de Santa Elena, mi alma máter. Acababa de regresar de un viaje a Lima, y todos estábamos invitados a darle la bienvenida. Yo estaba deseando acudir a la fiesta y, además, me había resignado pensando que era demasiado joven como para ir a visitar a mamá al hospital. El día anterior, una enfermera así me lo había hecho saber, y su severidad hacía imprescindible que yo cumpliera aquella norma. Traté de persuadir a mi padre para que sencillamente no me obligara a ir, pero sabía que cualquier esfuerzo sería en vano. Nadie contradecía a papá, y menos que nadie, su hija de nueve años.

Cuando llegamos al hospital, me senté sobre la cama de mamá, charlando y riendo con mis hermanos. De repente, entró nuestra tía Julia, nerviosa e iracunda.

—¿Por qué no he sido informada del ingreso de mi hermana en el hospital? —Quiso saber—. He tenido que enterarme por terceros, y...

Su voz se fue apagando a medida que el reloj daba las 3:23 de la tarde. «Seguramente, el enfado de tía Julia no puede ser tan fuerte como para hacer temblar la cama y todo el resto de la habitación con tanta virulencia», pensé yo. Al minuto siguiente, escuché el ruido sordo de una enorme tormenta que se aproximaba. Entonces, los vidrios de las ventanas temblaron y el depósito de agua del cuarto de baño de mamá comenzó a gotear.

—¡Mantened la calma! ¡Se trata de un terremoto! ¡Vamos hacia la entrada principal! —ordenó mi padre.

En un instante, le seguí, haciendo caso instintivamente de sus órdenes.

Mientras nos apiñábamos junto a la entraba principal de la habitación, comenzamos a rezar.

—¡Gracias a Dios que hemos comulgado esta misma mañana! ¡Estamos dispuestos a morir, si así tiene que ser!

Mi angelical hermana mayor me contempló con una mirada resuelta. La estreché entre mis brazos, rezando y acobardada por el miedo. No podía soportar la idea de perderla a ella o a mi propia vida, de renunciar a todo lo que tanto quería. La niebla, el polvo y la tierra llenaron la habitación, sumiéndonos en un sueño, la verdadera pesadilla del poderío iracundo de la naturaleza. A continuación, tuvo lugar el caos, la sangre manó por el suelo —los remanentes de la vida sagrada—, de las madres que estaban dando a luz en el ala de maternidad. En español, utilizamos esa expresión, «dar a luz», con el significado de traer al mundo un bebé. ¿Qué fuente de vida puede ser mayor que la de la propia luz? Sin embargo, en aquellos momentos, rodeándonos, era la oscuridad la que reinaba, y se oían voces gritando en plena confusión y agonía.

Papá, nuestro valiente comandante de campaña, era el pilar de nuestra fortaleza y aplomo.

—¡Mantened la calma! —continuó gritando, mientras trataba de encontrar algún refugio.

Al principio, decidimos que bajaríamos las escaleras por las que habíamos entrado, pero mamá sugirió que atravesáramos un patio situado detrás de su habitación que daba a un jardín lleno a reventar de hermosísimas flores. Tras el cataclismo, la vida fue literalmente arrancada de sus raíces, y aquel lugar se convirtió cruelmente en una fosa común, sumida en la niebla y el polvo. Se me puso el corazón en un puño y me dio la sensación de que una corriente eléctrica me atravesaba todo el cuerpo. El hedor de los cadáveres en descomposición inundó mi sentido del olfato mientras se me llenaban los oídos con los gritos de angustia, miedo e indefensión de las víctimas. Luchando por recuperar el aliento, me tembló todo el cuerpo, pero logré avanzar, como un autómata programado para sobrevivir. Niños pequeños, asfixiados por el polvo y ensangrentados de pies a cabeza, yacían sin vida, que les había sido interrumpida bruscamente en la flor de su infancia. A nuestro alrededor, los encargados y voluntarios de los servicios de emergencia apilaban los cadáveres de las víctimas en una fosa común. Nadie —y menos aún, unos meros niños— deberían soportar o presenciar una estampa tan cargada de desesperación y dolor, pero no teníamos elección. Éramos como muñecos a merced del destino, esa fuerza motriz, a veces tan despiadada, que dirige nuestras vidas. En un momento dado, se me activó un mecanismo de defensa en mi interior y me desvinculé del desastre, concentrándome únicamente en mi propia vida y la de mi familia. Los intentos de mi padre por mantenernos seguros se veían interrumpidos constantemente por réplicas, que transportaban a estados intensificados de alerta y pánico.

Repentinamente, divisé a un hombre que más tarde mi hermano reconoció como profesor suyo, llevando sobre sus hombros a su esposa, que había sido herida de muerte.

—¡Por favor, que alguien me ayude! —rogó—. ¡Mi mujer se está muriendo y mis hijos todavía se encuentran en casa! ¡Tengo que regresar para ayudarlos!

Mi madre le ofreció un poco de agua que había sacado de su habitación, pero no existía ni la menor esperanza de resucitar a aquella mujer. Expiró instantes después, y su desconsolado esposo se apresuró a volver a casa para rescatar al resto de su familia. Más tarde, nos enteramos de que había perecido en el intento: fue un mártir, cuyo heroísmo nunca olvidaré.

Aquella noche, acampamos en el exterior del hospital, en la camioneta de papá, que él cubrió con una lona de arpillera, empleada para la protección y el aislamiento de productos comestibles. Dormir resultaba imposible, pues la Tierra seguía temblando sin cesar. Por todas partes, los gritos y lamentos de los desesperados supervivientes reverberaban en el aire, y nosotros aprovechábamos cualquier oportunidad para sentarnos y rezar el rosario. Mamá era —y sigue siéndolo— profundamente religiosa, y aquella era su única forma de consuelo.

Al día siguiente, decidido a evitar que presenciáramos mayores tragedias, papá nos llevó a un lugar a las afueras de la ciudad de Huaraz. A pesar de que Ernesto, un tío lejano, vivía cerca con parte de su casa todavía intacta, la estructura corría peligro de derrumbarse a causa de las réplicas. No queriendo encarar el riesgo de permanecer entre cuatro paredes, establecimos al aire libre nuestro hogar temporal con mantas del hospital, entre las cáscaras de maíz que normalmente cubrían el suelo en época de cosecha. Gracias al cielo, no estábamos en temporada de lluvias. Como gotitas de una poción mágica, en aquellos momentos dábamos la bienvenida y apreciábamos hasta los milagros más ínfimos. Por decirlo suavemente, la comida escaseaba, pero papá logró conseguir una caja de manzanas, galletas y manzanilla. Alguien nos dio una olla de barro, en la que mamá cocinaba en el suelo con piedras como peana. Papá encontró madera para encender un fuego, y nos las apañamos con aquella existencia improvisada, agradecidos de estar vivos.

Aproximadamente cinco días después de que el mundo se desplomara sobre nosotros, en mitad del caos, apareció nuestro abuelo paterno, ataviado con su poncho y su abrigo de alpaca, a lomos de su caballo de más confianza: su fiel amigo y compañero, *Mauro Mina*, bautizado así en honor del famoso boxeador peruano. ¡Qué incorporaciones neurálgicas supusieron ambos para nosotros, nuestros relucientes ángeles de la piedad, que se aproximaban a nosotros agotados pero sin vacilaciones a través de la polvareda! Contemplamos lo que nos dio la sensación de ser una aparición, y procuramos contener las lágrimas. Había venido el sólido e inquebrantable roble de nuestra familia. Pero ¿cómo? ¿Cómo podía ser?, pensamos, sin apenas poder respirar. Resultaba imposible creer que mi abuelo hubiera recorrido una distancia tan grande desde su remoto hogar en las montañas de Huacachi, por un terreno extraordinariamente agreste y complicado. Pero sí, ¡era él! En vano, buscamos un lugar para que el abuelo pudiera descansar su agotada cabeza, descalzarse y poner en alto los pies, sin duda llagados por haber tenido que caminar por los estrechos y difíciles senderos por los que *Mauro Mina* no podía transportarlo a él. ¡Qué sacrificio! ¡Qué grandeza! Después de recuperarnos de la conmoción, descubrimos las razones del arriesgado viaje del abuelo. Creyendo que todos habíamos perecido, había venido a recuperar nuestros cuerpos. Este resuelto e increíble hombre que llegaría a vivir más allá de los cien años —casi hasta el final mismo en posesión de todas sus facultades— se derrumbó entonces, entre sus seres queridos, y sollozó. Nunca jamás olvidaré la escena de los ojos de papá brillantes por las lágrimas al ver a su queridísimo padre.

—¡Papá! —gritó.

Por vez primera en mi corta vida, vi ante mis propios ojos a mis dos pilares estrecharse entre sus brazos, desmoronándose. Apenas comprendían que su instintiva entrega a la emoción no era más que otro aspecto adicional de su fuerza y valor mutuos. Todos nos abrazamos y lloramos, sorprendidos y sobrecogidos. Aquellos momentos fueron gloriosos —incluso en mitad de un desastre así—, pues respirábamos y estábamos listos para seguir adelante, costara lo que costara.

A lo largo de sus dos meses de estancia con nosotros, el abuelo soportó situaciones con las que jamás había soñado. En medio de la naturaleza, él llevaba una vida bendecida por el aire puro, el agua, el ejercicio y la comida saludable. Aquellos elementos básicos definían no solo su vida, sino su identidad misma. Por eso, es fácil imaginar su conmoción y consternación cuando le obligaron a ponerse la vacuna contra el tifus. Él creía que aquella era algún tipo de trama conspirativa de la civilización para destruir la felicidad fundamental de aquellos se resistían a las intervenciones médicas convencionales, como las vacunas o las medicinas. Yo comprendía las reservas del abuelo, pero, en realidad, no le quedaba elección, dadas las circunstancias. Las consecuencias de desafiar sus convicciones podrían haber sido fatales. Comprendiendo aquello, logró superar su mal humor y regresó a casa sano y salvo, y aliviado por haber escapado de las garras de la muerte.

Dado que las carreteras estaban bloqueadas y nuestros tendidos eléctricos habían quedado completamente destruidos, no teníamos manera de reunir comida y provisiones. La única fuente de dichos lujos eran los aviones cargados de comida en lata, carne y leche, que periódicamente dejaban caer todos estos objetos sobre nosotros. Más tarde, cuando el gobierno finalmente evaluó la magnitud del horror y la destrucción, llegó el ejército y montó tiendas que hacían las veces de hogares temporales. Nos quedamos allí durante unos meses, hasta que se construyeron casas prefabricadas. A medida que pasaba el tiempo, comenzó a llegar ayuda humanitaria de diferentes países. Recuerdo particularmente la intervención de la gente proveniente de Rusia que no hablaba ni palabra de español. Nuestra comunicación no verbal, mediante gestos, hacía milagros, ayudándonos a acceder a la comida, la ropa y otras necesidades básicas.

Nos apañábamos con lo que teníamos, ideando también métodos de diversión. Nuestras reinas del glamour de papel fueron sustituidas por muñecas hechas de cáscara de maíz y, a veces, incluso las reemplazábamos por jugar en el barro. La preciosa muñeca de Laura que papá le había comprado aquellas alegres Navidades se perdió irremediablemente, pero su compañera se había salvado, gracias al ingenio de papá, que la recuperó al volver al lugar en el que había estado situado hasta ese momento nuestro hogar, ahora en ruinas. Mamá hizo un gran esfuerzo reparando a mi dañada compañera, y Laura y yo jugamos juntas con ella. También jugábamos en el riachuelo y trepábamos a los árboles, donde me enviaban a mí específicamente para recoger unas bayas silvestres llamadas capulíes. Una tarde, después de comer demasiadas de aquellas deliciosas frutas, bajé del árbol sintiéndome ligeramente mareada e indispuesta. Aunque no me gustó la sensación, sacié totalmente mi apetito por aquella exquisita fruta. Después de que el mundo se desvaneciera, todo lo que hacíamos era una manifestación de esperanza, que conformaba los ladrillos básicos de nuestras vidas hechas trizas.

El aliento vital era realmente lo único que nos quedaba. Anhelábamos tener algún minúsculo trozo de terreno al que llamar hogar, pero al principio aquello no pasaba de ser una mera entelequia. Nuestro paraíso de adobe había quedado completamente demolido, y sus esparcidos remanentes pavimentaban las estrechas callejuelas de nuestro vecindario. En retrospectiva, comprendo que incluso aunque hubiéramos escapado de la casa, habríamos perecido sepultados allí mismo, en la calle, enterrados en una fosa común. Solamente papá y Tomás fueron a presenciar el desastre y la carnicería de nuestro vecindario destruido. Al hacer tal cosa, probablemente tuvieron que reunir el coraje similar al de soldados condecorados, pero mostraron tal estoicismo sin precedentes que nunca supimos lo que estaba pasándoles por dentro: el alcance de su angustia y su intensa emoción.

Con toda probabilidad, papá encontró los restos de nuestros queridos animales, entre ellos, a mi hermosísimo *Marcelino*, que aquel espantoso día cantó por última vez. Sin embargo, no se dijo ni una sola palabra sobre su fallecimiento. Siempre con nuestros intereses en mente, papá cargó la tragedia solamente sobre sus propios hombros y, muchas veces, en silencio. En ocasiones, en nuestra limitada experiencia humana, las palabras resultan herramientas inadecuadas con las que acceder a la verdad inexplicable e indescriptible. Baste decir que todos aquellos que perecieron aún perviven en mi corazón.

Durante aquella época, llegaron a la ciudad muchos impostores: personas que fingían ser víctimas, pero que en realidad estaban tratado de hacerse con terrenos y otros bienes inmuebles de forma ilegal. Cuando Tomás intentó recuperar parte de nuestras posesiones de entre los escombros, presenció de primera mano la intromisión de uno de esos extraños. Una de esas víctimas fraudulentas se le acercó, alegando que su familia estaba enterrada en aquella zona y que necesitaba ayuda para encontrarlos a ellos y sus objetos personales. Tomás encaró al hombre, preguntándole:

—¿Quién es usted? ¿De qué está usted hablando? —Al haber pillado al hombre en una mentira, mi hermano sentenció—: Ni mi padre ni nosotros, su familia, hemos fallecido.

Al oír aquellas palabras, el vil intruso huyó de la escena. La tragedia saca tanto lo mejor como lo peor de la gente, y especialmente durante las primeras horas y días tras el desastre, la humanidad desplegó su espectro completo de defectos y cualidades.

Se creó tal confusión y destrucción a causa del terremoto, que el gobierno, incapaz de verificar o corroborar la información que le llegaba, asignó tierras a todos aquellos que reclamaron derechos sobre ellas, incluso aunque no hubieran vivido ni un solo día en la vieja Huaraz. Como consecuencia, mi padre perdió la gran mansión que había comprado gracias a su duro trabajo y su sacrificio. No solo habíamos perdido nuestro hogar, nuestros efectos personales y el negocio de mi padre, sino también aquella preciada adquisición: un símbolo y recordatorio de sus incansables esfuerzos y su excelente reputación. Antes del sismo, habíamos anhelado mudarnos a aquella mansión, que había estado situada justo junto a nuestra casa familiar. Antiguamente, había sido propiedad de la élite de Lima y estaba arrendada al Ministerio de Agricultura. Desgraciadamente, no estaba escrito que aquel lugar fuera a ser nuestro. Sentí lástima por mi padre pero, a aquella tierna edad, aprendí a poner la vida en perspectiva. La capacidad de resistencia era un componente esencial para la supervivencia, y nadie ejemplificaba mejor ese rasgo que mi padre. Nosotros lo tomábamos como ejemplo. Antes de la gigantesca limpieza de nuestra vieja ciudad y del desembolso de tierras por parte del gobierno en favor de los desplazados, nos asentamos durante un par de años en las afueras, en un lugar llamado Nicrupampa. Logramos subsistir allí en una tienda, agradecidos por al menos tener un simple techo sobre nuestras cabezas y por el enorme privilegio de poder seguir respirando.

Aunque lo que nos rodeaba y nuestro modo de vida había cambiado drásticamente, en mi subconsciente, el mundo se había renovado, al igual que Marina. En mis sueños, la buscaba y me preguntaba dónde se encontraba. Su madre siempre me decía lo mismo:

—Está en Europa y volverá cualquier día de estos.

Yo creía de todo corazón mi ensoñación, hasta que un día, una amiga del colegio me reveló la horrible verdad: Marina había perecido sola en su casa con su perro, mientras que sus dos hermanas sucumbieron a la devastación en otros lugares distintos. Milagrosamente, sus padres y sus dos hermanos se encontraban cerca de la plaza principal y habían logrado sobrevivir. Aquellas noticias me sacaron de mis casillas; apenas podía creérmelo. Muchas veces, vi al padre de Marina, siempre vestido de negro, símbolo de su luto perpetuo. Trabajaba en el tribunal superior de justicia, y había encargado que le construyeran una oficina provisional en las cercanías. Yo podría haber tenido muchas oportunidades de hablar con él, pero no me atrevía a acercarme o a abordar el tema, por miedo a escuchar de nuevo aquellas crueles palabras: Marina ya no estaba entre nosotros. Entretanto, su madre parecía una sombra, consumida por la pérdida de sus tres hijas y viviendo en un abismo de dolor. En una ocasión, incluso llegué a ver a sus hermanos caminando por la ciudad. Su pausada reserva lo decía todo. Las palabras no servían, dejando una vacua sima de sentimientos no expresados, especialmente los de la propia Marina. Nunca tendría la oportunidad de decirle cómo me sentía, lo apenada que me había quedado por no haberme reconciliado con ella a causa de nuestra absurda discusión. La culpa invadía todo mi ser, pero sencillamente era demasiado tarde. Yo era demasiado joven como para soportarlo o para tener la capacidad de analizar el sentido de la muerte. El concepto de finitud me resultaba odioso, pero estaba aprendiendo... demasiado deprisa.

Más tarde, descubrí gracias a la prima de mi amiga Inés lo que le había sucedido a su familia. Al parecer, el terremoto no afectó con tanta gravedad en Yungay, pero, diez minutos después, un trozo del glaciar más grande, el Nevado Huascarán, cayó en el lago Yanahuin, provocando una avalancha. Presa del pánico, la gente corrió en distintas direcciones hasta que, finalmente, alguien los guió hasta el cementerio, el lugar más alto de Yungay. Allí, una estatua de Cristo con los brazos abiertos (que sigue estando en el mismo lugar actualmente) dio la bienvenida a los refugiados. Todo el mundo corrió hacia esa zona, salvo el padre de Inés, cuyo peso le impidió seguir avanzando. Mientras seguía a su familia, sufrió un ataque al corazón y, viendo que el final de su camino estaba próximo, les dijo que se marcharan sin él y que se salvaran ellos. Antes de hacerlo, presenciaron cómo fallecía. El insuperable dolor de aquella tragedia afectó para siempre a la familia, incluida a Inés, a la que me encontré nueve años más tarde mientras yo trabajaba de enfermera militar. Había recorrido todo el camino desde Trujillo, donde ella y su familia se habían mudado justo después del terremoto, para visitar a su madre, que convalecía en el hospital. En aquel momento, yo iba vestida con mi uniforme militar, haciendo realidad aquella aspiración infantil nuestra. Intercambiamos una mirada, pero Inés pareció no reconocerme. La mente tiene métodos para protegerse de aquellos recuerdos insoportables que le son demasiado poderosos como para revivirlos. Sospecho que eso era lo que sucedía en su caso. Su padre había sido nuestro médico de familia, y su madre era buena amiga de la mía. Dado que nuestras vidas habían estado tan entrelazadas, yo sabía demasiado. Nuestros caminos no volvieron a cruzarse y, de nuevo, de algún modo, entendí por qué. Yo había formado parte de un mundo que había desaparecido en la bruma: un recuerdo distante que ya no existía.

¿Y qué pasó con Santa Elena, mi antigua escuela primaria, que celebraba el regreso de su madre superiora? Todo el edificio se derrumbó, con un par de miles de personas en su interior, una tumba de piedra para muchos de los inocentes de nuestro país y algunos de sus valientes padres que asistían a la festividad de aquel día. La enorme cantidad de fallecidos se debió principalmente a una bienintencionada aunque insensata monja que le dijo a todo el mundo que mantuviera la calma e insistió en que había que cerrar la gran puerta de metal que daba al exterior. La plaza principal quedaba cerquísima, pero debido al trágico error de aquella monja, casi todo el mundo murió. Unos pocos afortunados lograron romper a golpes la parte inferior de cristal de la puerta y escaparon, huérfanos y en soledad. Mi escuela secundaria, Santa Rosa de Viterbo, también se derrumbó, pero se erigió una estructura prefabricada a las afueras de la ciudad. Más tarde, se construyó un edificio permanente en su lugar original. Esa escuela ha seguido en pie hasta ahora —el monumento vivo del poder del espíritu y la voluntad humanas—, al igual que las familias, como la mía, que desafiaron la ira de la Tierra y sobrevivieron, contra todo pronóstico.

Cada segundo era precioso durante aquellos días, y, más tarde, a lo largo de una época aparentemente interminable. La tragedia me inculcó la noción de falta de permanencia, algo a lo que la mayoría de los niños apenas están acostumbrados. Incluso más que antes, llegué a comprender el valor inherente de las personas —esos seres queridos que tanto significaban—, aquellos que, en un abrir y cerrar de ojos, podían desaparecer sin más de la faz de la Tierra. Al comprender aquello, percibí la importancia del desarrollo propio, de aquellas cualidades humanas que me guiarían en la vida: autosuficiencia, empatía, compasión y amor. Entonces apenas sabía dónde o cómo canalizar aquellos sentimientos. Cada día se convertía en un proceso de crecimiento y comprensión: una evolución hacia un modo de vida totalmente nuevo.

Capítulo 3

Una energía vital en mitad de las ruinas

En los días siguientes a nuestro Apocalipsis personal, resultaba difícil marcar la diferencia entre dónde acababa la muerte y dónde empezaba la vida, y viceversa. Lo único que estaba claro era que nosotros —todos los integrantes de nuestro círculo familiar más inmediato— habíamos sobrevivido, a diferencia de muchos otros (se estimaba que la cifra de muertos ascendía a más de setenta mil personas). La devastación de nuestro mundo tal y como lo conocíamos era de tal magnitud que desafiaba a cualquier comprensión. Tampoco había palabras para describir adecuadamente las desgracias que nos rodeaban: enfermedades, fosas comunes, carreteras cerradas, escasez de recursos y agitación generalizada, cosas a las que ningún ser humano debería verse obligado a enfrentarse; pero allí estábamos nosotros, vivos, en medio de todo aquello. Nuestra gratitud era tan infinita como el propio universo, aquella basta inmensidad que no había sido afectada por el desastre (¿realmente existía algún lugar así?). Dado nuestro estado de suma gratitud por cada aliento que exhalábamos, nos absteníamos de comentar nuestra difícil situación —entre nosotros y ante terceros— y sencillamente permanecíamos en un estado de tranquila paciencia y resignación. Por supuesto, para mí, la pérdida de mi querida amiga, Inés, y de mi apreciada amiga, Marina, me provocó una angustia indescriptible, pero la soporté en silencio. En medio del caos, no existía ningún tipo de orientación psicopedagógica, y nosotros mismos teníamos que gestionar nuestros padecimientos como podíamos. Por decirlo suavemente, aquello no era tarea fácil para los que contábamos con pocos años, pero ¿qué elección teníamos? Durante aproximadamente un año, continué soñando con que Marina regresaba de Europa. Por desgracia, la dulce culminación de aquel sueño quedaría confinada para siempre al mundo de mi propia imaginación.

Una importante fuente de sustento durante aquella época fue mi amistad con Adriana, una niña que conocía desde la guardería y una de las pocas alumnas del Santa Elena que sobrevivió al terremoto. Este milagro se debió a que su hogar estaba situado en El Centenario, fuera de la zona en la que tuvo lugar la mayor parte de la devastación. Su padre, que era veterinario, solía regentar una tienda frente a la de papá en la vieja Huaraz, donde vendía toda clase de productos agrícolas. Después del terremoto, Adriana y yo volvimos a retomar el contacto. Papá abrió un supermercado provisional donde también vendía sus productos al por mayor a minoristas. El padre de Adriana era el dueño de la tienda adyacente, una imitación de su antiguo establecimiento. Ambos comercios se encontraban en la avenida Fitzcarral, en las afueras de Huaraz, lo suficientemente lejos de la ciudad como para haber escapado a la destrucción. Adriana, su hermana y yo solíamos ayudar en los respectivos negocios familiares. A menudo, nos reuníamos a la hora del almuerzo para charlar y evocar imágenes y recuerdos del pasado. ¡Qué extraño resultaba ser tan jóvenes y a la vez tan meditabundas! La juventud no debería tener pasado, pero el nuestro había quedado permanentemente unido a la conciencia colectiva de Perú, independientemente de quién estuviera pensando, por lo que atesorábamos aquellos momentos pasados, cuando la satisfacción permanente parecía algo más bien poco seguro. Cuando Adriana se marchó a estudiar a Lima, nos separamos, reuniéndonos de nuevo durante sus intermitentes visitas a Huaraz, manteniendo siempre nuestra rápida amistad. Durante aquel periodo, su hermana, Bárbara, y yo pasamos aún más tiempo juntas en nuestra ciudad natal. Resultaba un gran alivio tenerla cerca. Más tarde, Laura y yo también asistimos a clase en la capital, pero Adriana vivía demasiado lejos de nosotras en Lima como para seguir manteniendo nuestros encuentros. Por eso, esperábamos a que llegaran las vacaciones para regresar a casa, a nuestra pequeña ciudad de Huaraz, donde se daba por hecho que haríamos vida social con la familia y los amigos. De algún modo, mi conexión con Adriana y Bárbara era —y siempre ha sido— indeleble. Supongo que todo lo que habíamos soportado mutuamente unía inextricablemente nuestros corazones. Incluso hoy en día, Adriana y yo recordamos aquellos días lejanos. Ella ahora reside en Suiza y nos ponemos al día gracias a ese increíble medio de comunicación que es Facebook. ¡Vaya trayectoria de memorias imperecederas! El tiempo tiene alas y nos transporta en su lomo, pero la constancia del cariño nos ancla a lo familiar, a la experiencia compartida.

Aparte de Adriana y de mi querida hermana Laura, que, independientemente de las circunstancias, irradiaba cariño y alegría por el mero hecho de existir, yo obtenía la mayor parte de mi inspiración de papá, cuya estoica firmeza a la hora de adaptarse a nuestra situación resultaba verdaderamente heroica. Al igual que su padre, era una roca en aquellos tiempos de sequía emocional y caos sofocante, un rasgo de su personalidad que todavía alberga en su interior. Su entereza de carácter y su fortaleza física solo se igualaban, y siguen haciéndolo, a sus valientes e inquebrantables principios. Sirva a modo de ejemplo la siguiente anécdota: Hace varios años, uno de sus empleados (a quien sus compañeros lo apodaron en broma «Mala Noche» por sus constantes quejas de haber pasado una mala noche) tuvo un accidente fuera del lugar de trabajo. Conmovido por la mala fortuna de su empleado, papá se encargó de abastecer a Mala Noche y a su familia durante su periodo de convalecencia. Cuando la gente puso en duda las acciones de papá —especialmente dado que el accidente había tenido lugar durante las horas fuera del trabajo—, nuestro padre clara y decididamente respondió:

—Este es un buen hombre. No tiene a nadie y necesita que alguien lo ayude a él y a sus seres queridos.

Y eso fue todo. ¿Quién podría discutir un razonamiento tan impecable?

Haciendo gala de tal convicción tras el sismo, papá jamás se quejó de lo que habíamos perdido. Más que nunca antes, parecía un soldado en el campo de batalla: un hombre de acciones más que de palabras. A medida que el clima se hacía más y más inclemente y la supervivencia en las tiendas era cada vez más incómoda, nuestro protector consumado nos llevó a una pequeña parcela de terreno en Nicrupampa, lejos de lo peor de la catástrofe. Como ya he mencionado, vivir en la casa de mi tío, que seguía valientemente en pie, no era una opción para nosotros entonces. Solo de pensar en meternos bajo techo durante cualquier periodo de tiempo —y menos con vistas a instalarnos— nos resultaba totalmente impensable. Y así, nuestra pequeña parcela de civilización se convirtió en nuestro hogar, donde gozábamos de lujos (en absoluto estoy utilizando este término de forma laxa aquí) como poder plantar maíz, patatas, zanahorias y toda clase de hierbas que nos servían de sustento. Era allí donde solíamos acudir durante la cosecha para consumir deliciosas «pachamancas», carnes cocidas de diferentes tipos, preparadas sobre piedras calientes (el término proviene del quechua y significa literalmente «olla de barro»).

Nuestro hogar temporal estaba hecho de paja, barro y un techo de aluminio, que se denominaba «techo de calamina», hecho de chapa ondulada de aluminio, unido con clavos para estabilizarlo ante las fuertes ráfagas de viento. Nuestra cocina de carbón, que mamá llamaba «vicharra» era extraordinariamente rudimentaria y estaba hecha de adobe. Mamá solía cocinar todas nuestras comidas en aquel artilugio, empleando ollas de arcilla, al tiempo que los ojos le lloraban profusamente por el humo mientras removía el contenido con una cuchara de madera. Con razón, cabría pensar que la comida preparada en aquellas condiciones no estaba sabrosa pero, de hecho, sucedía todo lo contrario. El aroma y la sustancia de la sabrosísima cocina de mamá desafiaban cualquier condición climatológica. Para compensar nuestra falta de electricidad, papá compró una lámpara de gas que tenía una bombilla con aspecto de mecha. Aquella tenue luz en la oscuridad se convirtió en nuestro santuario, en torno al cual nos reuníamos a charlar, a jugar a las cartas o a leer por la noche. Su brillo acogedor representaba nuestra metáfora de energía vital, inherente a nuestra capacidad de resistencia colectiva y de adaptación, mediante el cariño y la solidaridad. La iniciativa propia y la ingenuidad eran componentes esenciales de supervivencia en aquellos tiempos. Recuerdo haber tenido que aguardar largas filas junto a mi familia para conseguir agua limpia de los camiones cisterna de salvamento, para después llevarla en cubos llenos hasta nuestra choza. Aquellos cubos pesaban tanto como yo misma. Supongo que esto explica, en parte, que actualmente tenga tanta fuerza en el tren superior de mi cuerpo. Realizábamos aquellas tareas con diligencia, para evitar consumir el agua contaminada que había infiltrado los arroyos y generado enfermedades como la fiebre tifoidea.

Por fortuna, las aflicciones más graves que ponían en peligro la vida pasaron de largo ante nuestra puerta. Por la noche, sin embargo, me atenazaba persistentemente una horrible sensación en la garganta, acompañada de un extraño ahogo, como si la abrumadora conmoción del sismo todavía se alojara en el interior de mi garganta: una manifestación literal de mi estado de conmoción tras el desmoronamiento de mi mundo. De repente, me despertaba asustada, boqueando en busca de aire, tratando de determinar la causa. También despertaba a mis padres que, alarmados por la interrupción imprevista de sueño —su único momento de tregua de los esfuerzos por sobrevivir—, corrían a mi lado, igual de asustados que yo y sin saber qué sucedía. Ahora que conozco las técnicas y filosofías de la medicina tradicional de la antigua China, comprendo que mi Qi (también llamado Chi) se vio afectado por el influjo de estrés y otras potentes emociones. El Qi es la energía vital que circula por nuestros cuerpos. La enfermedad y otras toxinas pueden interferir con el flujo de esta energía y provocar que el cuerpo reaccione negativamente. Cuando el Qi se atora o se estanca, se produce la enfermedad. Cuando hay enfermedad, debe restablecerse el flujo del Qi. Para hacer tal cosa, debe eliminarse la interferencia. En Perú, las curanderas están bien versadas en el arte de restaurar el flujo de energía. En retrospectiva, las considero versiones de sus homólogas del antiguo Oriente, solo que provistas de otros métodos distintos. Por ejemplo, frotaban huevos frescos por todo el cuerpo mientras pronunciaban plegarias, o introducían en el cuerpo conejillos de indias vivos que se encargaran del trabajo. Solo de plantearme ese último método hace que todavía sienta picores, y una descripción gráfica no tendría ninguna utilidad aquí. Afortunadamente, en mi caso, mamá llamó a una curandera para que empleara la técnica de los huevos y las oraciones, al mismo tiempo que me administraba hierbas calmantes. *Voilà!* Después de un par de meses, me recuperé. No hace demasiado tiempo, alguien de mi oficina con síntomas idénticos experimentó una total recuperación cuando le apliqué un tratamiento de acupuntura. El éxito de dicho tratamiento corrobora mi teoría de que la interferencia con la energía vital puede provocar enfermedades. Los tratamientos de barro, otro método de curación, me ayudaron con mis problemas digestivos. Aún puedo recordar a mamá poniéndome el barro sobre el vientre, esperando a que se secara, para después retirarlo. El tratamiento funcionó y, a partir de entonces, siempre me sentí totalmente recuperada. En los últimos años, he visto con mis propios ojos los efectos reparadores de la medicina alternativa y creo sinceramente que su uso debería respetarse tanto como las técnicas occidentales tradicionales.

A pesar de los efectos postraumáticos del terremoto, también disfrutábamos de momentos de frivolidad, que provenían en su mayor parte del tío Rubén. Su iglesia bautista se encontraba en una tienda cercana, a la que acudían predicadores a dar sermones ante una admirada multitud, sentada en sillas que se hallaban meticulosamente alineadas. Rubén, que residía con unos parientes vecinos en aquella época, nos visitaba con frecuencia, Biblia en mano, tratando de persuadirnos alegremente a Laura y a mí de que cantáramos himnos religiosos. Mamá nos permitía participar en las canciones y sermones de Rubén a condición de que siguiéramos siendo católicas. Por supuesto, aceptamos, y formamos una pequeña congregación que respetaba profundamente a nuestro fascinante tío. La historia de Rubén es extraordinaria, pues su creencia fundamental era el ateísmo, es decir, hasta que se enamoró perdidamente de Rubí, una devota bautista. Rubén se convirtió para poder proseguir su vida junto a ella y, al hacerlo, se involucró en la fe aún más que aquellos que habían nacido en la fe misma. La hermana de papá, la tía Emma, nos contó la historia de cuando asistió a la ceremonia de bautismo de Rubén y su entrada en la fe. El ritual consistía en múltiples inmersiones en una piscina de agua, que convertían al no creyente en el devoto más ardiente posible. ¡Ese es el poder transformador del amor!

Así es el río de la vida, avanzando palmo a palmo, cambiándolo todo mientras fluye por su curso. Lentamente, las circunstancias fueron alterándose cada vez más para nosotros también, y nuestros días a merced de los elementos llegaron a su fin. Finalmente, nuestra existencia dejó de ser un esfuerzo consciente. A medida que se disipaban las réplicas del terremoto, nos fuimos sintiendo más cómodos quedándonos bajo techo. El tío Ernesto nos acogió en su ruinoso hogar, proporcionándonos un dormitorio grande, un armario y una sencilla cocina. En torno al patio principal de tierra, habían florecido los rosales y otras flores que desprendían su fragancia, estallando de vida y desafiando el reciente estallido de ira de la naturaleza. En aquel insigne lugar, entre las rosas en flor, tuvo lugar un desgraciado acontecimiento que, literalmente, me dejó marcada de por vida. Era un día hermosísimo, con un cielo brillante y azul, una de esas tardes en las que todo parece estar en el mundo tal y como le corresponde. Había regresado a casa de la escuela en El Centenario, donde Santa Rosa de Viterbo había sido reconstruida temporalmente. Llevaba puesto mi uniforme, un almidonado suéter blanco y una falda gris oscuro, firmemente ajustada a la cintura. Mamá me dio la bienvenida y me preguntó si podía ir hasta un antiguo armario y sacar de él un poco de arroz. Obedientemente, fui a hacer lo que me pedía, pero, tras varios minutos, no logré encontrar lo que estaba buscando, así que decidí ir abriendo cada uno de los envases que se encontraban allí. Mientras estaba inclinada, un ratón se me metió por el almidonado cuello de mi suéter, correteándome espalda abajo y quedándose atrapado por la ajustada cintura de mi falda. En mi mente, imaginé a la criatura gritando: «¡Estoy atrapado! ¡Ayuda! ¡No hay salida!», ¿o aquella era mi propia voz aterrorizada? Presa del pánico, comencé a correr frenéticamente en círculos, hasta que me mareé tanto, que terminé cayendo sobre los rosales y una espina se me clavó en el lóbulo izquierdo de la oreja, justo detrás del agujero del pendiente. La sangre manó por lo que parecía ser cada uno de los poros de mi piel. Mi suéter quedó totalmente ensangrentado en el lado herido, como si me hubiera destrozado la metralla. Me puse en pie, sumida por la conmoción y la incredulidad, para descubrir que mi atacante había desaparecido sin dejar rastro, y no volvió a vérsele de nuevo. Huelga decir que, a partir de ese día, desarrollé una fuerte aversión por los ratones y, francamente, por las rosas también y si, por un segundo, logro olvidar que tuvo lugar ese incidente, solo tengo que mirar la prueba inequívoca: una cicatriz detrás del lóbulo de mi oreja, la prueba fehaciente de lo que ocurrió en realidad.

Como todas las cosas en la vida, una fuente de dolor en un caso también puede ser origen de placer en otro. En una esquina de aquel mismo patio, había un dispositivo que tío Ernesto llamaba «el batán», una piedra ovalada, con forma de huevo, que utilizaba como una especie de batidora para preparar las salsas de chili más deliciosas del mundo, hechas con hierbas del jardín. Después de limpiar la piedra, mamá machacaba pimientos picantes sobre ella y los colocaba en un recipiente aparte, añadiendo limón, sal, especias, queso fresco y cebollino, para crear su famoso ají con huacatay, una deliciosa salsa picante peruana con patatas. El huacatay, mi condimento favorito, está emparentado con la caléndula y el estragón. No tengo que hacer ningún esfuerzo de memoria para volver a oler su aroma, viajando atrás un tiempo inconmensurable, uniéndome a un momento ya pasado... pero ¿es eso posible? A medida que me permito continuar mi viaje cognitivo-olfativo, detecto el sabroso aroma del bizcocho de mamá, hecho con huevos y pasas sobre la cocina de ladrillos y adobe. Todos los sábados, cuando mamá preparaba aquel manjar, esperábamos a que la masa subiera y alborotábamos en torno a la mesa de madera, dándole diferentes formas con los dedos a aquella maleable sustancia. Para obtener fruta fresca, acudíamos directamente a la fuente: los melocotoneros y perales de las tierras de tío Ernesto, que parecían poblar toda aquella zona y producir su néctar especialmente para nuestro deleite. ¿Cómo era posible que surgiera una abundancia así tras el caos? Al ser simplemente una niña de nueve años, vivía felizmente en la ignorancia con respecto a aquella cuestión. Ahora, tras haberme distanciado geográficamente, puedo atisbar por la ventana de mi pasado y formarme un punto de vista objetivo. En realidad, con total sinceridad, reconozco de buen grado que me siento mucho más cerca de aquella época de lo que conscientemente me doy cuenta en cualquier momento dado. A medida que voy redactando mis recuerdos, lo revivo de nuevo, como un ave emigrando con las estaciones, regresando infinitas veces a su hogar primigenio.

Si la soledad alguna vez se arrastraba por debajo de nuestra puerta, siempre podíamos contar con tía Julia, la más joven de las dos hermanastras de mamá, que se encontraba en el hospital con nosotros cuando tuvo lugar el sismo. Sorprendentemente, ella y su familia de diez hijos habían sobrevividos todos, dada la distancia geográfica a la que se encontraban del epicentro. Durante nuestras visitas semanales a su casa, mamá transportaba entre sus brazos un paquete de colada seca al sol, con la intención de utilizar la extraña y potente plancha de tía Julia. Para llevar a cabo la simple tarea de planchar, mamá tenía que verter carbón por una abertura de la parte superior. Entonces, para evitar que la ropa se manchara de hollín, limpiaba el artilugio con cera. Una vez que la plancha estaba lo bastante caliente, pasaba a presionar y alisar meticulosamente nuestra ropa, las sábanas y el resto de ropa de cama. Mientras tanto, Laura y yo escuchábamos a hurtadillas los animados cotilleos de las mujeres. En ocasiones, nuestros primos venían a nuestra casa para pasar el día jugando al escondite, a subirnos a los árboles o a recoger fruta. Recuerdo con claridad nuestros juegos en los campos, con la boca cubierta de zumo de frambuesa o de peras amarillas, verdes, púrpuras o naranjas. Estas últimas provenían del higo chumbo, una exótica fruta de sabor peculiar que crecía en las regiones altas que bordeaban el arroyo. Cubiertas de minúsculas espinas, eran ricas en vitamina C. Laura y yo las pelábamos cuidadosamente una a una, para no herirnos antes de ingerirlas, cosa que hacíamos por pura glotonería, no por necesidad ni por hambre. Nos reíamos de la miríada de colores que nos adornaba el rostro, confiriéndonos el aspecto de payasitas de circo reconvertidas a ninfas del campo. Éramos niños de la tierra, aquella formidable madre que nos había traicionado hacía tan poco tiempo. Resultaba difícil comprender que aquella que nos alimentaba nos hubiera podido causar tanto dolor y destrucción.

Retomar la rutina de nuestras vidas resultaba casi surrealista, especialmente en lo referente a las actividades escolares. A pesar de que el nombre de la escuela era idéntico, sus pobladores habían cambiado. Todo el mundo era nuevo —monjas, profesores, compañeros de clase—, como si hubieran surgido de la propia reconstrucción, plantados allí como mobiliario, como si me dijeran:

—¡Bienvenida a un reconstituido mundo totalmente nuevo, completamente extraño!

Nada parecía lo mismo. Puede que la gente simulara una especie de normalidad artificial, pero todos éramos profundamente conscientes de lo que nadie deseaba admitir: nuestras vidas habían muerto y no podríamos recuperarlas jamás. Y, aun así, teníamos que seguir adelante. Se nos había concedido una segunda oportunidad, y no había tiempo que perder.

Por razones obvias, me resultó difícil hacer nuevos amigos en aquella época. Cuando el impacto de la pérdida es tan grande como lo que habíamos experimentado, resulta extraordinariamente doloroso —y aparentemente imposible— superar el miedo que se anida en tu corazón, susurrando: «¡Cuidado! ¡Podría volver a suceder!». Incluso ahora, la débil resonancia de la duda se asoma en diferentes momentos de mi vida, surgiendo en mitad de distintas relaciones, determinando cómo reaccionaré ante determinadas situaciones. Volveré a mencionar esta epifanía personal más adelante, pero, por ahora, baste decir que aquellos días tras el desastre, pasé la mayor parte del tiempo a solas. No obstante, sí que trabé relación con Singa, una muchacha alta e inteligente, que me ganaba una y otra vez al ajedrez. A pesar de su inteligencia, noté que Singa se sentía ligeramente acomplejada, dada su postura encorvada. Tenía todas las razones del mundo para caminar erguida, pero, dado que la naturaleza la había dotado de dones anatómicos distintivamente femeninos (que, según creo, ella consideraba demasiado prominentes), se agachaba deliberadamente, como si pretendiera esconderse. Yo no alcanzaba a comprender por qué su madre no la regañaba por su postura, tanto emocional como física.

Pensándolo bien, yo misma sabía bien lo que era vivir acomplejada y no poco, precisamente. A medida que iba creciendo, las manchas de mi rostro se fueron haciendo cada vez más obvias, provocando que me sintiera torpe e incómoda, especialmente en presencia del sexo opuesto. No obstante, por el momento, simplemente me centraba en lo académico, que siempre había sido uno de mis puntos fuertes. Sin embargo, por alguna razón, no se me daba bien la geografía, y llamaron a mi padre para que hablara con el profesor. Bueno, dejadme que reformule esto último. Yo tenía clarísimo por qué me distraía y no lograba centrarme: mamá estaba embarazada. Después de once años siendo la más pequeña, la presencia de nueva energía vital estaba a punto de dominar a toda la familia. Dado que el vientre de mamá iba haciéndose más grande día a día y ya no podía caminar, decidió llevarse a Laura con ella a Lima para descansar y visitar a mi hermano. Tomás ya se había marchado a la capital para asistir a una prestigiosa escuela jesuita. Así las cosas, yo me quedé sola en la casa con papá y Victoria, nuestra joven e iletrada ama de llaves. El momento no podría haber sido peor. Una mañana, me desperté para encontrarme en medio de un charco de sangre. Pensé que me estaba muriendo y no supe qué hacer a continuación. Sumida en el terror, no lograba comprender por qué Victoria celebró con júbilo que por fin me hubiera hecho mujer. Me sentí miserable. ¿Por qué no me había hablado mamá sobre esto? ¿Por qué tenía que abandonarme en un momento en el que mi furiosa pubertad me dominaba como un dragón comefuego, amenazando con devorar toda mi juventud? Todas estas preguntas me abrumaban y me confundían y me sentía totalmente sola, con aquella prueba más de la desatención de mamá, quizá la mayor: su ausencia en un momento en el que mi vida estaba cambiando. Me sentí aliviada al ver a Victoria limpiando todos los indicios de lo que había sucedido, y porque juró guardar el secreto y no contárselo a papá. Me estremecía solo de pensar en el posible bochorno de una revelación así, especialmente a mi austero padre, que no me habría ofrecido absolutamente ningún consuelo. ¿Cómo podría? Si aquellos asuntos eran tabú para mamá, ¿cómo podría yo sacarle el tema a papá? Tras un rato de soledad y meditación, logré calmarme y comprender (aunque todavía no sé cómo) que, como todos los demás, yo era una peregrina viajando por el mundo. Con aquella perspectiva en mente, mi dilema en la clase de geografía finalmente disminuyó de importancia y, gracias a la ayuda de un tutor, saqué una nota final más que respetable.

Entonces, llegó el día. Papá vino y me dijo:

—¡Mamá ha tenido gemelos!

Me desplomé en el suelo. Una oleada de emoción brotó de mi interior. Solo de pensar que tenía dos hermanos —uno de complexión clara, el otro, más bronceado— me resultaba verdaderamente asombroso. Era como si Papá Noel hubiera llegado con antelación y hubiera logrado desafiar todos los obstáculos, incluso las carreteras cortadas. Bueno, al menos, el cielo se había despejado... Por lo que todo el mundo sabía. Mamá y Laura tuvieron que quedarse en Lima durante un tiempo, porque uno de los bebés había sufrido complicaciones menores, de las que afortunadamente se recuperó con rapidez.

Cuando papá y yo fuimos a recibir al aeropuerto a mamá, a Laura y a los preciosos recién llegados, me embargó la alegría y el entusiasmo. Había extrañado tanto la presencia de Laura que cuando surgió de la terminal con uno de los bebés en los brazos, se me aceleró el corazón. Mamá la seguía de cerca con el otro. Nuestro reencuentro fue dulce. De repente, paseé la mirada y me di cuenta del atractivo de la gente que me rodeaba: los bien parecidos pilotos y azafatas, y sus hermosos atuendos. ¡Vaya, qué celosa me sentí! Volví a recordar mis manchas y me acobardé, sintiéndome retraída y solitaria. Entonces, mi mente viajó a un lugar prohibido, aquel espacio oscuro y vacuo de duda sobre mí misma, que me decía que los gemelos, con toda su inocencia, me robarían lo que más anhelaba: las atenciones de mamá. De hecho, ni nadie de mi familia ni yo nos dimos cuenta de toda la responsabilidad que acarreaba el cuidado de los nuevos bebés, pero, en última instancia, el trabajo extra no tenía importancia. El cariño siempre supera los desafíos y, de nuevo, como siempre antes, logré encontrar mi camino.

Cuando tenía once años, a la espera de nuestro regreso a nuestro hogar permanente en Huaraz, mi familia y yo nos mudamos a otro terreno en Nicrupampa y residimos allí durante tres años, en una casa de adobe construida por mi padre. El lugar era algo más confortable, con comodidades como cuartos de baño en el interior de la casa, agua corriente y electrodomésticos infinitamente mejores para mamá. En el seno de aquella comodidad relativa, nuestra familia continuó creciendo. Dos años después de que nacieran los gemelos, llegó Beatriz, la última hija de mis padres y el bebé que todos nosotros adoramos y que se parecía extraordinariamente a Laura.

La presencia de nueva vida nos sirvió de reconstituyente a todos nosotros. Laura y yo mimábamos a nuestros hermanos pequeños como si fueran hijos nuestros. Nuestras vidas retomaron una especie de carácter asentado, como si nuestra tragedia hubiera tenido lugar en el interior del lienzo de un pintor impresionista: borroso, pero cargado de color, y pintado con un pincel de esperanza.

Capítulo 4

A la sombra de la luna llena de otoño

No sé cuál fue el momento preciso en el que se apoderó de mí el primer signo de femineidad. Sencillamente, trepó sigilosamente por mi interior, como el ratoncillo que había encontrado un hogar en mi almidonado suéter blanco en el jardín de tío Ernesto. En vano, busqué a alguien que me proporcionara respuestas y encontré a mamá, pero ella no estaba allí. Aunque tenía su presencia física ante mí, su falta de apoyo emocional me hizo sentir menesterosa. Mientras que ella cuidaba de Roberto y de Juan y, más tarde, de Beatriz, yo me sentía cada vez más aislada. Aunque adoraba a los gemelos y a mi hermana pequeña, debo admitir que estaba celosa de su posición en el centro del universo de mi madre. Gracias a Dios, con la intervención de Victoria, nuestra joven ama de llaves, y las explicaciones ocasionales del instructor de educación sanitaria de la familia, tuve mi primer contacto con el asunto de la sexualidad humana. En realidad, todo aquel interrogante me resultaba totalmente extraño. Al sentirme torpe por mis manchas faciales y un grave acné, que eran lo que me arruinaba la vida, anhelaba, como la mayoría de los preadolescentes, que me apreciaran y me admiraran.

En lugar de que me cuidara, me ridiculizó una de las personas que tendría que haber sido más cuidadosa: nada menos que una de mis profesoras, cuyos comentarios insultantes y deliberadamente descarados sobre ciertos alumnos delante de toda la clase me provocaban escalofríos. Cuando mis manchas aparecieron un día, dejándome unas vergonzosas marcas rojas en la cara, aquella mujer no pudo guardar silencio.

—¿Se puede saber qué te ha pasado? —exclamó, como si yo me hubiera caído dentro de un bote de pintura.

Intuitivamente, al tener más experiencia en cuanto al tacto que aquella mujer, aun siendo ella mayor que yo, me contuve y no le contesté. A la mañana siguiente, el castigo divino cayó sobre ella, como un pájaro al viento, cuando entró en clase con un ojo morado. Verdaderamente, yo no le deseaba ningún mal, pero no pude evitar percibir la ironía de la situación. Y más que nada, deseaba devolverle la pregunta: «¿Se puede saber que le ha pasado?», pero de nuevo, la discreción me impidió hacerlo.

Por aquella época, a la edad de once años, comencé a asistir a mi primer curso en el instituto. Es importante aclarar que, en Sudamérica, el quinto grado es el último año de la escuela primaria, después de la cual, los alumnos emprenden su primer curso de secundaria. A la espera de la reconstrucción de Santa Rosa de Viterbo en su emplazamiento original en Huaraz, asistí a clase en un edificio prefabricado ubicado a las afueras de Nicrupampa. Como ya he mencionado anteriormente, la vida no me resultaba sencilla allí, pero me metí de lleno en las actividades extracurriculares como método de distracción y escape del mar de emociones y preocupaciones que me asaltaban constantemente. Aprendí a tocar la batería; una hazaña que no se solía fomentar ni cultivar en niñas. Las féminas tenían su lugar, y ese no era precisamente esforzarse en una actividad así, pero yo destaqué y disfruté concienzudamente de aquella habilidad. Para mí, era importante desafiar a la suerte y mejorar mis talentos y propensiones, a pesar de las limitaciones impuestas socialmente, por lo que es algo que nunca he dejado de hacer. Durante mi segundo y tercer curso, cultivé el gusto por el voleibol y me convertí en la capitana del equipo, teniendo que levantarme a las 6 de la mañana para entrenar. Aquel horario tan estructurado confería contexto a mi vida, y la sensación de tener un propósito, aparte de servirme como entretenido pasatiempo. También me uní al coro de la iglesia y aprendí a montar en bicicleta, cosa que implicaba el esfuerzo de estirarme para que, a pesar de mi corta estatura, pudiera alcanzar los pedales de la bicicleta de mi hermano. ¡Qué duro era! A pesar de todo, acogí con gusto aquel desafío.

En torno a aquella época, conocí a dos hermanas, Anna y Mariela, con las que practicaba equitación. Anna iba al colegio con Laura, y Mariela estaba en mi curso. Desgraciadamente, Mariela falleció de apendicitis a la edad de 13 años, y todos nos sentimos destrozados por la pérdida. A pesar de que era una amiga superficial, ninguna vida pasa por este mundo sin dejar un toque único de luz. Todavía hoy recuerdo a Mariela. El dolor producido por su pérdida es difícil de olvidar. Anna resultaba magnética, al menos, en cuanto a lo atractiva que resultaba para el sexo masculino. Era el alma de todas las fiestas, y los chicos revoloteaban en torno a ella, con la intención de charlar o bailar. En cuanto a mí, nunca podré insistir lo suficiente en la magnitud del complejo producido por las manchas de mi rostro; sin embargo, dado que no podía confiar realmente en nadie (excepto en mi queridísima hermana, Laura), aparentemente no decía nada, pero me pasaba la mayor parte del tiempo preguntándome si habría ocultado correctamente los indicios de mi vergüenza. Menos mal que Laura siempre venía a mi rescate, presentándome a todos los chicos, ayudándome a superar mi agitación interna que solo ella podía percibir y que se preocupaba de gestionar. En todo momento, hacía todo lo que estaba en su mano para aligerar mi difícil situación. Si yo decía:

—Me gusta ese chico. Es muy mono.

«Ese chico» se presentaba (y no por casualidad precisamente) en alguna de las fiestas de mi hermana.

—¡Ven aquí! —le decía emocionada Laura, haciéndole un gesto con la mano al objeto de mis atenciones—. ¡Quiero presentarte a mi hermana pequeña!

Tímida y apocada, yo respondía con poco entusiasmo, pero con orgullo, porque me encontraba junto a mi hermana mayor. Ella era además mi icono de belleza, sentido común e inteligencia. Cualquier incomodidad que yo pudiera sentir se veía mitigada por la naturaleza abierta y gregaria de mi hermana. Sin embargo, en ausencia de Laura, tenía que enfrentarme por mí misma en lo que a romances se refería. A los catorce años, conocí a Carlos, una de las figuras más enigmáticas con las que me había encontrado jamás. Era un muchacho dulce, un año mayor que yo, con el que había mantenido amistad durante un año. Nuestra conexión se inició en el coro, cuando una monja nos emparejó para que fuéramos a pedir juntos contribuciones para la iglesia. Mucha gente pensaba que nos parecíamos, con nuestro pelo color rubio cenizo y nuestra complexión clara. Alto y guapo, Carlos siempre había tenido el aspecto de un joven noble —siempre limpio y flamante, sin un solo cabello fuera de lugar— se ponía ropa claramente importada del extranjero (algo que no era más que pura conjetura por mi parte). Si hubieran tenido que elegir a alguien para aparecer entre las páginas de una revista de moda, Carlos hubiera sido el perfecto ejemplo de dignidad, respetabilidad y donosura, aunque, tengo que admitirlo, su intelecto no iba a la zaga. Sin embargo, lo que le faltaba de materia gris lo compensaba con creces en personalidad. Su procedencia fue siempre un misterio para mí, pues nunca hablaba de sus padres ni de su linaje. Al parecer, vivía con su tía, pero yo nunca la vi. De algún modo, la naturaleza clandestina de Carlos lo envolvía en un halo de misterio. Le gustaba enormemente a todo el mundo —incluidas a todas las chicas, por supuesto—. Es posible que fuera por las mismas razones por lo que mis padres le tenían mucho cariño. A papá le gustaba que lo ayudara en la tienda y apreciaba su habilidad para congraciarse con los demás de la forma más amistosa posible. En resumen, no había ninguna razón para no sentir aprecio por Carlos.

Lo que mis padres no sabían sobre mi amigo —al margen de su misteriosa herencia ancestral— era que se había convertido en mi novio. Teníamos una especie de relación amorosa adolescente, que comenzó con mi primer beso. Mientras regresábamos un día a casa desde el colegio, con mis libros en brazos de Carlos como era su costumbre, dimos un rodeo por una pequeña zona boscosa, donde me besó. Me sentí aterrorizada al recordar toda clase de cosas, especialmente, que podía quedarme embarazada debido a aquel beso. Me sentí tan abrumada, que me temblaron las piernas del mismo modo que cuando tuvo lugar el terremoto. Solo hice partícipe a Laura de mi secreto, y ella me aseguró repetidas veces que mis temores eran infundados. Me sentí incómoda y tonta, sin saber que hacer. No obstante, sin que mis padres lo supieran, continuamos viéndonos.

Una tarde, habíamos planeado ir a ver una película en una sesión matinal, y Laura me acompañó hasta el cine. Mi hermana ya era estudiante universitaria, y estaba en casa en Huaraz de vacaciones de sus estudios de Derecho en Lima. Ella nunca daba por hecho el tiempo que pasábamos juntas y me proporcionaba su apoyo siempre que se le presentaba la ocasión. El suspense empezó a acumularse mientras esperábamos... y seguíamos esperando. Tras diez minutos, Carlos no apareció, y nosotras nos marchamos. Ya veis, en mi cultura, resultaba inaceptable que las mujeres tuvieran que esperar a los hombres. Así pues, para colmo de mi decepción, tuve que aceptar que me habían plantado, dejado de lado, y cualquier otra expresión empleada para describir aquel columpio de emociones que inevitablemente culminaba en un abrumador sentimiento de rechazo. En realidad, nunca quise a Carlos, ¿cómo podría? En aquel momento, apenas sabía lo que significaba «querer», y mucho menos los sentimientos que acompañaban aquel término. Y, aun así, lo que había sucedido era un golpe, y sabía que tenía que recuperarme: debía hacerlo. Todavía tenía mucha vida ante mí. Mi cuerpo estaba cambiando físicamente y, aunque no comprendía por completo aquella evolución física natural, sentía intuitivamente que lo más sencillo era rendirme a las fuerzas de la vida, aquellas en mis mundos externo e interno.

Siempre a mi rescate, Laura, mi ángel de la guarda, me invitó a una fiesta aquella noche, a la que asistirían amigos suyos de la universidad, todos ellos mayores que yo. De hecho, yo era allí la única estudiante de instituto. Poco después de mi llegada, localicé a un hombre alto, de complexión morena, delgado y exquisitamente atractivo que tenía cerca de veinte años. Laura me leyó la mente y me lo presentó.

—Este es Lorenzo —me dijo—. Es estudiante de Derecho en Trujillo.

Lorenzo me preguntó si quería bailar y, en aquellos momentos, nos comunicamos una serie de sentimientos tácitos. Se bailaba mucho en mi país natal, Perú. Era nuestra forma de divertirnos y conocer a gente. Para mí, aquel interludio representó uno de los acontecimientos más fundamentales de mi vida.

Lorenzo y yo creamos instantáneamente un vínculo, y me preguntó si le permitía acompañarme a casa. Laura y su novio, Xavier, caminaban delante de nosotros, en su papel de silenciosas carabinas. Cuando nos detuvimos junto a la puerta de mi casa, Lorenzo me pidió que nos encontráramos al día siguiente. En aquel instante, sentí que caía totalmente bajo su hechizo, embelesada por su petición y sintiéndome privilegiada por que un hombre tan dotado quisiera salir conmigo. Acepté con entusiasmo su invitación y el resto de la noche sentí la impaciente anticipación ante nuestra siguiente cita. Durante el curso de un mes, salimos varias veces, compartiendo momentos inestimables, cuyos remanentes todavía perviven en mi memoria como duendecillos menudos, bromeando y burlándose de mí a ratos, recordándome un pasado muy distante en el tiempo, pero que aún resuena en mi corazón.

Para ilustrar lo profundamente arraigadas que están todavía mis experiencias formativas, ha llegado la hora de hacer una digresión. Con este propósito, permitidme que viaje al presente, el único punto de referencia real para momentos pasados o futuros y el revelador definitivo de la verdad. El otro día, mientras estaba sentada en un banco del parque, tomando notas para el presente libro, dos ancianitas que conocía se me acercaron y me preguntaron qué estaba haciendo.

—Estoy escribiendo un libro —respondí, dejándoles sitio a las señoras para que se sentaran junto a mí.

—¿Sobre qué? —me preguntaron ambas, casi al unísono.

—No se lo puedo contar ahora. Es un secreto —respondí, sonriendo.

—Bueno —contestó una de las ancianas, mirándome fijamente—, pues solamente lo leeremos si es picantón.

Aunque domino el inglés (tengo que aclarar que estaba charlando con ellas en este idioma), todavía hay palabras que necesito mirar en el diccionario. Cuando descubrí el significado del término que la anciana señora había empleado para decir «picantón», me eché a reír descontroladamente y decidí atender a su petición. Pues bien, como ya sabéis, me educaron las monjas, en una sociedad anclada en códigos de conducta rígidos —y me atrevería a decir que la mayor parte de las veces dictatoriales—, especialmente en lo relativo a los menores. Por lo tanto, podéis imaginar mis reservas a la hora de relatar cualquier cosa remotamente salaz. Además, ¿qué bien haría eso?, me pregunto a mí misma. Bueno, ahora ya lo sé. Actualmente, sirve para satisfacer la curiosidad ligeramente lasciva de dos venerables ancianitas y, posiblemente, de otros lectores cuyo interés en asuntos de naturaleza romántica debe cubrirse también. Por lo tanto, en deferencia a estas personas y, al mismo tiempo, prescindiendo de cualquier decoro en general, paso a relatar mi historia de amor con Lorenzo, el primer hombre al que le entregué mi corazón.

Durante aproximadamente un mes, experimentamos la felicidad de salir juntos. Él me tocaba y me acariciaba en lugares que yo ni siquiera sospechaba que existían, encendiendo en mí la sensación de lo que verdaderamente significaba convertirse en una mujer y serlo. Cuando me besaba, el mundo entero parecía desvanecerse, cuando me susurraba palabras de amor al oído, temblaban los cimientos... esta vez con emoción, éxtasis y deseo. En efecto, experimentaba un terremoto interno de una magnitud mucho mayor que nada que pueda describirse con palabras.

Una noche, tras un acontecimiento deportivo en mi instituto, Lorenzo me recogió y me llevó a dar un paseo a la sombra de la luna llena de otoño. Percibiendo que necesitábamos privacidad, Laura nos dejó solos, acordando que se encontraría con nosotros de nuevo en casa. El romance que experimenté aquella noche no habría podido imaginarlo ni en mis sueños más peregrinos. La química que compartíamos era, literalmente, palpable: una fórmula mágica de tiernos abrazos y besos apasionados, que nos fundían en uno solo. Arropada en los cariñosos y cálidos brazos de Lorenzo, contemplé la luz de la luna reflejada en sus ojos, asegurándome la fidelidad de su corazón. Su boca pronunciaba palabras de amor eterno.

—Te llevaré conmigo allá donde vaya —prometió.

Indeleblemente grabado en mi alma, el discurso de Lorenzo y su comportamiento dotaban de significado a los cambios pubescentes que estaban teniendo lugar en mi interior.

Una y otra vez, Lorenzo estaba allí para mí, queriéndome y haciéndome sentir especial. Durante nuestros paseos por el bosque, me cantaba canciones de amor, tocando cada nota de su guitarra con mi nombre. Atraía todo mi ser con suaves besos tras las orejas y en el cuello, cubriéndome de extasiadas caricias, haciéndome bailar en el séptimo cielo. Estaba viviendo por completo un sueño, la fantasía de cualquier muchacha joven de ser deseada. Durante un breve periodo de tiempo, me deshice de todos mis sentimientos de timidez producidos por las manchas de mi labio inferior y mi mandíbula. El amor de Lorenzo las hacía parecer prácticamente imperceptibles a mi vista. Eso es lo que hace el amor: se desprende de las capas, de la fachada de la llamada imperfección, para revelar la esencia de una persona, en mi caso, de una muchacha de quince años, locamente enamorada y bullendo de más emoción de la que hubiera sentido hasta entonces. Sin embargo, cuando mi padre me descubrió un chupetón en el cuello un día (capilares rotos provocados por uno de los ardientes besos de Lorenzo), aquello fue el preludio del final de mi alegría. Efectivamente, papá puso fin a las llamadas telefónicas de Lorenzo, insistiendo en que era «demasiado mayor» para mí, y demasiado persistente. Prohibió todas nuestras conversaciones, advirtiendo a mamá que no debía permitir que Lorenzo hablara conmigo. Así, comencé a ver a mi amado a escondidas, sin que mis padres lo supieran. Mis amigos venían de clase a buscarme para llevarme con él. No sabía qué más podía hacer. Una noche, un grupo que cantaba serenatas se congregó en el exterior de mi ventana para cantarnos a Laura y a mí. Papá estaba roncando profundamente, pero yo sabía que, en realidad, estaba despierto y en pleno uso de sus facultades. Tenía que haber oído la música, pues todos lo hicimos y, al día siguiente, todos teníamos oscuros círculos bajo los ojos por la falta de descanso. Era costumbre que el padre de la muchacha a la que se dedicaba la serenata invitara a su admirador y a los que le seguían a tomar café o té, pero no fue así en el caso de nuestro padre. En asuntos del corazón, especialmente si se trataba de proteger el de su hija, papá era inflexible.

Tras un glorioso mes de pasión y promesas, Lorenzo tuvo que regresar a sus clases de Derecho en Trujillo, que se encontraba aproximadamente a ocho horas de Huaraz. Me dijo que me escribiría, prometiéndome su amor inquebrantable. Yo le creí. Durante una temporada, llegaron sus cartas: cuatro en total —plagadas de poéticos refranes y palabras de compromiso—. Entonces, repentinamente, su correspondencia llegó a su fin. Cuando acudía a la oficina de correos esperando expectante una carta, volvía siempre con las manos vacías. Incluso la encargada de la oficina de correos sentía lástima por mí y bajaba la mirada abatida, como si estuviera reflejando mi propio espíritu apesadumbrado con su empatía. Sin razón, causa, ni explicación, Lorenzo había desaparecido de mi vida. Como es de imaginar, aquello me partió el corazón.

Entonces, una tarde, de repente, vi a Lorenzo, caminando por la calle en El Centenario, por la acera opuesta donde nos encontrábamos mi madre y yo. Pensé que había visto un fantasma, pero mirándolo con más detenimiento, supe que, de hecho, era él, a la vista de todos.

—¿Qué sucede? —me preguntó mamá.

Me quedé sin habla al verlo, aquel cruel rompecorazones... ¡de mi propio corazón! ¿Cómo podría haber hecho algo así? ¿Cómo podía estar con... con aquella hermosa mujer que llevaba del brazo y a la que abrazaba seductora y apasionadamente? «¡Aquella podría ser yo!», gritó angustiado mi corazón. Me sentí tan insignificante, tan poco digna de Lorenzo... Él nos vio, pero fingió que no se había dado cuenta. ¿Qué había hecho yo? ¿Se debía a que no era atractiva? ¿Hacía que se sintiera avergonzado, incómodo? Fuera de mis casillas, sentí un torrente de tristeza subiéndome por mi interior, eclipsando toda la euforia desenfrenada de la energía libidinosa que había evocado para mí él en el pasado, cosa que todavía ocurría. No podía evitarlo.

El momento de mi graduación se iba acercando: era hora de celebraciones y fiestas. Yo no quería formar parte de ninguna de ellas, pero mi amiga, Charo, trató de convencerme de que olvidara mis problemas yendo a una de aquellas reuniones. Después de mucho forcejear, acabé capitulando. A medida que la gente empezaba a bailar, levanté la vista para a toparme... nada menos que con Lorenzo, que entraba con la misma gracia con la que lo había visto en la ciudad. Acobardándome solo de pensar en encontrarme en la misma habitación que él, deseé que me tragara la Tierra. Así pues, Charo me sacó de allí a otra sala, donde bebí mucha más sangría de la cuenta. Poco tiempo después, Laura vino a recogerme, y ella y Charo me llevaron a una cafetería, donde me recompuse —aunque solo fuera de forma transitoria— gracias a una taza de café y un montón de chicles de menta para enmascarar el olor a alcohol. Si me hubiera enfrentado a mis padres en aquel estado, habría sido un desastre, una auténtica sentencia de muerte emocional. Cuando llegamos a casa, mamá preguntó por la fiesta, y yo respondí que no me encontraba bien. Después de que Laura me diera té caliente, me fui directa a la cama: a sollozar durante toda la noche. Solamente mi hermana y Charo se enteraron de la verdad de aquella angustiosa experiencia.

Pronto, llegó la hora del baile de graduación, pero yo no tenía acompañante. Me quedé asombrada cuando Laura sugirió que se lo pidiera a Lorenzo. Todo indicaba en contra de aquello, pero, en ausencia de alternativas, así lo hice, a regañadientes. Mi hermana pensaba que una última alegría le sentaría bien a mi corazón antes de marcharme a la universidad en Lima, donde mis estudios, los nuevos amigos y las nuevas clases harían que mis pensamientos sobre Lorenzo desaparecieran para siempre.

Cogí el teléfono con una resolución temblorosa (que no deja de ser una contradicción de términos, pero mi alma estaba llena de oposiciones por entonces).

—Lorenzo —dije, tras oír su voz—. Mi hermano, Tomás, iba a llevarme al baile de graduación, pero no ha podido ausentarse de sus clases en Lima. ¿Puedes llevarme tú?

«¿Qué estás haciendo?», se preguntaba mi agitado corazón. Apenas tuve tiempo de reformular aquel pensamiento, cuando Lorenzo respondió:

—Ahora te llamo yo.

Mientras esperaba, ponderaba sin cesar las posibles razones que tendría para rechazarme... una vez más. Entonces, sonó el teléfono, y yo corrí como un rayo a contestar, para escuchar la voz de Alfonso, un amigo de la familia.

—¡Hola, Isabella! Lorenzo no puede llevarte al baile, pero yo sí.

«¿Qué acaba de suceder?», me pregunté a mí misma conmocionada y sorprendida. Así pues, convencida de que no tenía otro recurso que recomponerme y, sencillamente, ir al baile, fue exactamente lo que hice. Mis padres no pusieron pegas a que asistiera con Alfonso, que era un amigo al que respetaban. Ataviada con un hermoso vestido de terciopelo rojo y con la melena suelta y ondulada, me sentí casi etérea, dispuesta a disfrutar lo que debería haber sido una de las noches más memorables de mi vida —o, al menos, reunir fuerzas para soportarla con dignidad—.

La definición de la palabra «memorable» es crucial aquí, dado que la noche efectivamente fue inolvidable, pero no el sentido positivo de la palabra. Mientras bailaba con Alfonso, fundiéndome informalmente con la multitud, allí estaba de nuevo... ¡Sí, era Lorenzo! No podía creer mis ojos y, esta vez, lo acompañaba otra chica, quizás aún más bella que la primera. Alfonso y yo continuamos bailando, y las cadencias de la música reverberaban subiéndome y bajándome por la columna vertebral... ¿o se trataba de ira que sentía? Había sido rechazada, una vez más. Después de tres o cuatro bailes, Lorenzo se acercó y me preguntó si quería bailar con él. No sé por qué, pero acepté instintivamente. Supongo que había dejado mi corazón a la sombra de la luna llena de otoño. La estación había cambiado, pero mi amor no había perdido constancia. La juventud es alocada, ciega, impetuosa e incontenible, incluso ante un rechazo flagrante. En medio del baile, Lorenzo me espetó una sentenciosa confesión espontánea:

—Tú eres solo una chiquilla.

Pensé que sus palabras no eran más que un cruel engaño que enmascaraba sus verdaderos sentimientos: que yo era horrible y que él no me deseaba. Instantáneamente, me vinieron a la mente mis manchas faciales. «Se está compadeciendo de mí, poniendo mi edad como excusa para no decir lo que realmente piensa», me dije a mí misma. Aquello era demasiado para que yo pudiera afrontarlo, así que, tras una breve pausa, le espeté:

—Eres un hombre muy complicado. No te comprendo y lo mejor será que no vuelva a verte jamás.

Tras decir aquello, recogí mi abrigo y le pedí a Alfonso que me llevara a casa. Me estaba muriendo por dentro, experimentando una especie de segundo terremoto, la sacudida de un planeta: del microcosmos de mi propio pequeño mundo. Añoraba al Lorenzo que había conocido, al hombre que, bajo la luz de la luna, había jurado amarme eternamente. Mis sentimientos se dividían entre el deseo y la retirada. No estaba en mi naturaleza rogar y, además, de haberlo hecho, lo único que habría conseguido hubiera sido provocarme más daño y degradación. ¡No! Tenía que mantenerme firme, que reclamar mi derecho a hacer gala de mi propia identidad, libre de Lorenzo. Él no me conocía realmente y, para ser sinceros, yo todavía tenía que descubrirme a mí misma. Tenía toda mi vida ante mí, pero eso no lo sabía yo entonces. Lo único de lo que estaba totalmente segura era que me sentía profunda y desesperadamente miserable, una sombra de mí misma. Mi única distracción era el hecho de que tenía un futuro aguardándome en Lima, la capital, donde estaba a punto de explorar un mundo totalmente nuevo —un lugar que se desplegaría ante mis pies como una alfombra formada por diferentes experiencias—, un batiburrillo de alegrías y penas, cuya magnitud, en aquellos momentos de aislamiento y dolor de corazón, apenas podía empezar a comprender.

Capítulo 5

Trampolines hacia la evolución

A medida que el tiempo pasaba, yo también me iba desarrollando. A la edad de quince años, mis sueños resplandecían ante mí como rayos del sol mañanero, y cada día que transcurría, me atraían más y más para que me empapara en ellos y modelara mi futuro. No obstante, en realidad, seguía siendo una cría en muchos aspectos, siempre a la sombra de Laura, emocionada por que me incluyera en su mundo y sus iguales me aceptaran. A diferencia de la mayor parte de las hermanas mayores, ella me hacía participar en todo sin avergonzarse, cultivaba mi felicidad y se ocupaba de mi comodidad con tanto cariño y consideración como no había recibido de ningún otro ser humano. La delicada dulzura de Laura y su afable personalidad le granjeaban el cariño de prácticamente todo el mundo.

No era sorprendente que mi hermana fuera la favorita de mis padres, a menudo a causa de la negativa de mamá a la hora de atender los problemas que me concernían a mí. Nunca cuestioné por qué mi querida Laura gozaba de su privilegiada posición. Únicamente, reflexionaba sobre las razones del rechazo hacia mí. Tardaría varios años en reconciliarme con este asunto tan complejo y, como relataré a su debido tiempo, acabé por hacerlo.

El hecho de conseguir dar por cerradas este tipo de cosas finalmente les llega a aquellos que porfían y luego aguardan pacientemente a que las respuestas fluyan de forma natural. Sin embargo, durante mi adolescencia, aquella comprensión todavía no había tomado forma. Resultaba extraordinariamente difícil entender mi situación a ojos de todo el mundo (excepto de Laura) de muchacha fuerte e independiente, capaz de arreglárselas sola, sin necesidad de intervención materna. La manifiesta falta de implicación de mamá en mi mundo se hacía patente incluso en ocasiones trascendentales como cuando llegué a quinceañera (fiesta de celebración de mis quince años, una fecha de importancia similar a las de los «felices dieciséis» en Estados Unidos). Aunque nunca pude llegar a determinar la causa, me dejaron sola en aquella feliz ocasión, ahogando mi soledad, literalmente, en una botella de whisky que elegí para experimentar con el objetivo de levantarme a mí misma el ánimo. Tomé como ejemplo a diferentes adultos que había observado, y no veía por qué no funcionaría aquel método conmigo. Aquel odioso brebaje casi me hizo vomitar y, en un esfuerzo por, literalmente, endulzar la agonía, le añadí azúcar. Por supuesto, la diferencia resultaba insignificante, y tras haber engullido un buche de aquella horrible poción, me quedé dormida. Cuando los demás llegaron a casa y me encontraron sumida en mi sopor etílico, me explicaron que habían entrado a robar en la tienda de papá y que aquel desgraciado incidente había impedido la celebración de mi cumpleaños. ¿Era acaso una coartada plausible? Puede que sí, y ahora mismo no la cuestiono, pero me resultó doloroso creer que me habían despojado del reconocimiento de un día tan fundamental en mi vida. Laura no estaba en casa en aquella ocasión. Sin lugar a dudas, ella nunca habría permitido que nada echara a perder mi alegría, ni siquiera un robo.

Mi hermana y yo éramos como gemelas. Aprovechábamos la más mínima oportunidad para pasar tiempo juntas. Durante una tarde memorable, mientras salíamos de una tienda en El Centenario, nos topamos con Enrique, el novio de la amiga de Laura, Elena. Recordaba haberle conocido un año antes en una de las fiestas de mi hermana. En aquella época, el muchacho alto, de pelo ondulado y tez clara que se dedicaba a piropear a la hermosa y enormemente popular Elena, apenas dio muestras de darse cuenta de mi existencia. Como es natural, yo envidiaba el magnetismo femenino de Elena y el hecho de que tuviera un novio tan atractivo. En aquella ocasión en la que nos encontramos por casualidad fuera de la tienda, Laura me presentó como su hermana pequeña. Tras intercambiar de pasada los saludos de rigor, Enrique prosiguió su camino, aunque reaparecería más tarde cuando yo ya estaba en la escuela de enfermería de Lima, para hacer las veces de amigo omnipresente y guía turístico... Bueno, al menos, al principio.

A medida que pasaban los días, rememoré aquellas obras de teatro escolares con Marina e Inés en las que las tres hacíamos de enfermeras. Me prometí que cumpliría aquellos sueños infantiles y, al mismo tiempo, actualizaría mi potencial e inclinación por la práctica de la enfermería. Sin razón o causa que pudiera retrasar lo que yo consideraba inevitable, solicité, a la edad de dieciséis años, plaza en la escuela militar de enfermería en Lima. Y así, la muchacha de montaña se aventuró a lanzarse a la vida de la urbe.

¡Menuda transformación atmosférica y cultural! El propio aire que respiraba estaba cargado de los humos —especialmente en el centro de la ciudad— producidos por los tubos de escape de coches y autobuses que lo atestaban todo. Estos vehículos iban llenos a reventar de pasajeros, como sardinas en lata, y pululaban en todas las direcciones hacia sus múltiples destinos, a un ritmo que dejaría asombrados a los corredores de los cien metros lisos. El ritmo de la ciudad era tan frenético, que solían omitirse los sufijos de las palabras. ¿Por qué molestarse en enunciarlos si todo el mundo podía averiguarlos fácilmente? Sencillamente, no había tiempo que perder. Presenciar y experimentar todo aquello era más de lo que podían soportar mi corazón y pulmones, pequeños y pueblerinos. Realmente, me sentía abatida: tenía náuseas y mareos, y me sentía enferma en general, hasta un punto que jamás había experimentado antes. Afortunadamente, mi casa, que compartía con mi hermano, Tomás, y con Laura, estaba ubicada en un barrio a treinta o cuarenta minutos del centro de la ciudad. Tomás estudiaba medicina y Laura estaba finalizando sus clases preuniversitarias de derecho.

Vivir con Tomás no resultaba nada sencillo. En cualquier situación, su *modus operandi* consistía en mantener a sus hermanas pequeñas en la periferia de su círculo social, como si nuestra presencia de algún modo disminuyera los estándares que él y sus amigos siempre se esforzaban por mantener. Con frecuencia, los altercados verbales entre mis hermanos me hacían sentir desplazada y extraordinariamente incómoda. Por mi parte, las manchas de mi rostro me venían a la mente como la causa principal del maltrato de mi hermano. Pensaba que se avergonzaba de mí, que yo no era lo bastante buena. Aquellos sentimientos de estar fuera de lugar únicamente servían para exacerbar mis miedos existentes al estar en un entorno nuevo y tener que encarar a nuevas personas que, sin duda, también me juzgarían.

Durante un periodo de tiempo, creí que había establecido conexión, mediante contacto visual de un lado al otro de la habitación, con Paulo, uno de los amigos de Tomás —un hermoso joven de pelo rubio y ojos azules—, cuyo atractivo aspecto aparecería ante mí de nuevo años más tarde, no en la persona del propio Paulo, sino en alguien que se parecía extraordinariamente a él. Es curioso cómo la vida puede llegar a cerrar el círculo. De nuevo, mis pensamientos me toman la delantera. En cualquier caso, la cuestión aquí es que, Paulo era como un fantasma, dejando a un lado lo que podría haber ocurrido si yo me hubiera aventurado a hablar con él. Con mucha frecuencia, ciertos acontecimientos no se materializan en la realidad, aunque deseemos o esperemos que lo hagan.

No solo me absorbieron los cambios en mi mundo inmediato, sino que me abrumaron todavía más las diferencias en el nuevo y totalmente extraño ambiente que me rodeaba. Todo resultaba distinto de lo que yo había estado acostumbrada a ver y oír... La música, la comida e incluso la forma de vestir. En un esfuerzo por luchar contra el calor, la mayoría de la gente llevaba ropa ligera. Mi tono de tez rojizo provocado por el oxígeno de la alta montaña parecía incongruente con los morenos rostros de los habitantes de la ciudad. Aun así, a pesar de todas las anomalías y disonancias que me rodeaban, sabía que estaba donde debía, en un lugar en el que labrarme mi futuro.

La prestigiosa escuela de enfermería recibía varias miles de solicitudes para cubrir únicamente cerca de cincuenta plazas. No estoy segura de los datos exactos, pero el número de plazas era muy reducido en comparación con el de candidaturas. Mi ferviente esperanza de ser aceptada estuvo a punto de irse al traste cuando suspendí el examen físico a causa de mi estatura. Que me dijeran que era demasiado bajita fue devastador. No obstante, alguien me comentó que se habían hecho excepciones en el pasado ante aquel tecnicismo. Así pues, papá acudió a un oficial de alto rango que conocía y le convenció para que me permitieran presentarme a las partes académica y psicológica de la prueba. Si hubiera suspendido la parte académica, habría sido el fin. Me sentí tan agradecida por aquella oportunidad, que trabajé con toda mi alma para cumplir mi objetivo último. Tuve que aguardar tres desesperantes semanas para recibir los resultados: probablemente, el periodo de tiempo más largo de toda mi vida. Como de costumbre, Laura, mi ángel de la guarda, esperó conmigo y, cuando llegó el momento, me acompañó a la escuela para ver los resultados. Casi me desmayé cuando me enteré de la noticia: Yo había sido una de las pocas estudiantes aceptadas en el programa. Rebosantes de alegría, mi hermana y yo llamamos a papá para comunicarle la buena nueva. Aquel, verdaderamente, fue un momento de celebración.

Para entonces, con el objetivo de cumplir los requisitos de aquel estricto programa, me corté mis largos cabellos rubios en una corta melenita, como la de un muchacho. Fue en aquella época de transición cuando volví a relacionarme con Enrique, mi guía a la diversión de todo tipo. Nuestra conexión floreció rápidamente hasta convertirse en una inquebrantable amistad. Me enseñó la ciudad, llevándome a lugares que jamás habría imaginado que existían: el zoológico, restaurantes elegantes y el teatro. Solíamos ir al cine, charlábamos, intercambiábamos pueriles bromas y, sencillamente, disfrutábamos con la compañía del otro. Por alguna razón inexplicable, me sentía cómoda con aquel muchacho extraordinariamente encantador que parecía saberlo todo, al menos, a mi juicio. En aquella época, Enrique y su novia, Elena, habían puesto fin a su relación. Ella se había ido a estudiar a Rusia, una decisión que le provocó a mi amigo no pocos sufrimientos. Sumido en su desgracia, confió en mí y se sintió agradecido por contar con alguien que le escuchara. Por mi parte, no podía estar más contenta de poder distraer mis pensamientos de mi corazón roto recientemente por Lorenzo. Supongo que podría decirse que Enrique y yo estábamos ambos en el lugar adecuado en el momento preciso. Por razones que todavía no puedo llegar a discernir, a él nunca parecieron importarle mis manchas, que entonces eran visibles si no las ocultaba con un toque de maquillaje corrector. Sencillamente, Enrique me aceptaba sin condiciones. Cuando me corté el pelo, se quedó asombrado, pero finalmente declaró:

—Solo es pelo, y estoy seguro de que podrás volver a dejártelo crecer en menos de lo que canta un gallo cuando termines tus estudios. Ya sé lo mucho que significan estas clases para ti. Así pues, ¡felicidades!

Me alegré de contar con su aprobación, agradecida de que, con Enrique, no tendría que intentar ser otra persona diferente de mí misma.

Tener un aliado, aunque suponía un alivio enorme, aun así no podía protegerme de la dura realidad de mi nuevo entorno. La idea de emplear protección solar me resultaba inconcebible: una chica de montaña que había crecido con el aire fresco y la radiante luz del sol, sin miedo alguno a quemarme. ¡Menuda sorpresa desagradable me valió aquello! Un día, dos de mis compañeras, Carolina y Linda, me invitaron a ir a la playa. En aquella época, la playa era un concepto novedoso para mí. Al volver, me percaté de que se me había puesto la piel rojísima. Unos días más tarde, empezó a oscurecérseme y comencé a pelarme. No pensé mucho en ello, pero, una semana más tarde, tras haberme aventurado a ir a la playa a tomar el sol de nuevo, tuve que acudir a urgencias, donde me diagnosticaron quemaduras de segundo grado en la espalda. Dormir boca arriba resultaba increíblemente doloroso y, durante dos semanas, tuve que ponerme vendas y apósitos de gasa. ¡Imaginaos! En mitad el intenso calor estival, ¡y yo tenía que andar por Lima ataviada como un jugador de fútbol americano! Esa experiencia me enseñó a ser mucho más cuidadosa y a estudiar mi entorno un poco más antes de aventurarme a algún lugar nuevo. Más de lo que me imaginaba en aquel momento, aquella lección me serviría enormemente en el futuro. El tópico es cierto: a veces, el dolor es el precursor necesario para evolucionar, especialmente cuando la incomodidad genera concienciación.

Una vez que me quité el peso de encima de haber sido admitida en la escuela de enfermería, me enfrentaba al desafío aún mayor de permanecer en el programa. A lo largo de la formación básica, muchos cayeron, y también lo dejaron un par de estudiantes durante la instrucción en quirófano. Recuerdo vívidamente que tras contemplar una operación de corazón en nuestro primer año, una de las muchachas se puso repentinamente pálida y se desmayó encima de mí. Ella y un par de estudiantes más no regresaron tras aquel incidente. Yo, por el contrario, me sentía intrigada por toda la experiencia de presenciar por primera vez un corazón humano mientras bombeaba de forma autónoma la fuerza vital por todo el cuerpo. Qué perfecto es el diseño, misterioso e intrincado, de la naturaleza. Para mí, no había duda alguna de que aquel era el lugar adecuado para mí: esa era claramente mi vocación. Sinceramente, consideraba toda aquella experiencia algo profundamente conmovedor. Una experiencia así me proporcionaba una motivación añadida para estudiar con aún más ahínco. El poco tiempo libre que me quedaba lo pasaba socializando, labrando amistades imperecederas, mientras me dedicaba a estudiar doce horas al día, cinco días a la semana y medio día los sábados. Nuestra formación era casi tan rigurosa como a la que se someten los estudiantes de medicina en Estados Unidos. Bajo el gobierno militar, recibíamos asistencia económica para comprar los libros y uniformes, además del alojamiento y manutención.

Vivir a una manzana de la escuela era todo un lujo. Literalmente, podía caerme de la cama y ya estaba en clase. A pesar de esta gran ventaja, tenía tendencia a llegar tarde: un hábito por el que prácticamente recibí una seria reprimenda. Puede que, subconscientemente, estuviera empleando mi libertad e independencia para compensar todos los años que había pasado bajo el puño de hierro de las monjas. Mi única fuente de sustento y seguridad residía en mi capacidad para destacar académicamente. Era la más joven y la más bajita de mi grupo, y me sentaba en el fondo de la clase con un grupo de amigas más altas que yo. Mi padre acudió a la escuela un día para informarse sobre mis progresos y se enteró de que yo estaba entre las primeras de mi clase. Más tarde, se pasó por mi apartamento y

ISABELLA TANIKUMI

me dejó un paquete con una nota en mi puerta. «Estoy muy orgulloso de ti. Estás entre los mejores estudiantes del programa, pero tienes que llegar a clase a tiempo». El paquete contenía un gran reloj despertador: un dispositivo de advertencia para que yo cumpliera con mi horario y una promesa implícita para con mi padre. Su aprobación y orgullo me proporcionaron la inspiración necesaria para cumplir lo prometido, y no volví a llegar tarde nunca más.

Cuando tocó estudiar la sexualidad humana, me puse coloradísima de vergüenza. Con las monjas, aquel tema siempre había sido tabú. Desesperadas por evitar la ira divina, algunas niñas de mi instituto que se habían quedado embarazadas, abandonaban las clases y se casaban, para no volver jamás. Por lo tanto, la transparencia con la que se trataba aquel tema en la escuela de medicina era una nueva dimensión completamente diferente para mí, algo a lo que tuve que acostumbrarme, lenta y paulatinamente.

Cuando vuelvo a pensar en ello, veo que mi reticencia se debía, sin lugar a dudas, a un incidente específico que tuvo lugar en cuarto curso, un año antes del terremoto, mientras yo asistía a clase en Santa Rosa de Viterbo. Como todos los niños pequeños, la forma humana me producía curiosidad. Quizás, el hecho de que no pudiéramos hablar abiertamente del tema con los adultos hacía que el enterarnos de aquellas cosas resultara aún más tentador. Un día, revolviendo en el desván de nuestro negocio familiar, encontré lo que pensé que era un libro de tebeos, que

312

representaba una serie de desnudos dorsales. Nadie de mi familia inmediata solía leer cosas así, por lo que atribuí su pertenencia a alguno de los trabajadores. Yo tenía alrededor de ocho años, y mi interpretación de aquellas fotografías reales se limitaba a una vaga diversión. De hecho, lo que estaba contemplando era pornografía. Solté una risita al ver la anatomía humana al desnudo. Al día siguiente, cometí el error fatal de llevar mi «tebeo» al colegio. ¿Yo qué sabía? Pensaba que las fotografías harían reír a mis compañeros. Al principio, su reacción fue precisamente la que yo había anticipado, pero cuando Carla, el ojito derecho de la profesora, posó su mirada en el libro, el ambiente cambió por completo. Cuando ella le entregó la prueba incriminatoria a la Srta. Cecilia, una solterona de rostro pétreo y la más estricta de mis profesoras, noté que se me aceleraba el corazón. Entonces, la Srta. Cecilia clavó en mis ojos una mirada sabelotodo. En aquel momento, creí que mi vida había llegado a su fin. Me pidió que me pusiera en pie y me golpeó con la temida regla, que se estrelló sin piedad contra mi mano varias veces. Retiré aquella mano dolorida y, entonces, ella me golpeó el doble de fuerte. La humillación era indescriptible. Delante de todo el mundo, me rebajaron, me menospreciaron y me degradaron, como si yo no fuera más que una simple delincuente. ¿Es esa manera de tratar a la inocencia, de castigar una fechoría perpetrada por pura inconsciencia? La pregunta es más que retórica, pues exige una rotunda respuesta negativa. Al día siguiente, mientras yo estaba en clase, vi a mi madre andando hacia el despacho de la directora. Por su solemne expresión, supuse que me había metido en un buen lío. Al parecer, la Srta. Cecilia, que era conocida de mamá, la había hecho llamar inmediatamente. Tuvo lugar otro episodio desmoralizante mientras volvían, una vez más, a minusvalorarme y a hacerme sentir poco digna.

Con el paso del tiempo, la historia se repetía, solo que esta vez, no fue tan grave ni la herida tan penetrante, aunque tuvo lugar una situación parecida. Exactamente igual que en la clase de cuarto curso, la conducta en la escuela de enfermería se controlaba hasta detectar la más mínima trasgresión. Sirva a modo de ejemplo la siguiente anécdota: Un día, yo estaba bromeando con unas compañeras sobre la pronunciación del profesor de nefrología de la palabra «haya» (la primera y tercera persona del subjuntivo del verbo «haber»). El profesor, cuya gramática no es que fuera precisamente impecable, cometía el error de decir «haiga». En el preciso momento en el que les comenté aquel error involuntario a mis cuatro compañeras, él volvió a soltar la palabra, lo que hizo que estalláramos a reír. Percatándose de la interrupción, el profesor ordenó:

—La señorita de pelo castaño claro, por favor, levántese y comparta la broma con el resto de la clase.

Allí estaba yo, de pie, muda, sin ser capaz de decirle cual era el objeto de nuestra mofa. Por orden del profesor, mis tres amigas también se pusieron en pie, una por una, igualmente incapaces de proferir sonido alguno. No había marcha atrás.

Habíamos desobedecido, cosa que era una infracción intolerable, garantizándonos que se informara de ello a nuestros superiores y que se nos impusieran cuatro días consecutivos de trabajos forzados: limpieza de los instrumentos del hospital. Aunque mis amigas se disgustaron, su lealtad para conmigo —y viceversa— evitó que ninguna de nosotras revelara nuestro secreto. Sencillamente, tuvimos que sobrellevar la lección acatando el castigo. Supongo que lo que no nos hiere, nos fortalece. Además, había que tener en cuenta que un poco de frivolidad lograba compensar la seriedad de nuestros estudios. Enfrentarse de cerca con situaciones de vida y muerte exigía indultos de vez en cuando, incluso si eso significaba embarcarse en alguna que otra incorrección pasajera. Entonces, yo era más fuerte que la alicaída niña de cuarto curso y estaba preparada para enfrentarme a cualquier desafío, y si eso significaba hacer un poco de servicio comunitario, transigí, de buen grado y decididamente.

En todo caso, enterrada entre mis libros, apenas tenía tiempo como para tomarme aquellas cosas con seriedad. El episodio del «haiga» simplemente me sirvió de recordatorio para no dejar que me afectaran pequeñas minucias y como claro indicativo de mi creciente fortaleza personal a la hora de resistir los envites de la vida. Ya no era ni una cría pequeña ni una víctima, sino que me había convertido en una participante total y convalidada de la experiencia humana. Y como tal, mi preocupación principal era estar a la altura del honor de formar parte del programa de enfermería y ser una de las mejores en mi profesión. Enrique,

que estaba estudiando ingeniería industrial en aquella época, siempre respetaba mi compromiso con mis estudios. Todavía estaba yo en mi primer curso cuando vino a mi casa y amablemente me trajo varios libros para ayudarme con mi proyecto de investigación de Psicología. En aquella época, contábamos con un invitado de honor: mi abuelo, que, en gran parte en contra de su propia voluntad, había venido a pasar unos días con nosotros y a visitar al médico ortopedista para que le examinara la cadera, que se había lesionado mientras montaba a su fiel caballo, *Mauro Mina*. Aquella lesión constituía una anomalía, algo totalmente fuera de lo normal. El abuelo parecía intocable, pero nos alegramos de poder hospedarlo durante su convalecencia. En todo caso, mientras Enrique y yo estábamos sentados en el sofá del salón, muy cerca el uno del otro para poder ver bajo las luces atenuadas, el abuelo entró y comenzó su arremetida verbal contra Enrique. Dirigiéndose a mi amigo en un tono severo, bramó:

—¡Ya sé cuáles son sus intenciones para con mi nieta, y debo advertirle que esta casa es de mi hijo! ¡Y como su padre, reclamo mi autoridad para ordenarle que abandone esta casa inmediatamente!

Sin proferir ni un sonido, Enrique acató lo que mi abuelo le exigía. La sobreprotección infundada del abuelo me provocó una vergüenza injustificada y comencé a sollozar. Inmediatamente, mi dulce abuela (que, por supuesto, había acompañado al abuelo para proporcionarle apoyo moral) vino a abrazarme y a consolarme mientras regañaba al abuelo por su comportamiento. Ante mis propios ojos, aquel anciano gruñón y aparentemente incorregible se transformó en un corderillo. Resultaba asombroso presenciar cómo mi abuela, que era como una flor delicada, lograba someter a aquel gigantón. Aunque hacía creer al abuelo que era él quien estaba al mando, ella era la que asumía el control discretamente. Para mí, aquel fue un inolvidable ejemplo del inexorable triunfo de la gracia y la belleza sobre el ilusorio dominio de la masculinidad. Y digo esto no como feminista, sino como humanista —con el firme convencimiento de que la amabilidad y la fortaleza no son mutuamente exclusivas—, independientemente del género.

Por supuesto, me disculpé profusamente con Enrique, cuya amistad conmigo nunca flaqueó. Aproximadamente un año más tarde, me pidió que fuera a dar un paseo con él por la playa para contemplar la puesta de sol. Atrayéndome hacía sí en el arrecife pedregoso frente al océano, me cogió por primera vez de la mano. Mientras contemplábamos la belleza del sol poniente, Enrique me besó. Yo me quedé pasmada —y profundamente sorprendida—, pues nunca lo había considerado más que un amigo. Respondí a su beso, sintiendo que la evolución de nuestra relación era tan natural como inminente el alba. Comenzamos a vernos con más frecuencia. Enrique venía a buscarme y me acompañaba a casa tras cenas y citas que nos hacían sentir como una pareja.

No obstante, más tarde comencé a percatarme de la afinidad de Enrique por el alcohol: una inclinación que me parecía inaceptable. Tuve que afrontar el hecho innegable de su flagrante alcoholismo cuando me llevó a una fiesta formal con sus padres. Me dejó sola toda la noche con ellos, básicamente ignorándome mientras bebía con sus amigos, parloteaba palabras incomprensibles y se comportaba como un bufón. Aquel comportamiento era abominable. Ya veis, en Perú, cuando un joven lleva a una chica a una reunión formal con sus padres, pasas a ser su novia de manera oficial y su futura prometida. Sin embargo, pronto quedó claro que Enrique me daba por hecho y salía conmigo por despecho tras su ruptura con Elena. En retrospectiva, tengo que confesar que yo tampoco estaba enamorada. Sin embargo, aunque comprendo esto, debo admitir, con el corazón en la mano, que cuando estaba sobrio, Enrique era todo un caballero, el sueño de cualquier mujer. Además, era muy romántico (aunque no tan ardientemente apasionado como Lorenzo). Me dijo que me amaba varias veces, y me trataba con sumo cuidado. Y, sin embargo, al emborracharse, me demostró que amaba el alcohol más que a nada o nadie que lo rodeara. Sencillamente, yo no podía competir. Está claro que sus padres se avergonzaron de su comportamiento en la fiesta de aquella noche. Su padre se disculpó y me acompañó a casa en coche, pero yo permanecí indiferente y seguí como siempre. Continué saliendo con él y disfrutando de nuestros momentos como pareja, pero no me sentía ligada a él de ningún modo. No le había entregado mi corazón. Ahora sé, sin lugar a dudas, que mi apatía era signo de indiferencia. Cuando todo terminó, continuamos siendo buenos amigos y, durante un considerable periodo de tiempo, ocupamos un lugar especial en el corazón del otro. Siempre me sentiré agradecida por el tiempo que pasamos juntos.

Cuando me encontraba en compañía de Enrique, la timidez originada por mis manchas faciales parecía convertirse en una preocupación sin fin. A pesar de mis mayores esfuerzos, siempre había algo o alguien que me recordaba lo que yo consideraba como una imperfección ineludible. Como consecuencia, relacionarme con los atractivos médicos y militares que me rodeaban (estos últimos solían ser las visitas de los pacientes ingresados en el hospital) suponía una inmensa presión. Algunos residentes y médicos muy insensibles a veces aprovechaban la oportunidad de convertirme en un espectáculo —mientras charlaban entre sí, nada menos— con el objeto de evaluar mi afección. Me sentía como si me hubieran convertido en un caso de estudio, un objeto sometido contra su voluntad al escrutinio de todos, aunque a nadie parecía importarle. Especialmente, durante mi formación clínica, algunos jactanciosos médicos señalaban descaradamente mis manchas, como si yo no estuviera allí mismo. Uno de aquellos dolorosos incidentes se me ha quedado particularmente grabado en la mente: Un médico sostuvo mi barbilla entre sus manos, sin pedirme permiso y, dirigiéndose a sus residentes, les preguntó:

—¿Esto es melanosis o melanoma?

Retirándome ligeramente, logré apartar la cara de sus manos. Me sentí humillada y desmoralizada más allá de todo límite y me pregunté para mis adentros: «¿Por qué yo?». Aquella situación sirvió para exacerbar los sentimientos que me había provocado el rechazo de Lorenzo. Pensaba que, a buen seguro, mi aspecto era la causa. El miedo a la exclusión y a los rechazos amorosos me engullía como una nube negra, y me ocultaba aún más tras un velo autoimpuesto de retraimiento (o esa era la sensación que producía mi comportamiento en los demás), pues ignoraba a todos aquellos que pudieran estar remotamente interesados en mí. Me relacionaba y me identificaba con aquellos que tenían cicatrices imborrables, pues me parecía que no había manera posible de borrar mi humillación.

Mi sentimiento de encontrarme fuera de lugar aumentó una tarde que un muchachito entró en la consulta de pediatría y comentó:

—Eres guapa, pero te tienes que borrar todas esas manchas de la cara.

Cuando le expliqué que no se podía, simplemente me miró con curiosidad. De nuevo, volví a subir mi escudo protector, hecho de acero. Cuando llegué a mi segundo año, un guapo residente se me acercó en las rondas clínicas para preguntarme si quería ir a cenar con él, pero lo rechacé categóricamente, asegurándole, aunque no era cierto, que me estaba viendo con otra persona. Sin añadir ni una palabra más, me marché. En mis momentos de tranquilidad posteriores, me avergonzaba al pensar en lo que había hecho. No, más bien, me odiaba a mí misma. Mi autoestima era tan frágil que no me permitía disfrutar de la compañía masculina. Alrededor de mis compañeros de trabajo me sentía igualmente incómoda, a menos, claro está, que conociera a la gente con la que me encontraba. En todo momento, llevaba encima barras de labios y maquillaje corrector. Sin aquellos instrumentos de defensa, me sentía desnuda, al descubierto, como si mis manchas fueran la prueba de algún delito. Aquel sentimiento de baja autoestima fue el sello distintivo de mi conducta en posteriores relaciones amorosas, sobre las que hablaré más adelante. Baste decir, no obstante, que lo que yo pensaba de mí misma en aquella primera época —básicamente, durante mis años de formación— se manifestó claramente en mi vida posterior y modeló profundamente mi carácter.

Me enorgullece decir que, actualmente, he evolucionado, y hago gala de la confianza que tengo en mí misma como si se tratara de la piedra preciosa más refinada. Si alguien osara tratarme ahora como hizo aquel médico altanero hace tantos años, le diría lo que pienso y reafirmaría mi personalidad.

—¡Quíteme las manos de encima! —le espetaría mi yo actual—. ¡No soy un objeto de exposición! ¡Préstele atención a los sentimientos de la gente antes de optar por emplearlos como conejillos de indias! El valor de cada persona no puede medirse. ¡Cómo se atreve a tratar a nadie como si fuera un monstruo de feria!

Por cierto, la mujer que, hipotéticamente, proferiría estas palabras ya no tiene manchas faciales. Ahora, echando la vista atrás hacia mi pasado, comprendo nítidamente que la fuente de mi enorme dolor sirvió, en realidad, de catalizador para mi crecimiento personal.

No obstante, algunas experiencias no sirven para ningún propósito aparente, excepto para demostrar la arrogante serenidad y falta de tacto de ciertas personas. Me viene a la mente un claro ejemplo. Continué aclimatándome a la ciudad saliendo con mi amiga, Carolina, que era aproximadamente siete u ocho años mayor que yo. Tenía la sensación de que ella y sus amigos eran muy sofisticados y me agradaba mucho estar con ellos. Una noche, fuimos a una discoteca donde un oficial de la marina, ataviado con su uniforme completo, me preguntó si quería bailar con él. Acepté. La pista de baile estaba a oscuras, pero por el contorno del rostro del oficial, supe que era extraordinariamente atractivo. Me atrajo hacia él y chocó contra mí deliberadamente en varias ocasiones. Entonces, cuidadosamente me cogió la mano y me guió hacia la zona inferior de su cuerpo donde albergaba sus atributos masculinos, que, lo único que puedo decir tratando de escoger un vocabulario lo más delicado posible, es que estaban en su máximo apogeo.

—Este es el efecto que tienes en mí —me dijo.

No sé cómo sería Adán, pero dudo que, de haber estado en el Jardín del Edén durante el Génesis, hubiera descubierto una expresión más prominente de masculinidad. Lejos de sentirme halagada, me produjo repulsión y me sentí ofendida por la osadía del oficial. ¿Cómo se atrevía? Sin duda, me veía como un objeto, más que como un ser humano. Confundida, conmocionada y temerosa, le dije a Carolina que quería marcharme a casa. Hasta ahora no había vuelto a contar esta historia. Ya había supuesto que tenía que esperar a mi renacimiento, una especie de génesis personal con introspección y retrospectiva sobre el mundo del que vine y el futuro al que me estaba encaminando.

Aun así, más trampolines hacia la evolución me esperaban cuando, durante mi tercer año en la escuela de enfermería, Carolina (que, por entonces, trabajaba en los departamentos de neurología y neurocirugía), me presentó a los médicos y enfermeras de las rotaciones, que me invitaron a formar parte de su equipo. En mi primera tarea como enfermera primeriza, Carolina me presentó al Dr. S., un fascinante neurocirujano, cuyo atractivo aspecto solo lo superaba su intelecto. De hecho, creo que me sentía atraída hacia él, pero desempeñaba más bien la figura de mi mentor que de un posible amante. Aunque estaba soltero en aquel momento, más tarde se casó con una de mis compañeras del departamento de neurología.

En una ocasión, yo estaba trabajando en el turno de noche, el Dr. S. me ayudó a ocuparme del cuerpo de un paciente que acababa de fallecer. Mi supervisor se enfureció y me reprendió con severidad por «no hacer mi trabajo». Instantáneamente, el Dr. S. salió en mi defensa.

—Isabella no me ha pedido que la ayude —insistió—. Yo me he ofrecido. Ella es nueva, y yo quería ayudarla.

Me sentí profundamente conmovida y nunca olvidé al Dr. S. por su amabilidad.

Desgraciadamente, el Dr. S. acabó por ser víctima de una destrucción autoimpuesta. Por muy brillante que fuera, su adicción al Valium y al alcohol terminó con él. Yo me enteré de esto por casualidad, cuando un auxiliar de enfermería que iba caminando rápidamente un día por la unidad, se chocó conmigo y se le cayó una bandeja de Valium por todo el suelo. Cuando le pregunté para quién era aquel medicamento, me respondió apresuradamente:

—No es para mí. Es para el Dr. S., que lo toma muy a menudo.

Me quedé conmocionada. Se lo conté a Carolina, que conocía los hechos, como todos los demás. Sin embargo, nadie se molestó por crear problemas por la adicción del Dr. S., pues era un gran profesional, incluso cuando, aparentemente, acudía al quirófano de neurocirugía bajo la influencia del alcohol y de medicamentos con receta. A pesar de aquella sorprendente realidad, siempre fue el mejor médico del hospital. Además, su autenticidad era uno de sus rasgos distintivos de carácter, y todo el mundo tenía únicamente cosas buenas que decir sobre él y sus tratamientos.

Cuando he dicho que sus adicciones terminaron con él, lo digo de manera totalmente literal. Muchos años después de que yo me marchara de Perú, su esposa trató de despertarlo una mañana, pero lo encontró inerte. Evidentemente, la noche anterior había vuelto a casa en estado de embriaguez y se ahogó mientras dormía. Como todos los que conocíamos al Dr. S., me venció la incredulidad y la tristeza. Me pregunté cómo podría haberle arrebatado la vida el alcohol a una persona tan brillante, atractiva y dotada como él. Nunca llegué a comprender una desolación semejante.

En retrospectiva, recordando el horror del prematuro fallecimiento del Dr. S., lo comparé a mi antigua afinidad por Enrique. Me di cuenta entonces de que, de haber seguido con él, habría terminado exactamente igual que la esposa del Dr. S. —una viuda desconsolada, lamentándose de la muerte sin sentido de su marido en la flor misma de su vida—, ¿y con qué propósito? ¡Por amor, está claro que no! Claramente, yo no estaba enamorada de Enrique, y estar con él habría supuesto un innegable sacrificio. Además, si él me hubiera querido realmente como decía, habría hecho todo lo posible por controlar su adicción, por amor, aunque no hubiera sido por nada más. Eso es lo que significa el amor: superar las debilidades y las flaquezas por un bien mutuo mayor. Quizás esto suene idealista, pero, especialmente si, en nombre del compromiso, uno no puede aspirar a lograr los principios de conducta más elevados, ¿cómo podemos los seres humanos esperar conseguir relaciones duraderas? El amor tendría que significar un toma y daca, un intercambio incondicional —en todos los aspectos—, con los ojos bien abiertos y la disposición para rectificar las imperfecciones evidentes que se interponen en el camino de la felicidad real.

Ahora comprendo que todas mis experiencias en la escuela de enfermería servían como anécdotas secundarias de la verdad. Con esto, quiero decir que, a medida que presenciaba y experimentaba más y más cosas, iba interiorizándolas silenciosamente, en diálogo conmigo misma. Sin definir mis acciones o intenciones, estaba haciendo balance de mi pasado que, mientras lo vivía, era una expresión rutinaria y mecánica de lo que yo era verdaderamente. Las imágenes reflejadas que resurgían para mí en el preludio de mi carrera profesional —la inseguridad, el miedo, las dudas sobre mí misma, un corazón hecho trizas...— colocaban en perspectiva todo lo que había pasado siendo niña. Estaba lista para seguir avanzando. De lo que no me di cuenta fue de que las crueldades de la vida podían golpearme de un modo que mi corazón apenas podría soportarlo —circunstancias que hasta me impedirían respirar—, incluso en los días más oscuros de mi vida, cuando no lograba encontrar razón alguna...

Capítulo 6

De héroes y cobardes

Si no llego a decidir convertirme en enfermera, lo más seguro es que hubiera estudiado medicina veterinaria. Siempre se me dio bien —y creo que sigue siendo así— trabajar e interactuar con nuestros amigos de cuatro patas, nuestros vecinos habitantes de este planeta. Parte de ser proveedora de cuidados y sanadora reside en la capacidad de sentir empatía por todos los seres vivos. El respeto y cariño por otras especies es parte integral de la experiencia humana completa. Por lo tanto, al escribir mi propia historia, sería una negligencia por mi parte si omitiera mencionar algunos seres importantes en mi vida que me han dejado una huella permanente en el corazón, cada uno de ellos de forma distinta, pero muy significativa.

Una de estas valientes criaturas pertenecientes a mi mundo fue *Clipper*, mi adorado perrillo de ojos azules, al que le enseñé a bailar y a hacer como que se fumaba un cigarrillo mientras se ponía a dos patas. Era monísimo. Fue mi perro mientras vivíamos en Nicrupampa. En aquella época, era una verdadera bola de pelo algodonoso, mi fiel compañero, que venía conmigo en la parte trasera de la camioneta de papá, disfrutando de las corrientes de aire que nos revolvían a mí el cabello y a él su pelaje: Mis largos mechones flotando a mis espaldas y el suave pelo de *Clipper* agitándose de forma similar. Tras el terremoto, caminábamos juntos a través de las fangosas calles de Nicrupampa, húmedas y embarradas, como dos vagabundos en un mundo perdido. Por desgracia, tuve que dejarlo al cuidado de mi madre durante mis estudios de enfermería en Lima. Tendría que habérmelo pensado dos veces, porque *Clipper* desapareció de la casa y nadie supo qué había sido de él. Se me rompió el corazón.

Cuando regresé a casa por vacaciones en mi segundo año, visité un mercado al aire libre con mi madre y Victoria, la joven ama de llaves que me había ayudado a superar mis episodios de pubertad. De repente, un perro de aspecto desaliñado se me acercó y comenzó a saltar arriba y abajo junto a mí. Al principio, me dio miedo, ¡pero pronto me di cuenta de que aquel cariñoso can no era otro que mi *Clipper*, extraviado hacía tanto tiempo! Sorprendida, comencé a acariciarlo y a hablarle, hasta que una señora bastante corpulenta se aproximó y me dijo:

—¿Quién eres tú? ¿Mi perro te conoce?

—¿Su perro? —le pregunté yo a mi vez—. Yo soy la dueña de este perro.

La mujer pasó a explicarme que había encontrado a *Clipper* hacía un año. Estaba vagabundeando sin rumbo fijo, así que se lo llevó a casa, y lo apareó con su perra, con la que tenía cachorritos.

—¡*Clipper* es padre y tiene una familia propia! —exclamé, profiriendo un grito ahogado.

Con todo el dolor de mi corazón, me despedí de mi *Clipper* y de su nueva dueña. ¿Qué otra opción me quedaba?

Clipper me proporcionó esa otra opción. Parece increíble, pero mientras yo estaba en casa durante una visita de un mes, *Clipper* se presentó en la puerta, con cortes y laceraciones bajo un ojo... Aparentemente, eran las condecoraciones de haberse metido en una pelea de perros. ¡Incluso estando en peligro (o quizás, precisamente a causa de ello, en un intento por buscar ayuda), *Clipper* había recordado dónde vivía y quién era su dueña anterior! No era ningún cobarde. Sabía dónde podía encontrar un hogar y dónde le proporcionarían un tratamiento adecuado. Mientras escribo esto, tengo que contener las lágrimas solo de pensar en su inconmensurable devoción. Lo dejé entrar y fui a la farmacia a comprar los objetos necesarios para curarlo. Me puse guantes limpios, me ocupé de sus heridas, las lavé y lo acomodé en una cómoda caja con el interior acolchado. Lo mantuve allí, vigilándolo constantemente y sometiéndole a una dieta blanda. Transcurrieron un par de semanas, y a medida que se iba sintiendo bien alimentado y querido, mi *Clipper* comenzó a recuperarse y a correr por la casa, como nuevo. Durante su proceso de recuperación, sus hermosos ojos azules parecieron adquirir una especie de bizquera, confiriéndole un curioso rictus a su expresión. No pude más que echarme a reír, pues estaba más entrañable que nunca.

Para mi desgracia, la estancia en casa de *Clipper* solamente duró el tiempo que se prolongaron mis vacaciones de la escuela.

Cuando me marché a Lima, él decidió regresar con su familia. Aunque no volví a verlo nunca más, sigo visualizándolo en mi mente, siempre resucitando una época alegre que nunca volverá.

En mi tercer año de la escuela de enfermería, fui bendecida, una vez más, con otro tesoro de nuestro ecosistema terrestre. Laura y yo decidimos subir a nuestra terraza a contemplar el día de conmemoración del capitán Miguel Grau, héroe de la batalla naval de Angamos, que tuvo lugar en la Guerra del Pacífico (1879-1884). Durante este festejo, se veía a la gente haciendo saludos, con las palmas de las manos sobre el pecho, en gesto de solemne recuerdo. Mientras mirábamos a nuestro alrededor, Laura vio un pequeño periquito verde. Parecía bastante modosito y necesitado de un hogar. Eso es lo que al menos nosotras sentimos en el interior de nuestros corazones. Así pues, Laura echó su jersey sobre el pajarillo y nos lo llevamos abajo, a nuestra casa. De ese modo, comenzó la estancia de nuestro pequeño y hermoso *Miguel* con nosotros. Sí, lo bautizamos así en nombre del héroe y, claramente, estaba a la altura de aquel nombre. Al principio, por supuesto, se comportaba de forma tímida, pero después de que le recortáramos las alas y lo alimentáramos con migas de pan y fruta, pareció adaptarse bien a la vida en el hogar y se convirtió en una mascota extraordinaria. Cuando yo regresaba del hospital, allí estaba *Miguel*, dándome la bienvenida. A menudo, yo me colocaba un trozo de papel de cocina en el hombro, que él utilizaba como almohadilla para descansar, despegar y aterrizar, volando de acá para allá, como un minúsculo avioncito. Era verdaderamente encantador. Traté de enseñarle a hablar, pero, de algún modo, no estaba genéticamente predispuesto para la elocución. Al darse cuenta de aquella carencia, heroicamente trataba de proferir toda clase de sonidos para complacerme: borboteos, silbidos, ruiditos y gorjeos de todo tipo. Su devoción hacia nosotras era inagotable. Incluso cuando le crecieron las alas, nunca trató de marcharse.

Miguel desapareció durante un día entero, cosa que me produjo una gran angustia. Cuando volví a casa de la escuela, no lo encontré por ninguna parte. Ni siquiera nuestra ama de llaves tenía idea de dónde se habría marchado. Al anochecer, comencé a preocuparme y ofrecí una recompensa a lo niños del vecindario que lograran encontrármelo. «Debe haberse ido volando», pensé para mis adentros, tratando en vano de luchar contra la pena. Más tarde, esa misma noche, salí a la terraza, donde Laura y yo nos habíamos encontrado por primera vez con nuestro alado compañero. Suavemente lo llamé y oí: «¡Pip!». Y luego otra vez: «¡Pip!». Seguí el sonido y detecté que provenía del desván. Conforme iba siguiendo el silbido, crecía en intensidad a medida que me aproximaba. Entonces, de debajo de una sábana, el ruidito parecía emanar aún más alto... y allí estaba, mi héroe, casi asfixiado bajo su escondite. Se echó a volar, feliz como una perdiz —o más bien, debería decir: «Feliz como un periquito»—, agradecidísimo de que lo hubiera encontrado. Más tarde, descubrí que, cuando nuestra ama de llaves había subido al desván, *Miguel* debía de haberla seguido y se había quedado atrapado bajo la sábana. Todavía siento cómo se me acelera el corazón cuando pienso en el feliz momento en el que nos reunimos de nuevo.

Durante aproximadamente un año, mi delicado amigo continuó siendo la fuente de entretenimiento de todos aquellos que le conocían. La vecina de al lado tenía varios niños que le cogieron muchísimo cariño a *Miguel* y le pidieron a su padre ausente (que solamente visitaba a su familia una vez al mes) que les consiguiera un periquito exactamente igual que nuestro pequeñín. El padre, que al parecer les concedía todos sus caprichos, llegó a casa un día con un loro adulto parlante. Aquel pájaro era locuaz. Podría haberse presentado a algunas elecciones, con lo imponente que resultaba su pose y su capacidad para hablar. (No es mi intención ofender a los políticos con cargo, por supuesto. Cualquiera que ocupe un puesto así se sentiría bastante halagado de ser comparado con aquella espléndida criatura emplumada). Una tarde, los niños insistieron en que yo les llevara de visita a su diminuto homólogo; supongo que con la intención de alardear de las ostensibles diferencias que había entre ellos. *Miguel* no era un pájaro extravagante. Él se comportaba como él mismo, sin tratar nunca de impresionar a los demás, solo intentando agradar. No tenía nada especial que hacer aquel día en particular, así que hice lo que me pedían. Nunca olvidaré cómo mi lindo y diminuto héroe le echó un vistazo a aquel formidable pájaro y no perdió tiempo en echarse a correr. El otro arrancó a andar como un pato, siguiéndolo de cerca mientras le chillaba: «¡Cobarde, cobarde!». Aquel episodio fue tan desternillante, que se me saltaron las lágrimas, aunque a *Miguel* no lo divirtió en absoluto. Tuve que llevármelo a casa inmediatamente.

Varios meses más tarde, el perro de mi hermano Tomás, que se llamaba *Ramón*, un perro salchicha, se dedicó a jugar violentamente con Miguel, como tenía por costumbre. Cuando yo llegué a casa, me encontré a la ama de llaves llorando, con nuestro queridísimo pajarillo entre las manos. *Miguel* estaba expirando. Al parecer, *Ramón* le había golpeado con demasiada agresividad en el lugar equivocado. Laura y yo lloramos su pérdida. Es increíble cómo conmovió aquella criaturilla nuestros corazones y nuestras vidas con su increíble y dinámica personalidad y su ternura. ¡Con qué sorpresas puede bendecirte la naturaleza, simplemente si abres tu corazón, incluso a las formas de vida más insignificantes! Todos tenemos algo que enseñarnos los unos a los otros, y mi héroe me enseñó esta gran lección.

Deseábamos enterrar a *Miguel* en nuestro jardín, pero viendo lo tristes que nos habíamos quedado tras su pérdida, un amigo insistió en llevarse su cuerpecillo. No teníamos ni idea de cuál era su intención, pero le confiamos los preciados restos mortales. Pasaron dos semanas, y nuestro amigo regresó con la viva imagen de *Miguel* sentada en una rama, una creación taxidérmica. Entonces, tuvimos que cederlo de nuevo, cuando papá se lo llevó para guardarlo en una vitrina de cristal en su despacho. Bajo el minúsculo pajarillo hay una placa inscrita con su nombre, la fecha en la que lo encontramos, y la fecha en la que murió. De este modo, nuestro amigo quedó inmortalizado. En realidad, yo no sabía si sentir repulsión o agradecimiento, pero sospecho que, después de todos estos años, me decanto hacia lo segundo, junto con nuestros incontables recuerdos de cariño, diversión y risa.

Puede parecer extraño comparar una historia humana con las narradas aquí y, de hecho, no existe ninguna correlación aparente entre ellas y el acontecimiento que voy a relatar a continuación, excepto porque la verdad más profunda, como veréis, es que todas esta relaciones estaban imbuidas de los tres elementos siguientes: un inmenso cariño, el sentimiento de pérdida y la capacidad de pasar página.

Yo nací para ser una profesional sanitaria y, a lo largo de toda mi vida —hasta hoy mismo—, sigo comprometida con ese objetivo. Desempeñar un oficio en ese campo exige como características personales la compasión, la resolución y la capacidad de tener un propósito, características que pongo en práctica en todos mis círculos y a todos los niveles en los que interactúo: un intercambio generoso y desinteresado tanto con los seres humanos como con los animales. En el caso de los seres humanos, el cariño y amor mutuos son fuerzas que, cuando se comunican de forma sincera, nos proporcionan la posibilidad de trascender a todos los demás tipos de intercambio y alcanzan la máxima expresión.

Con Lorenzo, mi primer amor, se me presentó esa oportunidad dos veces. La primera tuvo lugar cuando yo era una jovencita adolescente que acababa de enamorarse, explorando el alcance de mi floreciente adolescencia y anhelando el afecto y la aprobación de los demás. El segundo episodio aconteció durante mi último año en la escuela de enfermería, cuando yo tenía dieciocho años. Para mí, durante aquel paréntesis, las cosas habían cambiado. Prácticamente de la nada, recibí una llamada de mi tía, que estaba saliendo con el tío de Lorenzo. Frenéticamente, me contó que Lorenzo y su nueva novia, Zoila, habían sido víctimas de un terrible accidente. Mientras cruzaban la calle, un automóvil con un solo faro (por lo que, erróneamente, lo tomaron por una motocicleta) los atropelló frontalmente. Sin posibilidad de apartarse al borde de la carretera, ambos fueron víctimas del impacto. Milagrosamente, Zoila solo padeció laceraciones y una contusión, pero Lorenzo salió bastante peor parado. Tenía múltiples heridas faciales y fracturas por todo el cuerpo, la más grave de las cuales era la del fémur. Para colmo de males, se quedó inconsciente y permaneció en coma durante quince días. Comprendiendo que Lorenzo necesitaba inmediatamente una intervención médica experta, mi tía me convenció para que intentara que lo admitieran en mi hospital, que era uno de los más prestigiosos de todo el país. El problema era que Lorenzo no formaba parte del ejército, así que, haciendo un gran esfuerzo emocional —y con no poca buena fortuna—, tuve que mover unos cuantos hilos.

La suerte quiso que Ana, una de mis compañeras de clase, tuviera una relación con el director general del hospital, al que llamaré Dr. B. Audazmente y reuniendo todo mi valor, le pedí a Ana que me presentara al eminente galeno con la intención de discutir la premura del caso de Lorenzo. Ana así lo hizo, y yo fui al despacho del Dr. B, vestida de punta en blanco y armada de valor gracias a mi profunda convicción. Le expliqué la situación de Lorenzo y le pregunté si «mi primo», a pesar de no pertenecer al ejército, podía ser ingresado en el hospital. Guiñándome el ojo con una expresión pícara, el Dr. B. respondió:

—Si es para tu primo, entonces, por supuesto.

Exhalando un suspiro de alivio, me marché a casa para contárselo a mi tía que, a su vez, le comunicó la noticia al padre de Lorenzo. La gratitud de aquel hombre fue verdaderamente abrumadora. Yo me sentía también demasiado feliz por haber sido de utilidad. El corazón nunca olvida y siempre mantiene una puerta abierta, aunque no de forma romántica, sí de otras maneras, a veces incluso más significativas.

Así pues, mi antiguo amor fue transferido de un hospital de Trujillo al cuidado especializado del lugar en el que yo trabajaba. Para entonces, Lorenzo ya había salido del coma, y yo me sentí emocionada ante la perspectiva de volver a verle después de tanto tiempo. Por supuesto, aún estaba muy débil e indispuesto, pero me reconoció. Los detalles de su pasado, sin embargo, seguían resultándole poco precisos. Su fiel novia, Zoila, acudió religiosamente todos los días para velarlo y para atenderlo y estar junto a él. Incluso solicitó, y le concedieron, un puesto de nutricionista en un instituto cercano. Por muy mala suerte que yo hubiera podido tener en el amor, me conmovieron profundamente las atenciones que le prodigaba a su novio. Por eso, os resultará fácil imaginaros lo aturdida que me quedé cuando presencié el cruel rechazo hacia ella por parte de Lorenzo cuando recuperó todas sus fuerzas y el conocimiento.

—¿Todavía me quieres? —exclamó un día dirigiéndose a mí, agarrándome de la mano cuando fui a visitarle y a ver qué tal estaba en la sala de recuperación.

«¿¿¿Cómo???», me dije para mis adentros. ¿No me estaban engañando mis oídos? ¿Cómo podía estar pasando una cosa así? Había estado enamorada de un donjuán y, de haberme quedado con él, me habría roto el corazón en pedacitos y, probablemente, mi vida habría quedado desprovista de calidad y de la posibilidad de tener otras relaciones significativas. Lorenzo no representaba más que un fantasma, un mero producto de mi imaginación juvenil, aunque, no puedo negarlo, alguien a quien le había entregado mi corazón sin remordimientos. En aquel momento, allí en el hospital, me quedé helada, sin pronunciar palabra. Mi silencio simbolizaba una verdad infinita. Aquello sencillamente no era lo que debía ocurrir. Yo era algo mayor entonces y, definitivamente, más sensata y más capaz de tomar decisiones razonables, y eso fue lo que hice. Fue aquel un momento de confusión, pero me siento innegablemente orgullosa de mí misma. En aquel instante, rescaté a mi propio corazón.

Al igual que por *Clipper* y por *Miguel*, había sentido cariño por Lorenzo, le había querido con todo mi corazón, había hecho sacrificios y excepciones por él y, entonces, tuve que pasar página. Una vez más, debo explicar —aunque no me disculpo por ello— la aparente incongruencia de la historia de Lorenzo con respecto a las de mis adoradas mascotas, pero los tres elementos, el amor, la pérdida y la capacidad de pasar página estuvieron irrefutablemente presentes en cada caso. ¿No es acaso cierto que todos los interrogantes de la vida suelen girar en torno a dichos elementos? Puede que sí, pero debía avanzar mucho más y tenía mucho más por descubrir. Mi corazón no había terminado todavía de experimentar sentimientos, de hecho, todavía le quedaba mucho más. Lo que no podía imaginarme era lo mucho que me quedaba por invertir y, trágicamente, lo mucho a lo que tendría que renunciar.

Capítulo 7

La paloma

La paloma

Si a tu ventana llega
una paloma,
trátala con cariño,
que es mi persona.

Sebastián Yradier, compositor (1809-1865)

La vida está compuesta por una serie de elementos diametralmente opuestos —emociones, sentimientos y acontecimientos que normalmente recaen sobre nuestros hombros todos a la vez—, mezclas de alegrías y penas, dolor y placer, pérdidas y beneficios. Por lo tanto, resulta natural, queridos lectores, que mi propia historia contenga una amalgama de estas contradicciones. En este momento, llego a un punto de mi narración cargado de tristeza; un capítulo de mi historia en el que el pesar se posó en el alféizar de mi ventana como una siniestra aparición, transportándome a las profundidades más hondas de mi alma. Antes de poder seguir adelante, tuve que visitar de nuevo ese lugar —bastante en contra de mi voluntad y a pesar de la enorme desesperación y dolor que me produce—

hasta que, una vez más, pude renacer a la luz. No necesitáis asustaros o (absteneros de leer) lo que estoy a punto de relatar, porque estoy segura de vosotros también habéis experimentado fluctuaciones similares en la vida de muchas maneras distintas. ¿Quién podría ser inmune a algo así? Dadme la mano y acompañadme en este viaje a través de mi particular túnel de dolor, para que podamos salir de nuevo juntos a la luz.

Imágenes, sonidos, olores —todos ellos bullen ante mí como tenues recuerdos de mi pasado—, y todos forman parte del interrogante de los opuestos. Precisamente ayer, mientras iba de camino hacia una clase de pintura, un suculento aroma a comida china llenó por completo mi sentido del olfato. ¡Ñam! Kam Lu wantán frito, esa crujiente delicia china, ¡la favorita de Laura, y también la mía! «¿Dónde puedo encontrarla?», me pregunté a mí misma. Hasta ayer mismo, ningún restaurante chino que yo hubiera probado en Estados Unidos había logrado satisfacer mi petición. Y justamente ayer, un familiar antojo se me alojó en el cerebro, provocando que recordara un memorable momento del pasado, que nunca jamás podría volver a repetirse... Hasta ayer, cuando volví a experimentar aquel sabor. Durante mi primer año en la escuela de enfermería, probé aquel delicioso plato a escondidas. Ya veis, en aquella época me extirparon las amígdalas y tenía que guardar una estricta dieta compuesta únicamente por gelatina y líquidos. El hambre me dominó como un monstruo feroz, atrapándome entre sus garras. Y allí entró mi dulce hermana al rescate, como siempre solía hacer. Me hizo una visita en el hospital una tarde, en un momento en el que yo debía de tener seguramente el hambre pintada en la expresión de mi rostro.

—¿Cómo te encuentras, Isabella? —me preguntó mi hermana con ternura.

—Tengo muchísima hambre, pero no me permiten comer, y no lo soporto ni un minuto más.

—¿Qué puedo hacer por ti? —me preguntó mi benevolente salvadora, que resolvía todos mis males.

—Me muero por comer Kam Lu wantán frito —dije yo salivando, casi imaginándome el sabor de aquella delicia.

—Vuelvo en un momento.

Mi hermana se marchó a toda prisa y pronto regresó para colmar mi deseo. Ella siempre lograba cumplir y superar mis expectativas. Escondí el Kam Lu wantán frito bajo las sábanas, por si acaso entraba la enfermera y me sorprendía con las manos en la masa. Mi hermana, mi ángel de la guarda, se quedó junto a la puerta, vigilando, mientras me sonreía y me reprendía por masticar demasiado fuerte.

—¡Silencio! —Me ordenaba con dulzura, llevándose un dedo a los labios.

Efectivamente, en cuanto terminé de devorar la comida prohibida, entró una enfermera en mi habitación.

—¡Algo huele bien por aquí! —sentenció, contemplándome con recelo.

Laura y yo simplemente nos miramos, sin decir una palabra. Qué fechoría más sabrosa... ¡y que hizo que mi estado de salud empeorara! Un par de dosis de medicación antiinflamatoria para la garganta después, y me sentí como nueva.

Tenía la sensación de que todo eso había sucedido ayer mismo, ¿o no?, cuando probé el primer bocado de aquel familiar Kam Lu wantán frito y me deleité con su sabor. ¡Un momento! ¿Cómo he llegado hasta ese punto, es decir, hasta aquí? Ah, sí, de nuevo, hablaba de mi hermana. Fue ella la que me trajo a Estados Unidos y a mi actual estado de conciencia. Fue, y siempre será, mi hermana.

Una mañana, vestida con su jersey verde tejido a mano, pantalones negros y zapatos, con un bolso grande colgado del hombro derecho, Laura se giró de lado, en el exterior de la puerta trasera.

—¡Chao, Isabella! —me dijo, contemplándome con recelo y añoranza, como si la tristeza envolviera todo su ser.

Me pregunté por qué... y sigo preguntándomelo, aunque ahora no constituye un misterio tan grande para mí. Aquel estado de ánimo no era típico de mi Laura, normalmente tan risueña. Aparte de aquella breve despedida, no sucedió nada especial aquel día. En aquel momento, yo era enfermera diplomada y trabajaba en la clínica militar. Ocurrió que aquel era mi día libre, que solía pasar simplemente relajándome o viendo la televisión. Para ser sincera, ahora mismo no lo recuerdo. Disfruté de mi descanso, sin pensar en nada, simplemente deleitándome de la total falta de reflexión.

No me acordaba de que, justamente dos días antes de percibir aquella expresión triste de mi hermana tan poco habitual en ella, Laura había tenido una pesadilla de tal magnitud que se vino a dormir conmigo, en mi propia cama.

—¡He tenido un sueño terrible! —exclamó, profundamente angustiada—. He soñado que algo muy pesado me aplastaba todo el cuerpo y no podía moverme. ¡Tengo mucho miedo! Por favor, ¡déjame quedarme contigo!

No pude evitar recordar que, quince minutos después, ambas dejamos escapar unos gritos espeluznantes cuando nuestro hermano, Tomás, se abalanzó sobre nuestra cama con tal fuerza, que nos imaginamos que estábamos en medio de otro terremoto. Al ver la cama de Laura abierta aquella mañana y pensándose que nuestra hermana se había marchado para asistir a alguna fiesta con Xavier, había venido en busca de Laura.

—¿Cómo te atreves a asustarnos así? —exclamé.

Tras varios segundos de terror, comprendí que nuestro hermano se estaba comportando como de costumbre.

No me paré a pensar que, varias semanas antes, Laura se había encontrado con una vidente en la plaza principal frente al Tribunal Supremo, donde estaba llevando a cabo sus prácticas de Derecho. La mujer detuvo a mi hermana por casualidad —en gran parte contra su voluntad, pues Laura estaba a punto de montarse en el autobús— y le ofreció el siguiente consejo:

—¡Ten cuidado, niña! —exclamó, tomándola de la mano y mirándole la palma—. No vas a disfrutar de una vida demasiado larga. ¡Cuídate!

Aquel encuentro fue terriblemente extraño, especialmente dado que estas supuestas adivinas no ofrecían sus consejos sin más, ni hacían gala de sus habilidades sin algún tipo de compensación a cambio. Por supuesto, Laura no buscó, y ni siquiera lo quería, el consejo de la señora, y no pago ni un solo penique por aquellos comentarios no solicitados.

Fuera de sí por el miedo, mi hermana regresó a casa llorando a lágrima viva y me contó la historia.

—Si algo te pasara, ¡no podría seguir viviendo! —exclamó, abrazándome—. Espero que yo sea la que muera primero, ¡pues no podría soportar perderte! ¡Te quiero tanto! —Entonces, añadió—: Si algo me sucediera, piensa en mí, Isabella, y ten por seguro que estaré contigo. Te mandaré alguna señal.

Recuerdo que mi hermana solía cantar una canción sobre una paloma, titulada precisamente *La paloma*, que es muy conocida en muchos países en todo el mundo. De algún modo, siempre he asociado esa canción con Laura. Parecía ser tan apropiada para ella.

Si a tu ventana llega
una paloma,
trátala con cariño,
que es mi persona.

En aquella época, sabía que el símbolo de la paloma tenía un significado especial, pero no me imaginaba el profundo impacto que tendría en mi propia vida.

Como hermana pequeña de Laura, solo de pensar en su ausencia hizo que entrara en pánico. Me entristecí muchísimo y le dije que no debía volver a hablar o a pensar de aquella manera. Habíamos pasado tantas cosas juntas, incluido el catastrófico terremoto que había hecho pedazos nuestros sueños juveniles de felicidad perpetua, habíamos perdido a conocidos y amigos, habíamos soportado juntas males de amores, habíamos resucitado de nuestras cenizas entre risas... Y, a fin de cuentas, ¡habíamos sobrevivido! Por lo tanto, en cualquier momento dado, pensar en no tener a Laura a mi lado me resultaba inconcebible. A lo largo de todas nuestras sonrisas y lágrimas, ella siempre había estado allí para mí, como mi relaciones públicas, mi confidente y mi compañera: la mejor amiga con la que podía charlar hasta altas horas de la madrugada sobre cualquier cosa: libros, películas o la vida misma. Puesto que estoy predispuesta a buscar el placer —al igual que cualquier otro ser humano—, opto por evocar el néctar, la dulce contemplación de aquel día en Miraflores, un exclusivo barrio de Lima, con boutiques de ropa y otras tiendas de lujo. Mientras paseábamos juntas por allí, levanté la mirada y vi un hermosísimo y elegante vestido azul de alta costura con una banda en la cintura. Debieron de iluminárseme los ojos, porque mi hermana me contempló con una mirada de complicidad. Era capaz de percibir todas y cada una de mis emociones.

—¡Ni lo sueñes! —le dije yo—. ¡Es demasiado caro!

Poco tiempo después, Laura recibió su primer cheque por vender electrodomésticos en una feria internacional. En lugar en gastarse el dinero en sí misma, pensó en mí: exactamente como siempre había hecho. Cuando regresé a casa de la escuela, encontré una enorme caja en la mesa junto a mi cama. La abrí y encontré... ¡el vestido! Me emocioné tanto que casi lloré de alegría. Dentro, había una hermosa tarjeta que ponía: «Para mi hermana pequeña de tu hermana mayor, que te quiere».

No logro recordar nada ahora, excepto aquel cariño... y excepto que aquel día aparentemente ordinario, a las nueve de la noche, me estaba lavando el pelo inclinada sobre la bañera, cuando alguien llamó estrepitosamente a mi puerta. Era Tomás, que gritaba frenéticamente mientras sostenía los zapatos negros y el bolso grande de mi hermana.

—¡Laura ha sido víctima de un gravísimo accidente de coche! ¡La policía acaba de venir a traer sus pertenencias y la han llevado a urgencias de tu hospital! ¡Voy para allá ahora mismo!

Al parecer, un médico de mi hospital iba al volante del coche, algo muy peligroso, pues probablemente conducía en estado de embriaguez. Más tarde, me enteré de que, tras atropellar a mi hermana (que iba caminando al borde de la carretera), el médico entró en pánico, salió de su coche, la recogió del suelo (algo muy poco común, dadas las circunstancias) y la llevó a urgencias.

Me quedé totalmente aturdida. Con el pelo empapado y despeinado, agarré una toalla y corrí, a lo largo de una manzana entera, hasta llegar al hospital. Cuando entré en urgencias, conmocionada y calada hasta los huesos, oí que mi hermano gritaba:

—¡No, no, Dios mío, no! ¡Mi hermana está muerta!

Tras escuchar aquellas palabras, me desplomé en el suelo. Allí, sumida en mi angustia, abrí los ojos y percibí vagamente la imagen de un rostro familiar: el de Carlos, un médico y amigo de la familia. Él apenas me reconoció, pero cuando finalmente lo hizo, exclamó:

—¡Oh, Dios mío! ¡Es la hermana pequeña de Laura, Isabella!

Sometida al efecto de unos intensos sedantes, permanecí ingresada en el hospital aquella noche. Parecía que ninguna cantidad de medicación podría mitigar o eliminar mi angustia mental y emocional. Una fuerte sensación de conmoción me embargaba como la marea, robándome la vida, descentrándome. Mi anclaje, mi hermana, que hasta ese momento prácticamente había formado parte de mí, se había perdido para siempre. Permanecí despierta toda la noche, gritando y llorando por ella. Al día siguiente, mientras un amigo me acompañaba a casa, me encontré con mi padre, que entraba en ese momento en el hospital.

—¡Oh, Dios mío! ¡Mi hija está muerta! ¡No puede ser!

Le oí decir mientras nos abrazábamos brevemente.

No existía ningún modo de gestionar aquella horrible tragedia, salvo llorando, así que eso fue lo que hice: llorar y llorar días y días sin parar. Estoy convencida de que nunca dejé de llorar; simplemente, las lágrimas se agotaban en el depósito de mi corazón, de donde volvían a brotar cuando las imágenes, sonidos, olores y recuerdos de mi juventud me vienen a raudales a la mente, como torrentes de lluvia —y como rayos de sol—, otro ejemplo más de la yuxtaposición de opuestos.

Cuando mi paloma por fin se marchó, lo hizo con honores militares. El personal del hospital se quedó tan conmocionado por la muerte de mi hermana que celebraron en su honor un funeral y un entierro insignes. Como ya he mencionado, yo ya era enfermera en la clínica militar y el médico que la había atropellado también trabajaba allí. De ese modo, en administración pensaron que era apropiado celebrar aquel selecto tributo. Aunque yo me sentí profundamente agradecida por aquellas muestras de respeto y afecto, apenas podía albergar pensamiento o sentimiento alguno a medida que luchaba contra mi tendencia natural de perder y recuperar la conciencia, derrumbándome cada vez que aquello me sucedía. En el funeral de Laura, contemplé a mi bella durmiente vestida de blanco, con un cinturón azul ciñéndole la cintura y un ramo de rosas en las manos. Sospecho que mi aversión por este tipo de flores proviene, entre otras cosas, de aquella profunda tristeza.

Mientras tanto, me sentía desvinculada de mi cuerpo, como si mi cerebro me estuviera protegiendo del profundo dolor emocional ocasionado por aquel momento: las imágenes, los sonidos, los olores y toda la experiencia completa. Era como si mi cuerpo y mi mente, de algún modo, se hubieran separado el uno de la otra en un esfuerzo por mantenerme con los pies en la tierra —aunque, aun así, no estaba completamente presente— allí, en un lugar de indescriptible luto.

Laura recibió sepultura en el quinto nivel de un intrincado mausoleo ubicado aproximadamente a media hora de casa. La noche antes de que enterráramos su forma humana, me senté en nuestra terraza, implorándole que me diera alguna muestra de su presencia eterna.

—¡Por favor, te lo ruego, envíame una señal! ¡Dijiste que lo harías! ¡No puedo vivir sin ti!

Justo en aquel instante, un pedazo de una vara de metal que había descansado hasta aquel momento contra el fregadero de la terraza, se estrelló contra el suelo. Sobresaltada, corrí de vuelta a la casa, sin pronunciar ni una palabra a la multitud de invitados. Sin duda, habrían pensado que yo había perdido la cabeza. Sin embargo, yo sabía muy bien lo que sentía. Mi hermana me acompañaba. No obstante, sí confié en Carolina, mi buena amiga y compañera. A lo largo de nuestra trágica y terrible experiencia, ella me acompañó, ayudándome incluso a maquillar a Laura para el entierro. Carolina me contó que el tercer día tras la muerte de un ser querido, el difunto repasa las fases de su vida antes de adentrarse en la Eternidad.

Aquel tercer día, nuestra casa, una vez más, se llenó de gente: parientes y otros dolientes que venían de Huaraz y de muchas otras localidades. Ya que teníamos poco espacio para dormir, Carolina y yo quedamos relegadas a hacerlo en una caravana fuera de la casa. Aquella morada rodante, equipada con camas y otras comodidades, era del hermano de papá, Luis, que vivía en Estados Unidos. Mi tío esperaba que, quizás, mi padre pudiera ayudarle a vender aquella caravana. Sin embargo, por el momento, agradecimos tener la posibilidad de utilizarla como dormitorio en ausencia de otras alternativas. De repente, mientras me quedaba dormida por efecto de una píldora para dormir, me despertó una voz clara que susurraba mi nombre: «¡Isabella! ¡Isabella! ¡Isabella!». Me tembló todo el cuerpo y, pensando que era Carolina, que dormía en la cama junto a la mía, rápidamente levanté la mirada hacia donde ella se encontraba. Mi buena amiga se hallaba profundamente dormida, ajena a la voz que yo había escuchado. Me eché a llorar, gritando:

—¡Laura está aquí, Laura está aquí!

Carolina se despertó y corrió a mi lado para consolarme. Justo en aquel momento, escuchamos el aullido lastimero de un perro en el exterior: «¡Auuuuuuuu!». En mi país, existe la creencia generalizada entre los más ancianos (una especie de cuento de viejas) de que, cuando un perro aúlla de esa manera, es que ha visto a un fantasma. Si hay o no verdad en ello, cada cual que saque sus propias conclusiones. Lo único que yo sé es que, aquella noche, mi hermana se encontraba muy cerca de mí, lo suficientemente cerca como para darme su último adiós.

Unas semanas más tarde, aún me encontraba a merced de una pena indescriptible y no era capaz de dormir ni comer bien, pero vi a Laura, mi paloma, ante mis propios ojos. Ignoro si se trataba de un producto de mi torturada mente o de una presencia real. Me encontraba en mi habitación, tumbada junto a la cama vacía de mi hermana, cuando ella apareció, tan real como cualquier persona que he conocido, sentada ante su escritorio, estudiando sus libros de derecho. Traté de hablar, pero no logré pronunciar palabra. Lo único que pude hacer fue gritar.

—¡¡¡Laura, Laura está... aquí!!!

Mi padre vino corriendo, me estrechó entre sus brazos, me abrazó con fuerza y yo sollocé de modo incontrolable.

—Ya he perdido una hija y no quiero perder otra más —me dijo, mirándome con ternura—. Puede que sea buen momento de que le hagas una visita a tu tío Luis en Estados Unidos, como solías comentar que ibas a hacer en el pasado.

Sin la presencia de ánimo suficiente para aceptar o negarme, me plegué a la sugerencia de papá. Sabía que, como siempre, su intención era buena y no podía negarme a nada que él dijera, especialmente, cuando estaba pensando en mi propio interés, como siempre hacía. Así pues, sin tener totalmente la oportunidad de llorar mi pérdida, me vi obligada a prepararme para marcharme. Mi padre lo organizó todo con el tío Luis y el

Lions Club para que yo pudiera disfrutar de un visado de estudiante, y papá pagó una considerable suma por mi billete, más todos mis gastos. Mi futuro —al menos el más inmediato— había sido decidido por mí.

Al igual que mi paloma, yo iba a alzar el vuelo hacia un país lejano, mucho más allá de las nubes, donde el dolor y la pena no podían alcanzarme... Pero, ¡no! Yo estaba intensamente aferrada a la Tierra, todavía presa de mi irrefrenable dolor. Laura era libre y, en ese sentido, quizá, más afortunada que yo. Yo tenía que seguir adelante, pero ¿cómo? Sabía que mi hermana me echaba de menos, que pensaba en mí y que me quería tanto como yo a ella. ¡Oh, si al menos hubiera tenido una última oportunidad de decírselo! ¿Cómo iba yo a saber que aquella sería mi última ocasión? ¿Cómo podemos saberlo? Y, aun así, mi hermana vivía —y aún lo hace— en el interior de mi corazón y, como revelaré más adelante, ha regresado una y otra vez de formas misteriosas, enigmáticas y profundamente conmovedoras.

Capítulo 8

Transformaciones

Cuando mi queridísima Laura trascendió a otra esfera, yo también lo hice: a Estados Unidos, un lugar extraordinario y misterioso, del que no tenía absolutamente ningún conocimiento en aquellos días y donde las maneras de comunicarse, interactuar y vivir me resultaban totalmente extrañas. Tenía veintiún años cuando emprendí ese viaje interplanetario, con la línea aérea Ecuatoriana (una compañía ahora desaparecida) que me llevó hasta el Aeropuerto Kennedy. Aquella fue la primera vez que viajé en avión. Por decirlo suavemente, la sensación de ser totalmente ingrávida y de haber perdido por completo el control de mi destino resultaba sobrecogedora. En el interior de mi corazón, aún llevaba encima un peso que probablemente hubiera ocupado de forma incontenible cualquier espacio —por no hablar de la cabina de un avión—, pero no me atrevía a admitir aquella presencia —ni siquiera a mí misma— de ese penetrante y absoluto dolor mío. Me sentía muy pequeña, pero no insignificante. Sabía que me esperaba algo, algo quizá sorprendentemente agradable, pero aquello no era más que una efímera conjetura. En realidad, toda la experiencia se resumía en un enorme símbolo de interrogación.

Al provenir de un clima totalmente diferente, ataviada únicamente por un suéter con motivos peruanos, parecía como si acabara de salir de una cápsula cultural-temporal de otro mundo. Desconcertada y asustada (¿quién no lo estaría?), esperé con anticipación y suspense a que viniera a recogerme mi tío Luis. Eran las diez de la noche y yo tenía frío: una desagradable sensación a la que estaba muy poco habituada. De repente, un caballero de mediana edad de aspecto respetable y distinguido se me acercó y comenzó a hablarme en un torpe español.

—¿Puedo ayudarte en algo? —me preguntó—. ¿Va todo bien?

Algo en el rostro y los gestos del hombre hizo que me inspirara confianza.

—Se está haciendo muy tarde y estoy preocupada porque se suponía que mis familiares iban a venir a buscarme y no todavía no han llegado.

Debí de mirarle como un ciervo desorientado ante los faros de un coche.

Inmediatamente, el hombre se puso manos a la obra y habló con una familia portorriqueña: una pareja con dos hijas a los que llamaré los Ortega.

—Esta amable familia se quedará contigo mientras esperas a tu tío. Estás en buenas manos —me aseguró mi aliado.

Más tarde, aquel solemne y decidido buen samaritano me estrechó la mano, me deseo buena suerte y se marchó. Nunca lo olvidaré. Gracias, caballero, por haber sido el preludio de mi extraordinario viaje, ¡que aún sigue su curso!

Los Ortega y yo esperamos aproximadamente una hora, sin que tío Luis diera señales de vida. Así pues, ellos me ayudaron a utilizar el teléfono. Dada mi incapacidad para hablar inglés, aquel me parecía un instrumento aterrador.

La señora Ortega dejó un mensaje para la tía Carmela, la esposa de mi tío, y le comunicó nuestra ubicación en el aeropuerto y la información de contacto de la familia (incluida su dirección). Cerca de la una de la mañana, como no había ni rastro de mi benefactor, los Ortega decidieron llevarme a su casa, que se encontraba a aproximadamente media hora de distancia. Yo no tenía ni idea de dónde vivían. De hecho, desconocía totalmente cuál era la distancia entre Nueva York y Nueva Jersey, donde vivía el tío Luis. Al parecer, todos los lugares estaban muy separados entre sí y mis percepciones espaciales y de distancia en mi nuevo planeta eran, por el momento, nulas.

Una hora después de mi llegada al hogar de los Ortega, apareció por fin el tío Luis, con aspecto de esquimal, ataviado con un enorme abrigo. Al verle, me sentí como si estuviera viendo un rostro familiar en una tundra desierta. Nos intercambiamos los saludos de rigor, y el tío Luis les expresó a mis amigos su más sincera gratitud por su hospitalidad. Yo también le di las gracias a la familia por todo lo que habían hecho para hacerme sentir cómoda. De hecho, resulta poco común encontrar gente que realmente se preocupe y se desprenda de las fachadas y la circunspección para echarle una mano a alguien que lo necesita. Después de todo este tiempo, se impone la necesidad de que les dé las gracias de nuevo a aquellos extraordinarios corazones que tan generosos fueron conmigo.

Y así, me encontré en el interior del elegante utilitario del tío Luis, con sus ventanas y puertas automáticas y toda clase de sofisticadas tecnologías, que ni siquiera intenté ni empezar a entender. Lo que estaba viendo por la ventanilla era muchísimo más atractivo: altísimos rascacielos, enormes carreteras, y señales por todas partes en inglés, ese modo de comunicación intensamente difícil y aterrador que parecía estar más allá de mi comprensión. Lo que más me asombró fue el tramo de nuestro viaje a través del túnel Lincoln. El tío Luis se volvió hacia mí y me explicó con total naturalidad:

—Estamos pasando por debajo del río Hudson.

—¿Viajamos bajo el agua? ¡No puede ser! —exclamé yo, quedándome boquiabierta.

No lo sé con seguridad, pero me imagino que durante una temporada bastante larga al inicio de mi estancia en Estados Unidos, la mayor parte del tiempo, tenía una expresión petrificada pintada en el rostro.

Mi estancia en casa de mis benefactores fue breve: apenas duró unas pocas semanas. Aunque eran amables conmigo, no nadaban en la abundancia y no podían permitirse mantenerme durante un periodo más largo. Su hogar era pequeño, y yo tuve que meter a presión mis pertenencias en minúsculos armarios. Aun así, con el paso de los días, comencé a aclimatarme. Ver toda aquella hermosísima nieve el segundo día tras mi llegada fue una imagen especialmente fascinante. Nunca antes había sido testigo de un fenómeno así. Era enero, el mes más frío y borrascoso. Por supuesto, en Perú teníamos glaciares, pero la nieve se encontraba siempre a más altitud, nunca junto a nosotros, cubriendo el suelo que pisábamos. Bajo esa refulgente capa de esplendor invernal, aquel nuevo planeta tenía un aspecto de lo más tentador. ¡Si al menos hubiera podido compartirlo con Laura!

Con ayuda del destino y de tía Carmela, me matriculé en un programa de idiomas e hice buen uso de mi visado de estudiante. Nos enviaron unos impresos para rellenar, después de lo cual, asistí a una escuela de idiomas a aproximadamente cuarenta y cinco minutos de casa. No me sentía incómoda llamando «hogar» a ningún otro lugar que no fueran Huaraz o Lima, pero simplemente tuve que plegarme a los caprichos del destino. En la escuela de idiomas, conocí a una amable señora a la que llamaré Sra. N. que no hablaba ni palabra de español. Sin embargo, de algún modo, su corazón hablaba más alto que ningún otro idioma. De forma inherente, comprendía la difícil circunstancia en la que yo estaba —que me encontraba sola y necesitaba amigos—, así que decidió presentarme a su hija, Julie, que, en aquella época, se había tomado un semestre libre de la universidad.

Tengo que hablaros con más detenimiento sobre esta amistad, que se merece una atención especial, pues fue —y sigue siéndolo— una verdadera bendición en mi vida, lo mejor que habría podido sucederme en un momento en el que yo más necesitaba respaldo emocional, comprensión y apoyo. Con su metro setenta, ojos azules y pelo rubio, la belleza externa de Julie solo se igualaba a su imparable energía, vivaracha personalidad y contagioso buen humor. Aunque al principio no hablábamos ni una palabra de nuestros respectivos idiomas, nos comunicamos mediante gestos, fotografías e imágenes: un juego constante de charadas, del que disfrutábamos muchísimo. Poco a poco, a medida que empezaba a aprender inglés y le enseñaba a Julie un poco de español, nuestra comunicación fue haciéndose más fluida y nuestras interacciones más exhaustivas.

Durante este periodo, comencé a trabajar de niñera residente, cuidando de dos encantadores niños, Cameron y Melissa, de seis y ocho años respectivamente. Los adoraba y les cogí mucho cariño, y viceversa, hasta el punto de que Cameron preguntó por qué no podía ser yo su madre.

—Papá —dijo meditabundo el niño una noche en mitad de la cena—, si mamá se muere, ¿podrías casarte con Isabella, por favor? Quiero que ella sea mi mamá.

Todo el mundo guardó silencio.

—Cameron —le respondí yo, mirándolo con firmeza, pero también con benevolencia—, te quiero muchísimo, pero yo no soy tu mamá. Tu mamá está sentada junto a ti, y nadie puede ocupar su lugar.

Aunque mi inglés resultaba titubeante, creo que transmití mi mensaje a la perfección. Comprendí que la madre de Cameron debía de sentirse intimidada. Por eso, hice lo posible por comportarme de manera deferente con ella. Al mismo tiempo, me sentí intensamente halagada, percibiendo que el comentario de Cameron había encendido mis instintos maternales —por muy minúsculos que fueran en aquella época—, como florecillas germinando bajo las últimas nieves del invierno.

Y hablando del cambio de las estaciones, aquel fenómeno era un completo misterio para mí. Cuando el invierno se convirtió en primavera, Julie y yo salimos juntas a correr por el parque. Con entusiasmo, como un niño presenciando un acontecimiento fascinante, mi amiga me mostró las flores de los cerezos: ¡la vuelta a la vida de aquellos árboles, aletargados durante todo el invierno, transformándose en un magnífico despliegue de florecillas que poblaban sus ramas como pequeños duendecillos picaruelos haciendo uso de su magia! Nunca había visto una imagen más milagrosa en toda mi vida. A medida que la naturaleza se transformaba, yo también lo hacía, asimilando mi nuevo mundo y fundiéndome con él.

Mientras tanto, los días se convertían en meses, y yo continuaba aprendiendo inglés mediante un curso a domicilio que, dada mi falta de medio de transporte, me proporcionaba la escuela de idiomas. Esperaba con impaciencia la llegada de la Sra. D., mi profesora particular, una extraordinaria mujer que no solo me enseñaba el idioma, sino que también me exponía a la cultura estadounidense. Fue una época emocionante, y mis punzadas de dolor, aunque no se disiparon, lentamente empezaron a formar parte de mi tejido emocional: algo con lo que convivía diariamente, en contraposición con un enemigo al que combatir. Esta transformación se debió en gran parte a la luminosa presencia de Julie y a su capacidad para hacerme sentir cómoda, independientemente de dónde estuviéramos juntas.

Pronto, comencé a recibir clases de inglés como segundo idioma en una escuela de la zona. Allí, conocí a gente de diferentes países: Colombia, Italia, Grecia, India y muchos otros. Un hombre en particular, al que llamaré János, era un atractivo estudiante a piloto proveniente de Hungría, con el que labré una firme amistad. Me llevaba a cenar y a obras de teatro al centro de Nueva York y, en unos pocos meses, empezamos a salir juntos de forma oficial. Aunque yo ocultaba con diligencia mis manchas faciales, aquel asunto siempre fue un problema con él. Me sentía a gusto y, en mi interior, sabía que a János le gustaba tal y como era. Incluso me llegó a decir que, si alguna vez tenía un ataque de insomnio, podía llamarlo en cualquier momento de la noche. En una ocasión, aproveché su generosa oferta. Podéis imaginaros mi asombro cuando contestó el teléfono una mujer, que afirmó ser la novia de él, tras lo cual, interrumpí por completo mi relación con él.

Un año después de empezar a trabajar como niñera, mis servicios a jornada completa dejaron de ser necesarios, pues la madre de la familia comenzó a pasar más tiempo en casa. Me marché agradecida, despidiéndome de los niños con todo el cariño y los mejores deseos de mi corazón.

En la siguiente fase de mi evolución, trabajé para la Sra. C., una excéntrica octogenaria llena de energía. La Sra. C. era una mujer delgada de ojos azules y arrugas que se le acentuaban cuando sonreía. Con su cabello grisáceo recogido en un moño, era la perfecta estampa de anciana elegante. No obstante, sus costumbres podían llegar a ser bastante particulares, aunque yo le tenía aún más cariño por ello. Sus placeres favoritos eran el chocolate y leer la Biblia, y ambas cosas las compartía de buen grado conmigo. Su curiosa yuxtaposición entre los asuntos temporales y los espirituales siempre me hacía reír. Por la noche, venía a mi habitación en la segunda planta, abría mi cama, que parecía la de un hotel, y me dejaba una chocolatina de chocolate con leche sobre la mesilla de noche, acompañada en ocasiones por una copa de jerez Harveys Bristol Cream. Las chocolatinas y el licor a veces resultaban excesivos, y yo tenía que apartarlos de mí para evitar abusar. La Sra. C. me hablaba durante horas, relatándome las aventuras de su juventud y su vida en familia. Me decía «querida mía» y me mimaba como a una hija. Y exactamente como si lo fuera, hasta me impuso un toque de queda. Si, Dios no lo quisiera, no llegaba a casa a las ocho de la tarde, hacía que me buscara todo el departamento de policía del barrio. ¡Y era un milagro que no llamara también a la Guardia Nacional! Disfrutamos de muchos buenos ratos: yendo juntas a la iglesia más cercana, contemplando a nuestro perro correr por el patio y, en ocasiones excepcionales, yéndonos de tiendas. La Sra. C. era el altruismo personificado, siempre comprándome suéteres y vestidos, al mismo tiempo que se negaba a adquirir nada para sí misma.

La Sra. C. me animaba para seguir adelante con mi educación, que ella misma financiaba, junto con mi alojamiento y manutención. Incluso se interesaba por mi vida amorosa. No sé cohibió de comentar el atractivo de János. Resultaba divertido ver cómo lo contemplaba boquiabierta, casi como una deslumbrada jovencita. Sí, János efectivamente vino a visitarme, pidiéndome que volviera con él, pero eso era algo que no iba a suceder. Nuestra relación nunca llegó a ser muy profunda y, por lo tanto, no me resultó difícil cortar mis lazos con él.

En otra memorable ocasión, la Sra. C. me llevó a visitar a su hija a un pueblo vecino. Allí, conocí a Henry, el nieto de la Sra. C. Su carácter cordial y hospitalario me hizo sentir muy cómoda. Aproximadamente una semana más tarde, la madre de Henry se pasó por casa y me explicó que su hijo pensaba que yo era atractiva y quería invitarme a salir. La ansiedad se apoderó de mí y, dado mi insuficiente vocabulario en aquella época, apenas pude responderle:

—¡Vaya! ¡Qué mono es!

Al parecer, se tomaron mi reacción como un rechazo, porque ni Henry ni su madre volvieron a sacar el tema jamás. Dada mi baja autoestima, me obsesioné con aquel error comunicativo, y acabé por llegar a la conclusión de que, de hecho, yo debía de ser la que había tenido la culpa. Ya veis, solo de pensar en mis manchas faciales (por no hablar de su existencia) seguía creándome sentimientos de inferioridad, tanto subliminales como manifiestos, que yo empleaba de forma subconsciente o deliberada para justificar el rechazo. Como alternativa, a veces empleaba mi sentimiento de baja autoestima como escudo para protegerme de que me rompieran el corazón. Eso fue lo que sucedió con Henry y, como veréis, queridos lectores, con otros más adelante. También le di vueltas a la idea de que la madre de Henry pudiera haberlo desalentado para que no iniciara una posible relación romántica conmigo dado mi cargo de cuidadora sanitaria y nuestras dispares circunstancias socioeconómicas. Su familia era muy acaudalada, en cambio, yo no; por lo que, según razonaba yo, no era lo suficientemente buena para Henry. Aquel era el devastador mantra de mi bajísima autoestima. Gracias a Dios, esa cantinela ahora ha cambiado.

Uno de los acontecimientos más destacados de mi estancia con la Sra. C. fue que adoptamos una lanuda perrilla negra, *Maggie*. Me tenía mucho cariño y solía dormir en un sofá junto a mi cama. Éramos inseparables y siempre jugábamos juntas, y yo me encargaba de ella. Desgraciadamente, nuestra perra, que normalmente era una dulce mascota, detestaba al padre Othello, el director de la congregación de la Sra. C. que, junto con otros párrocos, solía venir a casa diariamente a ofrecerle a la Sra. C. su Sagrada Comunión. Mi protectora hada madrina era muy religiosa, leía vorazmente la Biblia, hablaba conmigo sobre el libro sagrado y practicaba su ritual diurno de recibir la Eucaristía. En una ocasión en particular, miré por la ventana y vi que nuestra perrita se había escapado y perseguía al padre Othello por el jardín, con su sotana sacudiéndose por la brisa. Como tenía un poco de sobrepeso, el pobre clérigo apenas lograba avanzar a trompicones, tratando de evitar la ira de *Maggie*. Aunque aquel incidente no fue cosa de risa, no pude evitar verle la gracia. Más tarde, *Maggie* volvió a entrar en casa con un trofeo colgándole del morro: un trozo del negro atuendo del padre Othello. «¡Oh, no! ¡Ahora sí que nos hemos metido en un buen lío!», pensé yo. Sonó el teléfono, y no era otro que el propio padre, totalmente atribulado, jurando que no regresaría jamás ni enviaría a ningún otro párroco a la casa a menos que «¡se deshagan de esa bestia!». Profundamente disgustada, temí por la suerte que correría *Maggie*, si saber cuáles serían finalmente las intenciones de la Sra. C. con respecto a mi fiel compañera. Cuando regresé de la escuela un día y corrí para jugar con mi amiguita, mis mayores temores se hicieron realidad. La Sra. C. me comunicó la noticia.

—*Maggie* se ha ido a vivir con mis parientes a otro estado —me dijo, con la voz cargada de compasión.

No volví a ver a *Maggie* nunca más. Y de nuevo, tuve que despedirme de otro de mis fieles amigos de cuatro patas.

Derramé infinidad de lágrimas aquel día. No podía evitarlo, pero sabía que tenía que pasar página. Aprendí que, como todo lo demás, la falta de permanencia forma parte del interminable ciclo de esa entidad en continua edificación y derrumbamiento llamada vida, un viaje en el que cada uno tomamos senderos divergentes. Si tenemos suficiente suerte, numerosos caminos convergen y se forman huellas, una al lado de otra, que simbolizan la amistad y el amor. A través de las lágrimas, la risa y la multitud de transformaciones tanto dentro como fuera de mí, mi viaje personal no había hecho más que comenzar.

Capítulo 9

Desvinculación

No cabe duda de que el deseo de mi padre de que yo abandonara mi hogar en Lima tenía un objetivo muy pragmático y razonable: disolver la abrumadora pena que embargaba a mi corazón. Sin embargo, descubrí que, en realidad, no existe ninguna manera de escapar de esos sentimientos que forman permanentemente una parte integral de la composición emocional de cada uno. De alguna manera, tuve que continuar con mi vida, a pesar de aquel omnipresente e insalvable dolor mío. Mi hermana no volvería jamás, y yo tenía que afrontar aquella horrible realidad.

Aparte de Julie, mi mejor amiga y principal fuente de consuelo, mi carrera era otra de mis tablas de salvación para mantenerme centrada. Solicité y satisfice los prerrequisitos para un programa de terapia física: el único de su clase en todo el estado de Nueva Jersey en aquella época. Había oído que los prerrequisitos de admisión eran extraordinariamente rigurosos y, a menudo, agotadores. No obstante, yo estaba decidida a estudiar hasta quemarme las pestañas para demostrarme a mí misma que podía hacerlo, y a todos los demás a mi alrededor. Durante las vacaciones de la escuela, decidí regresar en una corta visita a Perú, el origen de tantos recuerdos. Me había ido muy lejos de casa y, tras algo de deliberación y de hacer un examen de conciencia, me aventuré a regresar al lugar de la Tierra que me había dado y que me había despojado de tantas cosas. Julie me acompañó. Conocía el dolor emocional que me había producido la pérdida de mi querídisima hermana, Laura. Identificándose profundamente con mi desgracia, lloró conmigo y, con todo el cariño de su desinteresado y hermosísimo corazón, se ofreció a llenar el vacío que yo albergaba en mi interior. Pero ¿cómo? Pues haciendo las veces de mi hermana. Verdaderamente, fue tan fiel como podría haberlo sido cualquier hermana conmigo y, hasta el día de hoy, no he podido olvidar sus extraordinarios actos de amabilidad y devoción. No podía llegar a imaginarme hasta qué punto esta brillante presencia en mi vida podría llegar a influir tan positivamente en el curso de mi destino. Nunca nos damos cuenta cuando los ángeles bajan del cielo para caminar entre nosotros. Julie fue, y sigue siéndolo, el mío.

Cuando llegamos a Lima, visitamos la casa en la que yo solía vivir con Laura y Tomás y fuimos en autobús hasta el centro. Al mirar a mi alrededor, me sobrevino un sentimiento de pérdida, como si se me hubieran desgarrado partes de mi anatomía interna. Allá donde mirara, en cada esquina y entre la multitud, me faltaba mi hermana. Me tomé ingentes cantidades de Valium con receta para tratar de sobrellevar aquel dolor emocional, al tiempo que boqueaba en busca de oxígeno tratando de respirar. El aire mismo que inhalaba junto a Laura no hacía tanto tiempo, literalmente me asfixiaba en su ausencia. Padecí ataques de pánico y palpitaciones, hasta el punto de asfixiarme, cosa que tuvo como resultado que me hiciera falta someterme a un electrocardiograma. Me llevaron a toda prisa al hospital, a ese mismo edificio en el que solía trabajar, aquel cuyo personal tan bien conocía y donde recibí la noticia que tanto alteró mi vida de que Laura había fallecido. Había cerrado el círculo al regresar a aquel lugar. Fue como si el destino se estuviera burlando de mí. Un cardiólogo me examinó y me recetó grandes cantidades de Valium. A partir de aquel momento, me quedé totalmente enganchada. Al tomarme un Valium tras otro para enmascarar mi agitación interna, comencé a caer en una espiral descendente, hasta que un día, Julie me ayudó a liberarme. Me quitó el Valium de las manos, se hizo con todas y cada una de las botellas que yo tenía en mi poder, y allí, ante mis ojos, echó todas aquellas píldoras por el retrete y tiró de la cadena.

—A partir de ahora, no vas a necesitarlas —afirmó rotundamente mi ángel—. Yo seré tu Valium.

Prescindir de la medicación me salvó la vida. Aquel acto simbólico de echar al retrete las píldoras y tirar de la cadera también significó una purga de mi pena. A partir de aquel momento, el sostén de tomar medicación para camuflar mi dolor se convirtió en algo del pasado. En efecto, me purifiqué de la toxicidad de aquella pena insondable que me había carcomido por dentro: aquella angustia silenciosa, reprimida por mi precipitada marcha de Perú apenas una cuantas semanas después de la muerte de mi hermana. Hasta aquel momento, cuando Julie pronunció aquellas palabras de cariño y salvación, no pude liberarme de la tácita autodestrucción. Ojalá el mundo —y cualquiera que padezca dolor de cualquier tipo— pudiera contar con un apoyo como el que yo tuve entonces; alguien que nos diga: «¡A mí me importas! Por favor, ¡no te hagas más daño! ¡Te quiero!». Gracias, Julie, por ayudarme a afrontar mi tumulto interno y conducirme a la luz. De no ser por tu sabiduría, tu empatía, tu preocupación y tu cariño, no sería quien soy hoy, quien escribe estas páginas y quien vive genuinamente.

Una vez que me hube liberado de mi abismo emocional, nuestro viaje continuó por Cuzco y el Machu Picchu. Nos acompañó Carolina, mi fiel amiga de mis días en la escuela de enfermería. En primer lugar, volamos de Lima a Cuzco para aclimatarnos a la elevada altitud. Todos los que visitan esta región afirman que esa es la mejor manera de hacerlo antes de viajar al Machu Picchu, donde la altitud considerablemente elevada puede causar mucha impresión si no está uno preparado. Llevábamos puestos nuestros suéteres en todo momento, por lo que pudimos soportar las frías temperaturas que variaban entre 10 y 20 grados. Era la primera vez que estaba allí, y mis ojos no podían dejar de admirar la belleza que me rodeaba, verdadero alimento para el alma, llenándome de recuerdos que me acompañarán toda la vida. Un cielo azul brillante bailaba sobre nuestras cabezas, como dándonos la bienvenida a la región, preñada de antiguas estructuras construidas en los días de los incas, mis ancestros. En la antigüedad, Cuzco era la capital, el centro neurálgico de toda actividad. El término «Cuzco» (o

«Cusco») significa «ombligo» en quechua, el idioma inca, cosa que indica que Cuzco era el corazón o núcleo mismo de la nación. Hoy en día, los picos montañosos, los majestuosos templos y las estructuras de piedra esculpida y tallada atesoran los secretos del imperio inca, un pasado que nunca llegué a conocer, pero que tuve el honor de contemplar al presenciar el esplendor de aquel lugar. La Tierra tiene un lenguaje propio allí, y si uno escucha, puede oír los ecos de la verdad, la sabiduría, el sufrimiento y el triunfo.

Nos quedamos en Cuzco durante un par de días, donde hicimos excursiones al valle de Urubamba, con su imponente río y a Sacsayhuamán, una enorme fortaleza de piedra de casi diez metros de alto que parecía casi como si hubiera sido construida por gigantes. Con su forma de relámpago, el complejo amurallado tiene entradas y salidas simétricas de casi ochocientos metros de longitud. Los ajustes de altitud y mi propia agitación interna hicieron que fuera incapaz de trepar una pequeña pirámide, cosa que Julie y Carolina lograron hacer sin problemas. Tras nuestro regreso a Cuzco, fui sintiéndome poco a poco restablecida mientras bebía mate de coca y, de vez en cuando, llevaba un pequeño depósito de oxígeno portátil para ayudarme con mi ansiedad restante y con mi mal de altura.

Al día siguiente, fuimos a la ciudad sagrada de Machu Picchu, construida en la cima de una cadena montañosa. Nadie puede explicar por qué esta fascinante ciudad de piedra está ubicada precisamente allí. A nuestra llegada, vimos una fortaleza militar excavada en el interior de una sola roca, el famoso Templo de la Luna, con sus intricadas cuevas de exquisita construcción. Durante el momento culminante de nuestro viaje, mis intrépidas amigas y yo escalamos la pirámide de Intihuatana y vimos el reloj solar. Me sentí tan orgullosa y feliz, al mismo tiempo que deseaba que Laura pudiera haber compartido aquella fascinante experiencia conmigo. Al día siguiente, regresamos a Cuzco para pasar el último día y la última noche de nuestro viaje. Allí, socializamos con unos chicos muy monos, uno de los cuales me acompañó de vuelta a nuestro hotel. Julie y Carolina prosiguieron la fiesta durante toda la noche, mientras que yo sentí la necesidad de volver al hotel e irme a dormir. Así fue, pese a que un atractivo joven hubiera expresado interés en mí. Me marché, despidiéndome educadamente de él, y regresé a mi habitación, mientras que mis amigas disfrutaban de una noche de rebeldía.

Al día siguiente, embarcamos en el vuelo de vuelta a Lima, y mis amigas durmieron en el avión. Dado que la noche anterior yo había optado por actividades más descansadas que ellas, yo estaba completamente despierta y ansiosa por visitar a mi familia. Carolina regresó a casa, mientras que Julie se quedó con mi familia y conmigo durante unos días más antes de volar de vuelta a Estados Unidos. Una semana más tarde, tras mi visita a mi familia y un breve viaje a Huaraz, me marché de vuelta a mi nuevo hogar. Después de mis días de comunión con la naturaleza y los paisajes históricos de mi patria, me sentí renovada, dejando, como siempre, un trozo de mi corazón allí.

De vuelta en mi nuevo planeta al que había llegado a considerar mi hogar, descubrí, para mi sorpresa y júbilo, que me habían admitido en el exclusivo programa de terapia física. Mi diligencia y trabajo duro habían dado sus frutos. Poco después, me enteré de que mi hermano Tomás había decidido venir también ha Estados Unidos para proseguir su carrera de medicina. Me informó de que necesitaba un lugar en el que quedarse. Yo logré conseguirle alojamiento en casa de la incomparable Sra. C., quien, por el profundo afecto que me tenía y por cortesía hacia mí, le proporcionó gratuitamente alojamiento y manutención a mi hermano.

Aunque yo estaba ocupada resolviendo muchos asuntos, el viaje a Perú me había traído a la memoria vívidos recuerdos sobre la muerte de mi queridísima hermana, Laura. Independientemente de lo mucho que tratara de reconducir mis emociones, a veces recaía en un profundo y oscuro abismo de dolor por mi pérdida. Incluso aunque el viaje a Perú había servido de catarsis —gracias, sobre todo, a Julie—, no podía evitar completamente mis sentimientos de desconsuelo. Sin duda, Tomás también se sentía así, pero él nunca expresaba sus sentimientos. Puede que si hubiéramos sido capaces de comunicarnos más abiertamente, habríamos logrado tender un puente en el vacío que existía entre nosotros.

Ya veis, después de que Laura abandonara este mundo, yo tenía la sensación de que sus pertenencias no eran más que conchas vacías, naderías carentes de significado, obsoletas sin su presencia. Llegué a comprender que los objetos son, a fin de cuentas, totalmente superfluos, y que el dicho: «No te lo puedes llevar a la tumba» es más cierto que lo que ninguno de nosotros está dispuesto a reconocer. Mi dolor residía en que la propia Laura no estaba allí para experimentar la vida junto a mí, para celebrar los triunfos, para desesperarse ante las situaciones difíciles y para ser mi confidente, como siempre había sido hasta entonces. Solo mencionar su nombre me conducía a los más profundos abismos de la desesperación.

Aproximadamente por entonces, tuve un accidente de coche que dejó mi vehículo siniestro total, pero del que salí, gracias a Dios, de una sola pieza. Con el dinero del seguro, compré un flamante Toyota Supra, un coche de marchas, equipado con todos los servicios más modernos posibles. No obstante, fui dueña de aquel coche durante un cortísimo periodo de tiempo, pues Tomás rápidamente se quedó con mi nueva adquisición. Así pues, me vi obligada a comprar una destartalada ranchera de color mostaza a la nuera de la Sra. C. por 200 dólares. La única razón por la que hice aquella compra fue porque necesitaba transporte para ir y volver de la escuela. Como Tomás se quedó con mi coche nuevo, yo pasé unos agonizantes meses de verano, sacando y metiendo la cabeza por la ventanilla de mi desvencijada ranchera en un intento de respirar algo de aire fresco, pues carecía de aire acondicionado. Finalmente, acabó por convencerme de que le transfiriera la titularidad del coche. Para entonces, yo ya conducía mi Honda Accord rojo de segunda mano (el sustituto de mi difunta ranchera de color mostaza, que logré triunfalmente conducir con marchas: una dulce venganza. Mis esfuerzos autodidactas fueron todo un éxito). Estaba estudiando para un examen de Macroanatomía, diseccionando cadáveres, por lo que me sentía particularmente susceptible, como si mi propio corazón hubiera estado expuesto sobre la mesa, a la vista de todo el mundo.

Esos reductos de mi pasado —entre otras cosas, la subyugación que sentía en presencia de mi hermano— se instalaron como discordantes notas musicales en mi nuevo mundo. Fue aproximadamente en aquella época cuando conocí a Eduardo Davidio. Como ya he mencionado, estaba asistiendo a clase en un programa de terapia física extraordinariamente competitivo. El trabajo del curso implicaba que algunos de nosotros teníamos que asistir a las mismas clases que los estudiantes de medicina de primer año (por ejemplo, Macroanatomía y Embriología). De camino a clase un inolvidable martes por la tarde, vi a un joven alto, extraordinariamente guapo y de ojos azules que caminaba en dirección contraria. Cruzamos una mirada e instantáneamente me sentí como si furtivamente él hubiera mirado directamente en el interior de mi alma. Se me quedó paralizada la mente, aunque mi cuerpo siguió en movimiento mientras proseguía mi camino hacia mi destino. Aquel estado de inconsciencia me duró toda la clase, durante la cual estuve allí sentada, soñando despierta con el Adonis que me acababa de encontrar. En mi ensoñación, él me pedía salir, me agasajaba con tiernas atenciones, me admiraba y me hacía sentir especial. «¡Espera un minuto! —me gritó mi inseguro, tímido y desconsolado ser—. ¿Cómo puedes estar soñando estas cosas cuando tienes sobre tu rostro unas manchas que parecen de tinta, cuando has sido rechazada, cuando te han lastimado en el amor una y otra vez, y cuando apenas hablas inglés?». Aquella vocecilla negativa en mi cabeza y mi corazón ahogó cualquier posibilidad de esperanza. Aquella voz de miedo y autonegación era una mentirosa, pero no llegué a darme cuenta de ello.

Al día siguiente, mi compañera de clase y amiga, Sarah, me pidió que fuera con ella y un grupo de chicas a un restaurante mexicano cercano a nuestra escuela. Vacilé, conociendo la tendencia de la Sra. C. por tenerme controlada y por la timidez inherente a encontrarme en situaciones sociales que, al menos en mi mente, significaban tanto literal como metafóricamente tener que ocultar mis inseguridades. Sin embargo, después de que me insistieran un poco, decidí apuntarme. Poco después de llegar al restaurante, lo vi a él allí, al mismísimo Adonis, caminando hacia mí, como un holograma surgiendo de mi ensoñación. Sin poder creerme que sus ojos estuvieran fijos en una humilde servidora, la muchachita de montaña, me volví para mirar a mis espaldas, preguntándome la identidad de la afortunada que lo aguardaba. Cuando comprobé que no había nadie allí, rápidamente deduje, para mi sorpresa y asombro que, de hecho, yo era el objeto de sus atenciones. Tras empezar por presentarnos, charlamos durante largo rato, con la facilidad y la naturalidad de dos viejos amigos, esos que, de forma innegable, sienten una atracción mutua. No me atreví a admitírmelo a mí misma, a riesgo de que formular en alto aquel sueño hiciera que se desintegrara ante mis ojos. Hablamos sobre Perú y su cultura, cosa que parecía captar el interés de Eduardo, al tiempo que era un tema de conversación que a mí me resultaba cómodo. Mi torpe inglés de repente salía de forma fluida cuando hablaba sobre mi patria, puesto que había escrito varias redacciones escolares relatando mis experiencias y había desarrollado un holgado vocabulario sobre aquel asunto.

De repente, me di cuenta de qué hora era y anuncié que me tenía que marchar. Eduardo se había comportado de forma tan atenta y la conversación que habíamos compartido había sido tan maravillosa, que me resultó difícil marcharme, pero no tenía otra elección. Le expliqué que la anciana señora con la que vivía me esperaba en casa hacia las ocho, después de lo cual, llamaría a la policía y prácticamente denunciaría mi desaparición. A regañadientes pero gentilmente, mi amigo admitió que yo me encontraba en una situación apremiante. Me acompañó hasta mi coche y me dio un beso en la mejilla como dulce despedida, preguntándome si podía llamarme al día siguiente. Me puse tan nerviosa y emocionada, que apenas podía respirar. El aire a mi alrededor pareció cambiar, como si estuviera a punto de suceder algo espectacular. Y allí estaba, el protagonista de mi sueño de juventud, realmente pronunciando las palabras que mi mente había imaginado apenas unas horas antes. Él era real y deseaba estar conmigo, ¡conmigo!

Incluso ahora me siento un poco avergonzada de confesar que sentí que el teléfono no sonaba lo suficientemente rápido. Me imaginé aquella llamada como si fuera un meteorito a punto de caer del cielo y chocar contra mi vida para cambiarla para siempre. Cuando finalmente sonó el teléfono, mi corazón palpitaba como el de un purasangre a punto de ganar una carrera. Por alguna razón, desde el principio, la calidad y profundidad de aquella conexión adquirió un significado más allá de cualquier sentimiento que yo hubiera experimentado jamás. Quedamos en encontrarnos para una cena informal: simplemente iríamos a comer una hamburguesa con patatas fritas. De alguna manera, aquella decisión parecía lo más apropiado, dada la breve duración de nuestra relación.

Así pues, a las siete de la tarde aquella noche, Eduardo se presentó en la puerta de la Sra. C. Cuando entró en el recibidor principal, Tomás y él se estrecharon la mano brevemente. Mientras bajaba las escaleras, vi a mi pareja de pie junto a la puerta, con una chaqueta de color azul marino. Incluso con aquel atuendo informal, estaba elegantísimo. Mi hermano se comportó de forma rígida. Para colmo de males, era la hora del ritual habitual de la Sra. C. (una de entre sus muchas cómicas costumbres, aunque extraordinariamente particulares) de colocar su camisón sobre las cortinas de la ventana, para evitar que ningún posible espectador malintencionado curioseara a través de la ventana. Aquella extraña situación sería demasiado para un chico cualquiera, por no hablar de uno que hacía que se me detuviera el corazón durante varios latidos. Por esta razón, cuando Eduardo se hallaba en la entrada, yo salí a toda prisa, cerrando la puerta a mis espaldas, y diciendo simplemente:

—¡Vámonos!

Entramos en el coche y, por supuesto, traté de proporcionarle alguna excusa con la intención de encontrar una forma de compensar mi falta de hospitalidad.

—Siento no haberte invitado a entrar. Lo habría hecho, pero tenemos dentro de casa muchas antigüedades.

Adopté un aspecto bastante compungido mientras me preguntaba a mí misma de dónde diablos habría sacado un razonamiento tan inútil.

—Pero a mí me gustan las antigüedades —me respondió Eduardo, contemplándome con curiosidad.

Perfectamente consciente de mi descuido deliberado y percibiendo que no tenía escapatoria posible, no seguí hablando del asunto. ¡Me hubiera hecho falta ser un enorme mamífero marino para ser capaz de escaparme de aquella red! Y así, continuamos nuestro camino hacia la hamburguesería y, aunque la perplejidad de Eduardo no se mitigó, no podría haberse comportado de una forma más cortés. Una vez hubimos llegado a nuestro destino, su lenguaje corporal lo decía todo. En un intento por rodearme con el brazo, se sentó cerca de mí, me acercó las patatas fritas a la boca y se comportó de una manera tan simpática y encantadora que hizo que yo acabara totalmente loca por él. Sentía mi corazón palpitando con fuerza, como si cientos de mariposas hubieran ascendido a través de las paredes de mi estómago, provocándome cosquilleos y sensaciones nerviosas que no podía controlar incluso aunque quisiera y, creedme, ni siquiera lo intenté. Aquellas criaturillas aladas envolvieron todo mi ser, dejándome inútil y prácticamente indefensa. La fuerza del amor puede ser arrolladora: más intensa y dinámica que la reacción química más potente. Supongo que esa es la razón por la cual la atracción entre dos personas se denomina «química». Las luces que nos rodeaban no eran demasiado brillantes, por lo que no tenía motivos para cuestionarme el efecto de mis manchas faciales o a avergonzarme por ellas; y, aun así, había tantas cosas que quería decir y no podía... tantas inhibiciones que no lograban salir a la superficie, dada mi falta de fluidez al hablar. En particular, me obsesionaba el penetrante miedo de que la magia pudiera desvanecerse en un instante, al igual que había sucedido con Lorenzo, mi amor adolescente, que me había roto el corazón. Apenas podía creerme, por tanto, la existencia de aquella aura de atracción, tan evidente en todas las miradas de Eduardo: la profundidad con la que me contemplaba, como si me traspasara con la mirada hasta alcanzar el centro de mi ser. «¡Está claro que no! —me reprendió mi inseguro interior, sometiéndome a su siniestro control—. ¡No te dejes herir emocionalmente otra vez! ¡Guarda tu corazón bajo llave! ¡Nunca, en todo tu pasado, has sido considerada digna: ni por Lorenzo, ni por Tomás y sus amigos, especialmente Paulo, aquel joven atractivo de ojos azules y aspecto aristocrático, al cual te recuerda de forma inquietante tu actual acompañante! ¡El amor duele! ¡Ten cuidado! ¡Mantén las distancias!».

Más tarde, fuimos a un club nocturno cercano. Las luces estaban atenuadas, por lo que me resultaba más sencillo comportarme de una manera más desinhibida... bueno, al menos, ligeramente. Prestando atención a las mentiras de mi temeroso corazón, me cubrí con una armadura invisible formada por mi instinto de supervivencia y entré en la pista de baile con Eduardo tras nuestra cena informal. Una serie de intensas emociones en las que se entrecruzaban la atracción y el miedo me engulleron, con la inquietud brotando victoriosa de aquella batalla. Cualquier intento por vencer a este enemigo era en vano. Regodeándome en una trampa emocional de negatividad, me apresuré a volver a nuestra mesa tan pronto como sentí aquella sensación prohibida: cercanía y... amor. ¿Me atrevería a llamarlo amor? ¿Por qué me resulta tan tabú esta palabra? ¡Sí! ¡Yo quería a Eduardo! Por muy indeciso que pueda sentirse uno del amor a primera vista, puede existir y, de hecho, existe. Mi acompañante tenía una expresión de intenso desconcierto pintada en la cara. La confusión parecía habérsele quedado grabada de forma indeleble en su atónito semblante.

—¿Qué sucede? ¿Por qué has vuelto corriendo a la mesa tan rápido?

En un momento cargado de emoción y perplejidad recíproca por mi propio comportamiento, me quedé sin habla. Sencillamente, no sabía qué decir. Me sentí como si estuviera contemplando las emociones de alguien a quien apenas conocía: yo misma.

Queridos espectadores literarios, avanzad rápidamente cerca de tres décadas y sentaos junto a mí, en mi oficina del centro de rehabilitación. Conoced a una pareja de octogenarios, dos personas que se quieren mutuamente con tanto ardor y sinceridad como el día en el que se conocieron.

—Lo quise desde el primer momento en que lo vi —me explica la mujer en más de una ocasión.

El caballero se hace eco de exactamente los mismos sentimientos que su esposa, con la misma ternura. La pareja regresa a casa en un taxi, piropeándose y mimándose como un par de adolescentes. ¡Es una escena digna de ver!

Contrastad mi reacción en aquel memorable día: en la primera cita con Eduardo. Recordad al niño que me encontré en la consulta de pediatría, que me sugirió que me borrara las manchas: una verdadera imposibilidad (o al menos eso era lo que yo pensaba en aquel momento), un estigma que debía ocultar costara lo que costara, incluso a riesgo de parecer excéntrica a los veintitrés años de edad. «¡El amor duele! ¡Ten cuidado!», me coreaba sin cesar mi dolorido corazón.

Como es comprensible, Eduardo se quedó perplejo. Por muy urgente y fervientemente que lo deseara, yo no lograba romper el hielo, así que me escapé, sin proporcionar una explicación adecuada. En retrospectiva, ¿cómo podría haber penetrado a través de aquel férreo muro de miedo, edificado por un corazón rebosante de dolor? No tenía el ímpetu emocional ni los recursos necesarios para descifrar aquellas complejidades —al menos, no de forma consciente— como para levantar la cabeza el tiempo suficiente y declararle la verdad al hombre al que quería. Y así, él se quedó en la inopia, mientras que yo me concentré en conseguir una ruptura limpia, que me librara de la angustia. En realidad, sin embargo, me estaba muriendo por dentro. Me llevó a casa y, con un beso en la mejilla, nos separamos, con un silencio cargado de emoción.

No obstante, dos días más tarde, volví a ver a Eduardo de nuevo, porque estaba sentado, a la vista de todo el mundo, en la cafetería de la escuela con un grupo de amigos, todos ellos estudiantes de medicina. Tuve amplias oportunidades de acercarme a hablar con él, pero eludí lo que podría haber sido una grata manera de romper el hielo. Materializándose por los pasillos de mi pasado, me vino a la mente el pensamiento que resucitó al cruel médico que me había sostenido la barbilla entre las manos, pidiéndoles un diagnóstico a sus residentes, como si yo no fuera más que un objeto inanimado, que pudiera ser diseccionado por su cruel escrutinio y su insensible crítica. El objeto de mi deseo secreto me contempló con incredulidad, como si se le hubiera pintado un enorme signo de interrogación en el rostro, preguntándose por qué había cambiado tanto en solo dos días.

Aun así, Eduardo no se rendía fácilmente, aunque siempre siendo un caballero. Sigilosamente, se dirigió a la puerta de salida de la cafetería para esperarme. Cuando yo estaba a punto de marcharme, lo localicé contemplándome con su característica mirada penetrante y sentí como si hubiera metido el pie en unas arenas movedizas. Todo mi maquillaje corrector había desaparecido y, sin la suficiente cantidad, me sentí como un boceto a la espera de que el pincel y la paleta del artista me completaran. Aunque me encontraba en una estancia llena de gente, me sentí sola, desnuda, deseando con todas mis fuerzas poder esconderme. Allí de pie estaba Eduardo, mirándome más perplejo que nunca. No tuve más opción que huir —tanto de mí misma como de él— para liberarme de la vergüenza y la pena cuyos orígenes habían quedado permanentemente grabados en mi historia personal. Varias veces después de aquel incidente, siempre que veía a Eduardo con amigos, hacía todos los esfuerzos del mundo por evitarlo, y él lo sabía. En una ocasión, estaba a punto de entrar en clase de Anatomía, cuando noté un suave golpecito en la espalda, y era el mismísimo Eduardo, ofreciéndose a ayudarme con mis estudios de Miología. Sin saber cómo responder, me puse color escarlata y fui incapaz de pronunciar palabra mientras esperaba con impaciencia a que la puerta se abriera para poder escaparme. Cualquier otro joven, con mucha menos sensibilidad y compasión, habría huido lejos de allí tras un comportamiento tan extraño. En su lugar, él persistió, apareciendo por casualidad delante de mí, persiguiéndome con gracia, pero todo fue en vano. Eso no quiere decir, por mucha imaginación que le echara, que yo fuera indiferente. Todo lo contrario, me frustraban aquellos sentimientos autoimpuestos de inquietud que me hacían encontrarme tan fuera de lugar: dos malévolos espectros de mi propia creación, cerniéndose siempre sobre mí.

Una y otra vez, perdí mi oportunidad, hasta que un día, con mis manchas bien camufladas, me encontré con el Adonis una vez más, en un laboratorio ocupado normalmente por estudiantes de medicina. Allí, de pie detrás de mi instructor, a apenas dos metros y medio de mí, localicé a mi ubicuo y benévolo pretendiente. Me hizo un gesto, como si quisiera hablar conmigo. Quise huir de nuevo, pero sus penetrantes ojos azules me cautivaron. Más tarde, cuando me lo encontré en el pasillo y lo acompañé hasta su taquilla, reuní el valor suficiente para preguntarle si quería venir conmigo a la fiesta de Navidad de mi mejor amiga Julie en Nueva York. Al principio, vaciló, pero después aceptó, diciéndome que tendría que regresar a casa temprano para preparar un examen final que debía hacer al día siguiente. Más tarde, cuando nos encontramos por casualidad en el vestíbulo de nuevo, me pidió que quedáramos en su apartamento, que estaba más cerca de la ciudad que el mío. Aunque iba en contra de mis creencias internas y de mis costumbres, acepté, sintiendo que acceder a aquello era lo menos que podía hacer, dado el dolor que sin duda le había causado. En realidad, aquello estaba en las antípodas de mis intenciones, del grito de aquel insidioso mantra: «¡El amor duele! ¡Ten cuidado!». Mi *modus operandi* siempre había sido y seguirá siendo tratar a todo el mundo con el debido respeto y consideración: especialmente a aquellas personas a las que quiero. De hecho, seguramente debía de albergar ese último sentimiento por Eduardo, dado que nunca me había atrevido a proponer una cita o a atreverme a pisar el domicilio de un hombre yo sola. Aquella era verdaderamente la primera vez para mí, en todos los sentidos.

Ataviada con un vestido peruano creación de una amiga (una falda negra y un chaleco también negro con un suéter fino de angora azul debajo), el cabello rizado y suelto sobre los hombros y al volante de mi humilde automóvil de segunda mano, me presenté en el domicilio de Eduardo. Vi a mi acompañante a través de una de las ventanas mientras se aproximaba a la puerta. Vestido con unos pantalones de traje y sin camisa, era la viva imagen del esteticismo masculino. Dicho de un modo más coloquial, exudaba atractivo físico, cosa que no pude evitar percibir. Eduardo me pidió que me quedara en el salón mientras se cambiaba. Cuando salió de su dormitorio, me di cuenta de que llevaba una guitarra, que empezó a tocar, mientras cantaba la canción de los Bee Gees, *How Can You Mend a Broken Heart?* Aquella melodía tenía mucho que ver con mi involuntaria actitud distante. Eduardo comenzó a acariciarme los hombros de una manera muy íntima, pero, de repente, nos dimos cuenta de que era hora de que nos marcháramos a la fiesta.

Acordamos que llevaríamos mi pequeño Honda rojo, que Eduardo conducía con destreza. Por el camino, a petición suya, le fui leyendo preguntas de su examen final de Anatomía, vacilando al pronunciar algunas palabras en inglés, pero logrando un mejor resultado con aquellas de raíz latina. Me encontraba ligeramente nerviosa, pero la amabilidad de mi acompañante y su caballerosidad extrema al sujetarme las puertas para que yo pasara y, en general, al hacerme sentir toda una dama, hizo que me instalara en una zona de confort y seguridad. En la fiesta, no vimos separados por la multitud y, mientras mi querida Julie me presentaba a algunos de sus amigos, mi acompañante circuló entre la gente. Dado que no habíamos tenido la oportunidad de comunicarnos y teniendo en cuenta la presión impuesta por su examen del día siguiente, decidimos marcharnos temprano. Para mi sorpresa, acepté la invitación de Eduardo de entrar en su apartamento. No puedo mentir: Estaba nerviosa, pero la sensación de conexión que se había establecido entre mi nuevo amigo y yo trascendía una vez más a cualquier recelo.

Una vez dentro del apartamento, entramos en la oficina de Eduardo. Allí, en la pantalla de su ordenador, había una carta de una página que supuse que había sido escrita para mí. Mi creciente entusiasmo, unido a mi escaso vocabulario en inglés, me impidieron leer toda la misiva y, sin embargo, mi mirada recayó sobre la última línea: «Tu admirador secreto». Debí de demostrar cierta incomodidad, porque regresamos a la zona del pequeño salón, donde nos sentamos. Justo cuando Eduardo comenzó a masajearme los hombros, dije que me tenía que marchar. Me levanté y mi acompañante me condujo hasta la puerta. Con cariño y modestia, trató de besarme. Yo le ofrecí la mejilla. Eduardo adoptó una expresión solemne, y comprendí que se había quedado profundamente decepcionado. Me marché con el corazón en un puño. Una vez más, aquella fue otra oportunidad perdida que se me escapaba entre los dedos, como una bandada de esquivas mariposas. Sencillamente, no podía —o, más bien, no lo haría— permitirme la intimidad que tanto anhelaba, y no con cualquiera, sino con el hombre más entregado y encantador que había conocido jamás.

El ciclo de rechazo continuó su curso, a medida que yo persistía en mis intentos por ignorar a Eduardo. Cada vez que me topaba con él, daba todos los rodeos que fueran necesarios para evitarlo. Sin embargo, ni por un solo momento lograba quitármelo de la cabeza. De hecho, él inundaba mis pensamientos con una avalancha de emociones, ahogándome en un océano de sentimientos. Mis calificaciones empezaron a resentirse, y temí que me expulsaran del programa. Inquietud, autodegradación, pérdidas del pasado... Todo aquello estaba sumergido en el profundo y oscuro abismo de mi corazón. Quizás, en retrospectiva, mi postura puede interpretarse como un mecanismo de defensa. Antes de que me rechazaran, prefería adoptar la posición dominante, el poder de ser la persona que se retirara antes. No quería quedarme sola de nuevo —preguntándome a mí misma por qué, dándole vueltas, interrogándome y dudando de mí misma hasta el infinito y más allá—, todo por nada. Al hacer tal cosa, engañé a mi admirador, convenciéndolo erróneamente para que se creyera mi indiferencia. En realidad, no obstante, mi inseguridad era la culpable, la fuente de mi fingida actitud distante. No podía comprender como una tímida muchacha de montaña con tan poco mundo como yo podía atraer a un chico atractivo y elegante como él. Al proyectar mis propias dudas sobre mí en Eduardo, me saboteaba a mí misma y mi posibilidad de alcanzar el amor verdadero (es decir, lo que yo pensaba que tenía que ser la definición de «amor verdadero»: aceptación incondicional y un compromiso duradero). Siempre que veía a Eduardo, una tromba de emociones invadía mi ser, dejándome a su merced, como si estuviera yendo a la deriva en un inmenso océano sin bote de salvamento. Aun así, me sentía unida a él por una maravillosa sensación de conexión, algo que no había experimentado nunca antes. No obstante, como no me sentía digna, no tenía ni la menor intención de revelar mis verdaderos sentimientos.

Una tarde que Eduardo se hallaba sentado en el vestíbulo en un sofá, me acerqué a él con una carta en mano —una epístola inventada, llena de mentiras y más mentiras—, donde le contaba una tragedia que le había acaecido a alguien de mi pasado, alguien que me recordaba a él. Me inventé aquella historia como medio para rehabilitar mi reputación ante él, por no mencionar mi propia salud mental. Si alguien me pidiera que explicara qué contenía aquella carta, no podría, porque cuando te inventas una historia, surgen diferentes versiones del mismo relato y se vuelven contra ti, atormentándote. Decir mentiras significa no contar dos veces la misma historia. Si, por el contrario, tienes la verdad de tu parte, pueden darse diferentes versiones de la misma anécdota, pero siempre surge una esencia de veracidad —la verdad inalterable y empírica—, en palabras que nunca podrán distorsionarse.

Y así, con el espíritu más abatido del mundo, me escapé, una vez más, con un esfuerzo colosal de protegerme de lo que podría haber sido la relación más grandiosa y satisfactoria de mi vida. A causa de una serie de mentiras y de mi agitación interna personal, me quedé aprisionada en mi propia trampa y solamente gracias al paso del tiempo he llegado a comprender que únicamente yo podía liberarme mediante un continuo, concienzudo, jubiloso, misterioso y finalmente triunfante proceso de autodescubrimiento.

Capítulo 10

Tú estabas allí

Carta para Julie

Querida Julie:

En este punto de mi narración, he decidido detenerme para rendir homenaje a mi mejor amiga en este mundo: ¡sí, tú! Tú has sido la principal fuente de la que he extraído el valor para escribir este libro y componer los pasajes de mi historia y volver a revivir algunos recuerdos muy dolorosos y también otros alegres. Gracias a tu desinteresado corazón y a tu cariño sin condiciones, tú eres —y siempre lo serás— la personificación de la definición de la palabra «amistad». Cuando acababa de llegar a Estados Unidos, tímida y apocada, me acogiste bajo tu ala y me guiaste, me incluiste en tus reuniones sociales y me animaste a relacionarme con gente cuando yo apenas hablaba ni una palabra de inglés. Mis cicatrices faciales no te importaron. Me veías por lo que yo era realmente y sacabas lo mejor de mí. Mediante gestos, expresiones faciales y representaciones gráficas, me iniciaste en mi nuevo mundo. A todo le dabas un contexto —etiquetas y significados— y, gracias a ello, me proporcionaste un entorno en el que yo pude evolucionar. Reíste y lloraste conmigo, me abrazaste y me colmaste de apoyo como nadie más

390

logró hacerlo. Incluso me avisaste del paso de las estaciones, a medida que la naturaleza se cubría de blanco con su cíclico atuendo.

En mis momentos más bajos, cuando las luces del mundo se atenuaban y la esperanza no era más que una palabra vacía, tú estabas allí. Cuando la pena me consumía y me aferré a la ayuda artificial como fuente de energía, me levantaste y me mostraste el verdadero significado de la valentía: la importancia de reunir coraje interno para afrontar con la cabeza bien alta la vida, con todos sus más y sus menos. El día que hiciste que prescindiera del Valium que me habían recetado —aquellas minúsculas píldoras que enmascaraban esos sentimientos a los que no podía enfrentarme—, me liberaste del daño autoimpuesto y me mostraste el camino que conducía a la vida, la senda que tenía que recorrer sin mi hermana, sin olvidarla nunca, pero con paso firme y convencido, por mis propios medios. De no haber estado tú allí para abrazarme y guiarme, ¿quién sabe dónde estaría yo hoy? ¿Quién sabe cómo se manifiesta un dolor cuando se reprime constantemente? Tiemblo solo de pensarlo, pero no lo necesito, porque tú estabas allí.

Gracias a tu capacidad para llegar hasta mí, me rescataste de los estragos de un angustiado corazón y evocaste la sonrisa que hoy baila en mis labios. Tú estabas allí —y por eso, yo estoy para ti— ahora y siempre.

¡Muchas gracias, Julie!

¡Te quiero!

Isabella

Capítulo 11

Montañas y valles

En asuntos del corazón, no pasé una época demasiado próspera durante aquel periodo de mi vida, en gran parte, debido a la inseguridad producida por mis manchas faciales. No llegaba a comprender entonces lo que sé ahora: que aquellas manchas en sí no eran borrones en mi vida. Más bien, lo que me impedía conseguir alegría en el amor era la percepción que tenía de mí misma.

En cuanto a Eduardo, en realidad, no volví a verle mucho después de aquella funesta carta inventada que le había escrito, excepto por un par de encuentros de pasada. La primera vez que nos encontramos después de mi negativa reacción por escrito fue en las escaleras mecánicas. Mientras bajábamos (por desgracia, esa era la misma dirección que había tomado nuestra relación), Eduardo estaba de pie justo detrás de mí.

—¿Todavía sigues viviendo con aquella anciana señora? —me preguntó.

—Sí —le respondí, sin añadir nada más.

Eduardo pareció disgustado y decepcionado.

—¡Vas a pasarte la vida allí! —me contestó con dureza, dando a entender que yo estaba destinada a ser una solterona.

Se impuso el silencio durante unos segundos hasta que nos bajamos de las escaleras. Eduardo continuó su camino hacia la salida, mientras que yo giré bruscamente hacia la izquierda para entrar en la cafetería. ¡Qué tragedia experimentamos cuando las palabras fallan, cuando la falta de comunicación o la pérdida de expresión oscurece la verdad de lo que desearíamos expresar. Los sentimientos por sí solos no funcionan como mecanismos de pensamiento o habla. Ahora comprendo que, de nuevo, debería haber aprovechado la oportunidad de confesar lo que albergaba en el interior de mi corazón, pero, sencillamente, no pude. Las razones de mi reticencia aún se me escapan, pero, de nuevo, puede que no. Quizás no, ¡seguro! , tenía que evolucionar y crecer para poder ver toda la situación —y a mí misma— de forma objetiva y admitir mi valor intrínseco con o sin necesidad de aprobación externa. Aun así, el dolor de perder al que consideraba mi hombre ideal era más de lo que podía soportar. Me consumía el hecho de que yo misma había provocado que Eduardo se comportara de forma distante conmigo y, por lo tanto, yo misma lo hubiera apartado de mí, muy en contra de mis intenciones subliminales. El que no pudiera enfrentarme a él emocionalmente y que mi falta de soltura con el idioma dificultara cualquier intercambio significativo era, o así pensaba yo, por mi culpa, y de aquello solo podía culparme a mí misma. Ahora, me pregunto por qué había que buscar culpables. Lo que tenía con Eduardo fue un encuentro trascendental en mi vida —algo en lo que me volqué con toda mi esperanza y hasta mi último aliento— y seguí sintiendo todo aquello... hasta que decidí seguir adelante. Ninguna otra opción parecía posible o sostenible.

Parte del proceso de seguir adelante consistió en asentar mi carrera en Estados Unidos para conseguir el título de enfermera. Dado mi insuficiente conocimiento de la geografía estadounidense, pensé para mis adentros: «¿Por qué no trato de hacer el examen en California, que es el estado contiguo a Nueva Jersey?». ¡Piensa un poco, Isabella! En lo que se me antojó un vuelo interminable (casi siete horas), volé hasta California y me presenté a aquel examen, el más difícil de todo el país. Más tarde, me embarqué en una trepidante visita turística en autobús de nueve días. Durante el viaje, conocí a tres excéntricas señoras (a las que llamaré colectivamente las Clausen: Jane, Emily y Margret, la última de las cuales era la hija de mediana edad de Emily). Cuando descubrieron que yo era enfermera, se colgaron de mí como si fueran koalas, siguiéndome a todas partes. Sus divertidas travesuras me hacían reír y lograban que apartara de mi mente las tensiones de mi vida cotidiana. En los hoteles, se aseguraban de tener un amplio surtido de toallas y demás parafernalia, costumbre que ponía los nervios de punta al personal del hotel. Encontrarme con ellas también me hizo comprender que muchas veces las apariencias engañan. Margret, la señora de mediana edad, era aficionada a manipular a los que tenía a su alrededor, cosa que yo apenas podía comprender.

—Vamos a cenar a uno de los restaurantes más exclusivos de la ciudad —me anunció una noche.

—Pero ¿cómo? —protesté yo—. Si no tenemos reserva.

—¡Espera y verás! La sigilosa mirada de Margret me puso ligeramente nerviosa.

Cuando entramos en el ilustre establecimiento, Margret fue directamente hasta el maître y, dándose aires de dama de la alta sociedad, declaró:

—Clausen, reserva para cuatro.

—Lo siento, señora, pero no tenemos en la lista a nadie con ese nombre —le respondió el maître.

A continuación tuvo lugar la interpretación más asombrosa y digna de un Óscar de indignación e ira que yo haya presenciado jamás, antes o después de entonces. Margret comenzó a despotricar a voz en grito, expresando su terrible disgusto y amenazando con hacer pública la grandísima negligencia del personal del restaurante por no haber anotado nuestra reserva. Aquel jaleo seguramente se oyó hasta en Wisconsin, no me cabe la menor duda de que así fue. Para impedir que siguiera prolongándose aquella agonía —para todos los implicados—, el maître nos acompañó hasta una mesa. Cuando aquel episodio hubo concluido y ya habíamos salido de allí sin ningún percance, nuestra dramática acompañante se echó a reír a carcajadas. Me preguntaba cómo alguien podía vivir de esa manera, con aquellas costumbres tan ladinas, independientemente de la ocasión. Fue algo digno de contemplar y, aunque la comida fue lujosísima, de alguna manera, yo no lograba justificar la diatriba de Margret.

Aquella fue, sin duda, toda una experiencia. ¡Me pregunto dónde estarán esas mujeres ahora mismo! No volví a verlas jamás.

Una anciana señora que nos acompañaba en la visita en autobús también me proporcionó un recuerdo para mi álbum de recortes. Durante nuestro viaje, apenas cruzó conmigo una palabra, pero cuando las Clausen y yo fuimos a uno de los casinos del Lago Tahoe, vi a la señora (y aquí utilizaré ese término con cautela) jugando al póquer, sentada en una vulgar postura típicamente masculina, fumándose un puro con toda tranquilidad. ¡Apenas podía creerme que aquella fuera la mismísima pasajera taciturna del autobús a la que había visto apenas días antes!

Junto con aquellos cómicos interludios, también me detuve a disfrutar de las vistas. California es un estado muy hermoso. Las secuoyas me resultaron especialmente fascinantes. Su majestuosidad, alcance y fuerza vital me hicieron comprender que nosotros, los humanos, no somos más que minúsculas fracciones de un espectro completo de milagros que pueblan este planeta.

Cuando regresé a casa, me enteré de que había aprobado los difíciles exámenes de titulación de enfermería para California y que eran convalidables con Nueva Jersey. Eso significaba que podría practicar mis conocimientos en ambos estados. Me sentía en la cima del mundo, sentimiento que se debía a mis logros. Finalmente, era una persona válida, completa, libre de explorar los confines de mi potencial y de demostrarle a mi escéptico hermano que las mujeres (e incluso su hermana) podían, de hecho, labrarse una carrera inteligente y próspera.

Por supuesto, anhelaba compartir la gran noticia con mi «admirador secreto» (al menos, yo pensaba que así era como se llamaba a sí mismo en la carta por ordenador dirigida a mí que pude ver el día de la fiesta de Navidad de Julie). Una tarde, cuando vi a Eduardo sentado con dos de sus amigos a la entrada de la cafetería de la escuela, tuve la oportunidad de contarle brevemente que había aprobado los exámenes de enfermería de California. No pude evitar hablar con él en aquel momento y me atrevo a decir, que tampoco deseaba evitarlo. Algo dentro de mí buscaba la aprobación de aquel hombre que tantísimo me importaba. Me sentía exultante, pero mi emocionante logro adquiría un carácter especial cuando pensaba en compartirlo con Eduardo. Mi inherentemente baja autoestima debió de inspirar ese deseo. Colorada y nerviosa (pero con mis manchas faciales bien cubiertas), me aproximé a Eduardo, sin saber qué decirle, así que proferí algo estúpido, del estilo de: «Hay veces que a la gente le pasan cosas malas» (posiblemente, refiriéndome a la mezcolanza de invenciones que le había escrito). No sé si fueron aquellas palabras en particular las que salieron de mi boca en aquel momento. Fue como si estuviera tratando de rellenar el espacio para ocultar mi vacilación y mi incomodidad. El propio Eduardo adoptó un aspecto incómodo y confuso, ¡como si estuviera pensando él también lo excéntrica y extraña que yo era! Embargada por la vergüenza, me marché, de nuevo a merced de mis sentimientos internos de estar fuera de lugar, incapaz de dejar que la verdad saliera a la luz.

Aproximadamente un mes más tarde, mientras yo salía del lavabo de señoras de la escuela, vi a Eduardo apresurándose para entrar en clase. Al intercambiar brevemente unos breves saludos, nuestros caminos se cruzaron una última vez, para no volver a entrecruzarse jamás, o al menos, eso pensaba yo. La casualidad tiene maneras muy curiosas de revelarse. Pero no es momento de que me explique todavía. Para aquellos lectores que no soporten el suspense, solamente puedo decirles: ¡mala suerte! Tendréis que esperar hasta que se desarrolle mi historia.

Unos meses después de aquel efímero encuentro casual (por muy fortuito que fuera, había significado muchísimo para mí), un amigo, Ben, se me acercó y me informó de que Eduardo se había marchado a otro campus. Ben me transmitió el mensaje de que Eduardo me deseaba lo mejor y se preocupó por decirme que Eduardo se había prometido para casarse con una enfermera.

—¿Cómo sabes que eso es verdad? —le pregunté, tratando de contener mis emociones.

—Bueno, yo mismo he conocido a la chica. Lleva puesto un bonito anillo en el dedo. Lo mejor será que te quites a ese hombre de la cabeza —me dijo aquel amigo casi como una orden, como si estuviera intentando protegerme del dolor, al mismo tiempo que me planteaba la realidad del modo más duro imaginable.

Me quedaría muy corta si dijera que simplemente me sentí alicaída. Lloré durante todo el día, al menos en mi interior de mi corazón, y fui incapaz de centrar mi atención en las clases. Aquel dolor me embargaba de tal forma el corazón que apenas podía soportarlo. Querer y perder había sido una constante en mi vida, y no deseaba padecer aquel dolor. Quería deshacerme de él arrojándolo a un vasto océano para que se consumiera entre el oleaje de las profundidades marinas, en lugar de en lo más profundo de mi alma. Sencillamente, no estaba preparada para el desafío de soportar aquello a lo que no quería enfrentarme: Que Eduardo había desaparecido de mi vida para siempre. De algún modo, logré salir del abismo de dolor que me estaba engullendo, pero sin demasiado éxito. Estaba a punto de terminar mis clases. No podía dejar que todo por lo que había luchado y esforzado se fuera por la borda.

Mientras tanto, tenía la esperanza de que Tomás tuviera más suerte que yo en el terreno amoroso. No sé por qué me sentía así. Quizá sencillamente era por el parentesco que nos unía y por mi deseo de protegerle de algún modo. En retrospectiva, comprendo que, con toda probabilidad, él intentaba protegerme de las dificultades y durezas de la vida; y, sin embargo, lo que mi hermano no comprendía era que así me sometía a más presión de la que yo podía gestionar. Su temperamento a menudo me hacía la vida muy difícil, y me hacía desear que pudiera vivir separada de él geográficamente. ¡Sí, así era! La verdadera razón era que deseaba que mi hermano contrajera matrimonio. No puedo mentir.

Por las razones antes expuestas, me sentí aliviada cuando Tomás anunció que tenía novia. Yo percibía que la causa de esta decisión era la urgencia de mi padre por tener nietos, cosa que expresó en una conversación telefónica, y yo oí por casualidad una tarde.

—Hijo mío —le dijo papá a Tomás con su característico tono imperativo—, ¿cuándo te vas a casar y a darme nietos?

Después de aquella conversación, note que aumentaba el interés de mi hermano por casarse. Mientras tanto, yo buscaba mi propio camino en la vida, a medida que intentaba trepar la montaña del éxito. No sabía a dónde me conduciría aquel viaje, pero tenía que encontrar mi propio camino. Mi hermano no es que estuviera precisamente apoyando mi causa, y si yo misma no tomaba las riendas firmemente para encaminarme por el sendero de mi propio destino, nadie lo haría.

Desgraciadamente, algunas personas no tienen la buena fortuna de poder labrarse su destino, especialmente los ancianos. Con un enorme dolor de corazón, presencié como mi hada madrina quedaba a merced de un destino cruel e inexorable. A lo largo del tiempo, se fue haciendo evidente que las excentricidades de la Sra. C. no hacían más que contribuir a su declive. Nacida durante los años de la Gran Depresión, había aprendido a ser frugal y a ahorrar hasta llegar al punto de someterse a sí misma a privaciones, particularmente en lo referente a la nutrición. Esta negligencia de su propia alimentación me producía una gran preocupación, e hice todo lo que se encontraba en mi mano para contribuir al bienestar de mi benefactora. A veces, sin embargo, cuando la gente tiene sus costumbres fijas, no hay intervención que valga. Un día, oí un fuerte golpe y corrí a ver qué había sucedido. Allí, en el suelo de su habitación, encontré a mi estimada Sra. C. retorciéndose de dolor. Al parecer, se había caído, quizás intentando enchufar algo a la pared. Comprobé que su pulso se estaba acelerando y me di cuenta de que no podía moverse en absoluto. Daba la sensación de que se le había desencajado el hombro de su sitio. La pobre señora parecía desorientada y sufriendo una intensa agonía. Yo sospechaba que tenía una fractura, además de una contusión. Inmediatamente, llamé al 911. Finalmente, resultó que mis diagnósticos eran correctos. Después de aquello, mi querida Sra. C. se precipitó en una espiral descendente. La trasladaron del hospital a una residencia de ancianos y, a partir de aquel momento, fueron disminuyendo más y más nuestros contactos e interacciones. Aquella circunstancia se debió al hecho de que los parientes de la Sra. C. cayeron en picado como buitres para devorar los efectos personales y las demás posesiones de la anciana. Mientras que habían mantenido una actitud distante durante sus años de vitalidad y salud, los parientes de la Sra. C. vieron su situación de debilidad como una oportunidad para confiscar, despachar y reclamar las pertenencias de la anciana como si fueran suyas. Creo que mi relación con ella y su afecto por mí los consideraban como impedimentos para sus objetivos, por lo que la familia hizo todo lo posible por distanciarnos y, por eso, me prohibieron que la visitara.

Esforzándome por salir adelante, continué con mis estudios mientras trabajaba en el hospital de la zona como enfermera diplomada. Tomás ya se había mudado a un apartamento en las cercanías. Por mi parte, apenas ganaba suficiente como para costearme alojamiento y manutención en mi nuevo hogar con la Sra. Alan. Uno de los principales inconvenientes de vivir allí fue que tuve que renunciar a mi querido perro, *Shaggy*, que había sido mi compañero en casa de la Sra. C. El perrito, de aspecto parecido al famoso *Benji*, desgraciadamente se escapó de la familia a la que se lo había cedido, por lo que no albergaba esperanzas de volver a verle jamás. Una tarde, me pasé por casa de la Sra. C. para recoger algo que me había dejado allí y me encontré a una cuadrilla de pintores que estaban dejando la casa lista para ponerla en venta. Me preguntaron si yo tenía perro.

—Sí solía tener uno —respondí.

—Vale, pues un perro loco ha entrado en la casa, ha ido hasta esa habitación y ha comenzado a ladrarnos sin parar, y después ha salido corriendo a la calle, aullando como si no hubiera mañana —me contó uno de los pintores, señalando hacia mi antigua habitación.

Comencé a describir a *Shaggy* y, en efecto, los pintores confirmaron que era él quien había estado allí. Se me llenaron los ojos de lágrimas. Decidí sentarme y esperar a ver si *Shaggy* volvía. De repente, uno de los pintores gritó:

—¡Ahí está ese perro loco otra vez!

—¡¡¡*Shaggy*!!! —exclamé, incapaz de contener mis emociones.

Mi pequeña mascota estaba tan contenta de verme, que saltó y me saludó como si se hubiera hecho realidad su deseo de encontrarme. Su lealtad y gratitud me abrumaron y me sorprendieron en lo más hondo de mi ser. De haber sido diferentes las circunstancias, me lo habría quedado. No obstante, por desgracia, la Sra. Alan no podía tener perro. Se me partió el corazón en miles de pedazos cuando comprendí lo que era inevitable: Tenía que volver a desprenderme de *Shaggy* una vez más. La casa estaba a punto de ponerse a la venta, mis estudios estaban encarrilados y, sencillamente, no existía otra opción. Así pues, llevé a mi fiel compañero al refugio más cercano, suplicándole a la encargada que me llamara inmediatamente cuando le encontrara hogar a mi preciada mascota. Al día siguiente, recibí su llamada. Una mujer y su hijo lo habían adoptado. Eso significaba otra despedida más. Me enfrentaba a otra montaña que escalar y lo afronté con el valor de quien se ha visto abocado anteriormente a esas mismas circunstancias.

Otro inconveniente más de vivir con la Sra. Alan era su excesiva locuacidad, que lograba distraerme prácticamente siempre. En su presencia, mis momentos de estudio siempre se veían interrumpidos por su incesante conversación, y yo no lograba acabar de hacer nada. Aun así, seguí insistiendo, siempre recordando mis días con la Sra. C., cuya generosidad había inspirado que yo continuara con mis estudios y mi carrera. En una ocasión en la que, a pesar de que la prohibición de sus parientes que se oponían, me pasé a visitar a mi querida amiga, se aferró a mí, preguntándome:

—¿Dónde has estado? ¿Eres tú, mi Isabella? ¿Cuándo me vas a llevar a casa? ¡Llama a un taxi! ¡Por favor, llévame a nuestra casa! ¡Por favor, no me dejes aquí! —rogó.

Se me cayó el alma a los pies. Simplemente, no supe qué decirle, excepto que lo que ella deseaba no era posible. ¿Cómo podía decirle a mi bondadosa hada madrina que su casa ya había sido vendida y que no tenía otro lugar al que marcharse? No pude soportar verla en aquel estado, y no estaba en mi mano cambiar su situación. Con el corazón en un puño, le di un abrazo y un beso de despedida, para no volver a verla más. Me invadió un sentimiento de desesperación, pero no había nada que yo pudiera hacer. Solo podía querer a aquel bondadoso corazón —y decirle adiós—, tal y como había hecho antes en muchos sentidos y en numerosos casos en el pasado. Era como si los finales y los principios, las alegrías y las penas, las montañas y los valles fueran constantes en mi vida.

Una tarde, durante mi último año de estudios, justo antes de graduarme, pasé por una farmacia cerca de la antigua casa de la Sra. C. Por pura casualidad, la dueña me dedicó una mirada compasiva.

—¡Hola! ¡Hace mucho que no te veía! Lo he sentido muchísimo al enterarme de lo sucedido —me dijo, mientras le abonaba lo que le debía.

—¿Qué ha pasado? Mi sobresaltada expresión sorprendió a la farmacéutica.

—¿No te has enterado? —me preguntó.

—¿De qué?

—La Sra. C. ha fallecido. La farmacéutica me entregó el periódico del día.

—¿Cuándo? —pregunté, consumida por la pena, sin apenas mirar la necrológica.

—Hace poco. De hecho, hoy se celebra su entierro.

Me sentí como si una parte trascendental de mi propia vida acabara de llegar a su fin. Comprobé la hora del entierro de la Sra. C. y me di cuenta de que tenía bastante tiempo como para ir a presentar mis respetos, me metí en mi coche y me dirigí al cementerio. De camino, me detuve a comprar una rosa roja. Cuando llegué a mi destino, me di cuenta de que ya habían introducido el ataúd a dos metros bajo tierra. La ceremonia acababa de terminar, y no había otros amigos o familiares por allí. La reluciente y limpia tapa del ataúd todavía estaba al descubierto. En aquel momento, se reafirmó mi creencia sobre los momentos oportunos para absolutamente todo. Era como si la Sra. C. hubiera dicho: «¡Esperen un momento! Todavía tengo que decirle adiós a alguien especial». Los enterradores me preguntaron si quería estar sola. Les dije que sí. En aquellos momentos, abrí mi corazón, agradeciéndole a mi bondadosa hada madrina todo lo que había hecho para fraguar mi vida, especialmente en lo referente a haberme concedido el don de mi educación, que tan importante era para mí y sirvió como cimiento para mi futura carrera. Expresé mi gratitud por todos los buenos momentos que habíamos compartido juntas: las risas, las lecturas de la Biblia, el aprendizaje del inglés... por todo ello. Entonces, mientras me marchaba y dejaba que los hombres cubrieran el ataúd, me invadió una sensación de paz. Me sentí muy conmovida por que la Sra. C. me hubiera concedido el regalo de la despedida: aquella última expresión de deferencia, tan típica de ella. Aunque me sentía triste por haberla perdido, la oportunidad de haber podido dedicarle una reflexión personal me permitió cicatrizar heridas y me llenó de cariñosos recuerdos y gratitud. ¡Sra. C., siempre la llevaré a usted en mi corazón!

Y así, mientras un capítulo se cerraba, comenzó otro nuevo. Tomás contrajo matrimonio, para alegría de mis padres, que vinieron desde Perú con mis hermanos gemelos y mi hermana pequeña para asistir al gran acontecimiento, y se quedaron en Estados Unidos cerca de dos semanas.

A la espera del gran acontecimiento de Tomás, tuve que cuidar de mis hermanos pequeños. Para impedir que se aburrieran, conseguí que se apuntaran en una escuela parroquial, ocupándome yo misma de sus actividades y diversión mientras tanto. Estaba tan ocupada con las clases y atando los cabos sueltos, que aquella responsabilidad añadida era un impedimento bastante grande en una época tan crucial, aunque tener a mis hermanitos a mi alrededor era, por lo demás, fuente de mucha alegría. Mi familia me acusó de ser egoísta y distanciarme de ellos cuando, en realidad, lo único que deseaba era que mis padres comprendieran que mis planes y proyectos eran igualmente trascendentales que los de mi hermano. Así pues, después de la boda, mi familia regresó a Perú, dejándome en compañía de apenas unos cuantos amigos para celebrar aquel acontecimiento vital. Para desestabilizar aún más las cosas, las fotografías que Tomás se suponía que iba a tomar de mi día especial quedaron totalmente destruidas o borrosas cuando abrió su cámara de fotos. Y así, no quedó nada —ni siquiera las pruebas gráficas de aquella importantísima ocasión—. Por decirlo suavemente, me sentí desolada, pero, al mismo tiempo, orgullosa de haber llegado a aquel momento. Después de todo lo por lo que había pasado, internarme en los valles del sufrimiento, el miedo y la soledad —especialmente, sin la compañía de mi querida Laura— y escalar montañas emocionales bajo la luz del sol me hizo más fuerte de lo que nunca había sido hasta entonces. Por el camino, me sentí agradecida por haber contado con el apoyo de mis incondicionales aliadas —Julie, su madre y mi queridísima Sra. C.—, que fueron fortalezas aún más inexpugnables que las que había podido contemplar en mi viaje a Sacsayhuamán. Aún tenía un largo camino que recorrer, muchos valles que atravesar y muchas montañas que escalar, pero armada con los fundamentales ladrillos del amor, la esperanza y la confianza en mí misma, absolutamente todo parecía posible.

Capítulo 12

Libertad y complicaciones

Hasta aquí, mi vida había consistido en una serie de momentos circulares cerrados y epifanías, algunos de los cuales se produjeron por instigación propia y otros simplemente se trataron de los clarísimos designios del universo. Con el tiempo, he descubierto que cuando más nos esforzamos por que algo ocurra o tratamos de forzar el asunto, por así decirlo, menos tendrá lugar el efecto deseado, independientemente de lo organizado que sea el esfuerzo. Un buen ejemplo de esto era mi imagen propia, deslucida ese fatídico día en mi infancia cuando me caí sobre aquella fuente de natillas hirviendo, lo que posteriormente tuvo como consecuencia que me aparecieran mis manchas faciales, unas zonas de oscura hiperpigmentación con aspecto de borrones de tinta. De incontables maneras, tanto simbólicas como literales, aquel acontecimiento específico dirigió el curso de mi vida. Como consecuencia de mi baja autoestima y mi imagen deslustrada (que, según la opinión del niñito en la consulta de pediatría hace tantísimos años, tenía que corregírmelas borrándomelas), no podía ser totalmente yo, libre de interaccionar, relacionarme socialmente y proyectarme en el mundo tal y como me dictaban mis inclinaciones naturales. El deterioro visual de mis manchas faciales me transformaba en alguien a quien yo no reconocía y que no quería ser, corriendo constantemente a ocultarme, de forma bastante literal, siempre teniendo que llevar encima maquillaje corrector, pintalabios y otros tipos de herramientas enmascaradoras para camuflar aquellos estigmas que influían en casi cualquier decisión que tomara y cualquier movimiento que hiciera.

Un día, cuando menos me esperaba que me fuera a suceder algo tan trascendental, mientras estaba de pie en la cola de caja del supermercado, vi la foto de una chica con una marca en la mejilla muy similar a las mías. El titular hacía referencia a una hábil técnica de eliminación de ese tipo de marcas llevada a cabo por un famoso dermatólogo en Nueva York que, mediante un procedimiento de electrocauterización, era capaz de quemar la cicatriz no deseada. Prácticamente temblando de emoción, compré la revista y corrí a casa para leer en profundidad en el artículo. Sin malgastar ni un segundo en pensármelo dos veces, pronto me marché a la Gran Manzana para someterme a la intervención, sintiendo instintivamente que toda mi vida estaba a punto de cambiar. Emprendí sin compañía alguna aquel paso que me alteraría la vida. Por razones que no logro expresar —quizá porque compartir explicaciones y emociones haría que, de algún modo, disminuyera la intensidad de lo que estaba a punto de experimentar—, decidí afrontar en soledad aquel viaje profundamente personal.

Mientras estaba sentada en la silla con los ojos cerrados y protegidos, el médico fue quemándome las manchas del rostro, una por una. Cada ápice de dolor que sentí (y sí, por supuesto, sentí dolor, aunque estaba anestesiada) fue un ejercicio de lucha a muerte contra el enemigo: el estigma de mis cicatrices, que habían emponzoñado mi rostro como marcas de vil mugre que se resistían a desaparecer. En innumerables campos de batalla, aquellas naderías tan finas como el papel habían surgido como guerrillas insurgentes para conquistarme y frustrar mis alegrías presentes y futuras. Fueron ellas las que me despojaron de mi autoestima cuando aquel médico en el hospital en Perú sostuvo mi barbilla entre sus manos para mostrársela a sus residentes, como si yo fuera un monstruo de feria; hicieron que me acobardara ante mis admiradores; y fueron, o al menos yo así lo creía, la causa del rechazo de Lorenzo. Y lo que es más, me hicieron acobardarme ante Eduardo y huir de él, alguien a quien le tenía mucho cariño y con quien —de no ser por mis omnipresentes sentimientos de estar fuera de lugar— podría haber sido capaz de construir y mantener una relación duradera. Nunca lo sabré, y especular sobre ello en este punto solamente hace que esos espectros de mi pasado vuelvan a resurgir, pero en aquellos momentos en los que estaba sometiéndome al tratamiento, sentí ligereza de espíritu y que tenía un claro objetivo. Las implicaciones psicológicas y emocionales de lo que me estaba sucediendo solo pueden describirse como una vuelta a nacer, una renovación, un triunfo último de la voluntad sobre la adversidad. Por supuesto, el médico tenía poca idea, o ninguna, de que con cada movimiento de su mano estaba creando artesanalmente a una nueva persona. El precio desorbitado que costó la operación era algo secundario a todo lo que estaba experimentando en mi interior: la alegría y la exaltación de un destino totalmente nuevo.

Cuando terminó el tratamiento, mis labios y mi mandíbula inferior quedaron hinchados y protuberantes: una imagen no muy agradable. Me fui a casa y me acomodé entre mis cuatro paredes durante cerca de dos semanas, para escapar de la luz del sol y de la irritación resultante. Eso fueron instrucciones expresas del médico, y yo me cuidé de cumplirlas con fortaleza y resolución milimétricas. A medida que las heridas se iban curando, se convirtieron en costras oscuras y, tras dos semanas, comenzaron a pelarse y se desprendieron por arte de magia, como los restos de una serpiente mudando de piel. Hacia la tercera semana, mi hinchazón facial comenzó a disminuir. ¡Al fin era libre! Todas y cada una de las fibras de mi ser se revelaron cuando se me cayó el último resto de piel no deseada. El enemigo realmente había sido derrotado, dejando el país en guerra en un estado de pacífica alegría y renovación. Los daños del tumulto emocional y los ríos de dudas y complejos se derruyeron y se secaron como las ruinas de un antiguo reino olvidado. En su lugar, surgió una nueva parcela de confianza, que salía de las sombras, abrazando totalmente la luz, reverberando con energía vital.

Junto con mi nuevo ser, se me despertó el deseo de comprarme mi propia casa y declararme totalmente autónoma. ¡Oh, Estados Unidos, bella tierra de las oportunidades para aquellos que pugnan, muchísimas gracias! Mi generoso padre me ayudó con la compra, aunque yo ya estaba ganando un buen salario como terapeuta física en un hospital de la zona. Una amiga mía me habló sobre un inmueble que había descubierto a través de su marido, que era agente inmobiliario. La casa se iba a poner a la venta mediante subasta y, justo cuando todo estaba listo para que yo formalizara la compra y firmara el contrato, se presentó alguien con un número más bajo que el mío y prácticamente me arrancó el contrato de las manos. Por decirlo suavemente, me sentí decepcionada, pero tal y como lo quiso el destino, cuando se cerró aquella puerta, se abrió literalmente otra. Mi amiga me indicó otro inmueble que era el doble de grande, situado en un emplazamiento ideal para mis actividades cotidianas y mi estilo de vida. Creo firmemente en el yin-yang de la vida, y me parece que no deberíamos rebelarnos contra estos opuestos polarizados. La razón es que, justamente cuando piensas que tus sueños se han roto en mil pedazos, algo —o alguien— normalmente aparece para mejorar las circunstancias. Yo siempre he comunicado esta filosofía a la gente y he visto cómo se confirmaba una y otra vez. Justamente cuando piensas que toda esperanza es en vano y nubes de lluvia se ciernen sobre ti, repentinamente se despeja el cielo y, como un hermoso obsequio envuelto en papel de regalo, se asoma el sol y te sonríe desde el cielo.

A medida que las nubes se despejaban para mí, me puse en pie y acepté hacerme cargo de mi hermana pequeña. Esta circunstancia se debió a la insistencia de mis padres de que

Beatriz se encontraba en peligro de que la secuestraran terroristas peruanos que habían invadido el país en aquella época, asaltando a las clases acomodadas para que les entregaran grandes sumas de dinero. Amenazaban con que, de no recibir el dinero, secuestrarían a los hijos de estas familias, cuyo paradero y la ubicación de sus escuelas tenían sometidos a una constante vigilancia. Evidentemente, mamá y papá fueron víctimas de este chantaje y, sin saber a quien acudir, me pidieron que le proporcionara a Beatriz un refugio seguro. Aquella responsabilidad cayó sobre mí de forma bastante inesperada —y me atrevo a decir que supuso todo un desafío— justo cuando mi vida había comenzado a recuperar un poco de estabilidad, pero percibí el apremio de mis padres y accedí con mucho gusto. Hasta su primer año de universidad, Beatriz se quedó a mi cargo y me consideró como una especie de madre. Buscamos compañeras de piso y conseguimos formar un acogedor hogar. Se rumoreaba que alojarse en nuestra casa aseguraba conseguir buenos matrimonios, pues tras abandonar nuestro nido, la mayoría de las chicas que habían vivido con nosotras fueron tan afortunadas como para disfrutar de la dicha conyugal.

Durante esta época, tuve un pequeño choque frontal con el coche, que me provocó una lesión y dolores de espalda, cosa que me impidió ejercer de terapeuta física durante un tiempo. Aún con la esperanza de mantener mi espíritu emprendedor durante mi periodo de convalecencia, busqué trabajo y fui contratada como enfermera diplomada y encargada de la consulta de un médico de la zona. Un día, mientras abría el correo, vi un nombre que me resultaba familiar en uno de los informes quirúrgicos. Le pedí a mi jefe que me describiera al residente que allí figuraba. El médico me explicó que era alto, atractivo, rubio y de ojos azules. En aquel momento, se me cayó el alma a los pies, y el estómago se me subió hasta la garganta. «¡Es Eduardo!», exclamó mi corazón. Mi amor perdido, el hombre cuya presencia anhelaba, el hombre que apenas me conocía, pero que se había transformado en una imagen idealizada recreada y alimentada por mi mente y mi corazón, claramente tenía algún tipo de relación con el médico para el que yo trabajaba. Aquel era uno de esos momentos circulares que se cerraban, mucho más que una coincidencia. El instante en el que surgió el nombre de Eduardo, me inundaron la mente dispersos recuerdos, junto con más preguntas de las que posiblemente podía responder por mí misma. ¿Acudiría Eduardo a la oficina? ¿Tendría la oportunidad de volver a verle y, tal vez, reparar parte del daño que nuestra incómoda separación había causado? Por supuesto, no le dije ni una palabra al médico —ni a ninguna otra persona— acerca de que yo conocía a Eduardo ni compartí con él mis reflexiones internas. Justamente mientras andaba abstraída en estos pensamientos, se me acercó mi jefe y me preguntó si podía entrevistar a alguien para trabajar en la consulta, una mujer, que no era otra que... ¡¡¡la esposa de Eduardo!!! Todavía me acobardo solo de pensarlo. Aborrecía la idea de quizá tener que llevar a cabo una entrevista y explicarle complejos procedimientos a la mujer cuyo marido tanto había admirado y por el que aún albergaba profundos sentimientos latentes. Peor aún, no podía soportar el mero hecho de pensar que Eduardo pudiera visitar la consulta y descubrir que yo seguía soltera y sin compromiso.

Una semana después de que me pidieran que entrevistara a la mujer de Eduardo, se me curó milagrosamente la espalda, como por arte de una varita mágica invisible, y abandoné el trabajo en la consulta de aquel médico, para retomar mi puesto de terapeuta física. Necesitaba una vía de escape y creo que aunque hubiera estado atrapada en la mismísima boca del lobo, habría logrado escapar de allí costara lo que costara. ¿Qué acababa de suceder? Él estaba allí, pero volvió a desvanecerse; había aparecido y se había esfumado una vez más. Aquel patrón era inconfundible. ¿Acaso estaba persiguiendo a un fantasma, un mero producto de mi imaginación, para que se cumpliera mi deseo? Entonces, una vez más, él estaba casado y yo había estado a punto de tener que ponerme frente a frente a su esposa, ¡y nada menos que para contratarla! ¿Cuáles eran las posibilidades? ¿Aquel era acaso un cruel giro del destino, ofreciéndome un tentador bocado de la fruta prohibida, para después privarme de su dulzor? Mientras todos estos pensamientos inundaban mi mente, escaparse era mi único recurso, como de costumbre. Siempre me estaba escondiendo, huyendo, tanto de mí misma como de aquel a quien quería. No obstante, la verdad era que ya no tenía por qué escaparme.

Levantarme por las mañanas y mirarme al espejo había dejado de ser una pesada tarea o algo que me instigara miedo y angustia. Había logrado completarme por mi propio bien. Aunque no lo sabía entonces (¿qué persona joven, que lucha por encontrar un lugar en el mundo, posee tal conocimiento?), no necesitaba la adulación de otros. Tal vez, sin embargo, sí que sostenía esa idea, al menos, subconscientemente.

Para apartar de mi mente cualquier rescoldo de incertidumbre y las reflexiones sobre mi doloroso pasado, decidí celebrar mi recién descubierta libertad de las manchas faciales que me habían arruinado la vida hasta entonces emprendiendo un viaje de tres semanas por Europa: Suiza, Italia, Francia, Holanda, Austria y Alemania. Cinco amigos y yo nos embarcamos en aquella aventura: dos estudiantes de medicina, una enfermera, una psicóloga y una terapeuta física. Me alegró tomarme un tiempo de descanso de mi rutina diaria y empaparme de aire y de luz. A causa de la tremenda tragedia aérea de 1989 del vuelo 103 de la Pan Am sobre Lockerbie, Escocia, opté por utilizar la compañía aérea Lufthansa. Mis amigos, que cogieron un vuelo chárter por un precio considerablemente más bajo, se preguntaron por qué yo había decidido viajar sola, desembolsando tanto dinero. La respuesta está en que el conformismo nunca ha formado parte de mi naturaleza. Siempre dejo que me guíen mi cabeza y mi corazón, a pesar de las protestas y las sugerencias alternativas de los demás.

Sin embargo, empecé a cuestionarme a mí misma cuando, tras pasar los controles de seguridad, me detuvieron y me interrogaron sobre mi pasaporte peruano caducado. A día de hoy, sigo sin tener ni la más remota idea de por qué no reparé en aquello antes. Era, y sigo siéndolo, muy meticulosa con el protocolo, especialmente en lo referente a cumplir la ley. Aunque tenía una tarjeta de residente estadounidense en regla (lo que significaba que tenía residencia permanente en el país), mi pasaporte caducado podría haber hecho que me deportaran. Sin embargo, curiosamente, algo me dijo que debía mantener la calma, quizá porque tenía la verdad de mi parte. Atestigüé mi calidad de profesional de la salud y con total naturalidad, afirmé que estaba esperando la llegada de mis amigos en un vuelo chárter de Pam Am que había despegado del Aeropuerto Kennedy media hora antes que el mío. Percibí la comprensión de los funcionarios de aduanas, expliqué mis razones para viajar sola en Lufthansa y contesté a todas sus preguntas francamente y sin cortapisas. Cuando me los preguntaron, también les proporcioné los nombres de mis amigos. Claramente, no tenía nada que esconder. Gracias al diálogo cordial que mantuve con aquellos funcionarios, certificaron mi credibilidad y me proporcionaron un pasaporte temporal de seis meses de duración con el que podría viajar libremente dentro y fuera del país. Con un marcial «¡Bienvenida a Alemania!», el afable funcionario que me había concedido la libertad me estrechó la mano y se despidió. A lo largo de aquella dura experiencia, había comenzado a preocuparme por que mis amigos no me esperaran y, si no aparecía, me dejaran allí, perdida en un territorio extranjero y desconocido. Aunque no me faltaba experiencia en esas lides, temblé solo de pensarlo. La sala de espera era pequeña y estrecha, y no estaba equipada con las comodidades de hoy en día. Mientras esperaba durante media hora, el latido del corazón y el pulso se me aceleraron intermitentemente. Entonces, cuando ya había abandonado toda esperanza, llegaron mis amigos, aunque desaliñados y atolondrados tras su vuelo desde Bélgica (hacia donde los habían desviado a causa de turbulencias). Huelga decir que me sentí aliviada por dos razones: En primer lugar, porque mis acompañantes hubieran aterrizado sin percances, y en segundo lugar porque yo hubiera disfrutado de un agradable vuelo sin incidentes en otro avión diferente. De algún modo, siempre acababa mezclándome en situaciones poco habituales, pero en lo tocante a volar, la única opción que podía aceptar era tener un vuelo en calma.

Una vez que nos encontramos en tierra firme, nos sacudimos el polvo y viajamos hasta Mannheim. Mi prima, Sofía, estaba allí estudiando Económicas en la universidad, y mientras mis amigos hacían turismo, ella y yo aprovechamos la oportunidad de ponernos al día. Me resultó fácil y divertido estar con ella, especialmente en un país extranjero en el que no hablaba ni una palabra del idioma y no conocía a nadie. A pesar de todo, una vez más, aquello no me resultaba ninguna novedad. Una noche, cuando estábamos a punto de salir, recibí la contestación de una llamada de Johann, un joven al que había conocido años antes en una visita a mi ciudad natal en Huaraz. Una de mis amigas de la infancia me lo había presentado a él y a otro joven, ambos francamente atractivos y agradables. Mi relación de amistad con Johann, aunque fue breve, resultó memorable y, por ello, merece la siguiente digresión retrospectiva.

Cuando nos conocimos en Huaraz, Johann y yo, junto con otros, habíamos estado discutiendo sobre los extendidos rumores acerca de un indio peruano indígena, que supuestamente había sido abducido por los extraterrestres y al que estos lo habían curado de una grave enfermedad. Ahora bien, antes de que me acuséis de contaros cosas increíbles, tenéis que saber que esta historia la contaba el propio caballero, un hombre al que llamaré simplemente Diego. Mi padre y mis hermanos gemelos respondían de este milagroso acontecimiento del que habían sido testigos con sus propios ojos. Una cosa está clara: mi padre y mis hermanos no eran dados a contar mentiras. Al parecer, Diego mantenía una estrecha comunicación con aquellos supuestos extraterrestres que, según él mismo afirmaba, le curaron un brazo gangrenado. Papá me contó que cuando Diego le mostró la extremidad enferma, mi padre le aconsejó inmediatamente que fuera a ver a un médico, pero Diego insistió en que sus amigos extraterrestres lo curarían, tras lo cual, desapareció sin dejar rastro durante más de una semana. Cuando regresó, estaba completamente repuesto, gracias a los habitantes de otro planeta (qué planeta era específicamente es algo que todavía ignoro).

Siento un gran escepticismo por esos temas; y, sin embargo, después de haber vivido en un lugar en el que el misticismo es un modo de vida y los acontecimientos de origen desconocido (como avistamientos extraterrestres) a menudo se aceptaban como algo rutinario, trataba de mantener la mente abierta, mientras que me reía para mis adentros de la seriedad con la que se contaban esas anécdotas, si es que, en realidad, eso es lo que eran. Bajo ningún concepto intento trivializar sobre lo que escuché y vi, pero el cuento de Diego realmente parecía extraño, especialmente para aquellos que lo escuchan de forma indirecta. Para colmo, al parecer, Diego tenía la capacidad de hacer que su voz resonara por un receptor de radio si se hablaba cerca de la muñeca del brazo que los extraterrestres le habían curado. Los niños solían bromear sobre esto y apodaron a aquella emisora de radio Radio Shancayán, el nombre del pueblo natal de Diego. Escuchar todas aquellas historias no era suficiente. Con curiosidad creciente, mi amiga, los dos jóvenes y yo decidimos hacerle una visita a Diego. Allí estábamos, enfrascados en la conversación, cuando Johann, abrumado por el tema del que estábamos hablando, se puso en pie y se marchó, declarando:

—Esto es demasiado para mí.

Todos salimos de allí en fila, dejando a Diego con sus artefactos, o mejor dicho, sus conexiones electromagnéticas. Por decirlo suavemente, aquello fue toda una experiencia. El mundo está lleno de misterios, eso está claro, ¿y quién de nosotros tiene el monopolio de la verdad? Está claro que no reivindico la veracidad ni la rectitud. Simplemente, vivo mi verdad y disfruto compartiéndola. Si me paro a pensarlo, estoy convencida de que Diego hacía precisamente eso mismo.

En cualquier caso, regreso a mi narración sobre Johann: Durante el camino a casa después de nuestra charla con Diego, comenzó a mostrar interés en mí y me preguntó si podía acompañarme a solas. Percibí su decoro innato, por lo que no me podía negar. Cuando llegamos a mi casa, se lo presenté a mi madre, que nos recibió en la puerta, sin invitar, cosa que resultó llamativa, a mi nuevo amigo a que entrara. Más tarde, me explicó que, para su consternación, observó que Johann llevaba un pendiente, insignia inequívoca de que estaba interesado en gente de su mismo sexo. Ya veis, en aquella época, los pendientes estaban reservados para las mujeres. La valoración de mi madre fue tan vehemente, que me desanimó a que volviera a comunicarme con Johann y, sin embargo, logré mantener la amistad con él durante mi estancia de dos semanas en Huaraz. Johann era un verdadero caballero y me preguntó si podía escribirme cuando yo regresara a Estados Unidos. Accedí y, posteriormente, recibí la prosa más lírica que jamás he llegado a leer —en un perfecto español—, mucho más elegante y más gramaticalmente correcta que la de ningún hispanohablante nativo que me haya encontrado. Después de recibir su primera carta, me metí de lleno tanto en mis estudios de la escuela de terapia física que no pude contestarle. En su segunda misiva, Johann me pedía que fuera su acompañante en sus viajes por el mundo. Me sentí halagada, pero también me asusté un poco, pues apenas lo conocía, por lo que no podía plantearme en serio su proposición. Así es como perdimos el contacto, pero siempre guardé su número de teléfono. Nunca sabes cuando el destino puede llegar a unir caminos divergentes.

Y eso fue lo que pasó. Años después, cuando viajé a Alemania y me quedé con mi prima, Sofía, llevaba el teléfono de Johann encima. Quería que viera a la nueva yo a plena luz del día, no como antes cuando, ocultándome gracias a la oscuridad de la noche, mis oscuros secretos —mis manchas faciales— quedaban perfectamente camufladas y mis sentimientos de estar fuera de lugar me confinaban a la timidez. Por esta razón, podréis imaginaros mi emoción cuando, tantos años después, sonó el teléfono, ¡y escuché la voz de Johann en el otro extremo! Me explicó que sus intentos por ponerse en contacto conmigo no habían llegado a buen puerto, pues mi número de teléfono había sido desconectado y ya no residía en la dirección que le había proporcionado. Seguramente, él pensaba que nuestros caminos no volverían a cruzarse. Cuando lo hicieron, era demasiado tarde como para que compartiéramos un interludio romántico, ni cualquier otro tipo de relación sostenible. Por entonces, Johann se había casado con una hermosa muchacha italiana de la que estaba esperando su primer hijo: un niñito. Me embargó una mezcla de sentimientos de alegría y tristeza como las olas del impredecible océano de la vida. El amor no espera para siempre, surgen otras oportunidades, otra mueren y se encienden nuevas esperanzas. Y así fue en el caso de Johann y, si lo pienso, no puedo más que alegrarme de su buena fortuna.

Poco podía imaginarme, en los momentos posteriores a colgar el teléfono, lo que me esperaba. Ignoraba que, durante mi conversación con Johann, el enorme cepillo retráctil unido al secador de pelo que estaba utilizando, se quedó atascado y se enredó a mi larga melena. Todos mis intentos por liberar el cepillo fueron en vano. En un grandísimo acto de compasión y resolución, Sofía me puso un pañuelo en la cabeza y me acompañó, a pie, por las calles de Mannheim. Con el cepillo sobresaliendo de un lateral de mi cabeza, debía de tener el aspecto de uno de los compadres extraterrestres de Diego. En retrospectiva, la escena debió de ser para desternillarse, pero a mí me provocó una gran preocupación. «¿Cómo voy a ser capaz de deshacerme de este aparato?», me pregunté a mí misma, casi esperando escuchar ecos de algún consejo alienígena. Afortunadamente, me prestaron una extensa ayuda en el salón de belleza, donde las esteticistas trabajaron con mi cabello durante varias horas hasta que, finalmente, lograron retirar el cepillo. Lo mejor de todo —bueno, lo segundo mejor—, fue que no me cobraron ni un céntimo. Todo el mundo fue muy amable y me desearon lo mejor para mi viaje.

¡Y qué momento para viajar! ¡Se trataba de un periodo trascendental de la historia en el que *die Berliner Mauer* (el muro de Berlín), 140 kilómetros de largo que habían dividido Alemania Oriental y Alemania Occidental durante casi tres décadas en la época de posguerra de la Segunda Guerra Mundial, se estaba derrumbando ante mis ojos! El punto álgido de todo mi viaje europeo fue ir a ver el muro y sus dos lados —el antiguo bloque comunista soviético en el este y el oeste— finalmente liberados de la opresión de aquella barrera que los dividía. ¡Qué experiencia tan profundamente emotiva! Con mis propias manos, tuve el honor de arrancar un trozo del muro, una reliquia que conservo todavía hoy. Para mí, todo el acontecimiento guardaba simbolismo con mi propia vida: la derrota de las antiguas y erróneas concepciones sobre mí misma y la adopción de nuevas ideologías más sanas que me ayudarían a integrarme en el mundo de una manera más libre. Mientras inspeccionaba lo que, en su momento, fue el Berlín del este, percibí la desolación y lo gris que era, una especie de ciudad congelada, cuyos edificios tenían fachadas simétricas —un gran trabajo arquitectónico imponente, allí plantados, como centinelas petrificados—, hoscos ecos de un tiempo pretérito, que simbolizaban la muerte de aquella división. En comparación, el Berlín del oeste bullía de exaltación, abundancia y vida, al igual que Coblenza, Colonia y el Rin, el río más largo de Alemania. Allí, la gente cantaba y se agasajaban con camaradería, deleitándose con los sabores, los sonidos y las imágenes de la libertad. Y yo también lo hacía, mientras mis propios muros internos de opresión y de dudas sobre mí misma se derrumbaban una vez más. La libertad —ese extraordinario término, concepto y, finalmente, realidad— es inherente a todos nosotros. Independientemente de lo lastrados que nos sintamos por las circunstancias o por las cargas autoimpuestas del corazón y la mente, absolutamente nada ni nadie puede despojarnos de nuestra individualidad.

Hablando de libertad y de expresión individual, emprendí algunos memorables viajes secundarios por mi cuenta, en los que la falta de inhibición de la gente me dejó completamente sobresaltada. Experimenté estos choques culturales (que fueron prácticamente como relámpagos que cayeron sobre mí) mientras visitaba a viejos amigos. Una de esas experiencias tuvo lugar en compañía de Charo, una compañera del instituto que residía cerca de Salzburgo, Austria, con su marido. Puede que recordéis que Charo fue la heroína que me consoló durante aquel humillante episodio con Lorenzo. Entonces, muchos años después —lustros después de que aquel incidente tuviera lugar—, Charo me invitó a que visitara un terreno que poseía junto a un lago en un pueblo cerca de Salzburgo. Llegamos hasta allí mediante un barquito, casi tan minúsculo como el propio terreno, que consistía en un diminuto parche de tierra en el que, como mucho, cabían tres personas. Justo al lado del terreno, había dos hombres tendidos sobre toallas, tan naturales como cuando su madre los trajo al mundo, tomando el sol desnudos. Apenas podía creer lo que veía.

—Es mi imaginación, ¿o esos hombres están desnudos? —pregunté, casi atragantándome por la incredulidad.

Charo se echó a reír y me respondió:

—No, ¡es verdad! Ver a gente desnuda es extraordinariamente normal aquí, cerca de los lagos.

—¿De verdad? —inquirí, todavía casi respirando con dificultad—. La gente en América es mucho más conservadora y ni es sus mejores sueños se quitarían la ropa en público. Nadie creerá lo que acabo de ver.

Decidida a inmortalizar de forma fehaciente de la escena, Charo sacó su cámara de fotos y comenzó a fotografiar a los hombres. Conscientes de nuestra intensa curiosidad, aquellos amables hombres que estaban tomando el sol se pusieron en pie, posaron y nos saludaron, comprendiendo, sin duda, que lo que yo acababa de ver me resultaba extraño, si no extraterrestre. Durante un momento, sentí algo remotamente parecido a la experiencia de los avistamientos de Diego. ¡Ojalá él hubiera tenido una cámara de fotos! De no ser por el cine y la fotografía digital, las pruebas no pasan de ser meras elucubraciones. Bromas aparte, ¡aquella fue una escena inolvidable!

Cuando le hice una visita a mi amigo peruano, Emilio, que era estudiante de doctorado de Económicas en la Universidad de Heidelberg, me esperaba un panorama similar. Mientras dábamos un paseo por el campus, me sorprendí al ver a algunos estudiantes fumando y bebiendo durante los descansos entre clase y clase, costumbres que me eran totalmente ajenas. Más tarde, mientras Emilio y yo hacíamos un picnic con delicioso pan recién hecho y otros refrigerios cerca del lago, dos mujeres se sentaron cerca de nosotros y, sin aspavientos, comenzaron a desvestirse para tomar el sol. A Emilio no le llamó la atención, pero para ser sinceros, yo me sentí incómoda y me comí la comida a grandes bocados. Después, me apresuré a marcharme de allí, para protegerme de lo que mis ojos detestaban contemplar. ¡Imaginaos lo que era distanciarme de mi educación conservadora a una cultura en la que la libertad significaba deshacerse de las inhibiciones personales olvidándolas al viento! ¡Poco sabía la muchacha de montaña y poca capacidad tenía para llegar a imaginar las sorpresas que la vida acabaría por mostrarle!

En mis años adultos, a medida que iba formando mi personalidad, la definición de libertad dejó de ser tan decisivamente sinónimo de comedimiento físico, sino más bien de personalidad, inconformismo y convicción personal. Parte de aquella definición incluía aferrarme a mi estado civil de soltera. Aunque ya me había liberado de mis manchas faciales, seguía estando marcada emocionalmente por los rechazos del pasado. Deseaba ser cauta, quizá demasiado. Proteger mi corazón y encontrar a mi compañero adecuado eran mis principales objetivos. A medida que el reloj biológico comenzó a hacer tictac más y más alto, la preocupación de mis padres comenzó a intensificarse. Por consiguiente, al tiempo que iba acercándome a la zona de peligro de los treinta, con el riesgo inherente de que me tacharan de solterona, mamá y papá hicieron todo lo que estuvo en su mano para hacer las veces de casamenteros. Ya sé que sus intenciones eran buenas —como lo son las de todos los padres que quieren lo mejor para sus hijos— pero, ¿quién puede tomar mejores decisiones en asuntos del corazón que la propia persona en cuyo interior alberga el corazón en cuestión? Desgraciadamente, la bienintencionada instigación de mis padres siempre estaba presente, y en cuanto volvía a casa de visita, solían maquinar sigilosamente para emparejarme con innumerables solteros que ellos consideraban buenos partidos.

A principios de los noventa, volví a casa en Lima, donde, por entonces, mis padres estaban cómodos y bien instalados. Vino a recogerme al aeropuerto Enrique, el hombre cuyas costumbres alcohólicas habían impedido que mantuviéramos una relación más duradera años antes. Al llegar al aeropuerto, le vi sonriendo, afable y contento de verme. Me dijo que se había divorciado, que tenía dos niños y que gozaba de un buen trabajo de ejecutivo en una empresa internacional de fabricación. Me quedé impresionada, pero preferí ser cauta, acordándome de su comportamiento inadecuado durante nuestra juventud, cuando montó aquel jaleo en la fiesta a la que asistieron sus padres. Aún seguía estremeciéndome avergonzada al recordarlo, pero, como adulta que era, decidí perdonar y olvidarme de aquello. Enrique me llevó a casa y vino a visitarme todos los días. Una noche, durante la cena, sus atenciones culminaron en una proposición de matrimonio. Era tan sincero y serio con respecto a su propuesta, que no tuve corazón de rechazarlo inmediatamente, sino que le dije que me lo pensaría. Dado el estatus social y económico de Enrique, estoy segura de que cualquier cosa diferente de un «sí» le hubiera provocado una fuerte conmoción. Prácticamente, ninguna otra mujer lo habría rechazado. No obstante, yo me mantuve firme en mis convicciones, esperando con paciencia a que llegara mi oportunidad, con la intrínseca certidumbre de que él no estaba hecho para mí. Cuando regresé a casa y se lo conté a mis padres, se pusieron locos de alegría, especialmente mi padre.

—Él te quiere, Isabella. ¡Deberías casarte con él!

—¡Pero papá! —protesté yo—, a él le gusta el alcohol más de lo que me quiere a mí.

—Eres fuerte. Lograrás cambiarlo. Es muy buen partido, económicamente estable y está enamorado de ti.

—Por favor, perdóname, pero, con todos los respetos, no llevas razón, papá. Prefiero ser una solterona a casarme con el hombre equivocado. Espero que lo comprendas.

¡Me resultaba totalmente asombroso que mi padre hubiera levantado su prohibición contra casarse con hombres divorciados! Sin duda, estaba haciendo aquella excepción por el bien de su hija, que tenía cada vez más edad. Aunque se sintió profundamente decepcionado por mi decisión, percibió con toda la razón que no podría persuadirme.

Dudando sobre qué debía contestarle a Enrique y queriendo darle a mi admirador el beneficio de, al menos, un poco de consideración, decidí ponerlo a prueba. El novio de mi hermana pequeña Beatriz, Flavio, se ofreció amablemente a prepararnos la comida. Los cuatro —nuestro chef, Beatriz, Enrique y yo— disfrutamos de una suntuosa cena. Entonces, con la excusa de tener que hacer una llamada telefónica, me disculpé, dejando mi copa de vino intacta a la vista de todos en su lugar de la mesa. «Si Enrique se bebe el vino antes de marcharse, no me casaré con él», me dije a mí misma, aludiendo mentalmente a su insaciable sed por las bebidas alcohólicas. Espiándolo sigilosamente detrás de un panel de cristal, pronto lo vi bebiéndose el vino antes de ponerse en pie para marcharse. Y mi respuesta fue: ¡una rotunda negativa! Aun así, me comporté de forma discreta. Cuando nos despedimos, Enrique y yo nos abrazamos afectuosamente, pero supe, en aquel momento, que aquel sería nuestro último intercambio de afecto.

—¡Nos vemos mañana! —afirmó Enrique, como si nuestra cita del día siguiente ya fuera algo predeterminado.

Asentí educadamente y fui a llamar a la compañía aérea. Logré reservar mi vuelo un día antes y me embarqué en alas de la libertad, aliviada pero triste de provocarle dolor a Enrique al marcharme tan súbitamente y de forma tan irrevocable. De hecho, nunca supo lo que se le venía encima. Ni siquiera llegué a despedirme. Por mucho que comprendo que aquella omisión fue injusta, en aquel momento, no se me ocurrió ninguna otra alternativa. Sencillamente, no fui capaz de enfrentarme a él. ¿Qué le iba a decir?, «¿Tu amor por el alcohol supera tu cariño por mí, y tengo que protegerme a mí misma?». Cualquier intento de explicarme de aquel modo habría tenido como consecuencia que probablemente Enrique se hubiera puesto a la defensiva, hubiera desmentido mis afirmaciones y hubiera intentado tratar de convencerme con toda clase de zalamerías y promesas de que no sería así. Enrique era, y sigue siéndolo, un hombre muy bueno, pero yo decidí en ese mismo instante que, a menos que comprendiera el significado y el apremio de que debía abstenerse de beber alcohol, no podía ser mi marido. Como era de esperar, papá se sintió terriblemente consternado, al igual que el propio Enrique. Cuando regresé a casa, Beatriz encontró numerosos mensajes de él, a ninguno de los cuales yo di respuesta. No puedo negar que me arrepiento de aquel silencio. Nunca me olvidé de los buenos momentos que compartimos, lo amable que era conmigo, lo mucho que yo admiraba su intelecto y su genuino buen corazón... especialmente en aquella época en la que yo era nueva en Lima y él me enseñó la ciudad, haciéndome sentir cómoda y protegida. Todo tiene una razón, y yo me sentí agradecida de haber florecido en compañía de él y haber sido testigo de su generoso espíritu.

Al final, la vida siempre tiene una manera de atar los cabos sueltos para llenar el vacío de los corazones, dejando que pervivan los recuerdos agradables. No hace demasiado tiempo, telefoneé a casa de Enrique para saber cómo les había ido a él y a su familia durante el terrible terremoto de 2007 en Ica, Perú. Afortunadamente, todos habían salido ilesos. Los hijos de Enrique estaban estudiando en la facultad de derecho en aquella época, vivían con su madre y estaban creciendo maravillosamente. Me sentí tan aliviada y feliz al oír aquellas noticias de boca de la madre de Enrique, que me aseguró que le comunicaría las mías y mi información de contacto a su hijo.

Finalmente, mi antiguo admirador no llegó a devolverme la llamada. Como cualquier persona racional en mi situación, ni siquiera me molesté en plantearme la razón evidente. Habían sucedido demasiadas cosas entre nosotros, y yo había surcado varios océanos desde mis días con Enrique. Aún tengo que relatar los acontecimientos que tuvieron lugar durante los días posteriores, por lo que os invito cordialmente a que sigáis acompañándome.

Capítulo 13

Vuelco al síndrome de la solterona

Si lo pienso ahora, el hecho de que mis padres quisieran casarme resultaba verdaderamente entrañable. ¿Qué otra cosa podía significar, después de todo, esa intención, aparte de un genuino deseo de ver a su hija feliz? En retrospectiva, por muy desconcertante que fuera el asunto de su vocación de casamenteros, ahora comprendo, más que nunca, que simplemente se estaban esforzando por garantizar mi futuro. No obstante, por mi parte, casarme no era mi principal preocupación. Había logrado desarrollarme por mí misma y estaba totalmente preparada para enfrentarme al mundo, libre de las inhibiciones que me habían asediado en el pasado, y lista para explorar nuevas perspectivas de posibilidades. Solo entonces, pensaba yo, mi corazón estaría verdaderamente dispuesto para amar.

Tal y como he mencionado, una de mis principales diversiones era viajar. Experimentar diferentes países y culturas me permitía apreciar otras mentalidades, para captar el amplísimo macrocosmos que existía más allá de mí misma. Aparte de mi aventura por Alemania, son dignos de mención mis últimos viajes a Inglaterra con mi amiga, Donna. Pudimos ver muchos lugares históricos interesantes, como el palacio de Buckingham, la catedral de San Pablo, donde se casaron el príncipe Carlos y la princesa Diana, y la fascinante abadía de

Westminster, donde el príncipe Guillermo y Kate Middleton contrajeron matrimonio el 29 de abril de 2011. Allí, pude contemplar la tumba del famoso novelista Charles Dickens (1812-1870), donde sentí todo el peso de la historia. Después, viajamos a Stonehenge en Wiltshire, la grandiosa estructura circular de hace cuatro mil años, que me recordó a las pirámides del Machu Picchu. Al igual que en aquella magnífica edificación, Stonehenge era una imagen increíble de contemplar y su construcción está envuelta en un gran misterio. Desde allí, nos dirigimos hacia el norte a través de Salisbury, donde vimos una pequeña montaña con un caballo en el centro. Nuestro guía mencionó que los habitantes de aquella región habían informado de avistamientos extraterrestres. Hmmm.... Eso me sonaba familiar. ¿Acaso podría olvidar a Diego y sus amistades extraterrestres?

A continuación, dimos un rodeo para pasar por Bath, donde el príncipe Carlos iba a jugar un partido de polo. Decidimos asistir al partido y, para nuestra sorpresa, vimos a Su Alteza Real llegando en un Rolls-Royce de color verde oscuro y, después, estuvo a unos veinticinco metros de nosotras. Ver al príncipe fue uno de los verdaderos puntos culminantes de nuestro viaje.

A continuación, nos marchamos a Francia, donde navegamos por el río Sena alrededor de París y visitamos atracciones turísticas como el Museo del Louvre y el Museo de Orsay. Por supuesto, también vimos la imponente Torre Eiffel, la construcción más alta de París. Aquella monstruosa estructura me abrió los ojos ante el hecho de que todos nosotros sencillamente estamos metidos en nuestra propia esquinita del vasto universo, rebosando de emoción. Si nos atrevemos a mirar fuera de nosotros mismos y permitir que el mundo entre en nosotros, nuestros corazones y mentes se expanden hasta cotas inimaginables.

Nuestra gira por aquellos lugares fascinantes me ayudó a ganar perspectiva y a prepararme para las tareas que me aguardaban en casa. Para entonces, ya era Directora de los Servicios de Rehabilitación en un hospital de la zona. Entre nuestros servicios, se incluían terapia física y ocupacional, patologías del habla y del lenguaje, y audiología. También trabajaba a título privado para una señora encantadora de la que había cuidado desde que me terminé la escuela. No quería dejar aquel trabajo porque la señora era muy divertida y pretendía mantener al día mis capacidades como enfermera titulada. Además, tenía una consulta privada que se la había adquirido a uno de los fisiatras (un médico especializado en fisiatría) del hospital. Su consulta no estaba dando buenos resultados, así que me convenció para que yo me encargara de ella. Después de que nuestro hospital aprobara el proceso de acreditación de The Joint Commission (comisión conjunta para la certificación de organizaciones de atención médica, TJC, por sus siglas en inglés), me sentí motivada a probar suerte en la gestión de una consulta privada. Mi especialización: la terapia física. El esfuerzo era sobrecogedor al principio, pero con ayuda de Dios y algunas personas altamente capaces que trabajaban junto a mí, logré superar las dificultades a las que me enfrentaba, al mismo tiempo que compaginaba con mis responsabilidades en el hospital. Es sorprendente lo que una persona puede llegar a hacer si tiene la suficiente tenacidad y voluntad.

Previsiblemente, mi vida social se resintió durante aquella época. Apenas tenía tiempo para nada, y salir con hombres no entraba en absoluto en mi esquema. En pocas ocasiones, me enfrenté al dilema de si salir o no con alguien, cuando un médico al que había conocido hacía tiempo antes de abrir mi consulta privada me devolvió una llamada telefónica (que yo le había hecho con el objetivo de pedirle que me derivara pacientes). Me propuso «un paseo romántico por la playa y, después de eso, quizá podríamos hablar de negocios». Sentí una ligera intriga, porque a mí también me gustaba aquel médico, pero no me parecía correcto capitular tan fácilmente. Yo había hecho aquella llamada por motivos profesionales y, después de todo, no quería contribuir a crear confusión sobre aquel asunto. Después de anotar su número en el dorso de una tarjeta de visita, le respondí que le devolvería la llamada, pero nunca lo hice.

Poco después, me nombraron para que asistiera a una cena para el personal del hospital. Allí, vi a un hombre alto de aspecto llamativo y cabello negro de pie junto a una mujer rubia que pensé que era su esposa. Más tarde, mientras yo estaba sentada en un grupo, el caballero se me acercó y educadamente me preguntó si podía acomodarse a mi lado. Accedí, e iniciamos una animada conversación. Pronto me enteré de que Richard era productor de televisión para una cadena en español que, por casualidad, emitía muchos de los programas que yo había visto durante los ochenta. Era culto, amable y desplegaba un conocimiento impresionante sobre Sudamérica y, especialmente, sobre Perú. Y lo más sorprendente es que hablaba español con una soltura poco habitual para no ser su lengua materna. Su erudición y capacidad para charlar sobre una amplísima variedad de temas resultaban muy agradables. Aunque logró llamar mi atención, con el corazón en la mano, tampoco puedo decir que saltaran chispas entre nosotros. Aun así, cuando Richard me pidió mi número de teléfono, se lo di de buena gana e, involuntariamente, lo escribí en la misma tarjeta en la que había anotado el número del médico, mi aspirante a admirador, con el que no estaba escrito que fuera a darme ese paseo por la playa que él me había propuesto. Richard tardó dos meses enteros en pedirme una cita y, de sus muchas cualidades, la persistencia fue una de sus principales características.

Como ya he dicho, la tenacidad da sus frutos, y eso fue lo que hizo en el terreno romántico. Un año después de nuestro primer encuentro, el día de San Valentín, Richard y yo nos casamos. Su proposición de matrimonio fue digna de un caballero: elegante y romántica. Estábamos cenando en un restaurante, cuando se arrodilló y me regaló un hermoso anillo con un corazón de rubí, el precursor de un anillo de compromiso que, según me dijo, yo misma debía elegir. Al ser de gustos sobrios y sin complicaciones, le respondí que quería algo pequeño, acorde al tamaño de mi mano. Richard pareció perplejo, pues creía que a la mayoría de las chicas les gustaban los anillos grandes y ostentosos. Como ya he dicho antes, nada en mi naturaleza es fiel al conformismo.

Y hablando de bailar a mi propio ritmo: Antes de que nos casáramos, hice mis deberes y comprobé la credibilidad de mi prometido y su estado de salud. La tímida muchacha de montaña se había convertido en una concienzuda urbanita. Reconocía los riesgos implícitos a nuevas empresas, especialmente, una como casarse con alguien de cuyo pasado tan poco sabía. Por lo tanto, no estaba dispuesta a correr ningún riesgo. Reuniendo toda mi fortaleza y valor, llamé a su ex novia, la presentadora de un programa de entrevistas en una de las cadenas de televisión en español que yo solía ver. Sorprendentemente, aquella mujer era muy agradable, y no tenía absolutamente nada negativo que decir sobre Richard.

—Es un buen hombre —me aseguró.

Satisfecha, le agradecí que me hubiera dedicado parte de su tiempo, colgué el teléfono y le conté a mi prometido exactamente lo que había hecho. Él apenas pudo creerse mi atrevimiento, pero yo tenía que hacerlo. Entonces, tomé a Richard de la mano y lo llevé a mi médico de cabecera, insistiendo en que ambos nos hiciéramos una serie de análisis de sangre.

—Ya sabes que trabajo en el campo de la medicina y necesito cerciorarme de que ambos estamos sanos antes de casarnos —le expliqué.

Richard claramente comprendió que no tenía otra opción que cumplir mi deseo. Cuando me puse en contacto con mi médico para comunicarle mi exigencia de un examen de salud prematrimonial, me respondió en tono afable:

—¡Jamás había visto antes algo así! ¡Si cualquier mujer me obligara a someterme a una prueba como esa, la dejaría al instante! ¡Es demasiado! ¡Es usted algo fuera de lo común!

En todo caso, a continuación, procedió a extender las recetas para los análisis. Afortunadamente, ambos superamos la prueba de buena salud y nos dispusimos a iniciar nuestra vida en común.

Y así, después de asegurarse de que yo aceptaría —y de haber resuelto todos los imprevistos importantes—, Richard llamó a mi padre para pedirle mi mano en matrimonio.

—Con una condición —le respondió ceremoniosamente papá—. La boda ha de tener lugar en Perú.

Y así fue: con más de trescientos invitados, una banda de música bilingüe de cuarenta y ocho instrumentos, una tarta de bodas de diez pisos o más, y la sala de fiestas con la decoración más elaborada que os podáis imaginar. De repente, parecía que la aguja de mi reloj biológico estaba marcando las horas en sentido contrario, dándole, efectivamente, un vuelco a mi síndrome de la solterona, y mis padres celebraron el acontecimiento por todo lo alto. Mis invitaciones fueron simples pero elegantes, un hecho con el que hubo gente que discrepó, pues pensaban que tendría que haber sido más magnificente, pero sencillamente esa no era mi manera de hacer las cosas. Mi queridísima amiga, Julie, se encontraba en Washington en aquella época y no pudo asistir al festejo, pero sí que estuvo presente dentro de mi corazón. Mis damas de honor —mi hermana pequeña, Beatriz, y nuestra compañera de piso, Clara— estaban bellísimas. Yo llevaba un suntuoso vestido, un hecho que, me doy cuenta, contradice lo que he dicho hace un momento sobre mi carácter modesto. La única razón por la que abandoné el comedimiento en aquel aspecto no fue más que un mero impulso, porque era una forma de decir públicamente: «Vais a ver lo que es bueno». Anteriormente, había visitado una tienda de vestidos de novia en la que la encargada, una señora mayor, criticó mis gustos, hasta el punto de que llegué a rebelarme. Todas sus existencias estaban pasadas de moda y resultaban muy horteras, así que, en un momento de frustración, entré en una exclusiva tienda y adquirí un espléndido vestido con el que hacer mis votos. Solamente tuvo lugar un único contratiempo con el postizo de pelo que me iba a poner, que se enredó con otro al prepararlo para vuelo a Perú. No tuve otra opción que ponerme lo que tenía y aquello tampoco me afectó excesivamente. En ocasiones, simplemente hay que dejarse llevar y, en el esquema general de la vida, las minucias no tienen importancia. A pesar de las protestas de mi madre, yo misma me encargué de peinarme y de maquillarme. Todo el mundo se sorprendió de lo bien que lo hice.

Poco después de aquella memorable ocasión, fui bendecida al traer a mi hijo al mundo y un año y medio después, a mi hija. Aproximadamente en la época del nacimiento de mi hija, comencé a experimentar jaquecas, depresión y alergias. Un médico, que en aquellos momentos se alojaba en nuestra casa, se ofreció a aplicarme un tratamiento de acupuntura. Al principio, me mostré escéptica, pero el tratamiento funcionó como por arte de magia, además de inspirarme para proseguir mis estudios sobre medicina tradicional y de la antigua China. Llegar a dominar estas disciplinas me ha proporcionado un saber excepcional sobre los métodos alternativos de tratar muchos tipos de afecciones, complementando mi conocimiento de los tratamientos de medicina occidental. Esta práctica aún nos sirve a mi familia y a mí como medida preventiva para mantener nuestra buena salud. Siento un profundo respeto por la medicina oriental. Mientras yo acudía a la escuela, mi marido continuó y finalmente consiguió sacarse la carrera de Derecho. Nuestra familia prosperaba y yo disfrutaba a conciencia de mi papel de madre.

Mis hijos eran —y siguen siéndolo— el núcleo de mi ser, el centro de mi universo, y la mayor de las bendiciones que me han sido concedidas en mi vida: la culminación de todo lo que he hecho bien y por lo que tanto me he esforzado en conseguir. Por respeto a su privacidad, omitiré sus nombres. Os pido que tengáis indulgencia conmigo, pues compartiré unas pocas anécdotas sobre su niñez y sobre cómo han evolucionado. Una cosa es expresar sentimientos maternos habituales y otra bastante diferente es tener la fortuna de ser una madre que, además del tutelaje de sus hijos, también disfruta de tener la oportunidad de relacionarse con unos seres humanos extraordinarios en los cuales pervive su legado genético. Yo soy una de esas personas afortunadas. Suelo pensar en cómo los habría mimado su tía Laura, cómo los querría y los colmaría de regalos tanto de mimos como de objetos materiales. Esto me trae a la memoria que cuando nació mi hijo, la paloma volvió a visitarme, de forma bastante inesperada. Voy a narraros la historia porque sé, con todas y cada una de las fibras de mi ser, que Laura estaba allí. Yo me encontraba tendida en la cama del hospital cuando, de repente, se posó una paloma en mi ventana. No pensé nada del incidente, hasta que una enfermera comentó que nunca antes había visto ago así. Entonces lo supe: Laura había acudido a compartir mi alegría.

Vivamente consciente de los dones de la vida, mis hijos están creciendo en un entorno que nutre y capta la atención de sus curiosas mentes. Incluso cuando eran pequeños, tanto mi hijo como mi hija, cada uno a su manera, demostraban extraordinarias habilidades para comprender e interpretar su mundo con una sensibilidad e inteligencia que correspondía a niños de mucha más edad. Sirva a modo de ejemplo la siguiente anécdota: Cuando mi hijo tenía cerca de tres años, un día íbamos paseando por las cercanías del Museo de Historia Natural de

Nueva York. Repentinamente, desde su atalaya en la mochila para bebés donde lo llevaba, mi hijo dijo en alto:

—¡Sr. Suzuki, Sr. Suzuki!

Cuando le pregunté:

—¿Quién es ese?

Mi hijo exclamó:

—¡Yo lo conozco!

De repente, un hombre de pelo gris se nos acercó y preguntó por qué le habíamos llamado.

—¿Es usted el Sr. Suzuki? —le pregunté, sin apenas creerme lo que estaba pasando.

—Sí —me respondió.

Cuando interrogué a mi hijo para saber cómo era posible que lo conociera, mi pequeño prodigio declaró:

—He visto todas las cintas del cerebro y él estaba en ellas.

Todos nos echamos a reír, y el Sr. Suzuki dijo:

—Oh, pero eso fue hace mucho tiempo. ¿No eres demasiado pequeño para que te interesen esas cintas?

Al parecer, mi hijo insistía en que su niñera le había puesto aquellos vídeos, narrados por... ¡ya sabéis quién!: ¡El Sr. Suzuki! Mi hijo había asimilado su imagen como una esponja y lo reconoció incluso aunque hubiera envejecido.

Aproximadamente un año más tarde, cuando mi hijo tenía cuatro años, fuimos a ver una exposición en ese mismo museo. Íbamos caminando de la mano cuando pasamos por delante de un expositor donde el presentador estaba enseñando el hueso de un dinosaurio. Les pidió a los niños más mayores que lo identificaran, ante lo que mi hijo metió su cabecilla en medio del grupo y exclamó:

—¡Yo lo sé! Es una rótula. ¡Lo he visto en un libro!

Qué asombroso resultaba ser testigo del intenso interés de mi hijo... ¡e incluso más comprender que alguien tan joven podía lograr recordar un dato tan complicado!

En otra ocasión, asistimos a una presentación con animales vivos en un circo al aire libre en el noreste de Pensilvania, donde mi hijo capturó la atención de todo el público cuando identificó un lémur de cola anillada.

—¿Cómo sabes tú eso? —le preguntó el presentador, incrédulo.

Yo me quedé atónita. Entonces, después de hacerle más preguntas, mi niño le dio alas a su imaginación.

—Mi abuelo y yo hemos viajado a diferentes países, y uno de ellos fue Madagascar. Allí vimos muchos lémures de cola anillada.

—¡Oh! ¿De verdad? ¡Qué impresionante! ¿Y a qué otros países ha viajado? —preguntó el presentador, mirándome a mí.

No deseaba contradecir a mi hijo, así que sonreí discretamente e hice un gesto mudo de negación. A día de hoy, sigo sin saber cómo conocía mi hijo aquel animal. Seguramente solo había viajado a Madagascar en su propia mente o mirando fotografías.

Una de las características más tiernas de mi hijo es su indeleble cariño por su hermana pequeña. Desde que ella nació, él la ha protegido y avisado de las realidades de la vida, lo cual no quiere decir que ella, por derecho propio, no haya sido siempre un portento tanto de intelecto como de corazón. Por su parte, ella es la mismísima personificación de esos rasgos, pero a medida que los dos iban creciendo (y todavía hoy), mi hijo nunca le ha ocultado la verdad a su hermana. Lo compartía todo con ella, e incluso yo misma cuando le pedía que ocultara ciertas cosas a su hermana pequeña para protegerla. Por ejemplo, una noche, después de que se le cayera un diente, se rebeló contra la inminente visita del ratoncito Pérez. Después de arroparlo aquella noche e ir a ver cómo estaba una cuantas veces, lo encontré totalmente despierto.

—¿Qué sucede, cariño? —le pregunté.

—No quiero que venga el ratoncito Pérez, mamá. No quiero que me deje dinero.

Mi hijo fue tan insistente que, al final, no me quedó otra opción que contarle que el ratón Pérez no era más que un personajillo imaginario, aunque le rogué que no se lo dijera a su hermana. Iluminándosele los ojos, me respondió:

—¡Oh, muchas gracias, mamá! Ahora ya sé que tú eres no solo el ratoncito Pérez, sino también la liebre de Pascua y Papá Noel.

Poco después, recibí una llamada de la angustiada profesora de mi hija.

—Sra. TaniKumi, su hija les ha estado diciendo a los demás niños que Papá Noel no existe. ¿Sería usted tan amable de decirle que no fuera contándoles eso? Está arruinándoles las fiestas navideñas a todos los demás.

No pude creerlo. Mis hijos había conspirado para comunicarse el secreto sobre Papá Noel, y no había nada que yo pudiera hacer.

La curiosidad siempre impregna las mentes con sed de conocimiento. Mientras pasábamos con el coche una tarde junto a un cementerio, mi hija (que tenía aproximadamente tres años en aquella época) preguntó:

—Mamá, ¿qué es un cementerio?

—Eso es fácil de explicar, ¡yo te diré lo que es! —le dijo decididamente mi perspicaz hijo de cinco años—. Un cementerio es un campo muy grande de hierba, donde la gente tiene estatuas. Entonces, van allí a visitar las estatuas y rezan.

—¡Oh, muchas gracias! —le respondió mi hija, entusiasmada con la respuesta.

Poco sabía mi hijo lo agradecida que me sentí yo por no tener que explicar yo el sombrío significado de un lugar así. De algún modo, él siempre tenía una respuesta preparada para absolutamente todo, de forma inmediata y certera, demostrando una perspicacia asombrosa.

Quizá el ejemplo más conmovedor de la relación tan cercana que había entre mis hijos tuvo lugar cuando nuestra perra, *Magnolia*, enfermó después de consumir comida en lata en mal estado. Desgraciadamente, los riñones de *Magnolia* comenzaron a fallar. No quería traumatizar a mis hijos, y comprendiendo que no le quedaba mucho tiempo de vida, le pedí a mi marido que se llevara a *Magnolia* a un hospital en Pensilvania para que pasara sus últimos días en paz. Cubriendo de besos y abrazos a su mascota favorita, mi hijo y mi hija se despidieron de ella, creyendo, o al menos yo así lo pensaba, que nuestra perra iba a recuperarse. Aproximadamente un mes después, mi hijo se me acercó y declaró, con la madura resignación de alguien mucho mayor que él:

—*Magnolia* se ha muerto, ¿verdad?

—¿Por qué dices eso? —le pregunté, tratando de ocultar mi asombro.

—Mamá, te conozco bien. Si *Magnolia* estuviera viva, irías a visitarla todos los días. Como no lo estás haciendo, sé que ha muerto.

—Es verdad —le respondí, estupefacta de los poderes de deducción de mi niño—. No quise decirte nada porque no deseaba disgustaros ni a ti ni a tu hermana. Por favor, no se lo cuentes a ella. Eso sería demasiado para ella.

Aproximadamente un año más tarde, acudió a mi consulta de rehabilitación una mujer con un pequeño caniche. Mi hija, que dio la casualidad de que se encontraba allí conmigo aquel día, se arrodilló y comenzó a acariciar al perrito. A continuación, levantó la mirada hacia la mujer y le dijo:

—Yo tenía una perra. Se llamaba *Magnolia*, pero se murió hace un año.

Apenas podía creer lo que estaba oyendo. Aquel sentido común tan poco habitual, aquella tranquila determinación y aquella resignación eran dignas de ver. Su hermano le había contado la verdad, y ella lo había aceptado con resignación.

Junto con su agudo intelecto, las características más destacadas de mi hija son su agradecimiento por los pequeños placeres de la vida, su firme voluntad y tenacidad, su prontitud a la hora de dominar ciertas tareas y superar desafíos con desenvoltura y gracia, y su singular sentido común (es decir, un sentido común muy poco común en este mundo). Estos rasgos de carácter han ido evolucionando con los años y se han ido manifestando en cada fase de su vida. Cuando era un bebé, una vez me estaba observando mientras yo retiraba las etiquetas de la ropa recién comprada. Cogí una de las etiquetas, que tenía una imagen de un minúsculo osito, y se la entregué a mi niña. Demostrando el placer y el sentimiento más genuinos, levantó la mirada hacia mí y me dijo:

—¡Oh! ¿Es para mí? ¡¡¡Gracias!!!

Y sus enormes ojos casi se le llenaron de lágrimas de alegría.

La eficiencia del uso del teléfono móvil no se le escapó a la perspicaz e incansable mente de mi hija. Cuando tenía aproximadamente cuatro años y los móviles no eran tan omnipresentes como hoy en día, y mi práctica niñita nos explicó a mi marido y a mí que ir de compras no tenía que ser un ejercicio gimnástico de logística. Sencillamente, debíamos coordinar nuestros horarios por teléfono y encontrarnos a la hora que hubiéramos convenido.

—¡Qué tontos sois! —nos regañó cuando comprobó lo mal que nos habíamos planificado.

Cerca de la misma época, mi niña insistió en aprender a nadar por su cuenta. Estábamos alojados en un hotel, y su hermano ya se desplazaba cómodamente por el agua. Le pregunté si quería que la sujetara mientras intentaba nadar en la parte que no cubría de la piscina.

—¡No, mamá! ¡Quiero hacerlo yo sola!

Mientras la vigilaba, presencié cómo triunfaban su firme voluntad y determinación. Entonces, me distraje durante un instante, apartando la mirada. Cuando volví a mirarla, allí estaba ella, nadando por su cuenta.

En el transcurso de apenas una hora, a la edad de ocho años, mi hija logró aprender a montar la bicicleta que le había comprado por su cumpleaños y que había escondido en el garaje. Cuando llegó su día especial, dos de sus amigas y yo le dimos el regalo, que ella aceptó con gratitud y alegría. En menos de lo que canta un gallo, se montó en la bicicleta, con sus dos amigas corriendo equidistantes a cada lado, enseñándole y animándola. Unos minutos más tarde, miré por la ventana y la vi pasar a toda velocidad, ella solita. Su espíritu independiente era imparable. Me vienen a la mente multitud de recuerdos sobre lo difícil que resultó para mí aprender a montar en la bicicleta de mi hermano, siendo niña en Perú. Se me hinchió el corazón de orgullo.

Estas anécdotas sirven como ejemplo del enorme alcance e inspiración de los talentos y predisposiciones de mis hijos. Aunque admito que, con lo que he narrado aquí, puedo pecar de engreimiento, no creo que vosotros, queridos lectores, os vayáis a enfadar conmigo, especialmente si sois padres que, por serlo, tienen el derecho inalienable de elogiar las aptitudes de aquellas personitas a las que más quieren en el mundo. Siento un orgullo especial al saber que mis bendiciones más queridas, mis niños, algún día leerán estos fragmentos y comprenderán lo mucho que los quiero y los aprecio y la gran felicidad que ellos le proporcionan a mi mundo. Esos sentimientos suelen verse supeditados al fragor del día a día, pero nunca caen en saco roto. Estoy tan agradecida por tener la oportunidad de expresar estos sentimientos y de haber sido testigo del crecimiento y evolución de mis hijos. Y al hacerlo, veo el futuro. El pedagógico vocabulario de mi hijo y su omnipresente brillantez, y la sensibilidad y dedicación de mi hija nunca dejan de sorprenderme. Por encima de todo, ambos hacen que me esfuerce lo indecible por desarrollar lo mejor de mí misma. Siempre han sido —y siguen siéndolo— mi antídoto definitivo a mi síndrome de la solterona, y llenaron un vacío cuya existencia nunca antes me había dignado siquiera a reconocer.

Capítulo 14

Los patinazos de la falta de comunicación

La eternidad también florece en el cariño de los buenos amigos. Sin mi confidente, George (al que conozco desde hace ya siete años), no estaría hoy escribiendo este libro. Su amistad es muy significativa para mí. Él estaba empleado en una oficina junto a mi antiguo lugar de trabajo, y nuestra relación inicial se fundamentó principalmente en su habilidad con los ordenadores. No obstante, a medida que iba pasando el tiempo, llegamos a conocernos mejor y nos hicimos amigos. Finalmente, él empezó a venir a mi consulta para tratarse un dolor de rodilla. Este afroamericano alto, de figura imponente, es tan afable como sabio, y tan bondadoso como pragmático. Tengo sus opiniones en alta estima, y él me proporciona de buen grado una perspectiva masculina, que supone un grato contraste y un trampolín para mis propias interpretaciones y percepciones. Una noche, mientras estaba terminando mi ronda de casos de la jornada, George, mi último paciente del día, hizo una observación trascendental.

—Pareces tan preocupada... ¿Qué te inquieta?

Con la sensación de podía confiar en él, respondí, y se abrieron de par en par las compuertas de mi corazón, reconduciendo un torrente de recuerdos pasados y presentes, que me condujeron por las innumerables y variadas carreteras secundarias de mi vida.

He de reconocer que abrirle mi corazón a George era mi única válvula de escape en aquel momento, y vi aquella oportunidad como el único recurso para tranquilizar mi mente y corazón atribulados. Me hallaba en un estado de desconcierto, incapaz de concentrarme en el trabajo, ni, de hecho, en ninguna otra cosa. Allí, ante mí, al final de mi jornada laboral, contaba con el amigo que me hacía falta, una especie de voz de la razón, un oído dispuesto a escuchar el dilema moral que me había angustiado durante nada menos que veintiséis años: Todavía seguía perdidamente enamorada de Eduardo. Por una vez en mi vida, podía expresarme total y completamente, y sincerarme con alguien que era, de hecho, un aliado, alguien que me escucharía sin juzgarme o reprocharme nada, como un verdadero amigo. Durante dos horas, me senté junto a George y le hablé sobre los acontecimientos de mi pasado, y sobre el hecho de que la llama del amor, la pasión y la añoranza todavía inflamaban mi corazón por un hombre con el que mi falta de comunicación había destruido la posibilidad de tener con él una relación prolongada.

La extraña realidad de la situación era que mi marido, Richard, conocía todos los particulares sobre aquella llama. En un esfuerzo por ser totalmente sincera con él mientras estábamos saliendo juntos, le revelé mi omnipresente afecto por Eduardo, a lo que me respondió:

—Eso sucedió hace mucho tiempo, y probablemente no volverás a verle jamás. Además, yo haré que te olvides de él.

Pero ¿cómo podía olvidar, cuando había tantas palabras que habían quedado en el tintero, tantos sentimientos que no había llegado a expresar, tanta conexión entre nuestros corazones que, en aquel momento, apenas podía explorar dadas las dudas que sentía por mí misma provocadas por mis manchas faciales, la barrera del idioma y mis inseguridades concomitantes? Había evolucionado mucho desde aquellos años y, aun así, todo aquello seguía asediándome como una sensación crónica de algo desagradablemente familiar que bullía en el interior de mi estómago. Mi juventud ya había pasado. Y, aun así, seguía experimentando todas esas sensaciones a flor de piel. Y allí estaba George, mi querido amigo, que me escuchó con paciencia y me proporcionó buenos y razonables consejos. ¡No sé qué habría hecho sin él en aquellos momentos!

Mi respuesta a las preguntas de George de: «¿Qué te pasa? ¿Por qué estás tan preocupada?» fue prolífica. El hecho era que acababa de retomar la comunicación con Eduardo a través de la página web de nuestra escuela de medicina, enlazada directamente a Facebook. No había oído hablar de las redes sociales hasta que mi amiga de la infancia, Adriana (que ahora vive en Suiza), me inició en este milagroso medio de comunicación. Ahora, cuento en mi haber con un vocabulario totalmente nuevo, con expresiones que han adquirido una dimensión completamente diferente, como «añadir como amigo» y «dejar de seguir». Es una realidad paralela.

En todos los acontecimientos, ambos transmitimos una serie de mensajes por escrito, que comenzaron con unos cuantos saludos de rigor. Estos saludos iniciales fueron el preludio de nuestra relación por Facebook. Creo que nuestros intercambios comunicativos merecen una narración propia, especialmente porque a mi buen amigo, George, lo dejaron totalmente fascinado y porque siento que son muy reveladores de mi interacción con Eduardo. Bienvenidos al misterioso, distante y extrañamente íntimo mundo de las redes sociales para desgranar las palabras e imágenes que encendieron el definitivo romance del siglo que habría podido ser (sí, ya lo sé, soy una sentimental, pero así es como yo lo veo).

Una vez conectados a Facebook, escribimos:

Isabella: ¡Hola, Eduardo! Me he encontrado con tu fotografía en la página de la escuela de medicina. ¿Qué tal estás? Solo quería decirte hola.

Eduardo: ¡Estoy bien! ¿Y tú, qué tal? Te he enviado ahora mismo una solicitud de amistad.

Isabella: Acabo de terminar el trabajo. Me alegra saber de ti. Por supuesto, han pasado muchas cosas desde la última vez que te vi después de graduarme en la escuela de terapia física.

He trabajado en varios hospitales, he abierto mi propia consulta y he vuelto a estudiar para aprender acupuntura y medicina tradicional china. Cuéntame qué es de tu vida.

Sin responder, Eduardo esperó hasta esa noche para subir una enorme cantidad de fotos a un álbum, en los que aparecía en su lugar de trabajo, con sus queridos hijos, en partidos de hockey y todo tipo de instantáneas de corte personal. Con aquella información logró aumentar mi cariño por él aún más, si es posible. En aquel caballero mayor que el que yo había conocido, percibí la amabilidad y la gentileza del joven romántico en cuyos luminosos ojos azules me perdía constantemente, aunque fuera en silencio, únicamente en contemplación. Había sido demasiado tímida y poco clara para hacerle comprender la trágica realidad en un momento en el que las palabras eran lo que más importaba.

Sin embargo, las oportunidades hay que aprovecharlas, pues el momento es lo que importa —al menos, en lenguaje filosófico—, así que me decidí a integrar ese punto de vista en mi vida y a aprovechar las oportunidades. Así que cuando llegó el día de San Valentín, no perdí el tiempo y escribí un mensaje en clave en mi muro de Facebook. «Me voy a refugiar en mi escondite secreto —sin teléfonos, sin ordenadores, incomunicada—, pero antes, me gustaría desearos a todos un feliz día de San Valentín. P.D.: Soy Sarah Palin». En los comentarios, escribí: «Atención a mi mano». Y subí una foto de mí misma con ropa de hospital que me había tomado una amiga ex profeso. En la mano, me había escrito con un rotulador: «I <3 u» («Yo os <3», para los pocos que no lo sepan, <3 simboliza un corazón). Con aquello, me marché un viernes y regresé a casa el domingo (el día de San Valentín) emocionada, para comprobar mi página de Facebook y comprobar si mi mensaje habría sido recibido e interpretado correctamente. Para mi desilusión, aquel mismo día, Eduardo había publicado una foto de sí mismo con su prometida, acompañada del saludo: «¡Feliz día de SV a todos!». Yo lo interpreté como un mensaje directo hacia mí, comunicación no verbal que significaba: «Estoy prometido en matrimonio y voy a pasar el día con mi prometida».

Desilusionado y dolido, mi magullado ego me dictó que borrara todo mi mensaje y la fotografía, y los sustituyera por una de mi marido abrazándome con un fondo de una cascada. Una vez más, la foto de Eduardo cambió poco después, mostrándolo a él con su hijo de vacaciones. La pregunta era: ¿Se estaba comunicando Eduardo conmigo a través de fotografías? La semana siguiente, cuando cambió su situación sentimental a «soltero», me percaté de que uno de sus amigos le escribía: «Me he enterado de que ya no estás prometido». Eduardo confirmó: «Es cierto».

Aquel domingo, apareció otra visible foto de Eduardo con sus hijos jugando a un juego en el perfil de mi silencioso interlocutor, junto con un gesto de una mano exactamente igual que la que yo había publicado el día de San Valentín, con una excepción muy llamativa: no había nada escrito en ella. ¿Era una mera coincidencia o la imagen gemela de mi gesto, un mensaje recíproco de algún tipo? Me lo pregunto de forma retórica, por supuesto, porque puede que jamás lo llegue a saber. «¿Acaso importa a estas alturas?», me pregunto a mí misma, retóricamente, esperando en vano escuchar mi propia respuesta. Mi corazón, sin embargo, permanece en silencio.

Pasaron un par de semanas hasta que apareció el siguiente fragmento de un libro sobre budismo en el muro de Facebook de Eduardo: «Lo que somos ahora proviene de nuestros pensamientos de ayer, al igual que nuestros pensamientos actuales construirán nuestra vida mañana. Nuestra vida es una creación de nuestra propia mente. Optamos por actuar o hablar con una mente pura o impura, y eso marca absolutamente toda la diferencia». Cautivada por ese mensaje, supe que ese era el espíritu que me había conmovido tantos años antes: el corazón que, a pesar de nuestras dificultades comunicativas, era capaz de ver a través de la ventana de mi alma, y me hablaba de formas con las que hasta entonces nadie se había dirigido a mí antes. Respondí: «Hola, Eduardo. He estado pensando en lo que has escrito basándote en el libro que has leído. Es muy profundo. Supongo que nosotros mismos establecemos nuestros caminos en la vida, y depende de nosotros decidir sobre nuestras acciones y pensamientos. Con un poco de suerte, gracias a la bondad que albergamos en nuestro interior, podemos ser sinceros con los demás y con nosotros mismos. Hoy me gustaría ser sincera, porque no sé lo que traerá el mañana. He pensado en ti a lo largo de los años y lamento no haber sido sincera entonces, por miedo al rechazo, al fracaso y a la vergüenza, y mi temor a no conocer lo suficientemente bien el idioma con el que debía comunicarme contigo. Por eso, actué de forma tan ridícula. He madurado mucho desde entonces y me pregunto si algún día se nos presentará la oportunidad de conocernos mejor.

Al día siguiente, Eduardo escribió: «¿Con qué no fuiste sincera?».

«Buena pregunta —le respondí—. Me siento incómoda contestándote aquí».

«¿Prefieres mandarme un correo electrónico?», sugirió Eduardo, proporcionándome su dirección.

«Creo que estoy andando por la cuerda floja, ¡sin red de seguridad debajo!», me aventuré a decirle de momento.

«¿Por qué?», fue la respuesta.

«No es más que una expresión inocente —expliqué—. Para mí, significa que estoy un poco asustada y prefiero ser cauta. Supongo que por correo electrónico será mejor. Simplemente, dame un poco de tiempo».

«Envíame un correo», repitió Eduardo, aparentemente impaciente por recibir algún tipo de confidencia o explicación reveladora sobre lo que me estaba preocupando.

En un esfuerzo por explicarme, por tender un puente para subsanar el silencio y la falta de comunicación que caracterizó nuestra relación veintiséis años antes, le escribí la siguiente respuesta, poniendo cada milímetro de mi corazón y mi esfuerzo en cada sílaba. Teniendo en cuenta mi antigua barrera idiomática, aquella carta era una gran hazaña, una victoria sobre todas mis inhibiciones del pasado. Por fin lograba expresarme.

«Somos un producto de nuestro pasado. Desgraciadamente para mí, eso significó una relación fallida cuando tenía quince años y estaba en el instituto. Me enamoré de un estudiante universitario de Derecho de una prestigiosa facultad que posteriormente me dejó sin darme explicaciones. Que te rompan el corazón a una edad tan temprana no es fácil de superar. La carta que te escribí no era verdad, sino solamente la excusa que logré inventarme en aquel momento. Ahora, cuando echo la vista atrás, me resulta muy infantil. Estoy segura de que a ti se te habrá olvidado a estas alturas, pero yo no podría olvidarla. Lamento haberme comportado del modo en el que lo hice. Te tenía mucho cariño y te encontraba extraordinariamente encantador, atractivo y, sobre todo, inteligente. En aquella época, no logré un rendimiento académico demasiado bueno y estaba suspendiendo en todas mis clases. Entonces sentí que debía concentrarme en mis estudios. Y, además, para complicar las cosas aún más, mi inglés era bastante malo. Todos los días representaban un gran esfuerzo. No quería parecer una idiota a tu lado. No podía mantener una conversación larga con nadie y lo último que deseaba era causarte vergüenza delante de tus amigos. A veces, me resultaba tan difícil ignorarte. Tenía tanto miedo de la vergüenza. Fingía en las clases y cuando te tenía alrededor. Y creo que hice un buen trabajo con aquella charada. ¡Qué experiencia tan difícil fue aquella! Si ahora echo la vista atrás, veo lo mala que era mi situación. No entiendo cómo diablos logré triunfar entonces. Lo único de lo que me arrepiento es de que no tuve la oportunidad de explicarte todo esto hasta ahora. Creo que fue injusto para ambos. He pensado en ti todos estos años. Agradezco mucho lo que escribiste sobre el budismo, porque fue como abrirme una puerta para que ahora pueda estar diciéndote todas estas cosas. No creo que hubiera podido hacerlo de otro modo; y si, de hecho, las enseñanzas del budismo son correctas, no quiero dejar pendiente esto para tener que solucionarlo en mi siguiente vida. El mensaje más importante que deseo transmitirte es que esta estúpida muchacha que conociste ha madurado y necesita disculparse por sus acciones del pasado. Es lo que hay que hacer».

Ahora, si releo esta epifanía personal, puedo afirmar sinceramente que, quizá, se malinterpretó como una disculpa, espolvoreada solapadamente con sarcasmo por la frase: «No entiendo cómo diablos logré triunfar entonces» (que Eduardo pudo interpretarla como una afirmación de autoensalzamiento, es decir: «Estoy muy bien, gracias, y he triunfado en todas mis empresas»). Eso estaba lejos de mi intención y pudo ser otro patinazo más de la falta de comunicación.

Eduardo me contestó: «¡¡No hace falta que te disculpes! ¡No te guardo ningún rencor! ¡Continúa felizmente con tu vida y no pienses en el pasado así, por favor! ¡Te deseo lo mejor y toda la felicidad del mundo!».

Entonces, Eduardo cambió su estado en Facebook, en donde ponía: «Mi vida está completa.... No es perfecta, ¡pero está completa!». En su muro, escribió algo parecido a: «Algunas personas andan de acá para allá por la orilla, pero jamás reúnen el valor de cruzar al otro lado».

Apesadumbradamente, ahora percibo con claridad que mis palabras fueron interpretadas como indiferencia: una disculpa breve y brusca para alguien con el que me había encontrado por casualidad y con quien solamente había mantenido una relación pasajera. Mi corazón no se comporta de manera esquiva, especialmente en lo que se refiere a la gente a la que quiero. Eduardo formaba parte esta categoría y yo deseaba desesperadamente que supiera que, por mucho que lo intentara, siempre me quedaba corta, una vez más, tal y como yo pensaba. Me sentí dolida por que Eduardo me hubiera malinterpretado y le volví a escribir, en tono exasperado.

«¡Me siento como si alguien me acabara de dar con la puerta en las narices! Me voy a marchar durante unos días. He tenido una semana muy dura».

Tras recobrar la calma y regresar a casa, vi que había recibido una respuesta a mi mensaje. «Sí me acuerdo de ti, Isabella, pero de lo que no me acuerdo es de la carta que mencionas. ¿Puedes refrescarme la memoria?».

¿Cómo podía recordar una mentira? Como ya he mencionado, las mentiras son engañosas de por sí. Nunca puedes contar la misma historia dos veces. Así pues, me enfrentaba a otro atolladero moral más, por lo que lo consulté con George, que me aconsejó que me olvidara de esa misiva.

—Necesitas cerrar el capítulo referente a esa carta. Eso carece ya de importancia. Puedes empezar otro capítulo y comenzar de nuevo, si así lo quiere el destino.

Como de costumbre, mi conciencia racional, personificada en mi querido amigo, había hablado una vez más. Reuní el valor de contestar: «No creo que la carta sea importante a estas alturas. Quería desahogarme sobre algo que sucedió en el pasado. La carta era una manera de racionalizar mi incoherente comportamiento en aquella época. Ese capítulo de nuestras vidas ya está cerrado. ¿No estás de acuerdo conmigo?».

Reinó el silencio. Durante varios días, no hubo ni rastro de Eduardo en Facebook. Comencé a preocuparme y acudí a George una vez más en busca de consejo.

—Dale un par de días y si sigue sin conectarse, escríbele de pasada y dile: «Hola, hace tiempo que no te conectas. Simplemente quería asegurarme de que estás bien».

Capté el sentido inherente de esa frase, e hice lo que George me había recomendado y recibí una respuesta casi inmediata: «¡Gracias, estoy bien! ¡Ocupado, pero bien!». A partir de aquel momento, Eduardo comenzó a comunicarse de nuevo con su red de Facebook, revelando su intención de comprarse una motocicleta, a la que se refería como su «ciclomotor». Sin embargo, yo me confundí y pensé que lo que quería comprarse era una bicicleta eléctrica.

«Me alegra saber que te encuentras bien —le escribí, encantada de volver a tener noticias suyas—. No trabajes demasiado. Un maestro chino me advirtió una vez: "[El trabajo] extenúa tu esencia Yin y hace que envejezcas prematuramente". Tú todavía tienes buen aspecto, así que debes conservar tu esencia Yin. He visto que estás pensando en comprarte una bicicleta. Hace un año, estuve mirando la de Lee Iacocca. Creo que almacena la energía cuando pedaleas y me parece que hay una que es eléctrica con pedaleo asistido para las cuestas arriba». Sin saber que aquellas bicis eran solamente de segunda mano, le envié el enlace a Eduardo. Al menos, mis intenciones eran buenas.

Estaba claro que el tiempo no había obstaculizado las habilidades atléticas de Eduardo. De hecho, mencionó que tenía una bicicleta y que le ardían los muslos cuando pedaleaba cuesta arriba —una indicación explícita de que la juventud y el vigor aún formaban parte de sus cualidades—. Le comenté un par de veces los efectos beneficiosos de montar en bicicleta y le pregunté si había leído últimamente algún buen libro (al percatarme de que había hecho clic en «me gusta» en la cadena de librerías Barnes & Noble en Facebook). Me aventuré a pedirle que me recomendara algún libro. Menciono este detalle por lo que ocurrió a continuación. «Cada vez es más curioso curiosísimo» (por citar a la Alicia de Lewis Carroll): Una noche, me desperté después de haber soñado con que Eduardo estaba buscando con diligencia libros que recomendarme. Aquella misma mañana, me levanté y encontré su recomendación de *El código Da Vinci* y *Ángeles y demonios* de Dan Brown. ¡Fijaos que telepatía mental! Siempre sentí que existía el poder de la intuición entre nosotros.

Seguimos hablando un poco de todo, y entonces Eduardo me preguntó por mis hijos y mi trabajo, entre otras cosas. Después de alabar a mis hijos, me di cuenta de que ya le había hablado sobre mi trabajo y que la conversación estaba volviendo al punto de partida. Me sentí arrinconada. Aproximadamente en la misma época, Eduardo había estado comunicándose con una amiga por Facebook, loando las virtudes de hablar claro. «Dado que juego de portero, me gusta que la gente me lance tiros directos», dijo.

Percibí que era necesario que hiciera algo urgentemente y lo consulté con mi mentor.

—Es obvio, Isabella —me dijo George—, que él nunca te va a pedir una cita porque él está libre y tú no. Cualquier hombre honrado tendría problemas ante esa situación. ¡Así que es tu oportunidad de pedirle a Eduardo que salga él contigo!

Me quedé totalmente aturdida. La voz del pragmatismo me estaba incitando hacia el descaro, a tomar las riendas. Todo lo que pervivía en mi interior —las inhibiciones de mi pasado, la omnipresente rigurosidad y la cólera de mis profesoras, las monjas, los castigos infligidos ante la trasgresión o demostración de cualquier leve niñería infantil— invadía todos y cada uno de los poros y tejidos de mi piel

—¡No, no! ¿Yo? ¡No puedo hacer una cosa así! —dije en alto, pero algo dentro de mí me impulsó hacia delante; el deseo de hablar con candidez, abiertamente, sin reservas.

Había recorrido un largo camino desde la reticencia de la muchacha de montaña. Era un nuevo amanecer. «Di lo que estás pensando o calla para siempre», me dije a mí misma. Decidí jugar sobre seguro y le escribí lo siguiente a Eduardo:

«Estaría muy bien volverte a ver... para ponernos al día».

Veinte minutos más tarde, la flecha de Cupido cayó justo delante de mí.

«¡Guau! ¡Eso podría ser muy peligroso! ¡Sigues siendo muy sexy!».

Apenas sin saber qué responder y revitalizada con un subidón de ego y energía del tamaño del Everest, esperé a la mañana siguiente para responder.

«Correré el riesgo. Por cierto, el sentimiento es mutuo».

¿Era realmente yo, la tímida muchachita oriunda de Huaraz? ¡Sin duda, aquella niña había sufrido una transformación emocional y/o física! Fue una buena cosa que Eduardo no viera cómo me ponía colorada como un tomate ante la pantalla, mientras me fulminaba un relámpago que había permanecido inactivo durante tanto tiempo en mi corazón. Si aquellos sentimientos parecían adolescentes, abiertamente reconozco que lo eran y los experimentaba sin vergüenza, al permitir que fluyera como un océano mi aplazada exuberancia juvenil, reafirmada y fortalecida por una madurez y un conocimiento bien establecidos.

—¡Doble guau! —exclamó el hombre me estaba seduciendo verbalmente—. ¿Qué tienes en mente? —Entonces, rápidamente añadió—: Utilicemos el correo electrónico normal.

No logro relatar de forma adecuada mi alegría durante aquella época: fueron momentos en los que realmente me sentí liberada, desvinculada de mi pasado y del propio tiempo. La aceptación y el deseo de Eduardo por verme y comunicarse conmigo, sus aduladoras insinuaciones y expresiones de admiración me hicieron sentir completa. Tuve que pellizcarme para lograr comprender que el hombre por el que había suspirado durante más de un cuarto de siglo había vuelto a entrar en mi mundo de nuevo. El único vacío que quedaba por rellenar era mi deseo de hablar con él y volver a verle.

Fui a la tienda de Verizon Wireless de la zona para activar mi «teléfono rojo secreto», llamado así no por ninguna relación con la CIA, sino por mi intento clandestino de mantener privada la comunicación retomada con Eduardo. Una encantadora muchacha rusa (a la que llamaré Oxana) me ayudó y me hizo una fotografía, y me preguntó para qué era.

—Es para alguien muy especial de mi pasado con el que me he vuelto a reencontrar.

—¡Oh, eso es muy romántico! —exclamó Oxana, sonriendo de oreja a oreja.

Dado que tenía que marcharme al trabajo, me aconsejaron que regresara esa tarde para que me proporcionaran más explicaciones de cómo utilizar el teléfono. Le había dado a Eduardo mi número de teléfono de antemano. Aquella tarde, mientras conducía hacia la tienda, Eduardo me envió un mensaje de texto y me preguntó (haciendo referencia a un mensaje que yo le había enviado la tarde anterior, diciéndole: «Voy a soñar contigo»): «Bueno, cuéntame el sueño de ayer por la noche».

Sin poder creérmelo, detuve el coche y, sin saber qué decir, escribí: «Probablemente, debería susurrártelo al oído». Esa era sencillamente una forma de hablar. Nunca, ni en mis mejores sueños, pensé que se decidiría a llamarme, pero, cuando llegué a la tienda, justo cuando Oxana me estaba haciendo una demostración de las funciones del teléfono, entró una llamada.

—La está llamando —me dijo Oxana al ver el nombre de Eduardo en la pantalla. Y del otro extremo de la línea, brotó su voz. Mientras hablábamos, caminé hasta mi coche y comencé a conducir, olvidando lo estricta que es la policía sobre el uso de teléfonos móviles al volante. En aquella época, ni siquiera sabía como activar el altavoz. Sencillamente, estaba totalmente absorta en el momento. Todos los sentimientos de mi pasado me invadieron como la marea. Apenas podía creerme que estuviera hablando con él. Durante nuestra breve conversación, Eduardo me preguntó cómo iba mi matrimonio, a lo que yo respondí:

—Va todo bien.

—Si todo va bien —razonó—, ¿por qué estás hablando conmigo?

Evité contestar a aquella pregunta diciéndole que estaba nerviosa y preguntándole si podríamos volver a hablar esa noche. Aceptó, y yo continué mi camino para recoger a mi hija de su entrenamiento de *softball*.

«¿Realmente puede estar pasando esto?», me pregunté a mí misma, apenas sin saber cómo formular ni un solo pensamiento coherente. Aquella noche, me recompuse y le dije a mi familia que me quedaría a trabajar hasta tarde en la oficina. Aquello no solía ocurrir, por lo que mi encubrimiento de la verdad me hizo sentir muy incómoda. Aun así, la predominante y omnipresente energía que me fluía por mi interior me impulsó a que siguiera adelante con mi operación secreta y, gracias a mi teléfono rojo, iba correctamente equipada. Y así, allí me senté, en mi oficina, con el teléfono delante de mí, esperando a que sonara. Lo contemplé fijamente, como si fuera una criatura mágica, que atesorara el secreto de mi destino.

Precisamente a las 23:00 (la hora exacta a la que Eduardo había prometido llamar), sonó el teléfono y yo contesté. Y allí estaba de nuevo, aquella voz familiar aunque remota de mi pasado. Me sentí extrañamente completa, aunque desplazada: atrapada entre el mundo del ayer y otro bastante complicado al que debía enfrentarme. Aunque tenía mucho por lo que sentirme agradecida, me embargó el pesar por lo que podría haber sido, sin realmente saber si mi mente había inventado una historia insostenible o si la atención de Eduardo seguía siendo una inminente realidad, todavía posible. Lo único que sabía era que el amor no dice mentiras y que lo que yo sentía era tan real como cualquier cosa que hubiera experimentado en mi vida.

Los dos mantuvimos una larga y significativa conversación, en la que Eduardo me habló sobre la muerte de su padre, al que estaba muy unido, que había tenido lugar hacía unos años. Coincidiendo con aquel trágico acontecimiento, yo estaba recién casada, y me acuerdo de haber sentido una especie de pena inexplicable envolvió todo mi ser. Recuerdo que estaba absorta viendo un programa de la televisión, sin pensar en Eduardo en aquel preciso instante, cuando, de repente, su imagen me vino a la mente, y vertí lágrimas por él, una especie de luto que ni si quiera yo comprendía. ¿Fue aquel un sentimiento profético o mera coincidencia? Ahora, pensando en ello retrospectivamente, comprendo que aquellos sentimientos debían de indicar algún tipo de intuitiva conexión telepática y empática entre nosotros, similar a lo que ya he mencionado antes sobre la recomendación de libros que me hizo Eduardo. Nunca llegué a mencionarle aquel incidente a él porque, a veces, en la narración de ese tipo de acontecimientos se pierde su naturaleza visceral. Ahora, sin embargo, soy libre de ataduras, libre de vivir mi verdad.

En respuesta a la revelación de Eduardo acerca de la tensa relación que mantenía con su madre, le proporcioné un consejo personal. Le expliqué que yo también había experimentado una difícil situación similar con mi madre, que superé escribiéndole una larga y sentida carta, volcando en ella mis sentimientos de desatención y rechazo de mi juventud. La interpretación errónea de mi madre en relación con mi capacidad de recuperación y con que yo fuera capaz de mantenerme por mí misma me despojó de cuidados maternos, y su falta de intervención me hizo sentir sola y rechazada. «Perdona a tu estúpida madre», me respondió por escrito mamá en un momento de revelación personal. Tras aquel intercambio, nuestro vínculo se fortaleció y el amor consiguió construir un puente sobre el dolor de nuestro pasado. Ahora somos buenas amigas. Compartí aquella historia con Eduardo porque comprendía, de primera mano, que el perdón es la mayor panacea para curar todos los males. Al día siguiente, él condujo durante casi dos horas para ir a ver a su madre. Más tarde, vi que había un mensaje de su madre en su muro de Facebook en el que decía: «¡Gracias por tu maravillosa visita!». Lo interpreté como una afirmación que indicaba que habían logrado resolver sus diferencias, y me sentí halagada y feliz de que Eduardo hubiera seguido mi consejo.

Tras revelar que mi matrimonio había quedado desprovisto de cercanía emocional y física, escuché con mis propios oídos aquel tono de innegable dulzura y comprensión que había dominado mi corazón durante tantos años. Junto a las melifluas palabras de empatía y buenos deseos de Eduardo, se manifestaron sus explícitas y apasionadas declaraciones de lo que ocurriría durante nuestro encuentro: una unión de nuestros cuerpos y almas, descrita minuciosamente. Apenas podía creerme que aquellas palabras las pronunciara el hombre por el cual mis sentimientos se habían quedado congelados en el tiempo, marcados de forma indeleble en mi corazón. Ser libre de mis manchas faciales me permitía abrirme a la posibilidad de que realmente me quisiera y me deseara aquel hombre. No obstante, debo admitir que sentí una gran incomodidad manteniendo este interludio (que equivalió simplemente a un intercambio verbal de afecto) en secreto a mi familia. Aun así, sentía el insuperable impulso de explorar si mis sentimientos eran genuinos o si eran, simplemente, un subproducto de mis inseguridades pasadas, aquel deseo absoluto de tiempos pasados de encajar en el mundo sin el estorbo de mis marcas faciales. Retrospectivamente, puedo decir sin lugar a dudas que los sentimientos que albergaba solamente tenían que ver con el sincero anhelo de conectar con alguien a quien consideraba mi alma gemela.

Eduardo me pidió que nos viéramos y acordamos que nos encontraríamos el sábado, 1 de mayo de 2010. Al principio, él quería que nos reuniéramos en una cita romántica, para tomar una copa y después ir a su casa, pero yo no pude reunir el valor de aceptar aquella proposición, lo cual no quiere decir que estuviera totalmente en contra. Mi postura, de natural reservada, sencillamente dictaba en contra de una cita íntima. Por lo tanto, accedimos a encontrarnos en un centro comercial en el estado en el que él vivía, y yo iría hasta allí con el objetivo de verle. Mientras tanto, continuamos intercambiando correos electrónicos y mensajes de texto. Uno de estos últimos llegó aquel mismo día, tras una noche de desvelo y emoción, en la que apenas podía creerme los avances que Eduardo había hecho hacia mí. Los mensajes de texto a los que me refiero creo que estaban escritos para despertar mi necesidad latente por intimidad física, el deseo de que me desearan y necesitaran. Eduardo me presentó un currículum bastante impresionante: la muestra sin tapujos de sus atributos anatómicos en su máximo apogeo. ¿Necesito añadir más? En deferencia a aquellos que puedan acobardarse ante asuntos que inciten asuntos lascivos, les pido a los más atrevidos que utilicen su imaginación más vívida en este caso. Vuelvo a recordar a las ancianitas que me sugirieron que mi libro debía contener algún elemento picantón. Bueno, pues lo que vi cumple a la perfección —y acaso lo supera— esa descripción y, como tal, no puede ser material descrito con todo lujo de detalles por la muchacha culturalmente puritana que llevo dentro, aquella a la que las monjas regañarían con severidad por descripciones así de gráficas. Sí, esa muchacha todavía está ahí, si bien es cierto que de una forma más tenue, incluso tras mis atrevidas comunicaciones por Facebook y por correo electrónico. Podéis sacar a la chica de las montañas, pero seguirá habiendo ciertos elementos de ellas y de la vida que he conocido que no pueden desvincularse tan fácilmente de mi psique.

Por fin, llegó el día de nuestra cita. La noche anterior, me revolví en la cama por el insomnio, dando vueltas sin parar de un lado para otro, y al final conseguí dormir apenas cuatro horas. Literalmente, me estaba descomponiendo por pensamientos que me arrastraban en direcciones opuestas: por un lado, el enorme cariño que sentía por mi familia y, por el otro, el anhelo insaciable de estar con mi amor perdido hacía tanto tiempo.

Hago una pausa aquí para manifestar el debido respeto y reflexionar sobre las meritorias cualidades de mi marido, Richard, como padre: su devoción, cuidado y amor por sus hijos, su compromiso y promesa de hacerme olvidar a Eduardo. Simplemente no lo logró; nadie podría. En deferencia a la privacidad de mi familia, omitiré aquí referencias específicas a nuestra vida en común y lo que hemos pasado, y solo diré que la confusión que experimentaba —el anhelo por conseguir el amor verdadero— no se vio mitigada por mi matrimonio. En cuanto a mis hijos, que son mi mundo, no tenía la percepción de que mi amor por Eduardo fuera una trasgresión o una renuncia de mi responsabilidad y mi amor por mi hijo y mi hija. Ambas formas de amar son diferentes y distintas, y una de ellas no niega ni amenaza a la otra. Solamente puedes sacar lo mejor de ti mismo cuando eres sincero contigo mismo y con lo que sientes. Al expresarme abiertamente, me abro ante mis hijos como el ser completo e integrado que soy: un paquete integral, con todas mis cartas sobre la mesa. De ningún modo o apariencia eso hace que disminuya la profundidad de mi cariño por ellos. Todo lo contrario, así no estoy escondiendo nada. Sencillamente, estoy declarando: «¡Aquí estoy! Esto es lo que soy y os quiero con cada milímetro de mi corazón».

Este tipo de pensamientos se me ocurrían mientras deliberaba conmigo misma, con mi mente, mi cuerpo y mi espíritu. Supuestamente, tenía que llamar a Eduardo por la mañana temprano el día de nuestra cita pero, dado que no me acosté hasta las cuatro de la mañana y no me levanté hasta las ocho, no fue posible. Mientras tanto, a las seis de la mañana recibí un mensaje de texto que decía: «¡Buenos días!» de Eduardo, al que no respondí. No lo hice debido a los nervios que sentía, las extraordinarias prisas que me entraron por prepararme informalmente para el día y apresurarme a ir a la oficina para una cita que no podía cancelar. Había cambiado todo el resto de mis citas dada aquella ocasión trascendental. De hecho, había puesto toda mi vida en suspenso.

Mi interés por ocultar mis planes a ojos de mi familia oscurecía el resto de mis pensamientos. Todo el mundo estaba en casa. Les dije que iba a un centro comercial a reunirme con alguien que conocía, una media verdad que casi logró absolver mi conciencia culpable, y me preocupé de guardarme mi teléfono rojo secreto para que ellos no lo vieran. Contesté al mensaje de texto de Eduardo cerca de las 9:45, diciéndole: «¡Buenos días!». El silencio por su parte lo dijo todo. Supuse que Eduardo estaba disgustado, como le ocurriría a cualquier profesional de la medicina. En nuestros círculos (el de los profesionales de la salud), el que yo no hubiera respondido de inmediato probablemente se interpretaba como una omisión deliberada y grosera; pero, ¡repito que no era esa mi intención! Simplemente, me sentía muy emocionada y nerviosa. Algo me dijo que cambiara de planes y me diera media vuelta, pero, después de todos esos años, tenía que concederme aquel capricho, por mi propio bien. Me puse una ropa normal y corriente: vaqueros y una camiseta de tela vaquera, y me recogí el pelo en una coleta. Aquejada de mis habituales alergias estacionales (que empeoraron precisamente el día 1 de mayo por alguna razón), tenía los ojos hinchados. Mi falta de sueño se manifestaba en las bolsas que me salieron bajo los ojos, aquellos insidiosos ladrones de mi aspecto juvenil. Dado que no anticipaba un encuentro romántico ese día, me imaginé que iba vestida adecuadamente, pues solo deseaba conocer mejor a Eduardo. Además (y esto es importante), nos íbamos a reunir en un lugar cercano a mi finca; así, si por casualidad me encontraba con alguien conocido, podría decir simplemente que había pasado por allí de visita. Lo tenía todo planeado.

Tras recibir mi mensaje, Eduardo respondió: «¿Dónde estás?».

«Voy de camino».

¡Y vaya camino por el que iba! Estaba lleno de enormes camiones y otros vehículos que iban a la velocidad del rayo, provocándome un pánico terrible, pero conseguí reunir el valor para seguir adelante.

«¿Vienes hacia aquí?».

«Sí. No estoy segura de cuándo voy a llegar. ¿Digamos que a la una y media, y te llamo cuando llegue allí?».

«Vale, llámame entonces».

Mi sugerencia de llamar a Eduardo cuando llegara era pensando en su comodidad, una deferencia que él pareció ignorar. Nunca antes había hecho semejantes esfuerzos emprendiendo un viaje y aguardando a ningún otro hombre. (Bueno, excepto durante mi adolescencia, cuando esperé a Carlos, que no se presentó a la sesión matinal del cine. Aquello había tenido lugar hacía lustros, y la importancia de aquel incidente palidecía en comparación con lo que sentí en aquellos momentos justo antes de reunirme con Eduardo). Si un hombre realmente siente algo profundo por una mujer, reflexionaba yo, no debería dejar que lo esperara, tal y como yo hice. En su lugar, debería haberse ofrecido a esperarme él a mí. Todo el esfuerzo recaía sobre mis hombros. No obstante, me imaginé que, dado que yo misma había tratado tan mal a Eduardo durante nuestra época de estudiantes cuando él estaba tratando de acercarse a mí y yo lo evitaba constantemente dada mi falta de autoestima de aquella época, resultaba adecuado que ahora fuera yo la que me esforzara. Aun así, había algo que no encajaba. Me sentí particularmente incómoda, humillada y avergonzada cuando me encontré sola en mi destino, esperando a alguien que apenas días antes había sido tan abiertamente provocativo y había parecido tan emocionado por verme.

Cada quince minutos, Eduardo me enviaba un mensaje de texto, y en uno de ellos me preguntó: «¿Estás sola?». Le contesté: «Sí», pensando que lo preguntaba por una amiga que en un principio iba a traerme a mi destino, pero que lo canceló en el último minuto. Estaba claro que Eduardo pretendía mantener una conexión física conmigo.

«Estaré ahí en quince minutos». Los mensajes llegaban a oleadas, mientras yo acabé por sentirme frustrada por la espera.

«Me voy de compras. Llámame cuando llegues», le escribí.

Entré en una tiendecita donde vi un corazón de metal al que lo rodeaban las palabras: «¡Sueña, sueña, sueña!». ¡Qué pertinente en mi situación! De hecho, antes de que nos encontráramos, Eduardo había escrito en su muro de Facebook: «No lo sueñes, vívelo». Yo estaba viviendo un sueño, acaso persiguiendo un fantasma de mi juventud. Cuando Eduardo me llamó para decirme que había llegado, se estaba librando una batalla entre mi cabeza y mi corazón. En mi mente, trataba de encontrar excusas (una táctica mental que las mujeres solemos emplear cuando estamos enamoradas). «Después de todo, él es médico. Quizás ha tenido una emergencia, quizás he interrumpido su jornada laboral, quizás estaba cansado por exceso de trabajo... ¡Quizás!», mis pensamientos inventaban pretextos a toda velocidad.

Entonces, dentro de mi cabeza empecé a escuchar la canción de Bryan Adams, «Have you ever really loved a woman?», que aparecía en la banda sonora de la película de 1994, Don Juan DeMarco, protagonizada por Johnny Depp. Vi a Eduardo y me acerqué a él, avanzando en su dirección, esperando con ansia un beso. Puesto que ya le había visto en fotografía en Facebook, no me sorprendieron sus distinguidas y definidas facciones, cinceladas por algunos de sus rasgos de juventud. No obstante, me sentí ligeramente intimidada cuando mis dientes chocaron con él cuando traté de besarle. Su apariencia era fría y reservada, como un plato frío y metálico. No profirió ni una sola disculpa y no dijo nada por haber llegado tarde: ningún «Me alegro de verte», ningún abrazo. Me sentí como si fuera a desplomarme bajo mi propio peso por un horrible y desazonador sentimiento.

—¿Tienes hambre? ¿Has comido? —me preguntó Eduardo.

—No, ¿y tú?

Mientras le devolvía la pregunta, sentí que la presión se me acumulaba en la cabeza.

—Yo ya he comido —dijo Eduardo, mirándome como si realmente me hubiera visto el día anterior.

—Bueno, ¿y qué quieres hacer? —le pregunté, a falta de un diálogo más sustancial.

Nos decidimos a entrar en un restaurante normalito, donde podríamos beber algo fresco y combatir la sofocante temperatura de aquel día de mayo. ¡Qué adecuado! Con aquellas temperaturas, me sentí como si estuviéramos sobrevolando un desierto abrasador, y en mi interior, gritaba: «¡Colisión inminente, colisión inminente!». Llegamos al restaurante y nos sentamos uno enfrente del otro. Eduardo paseó la mirada por toda la habitación, por cada recoveco y esquina, y lo miró todo excepto a mí. Cada vez me estaba sintiendo más y más alterada y desilusionada. Y una vez más, tratando de tender un puente sobre nuestro silencio, me atreví a decirle:

—Bueno, entonces ¿dónde vas a llevarme?

—A ninguna parte. Solamente tengo un casco —me respondió él, refiriéndose al detalle de que había venido en su moto. Después, añadió—: Mi hijo está en casa. Vive conmigo.

En ese momento, nuestro diálogo descendió a las profundidades de... la nada. «¿Todo esto es un farol?», me pregunté a mí misma, tragándome la vergüenza y la incomodidad. Afortunadamente, la conversación mejoró mientras hablábamos, durante casi dos horas, sobre nuestras familias. Eduardo me confesó que había sido la víctima de abusos en su matrimonio. Me pregunté cómo alguien podría haberlo tratado tan mal y si su fría apariencia exterior tenía algo que ver con el muro que había construido a su alrededor.

—¿Cómo van las cosas en casa? —me preguntó, sin un asomo de su antigua amabilidad y simpatía.

—Mis padres están bien, gracias.

—No me refería a tus padres. Estaba pensando más bien en ti y tu familia.

Cuando decidimos pasear por el centro comercial, el brusco lenguaje corporal y las rígidas expresiones faciales de Eduardo se hicieron patentes.

—¿Cómo van las cosas entre tu marido y tú? ¿Qué piensa él de ti?

Por fin, Eduardo había preguntado por aquello que le producía curiosidad. Más que ninguna otra cosa, quería saber si se estaba arriesgando con una mujer felizmente casada.

—Mi marido piensa que yo soy insustituible —le respondí con candidez—. Pero yo no estoy segura de si le he querido alguna vez.

—Entonces, ¿por qué te casaste con él?

—Mi reloj biológico estaba sonando... ¿Quién sabe?

—¿A qué se dedica?

—Es abogado.

En ese momento, Eduardo se puso muy incómodo, y nuestra conversación volvió a disminuir y a apagarse. «¡Colisión inminente, colisión inminente!», gritaba mi corazón, con aquella sensación de ir a estrellarnos en mitad del desierto.

—Bueno, ¿y entonces qué te has comprado? —me preguntó Eduardo, sin verdadero interés.

Le mostré el pequeño corazoncito de metal, rodeado por aquel imperativo: «¡Sueña, sueña, sueña!». Eduardo continuó caminando con un aire arrogante y despectivo, tan diferente de cuando éramos jóvenes, tan contenido y engreído... Aun así, seguí caminando a su lado. No sé por qué. Parecía como si yo fuera masoquista. Quizás, subconscientemente, sentía que aquel era el resultado de mis desprecios pasados pero, ¿realmente lo era? ¿Aquel hombre que estaba junto a mí realmente me recordaba y albergaba los mismos sentimientos por mí que yo tenía por él? Claramente, no. No obstante, yo no lograba reunir el valor de marcharme de allí sufriendo, un acto que simplemente habría servido para exacerbar mis sentimientos de pérdida durante veintiséis años.

—¿Has hecho alguna vez kayak?

Aquella extraña pregunta de Eduardo me descolocó.

—No —le respondí, habiéndome acostumbrado a esas alturas a contestarle en monosílabos.

—¿Te gustan las motocicletas? —me preguntó Eduardo, buscando desesperadamente algo que pudiéramos tener en común.

—Me aterran las motocicletas.

—¿Por qué? Tú montas a caballo, y eso es lo mismo.

—Yo monto en un entorno controlado. Tengo dos amigos que murieron en accidentes de motocicleta —le respondí, esperando que Eduardo comprendiera que me importaba su seguridad y bienestar.

—También puedes morir simplemente cruzando la calle. —declaró Eduardo con decisión, y nada más.

Sus palabras me tocaron la fibra sensible. No creo que supiera nada sobre la trágica pérdida de Laura, mi queridísima hermana.

—¿No te preocupan tus hijos? —aventuré, queriendo hacerle entender que, si algo le sucedía a él, privaría a sus hijos de su compañía, del apoyo de su presencia y de un padre querido, y alguien por quien yo sentía un profundo cariño.

Por supuesto, en aquellas circunstancias, no podía dar rienda suelta a mis verdaderos sentimientos. Obviamente, la atracción física era su única motivación para reunirse conmigo y, para él, yo no parecía ser suficiente. Por mi parte, yo lo habría aceptado aunque hubiera estado calvo, envejecido y decrépito. Evidentemente, Eduardo se sintió extraordinariamente incómodo con mis comentarios. Caminamos hasta el otro extremo del centro comercial descubierto, bulléndonos la furia interiormente en silencio. Hablo por ambos porque estoy segura de que compartíamos un resentimiento mutuo en aquellos momentos. La decepción era mi guía constante y me sentí indefensa.

—Ya sabes —le dije, tratando de romper el hielo, aunque esta fuera una tarea ingente incluso para un maestro cinturón negro de kárate—, deberías sentirte muy afortunado por que haya recorrido todo este camino para verte.

La respuesta de Eduardo fue claramente mordaz y cortante. Comenzó a dar saltitos y a balancear los brazos mientras decía:

—¡Mira lo contento que estoy!

Nunca me había visto en una situación tan incómoda en toda mi vida, casi me sentía la víctima del aparente desdén y ridículo de Eduardo. El sentido común y la razón habrían dictado que me marchara sin más dilación, pero consideraba que aquello hubiera sido un acto de cobardía. Había llegado tan lejos, que no había forma de volver atrás. Algo iba francamente mal, y mi airado compañero había provocado un silencio entre nosotros tan denso como la niebla londinense. De nuevo, tratando de vadear la oscuridad, dije algo sin pensar.

—¿No me vas a dar un abrazo?

—¿Un abrazo? —Eduardo apretó bruscamente su cuerpo contra el mío. Estaba tan rígido como un tronco—. ¡Aquí tienes un abrazo!

¡Aquello iba mal, muy pero que muy mal! A medida que el grito de «colisión inminente» resonaba más y más alto en mis oídos, dije:

—¡Me siento muy incómoda!

—¡Yo también! ¿Dónde está aparcado tu coche?

—En el otro extremo del centro comercial.

—¡Te acompaño hasta allí!

Humillada y vencida, no tenía escapatoria. Tendría que haberle dicho:

—No te molestes. No necesito que me acompañes.

Sin embargo, el deseo de vencer a la adversidad me empujó a apretar los dientes y a mantener el tipo. Y así, no dije nada. Mientras caminábamos hasta la motocicleta de Eduardo, me dio su casco.

—Toma, ¡póntelo! Te llevaré hasta tu coche en moto.

No sé por qué acaté aquella oferta tan poco cortés. Montándome en la parte posterior, me senté a una distancia remota de Eduardo, agarrándome a su costado con las puntas de los dedos —apenas sin tocar al hombre al que tanto había admirado—, a ese hombre que había mutado para convertirse en mi oponente. Señalé mi coche, junto al que nos paramos y yo me bajé, mientras que Eduardo permaneció sentado en su motocicleta. Se me enganchó la coleta en el casco, una cruel metáfora de mi maraña de emociones. Finalmente, cuando logré soltarme, nos abrazamos, nos despedimos y Eduardo se marchó en su moto.

Arropada por la intimidad de mi coche, sollocé incontrolablemente. Decidí seguir mi camino para asistir a la segunda sesión de *El conejo Pedro*, la obra de teatro de mi hija, que mi marido y yo habíamos ido a ver la noche anterior. Sentía el corazón agitado y la sangre corriéndome a toda velocidad por las venas. Entonces, cuando bajé la guardia, aparqué y le envié un mensaje de texto a Eduardo.

«¿Qué ha pasado realmente hoy?».

«Unas cuantas cosas —respondió Eduardo—. Me sentía mal por que tú estuvieras casada, no noté que hubiera chispas entre nosotros, tal y como había esperado, y también nos separó una gran distancia».

«Eso era exactamente lo que me daba miedo cuando era joven. Esa situación me habría destrozado entonces, pero ahora soy mayor y puedo asumirlo. Necesito dar esto por cerrado para proseguir con mi vida. ¿Quizá podamos plantearnos la posibilidad de ser solo amigos?».

Lo que pensé que era el silencio de Eduardo detonó como si fuera una bomba en el interior de mi corazón. En realidad, sí me había contestado, pero yo iba conduciendo y me perdí su respuesta. Cuando llegué al colegio de mi hija y las luces se atenuaron en preparación para la obra, me senté allí, junto a una de las encantadoras amigas de mi hija, conteniendo las lágrimas. Nunca había sentido más gratitud por encontrarme sumida en la oscuridad. Entonces, me levanté, me disculpé y fui al baño. Allí, en medio de la confusión y la pena, vi otro mensaje de texto de Eduardo en respuesta al mío.

«Es mejor que olvidemos lo de hoy».

Interpreté el significado de estas palabras como: «Olvidemos que nos hemos cruzado alguna vez» y volví a echarme a llorar. Me sentí envejecida, fea y me dio la sensación de haber vuelto a mi antiguo capullo de falta de confianza en mí misma. Comencé a preguntarle a todo el mundo por mi aspecto físico, como si la convalidación externa de otros determinara mi autoestima. Por pura compulsión, volví a escribirle.

«¡Unas tetas, una nariz y un abdomen de mentira no son lo que yo soy! Yo soy cien por cien real —con los ojos hinchados y alérgicos, algunas arrugas y, de vez en cuando, algunos problemas dentales—, pero soy natural y real, y la gente debería aceptarme tal y como soy». Me sentí peor que miserable. En mi cabeza, mi aspecto físico volvía a aparecer como un posible elemento disuasorio para procurarme el afecto de Eduardo. Temía los estragos de la edad y del paso del tiempo, y le preguntaba a todo el mundo a mi alrededor si yo era víctima de la falta de atractivo y de la vejez. E incluso cuando los demás me aseguraban que no era ese el caso, me seguía sintiendo vacía, como si necesitara llegar a algún tipo de forma de dar por cerrado y de cicatrizar lo que había sucedido entre Eduardo y yo.

Nunca llegué a recibir respuesta a aquello, pero sí nos intercambiamos una serie de mensajes de texto en los que Eduardo me dijo que mi aspecto no había sido el desencadenante de su indiferencia. A mi vez, yo le dije que él tenía que afrontar la vida tal y como viene y comunicarse abiertamente con los que le rodean, pues si no, los sentimientos se estancan. Lo tranquilicé haciéndole saber que era consciente de que él había sido víctima de abusos en su matrimonio y la necesidad de que expresara lo que sentía, cosa que yo pensaba que estaba reprimiendo. Más tarde volví a escribirle, contándole que quería decirle algo interesante e importante, pero que, en aquel momento, estaba ocupada, preparando la fiesta de cumpleaños de mi hija. Me sentía dividida entre la necesidad —y el privilegio— de cuidar de mi niña, y el anhelo acuciante de hablar con Eduardo, al menos para suavizar los ásperos obstáculos provocados por la falta de comunicación. Eduardo insistió en que nuestras conversaciones se restringieran a Facebook, y que él no podía hacer las veces de mi terapeuta. Yo repliqué que no necesitaba tal ayuda, pues siempre he gestionado los asuntos que me han surgido enfrentándome a ellos frontalmente. Había sobrevivido a uno de los terremotos más devastadores que uno pueda imaginar, me había enfrentado a la muerte de una hermana a la que adoraba, me había echado sobre los hombros todos los obstáculos con los que la vida me había puesto a prueba con aceptación resignada y con desenvoltura... ¡Y Eduardo se atrevía a insinuar que yo necesitaba un terapeuta! Y aunque aquel atrevimiento fuera el colmo, aun así, lo perdoné. ¿Por qué? No lo sé. Quizás, porque me instaba a hacerlo por aquella imagen que se me había quedado grabada de forma indeleble en mi corazón: la representación de un alma amable y cortés, a la que yo nunca había llegado de abandonar en pensamiento, a pesar del tiempo y la distancia.

Y con respecto al «asunto interesante»: Dado que necesitaba hacer la compra para la fiesta, no podía enviar el mensaje de texto que debería haberle enviado, aquel ejemplo fundamental, cuando resultaba realmente oportuno. Perdí la oportunidad. Y así, mientras me sentaba en la tienda, esperando a mi hija, sola en un lugar oscuro, rodeada de los olores de perfumes y de la música estridente del hilo musical, me permití dar rienda suelta a mi pena. Lloré y le recé a Dios para que aliviara mi intenso dolor. Más tarde, mi hija vino hasta donde yo me encontraba y se dio cuenta de que tenía los ojos enrojecidos.

—¡Pobre mamá! —me dijo con empatía—. Debes de ser alérgica a algo que hay por aquí.

Mi ángel tenía toda la razón. No solo era alérgica al polen, sino a la tristeza que me invadía. De nuevo, otro paso en falso, otro fallo a la hora de escribir en un momento fundamental probablemente me había privado de cualquier esperanza de dar todo aquel asunto por cerrado de una forma positiva. No se pueden recuperar los momentos, pero nunca es demasiado tarde para decir lo que uno piensa.

Unas tres semanas más tarde después de nuestra desafortunada reunión, le envié el siguiente mensaje por Facebook a Eduardo: «Me siento muy confundida por las "chispas". Pensé que las sentíamos cuando éramos jóvenes. Supongo que ya no tiene ninguna importancia, pero la vida es corta. Por eso, he pensado que deberías saber lo siguiente: Ya sé que no quieres hablar conmigo y no espero nada más de ti».

Eduardo entonces mantuvo un intercambio de mensajes con un amigo, en el que citó a Confucio: «O bien lo haces o no. No existen los intentos». De nuevo, me pregunté si estaría intentando comunicarse conmigo de alguna manera. ¿Tenía que descodificar aquel mensaje como: «O te comprometes o no, pero no te quedes a medio camino»? Si su lenguaje se había convertido en un código, ¿a qué se debía? ¿A qué venía ese jueguecito?

Aproximadamente una semana más tarde, Eduardo tuvo la osadía de borrarme como amiga en Facebook, un movimiento que me dejó perpleja. Aun así, gracias los poderes de la red, podía seguir viendo sus fotos. Algo puede decirse sobre la comunicación directa, y donde hay una verdadera conexión, no existe la necesidad de subterfugios o evasiones de la verdad. Si me paro a pensar en ello, eso es precisamente lo que estoy haciendo ahora mismo: comunicar mi testimonio inspirado en Eduardo, contando la verdad y nada más que la verdad, así que,

¡ayúdame, Dios! En estos tiempos, el ordenador suele hacer las veces de un tercero a la hora de transmitir ideas y sentimientos entre la gente. Algunas cosas, por lo tanto, se pierden en esta transmisión electrónica (específicamente, la oportunidad de escuchar una voz, de interpretar una inflexión, de ver una reacción y de desarrollar una relación genuina con alguien).

Más tarde, tratando tender una rama de olivo felicitándolo por su cumpleaños, le escribí a Eduardo un mensaje temprano ese día: una especie de compensación por no haberle contestado de forma oportuna al mensaje de texto la mañana en la que nos encontramos. «¡Buenos días! ¡Espero que tu corazón esté lleno de amor, empatía y felicidad! ¡Espero que te encuentres bien! ¡Te deseo lo mejor! ¡Feliz cumpleaños! Isabella». Mi gesto de buena voluntad recibió como respuesta un silencio sepulcral. ¿Aquella indiferencia era ira, dolor, frustración o directamente rechazo? Una vez más, la evasión no verbal o la comunicación silenciosa simplemente provocaron que me preguntara de dónde fluían las emociones de Eduardo, o si, de hecho, habría albergado por mí algún otro sentimiento aparte del mero deseo físico.

Me guío por las enseñanzas de los sabios como Buda. Yo no hago teatro con el amor. No me dedico a fingir afecto y, para mí, el cariño tiene su base en el corazón y en un terreno humanístico común. Yo pensaba que Eduardo y yo estábamos conectados de muchísimas formas: intelectual, emocional, psíquica y físicamente. ¿Aquella conexión había sido una mera conjetura, un producto de mi imaginación o un subproducto de un sentimiento real y palpable? Solamente puedo contestar a estas preguntas con más preguntas aún y recorrer un círculo infinito de porqués y suposiciones.

Puede que, en retrospectiva, el viaje a los recovecos más ocultos de mi corazón fuera una forma de catarsis para volver regresivamente a mi pasado y revisar mi juventud, cuando el amor era un concepto mágico. Cuando uno es joven, la noción del amor no está contaminada por fachadas. Y como tal, existe en su forma más pura, y se introduce en nuestros corazones como un relámpago, dando pie a anhelos ocultos, a sentimientos a la espera de que los exploremos. Acaso la mujer en mitad de su vida necesitaba sentir de nuevo a la muchacha que lleva dentro, la mujer joven que todavía creía en el amor en su estado más ideal, manifestado como un impulso primario e irresistible.

La vida es un círculo completo y todo sucede por una razón. Cuando fui a la librería Barnes & Noble para comprar las novelas que me había recomendado Eduardo, comprendí que yo podría, de hecho, escribir la mía propia. La singularidad de mi realidad —el dolor, la alegría, el yin-yang de la vida— es lo que deseaba compartir, en honor al catalizador de mi corazón roto y con cariño hacia él, esté o no escuchando, pues está claro que cada historia tiene su mensaje. La mía tiene innumerables, concretamente la trascendencia literal de las cenizas, la tragedia que supone una pérdida, ser expuesto al ridículo, al desdén y a la degradación y, aun así, a pesar de todo ello, el triunfo de seguir siendo yo misma. Todavía quedan por escribir capítulos literales y metafóricos. Por eso, acompañadme un poquito más por los pasillos de mi vida, pues os ofrezco algunas reflexiones finales.

Capítulo 15

El despertar a la promesa

En esta época del año —las Navidades— flota en el ambiente un frío penetrante, cuando el cielo presagia nieve, el obsequio de la temporada. En esos momentos, cuando el muérdago y la magia dominan nuestro entorno, me invade una especie de melancolía nostálgica, recordándome el paso del tiempo y los cambios constantes que tienen lugar a nuestro alrededor. Es una época de gratitud y mi corazón se hinche con la sensación de apreciación omnipresente por tantas bendiciones, entre las que principalmente se encuentran mis hijos, otros miembros de mi familia y mis amigos. Le doy la bienvenida a mi marido, que regresa a casa después de un viaje. Nuestro intercambio es cálido, cimentando tácitamente el compromiso mutuo que compartimos como padres de nuestros más preciados dones, nuestros hijos. Aun todavía, quizá solamente en los momentos de quietud, pienso en Eduardo. Solo ahora, lo veo a través de un cristal, reflejando las sombras de un tiempo pretérito. En mi mundo del presente, contemplando todo lo que he sentido y experimentado, agradezco la oportunidad de haberle visto de nuevo y haberle dado expresión a intensos y genuinos sentimientos, alimentados por lo más profundo de mi corazón. Poca gente experimenta dichos sentimientos en toda su vida. El ciclo de la vida continua y hay estaciones del corazón. Los anhelos disminuyen con el tiempo y las circunstancias, pero negar su existencia es ser injustos con el pasado, el presente y el futuro indeterminado.

Aunque los flecos del tapiz de mi vida se entrecruzan entre el pasado y el presente, cada una de las hebras inextricablemente unidas unas a otras, yo les doy justificación y he hallado el equilibrio en mi vida en todos sus aspectos. He comenzado a pintar, un pasatiempo que me transporta a una odisea interior y me permite explorar mi lado creativo. Me siento muy orgullosa y feliz en compañía de mis caballos, esos sensibles seres que he llegado a apreciar gracias a mi abuelo. Disfruto mucho en compañía de mis pacientes y en mi labor de profesional de la salud y también de las artes de la curación, sintiéndome realizada todos y cada uno de los días gracias a la sabiduría y perspicacia de aquellos a los que les procuro cuidados. También he extraído de mi pasado el significado de crecer, cambiar y aprender. Las cenizas, el polvo y los escombros del devastador terremoto de Huaraz en mi juventud se han aclarado y ahora me encuentro en un país totalmente nuevo, a miles de kilómetros de mi hogar natal, totalmente equilibrada y ansiosa por vivir. Me detengo aquí para rendir tributo a las vidas perdidas y me comprometo a dedicarles mis buenas acciones presentes y futuras. Todavía puedo ver a mi querido abuelo montado en su fiel *Mauro Mina*, siguiendo adelante contra todo pronóstico, cargado de pragmatismo y resolución. Me imagino a mi hermosa abuela, reafirmando con dulzura su poderío femenino. Evoco a mi madre, que dejó que me desarrollara por mis propios medios y, aun así, me abrió en última estancia su pecho para confesarme su introspección propia y admitirme sus fallos (nadie en todo el planeta Tierra está libre de ellos). Escucho el eco de la sensibilidad de mi padre, su sentido de la justicia y su capacidad para reflexionar y ponerse rápidamente en acción. Ahora, casi con noventa años, todavía posee todas las facultades de su juventud (exceptuando su vista) y está dotado de una perspicacia que una vista clara y fina jamás le podría proporcionar. Pienso en mi hermano que ha logrado encontrar su lugar en el mundo, aunque ahora él y yo vivamos claramente distanciados el uno del otro. Espero que, con estas palabras, pueda extender la mano hacia él y volver a encontrarme con él de nuevo, tendiéndole una rama de olivo de aceptación e indulgencia.

Pienso en mi corazón juvenil hecho trizas —los que podrían haber sido— desde el rechazo de Carlos aquel día en el que le esperé en el cine hasta el paseo romántico con Lorenzo siendo una adolescente bajo la luna llena de otoño. Todavía siento el aguijón de la amabilidad de Enrique, unida a sus vicios y transgresiones, la glacial acogida de Eduardo durante nuestra última reunión... y me siento agradecida por todo ello: todo el interrogante de opuestos, el tira y afloja de la vida, pues he aprendido y he evolucionado tras estas experiencias, fortaleciéndome y ganando fuerzas para narrar mi historia.

Y luego está Laura, mi ángel, siempre a mi alrededor, garantizándome su presencia. No hace mucho, recibí una carta genérica del actor Richard Gere en el que pedía oraciones para el pueblo tibetano. No suelo leer este tipo de cartas, pero, por alguna razón, algo me impulsó a abrir ese mensaje. Leí todas y cada una de las palabras de la carta y después cogí entre las manos el paño de la oración que traía adjunto. Lo coloqué en el centro de la repisa de mi chimenea, bajo un hermoso espejo, y pronuncié una silenciosa oración de amor y buena voluntad por el pueblo tibetano, gente a la que considero pacífica y comprensiva. Siempre he sentido afinidad por ellos y sus buenas acciones. Un par de semanas más tarde, vino una nueva paciente a mi consulta. Mientras yo estaba tomando notas en su historial, cuando le pregunté por su ocupación, me reveló que estaba en el paro. Justo entonces, tuve que abandonar la habitación un instante. Cuando regresé, encontré a la mujer escribiendo algo en un trozo de papel.

—En realidad —me dijo—, soy vidente, y a veces recibo mensajes que tengo anotar. Cuando se marchó usted de la habitación, recibí un mensaje que creo que es de alguien muy cercano a usted. Ella me ha dicho que estaba allí, junto al espejo cerca de la chimenea aquel día.

Inmediatamente, reconocí que topar con alguien bienintencionado (incluso aunque sea un extraño) proporciona un inconmensurable sentimiento de paz, satisfacción y conexión con aquellos que hemos perdido. En el interior de mi corazón, sabía que Laura, efectivamente, había hecho acto de presencia silenciosa y poderosamente. En un esfuerzo por mantener el decoro profesional, sin embargo, me abstuve de reaccionar abiertamente. Mantuve la compostura, agradecí lo que mi paciente me acababa de decir y dejé pasar el asunto.

En la enredada maraña de la vida, las respuestas residen en las verdades subjetivas —los silenciosos susurros en el interior de todos nosotros— y la vocación de hacer el bien en el mundo reside en albergar sentimientos de empatía y solidaridad. Está todo ahí, alrededor de nosotros, surgiendo a la luz cuando nos esforzamos por buscar nuestras verdades individuales. Las enseñanzas budistas inspiraron las expresión de las mías propias.

Las respuestas también residen tras puertas cerradas, que tienen la posibilidad inherente de volver a abrirse, con una nueva revelación y comprensión. Este ha sido el objetivo de este libro, mi odisea personal, con la que he evocado la historia como trampolín para lo que queda por delante y, en última instancia, mi despertar a la promesa que crece en el origen de los días futuros.

Mis reflexiones y conversaciones con mi buen amigo, George, se prolongan hasta el presente. Hace poco, le conté un sueño que tuve hace tres años. Me encontraba en un serpenteante laberinto, a través del cual llegaba a la cima de una pirámide. Me dijeron:

—Lo verás allí (a Eduardo).

Yo continué mi camino. Allí, en lo que parecía una fortaleza china, me topé con una gran puerta. Llamé y un anciano contestó, diciéndome:

—¡Lo siento, pero él no se encuentra aquí! Y cerró de un portazo.

—Entonces, George —dije, mirando a mi amigo para que me diera su opinión—, ¿este sueño era un pronóstico de la realidad o solamente existía en mi subconsciente?

George levantó la mirada y me contempló directamente a los ojos, dedicándome una mirada de sabiduría.

—Eso solo lo puede decir el futuro —me respondió.

Algunas cosas han de quedar flotando en lo desconocido, hasta que llegue el momento adecuado de que las comprendamos. La puerta de mi mente y de mi corazón sigue abierta, dando la bienvenida a los obsequios de la vida y a todo lo que les queda por ofrecerme.

Printed in Great Britain
by Amazon

18992046R00294